Guardian of the Stone

Amity Grays

OMNIFIC PUBLISHING
LOS ANGELES

Omnific Publishing
1901 Avenue of the Stars, 2nd floor
Los Angeles, CA 90067
www.omnificpublishing.com

First Omnific eBook edition, September 2015
First Omnific trade paperback edition, September 2015

The characters and events in this book are fictitious.
Any similarity to real persons, living or dead,
is coincidental and not intended by the author.

Library of Congress Cataloguing-in-Publication Data

Grays, Amity.
   Guardian of the Stone / Amity Grays – 1st ed.
   ISBN: 978-1-623421-74-8
   1. Romance — Fiction. 2. Time Travel — Fiction.
   3. Knights Templar — Fiction. 4. Los Angeles — Fiction. I. Title

10 9 8 7 6 5 4 3 2 1

Cover Design by Micha Stone and Amy Brokaw
Interior Book Design by Coreen Montagna

Printed in the United States of America

To Lindsay, Shelley and Stephanie,
my friends and coaches:

To my family,
for having the pompoms out and ready
all the time and regardless:

Thank you. I love you all.

The Knights Templar was a Christian military order, existing from approximately 1118 to 1312. They are considered by many to be the greatest warriors of all time. In 1307, King Philip IV of France, who was greatly indebted to the order, had many of the Templars arrested. They were charged with various crimes against the church, and their confessions, drawn through torture, were used against them and the order which they served. On May 12, 1310, after recanting their confessions, fifty-four men were taken to the fields outside of Paris and burned at the stake.

Chapter One

Realm: Paris, France, May 12, 1310

Hundreds gathered in the courtyard outside the palace, anxiously awaiting a look at the condemned men. Whether it was morbid curiosity, despair, or disbelief that brought them, it didn't really matter. Their presence would bring neither comfort nor pain to the poor men who had already suffered the unthinkable. Betrayed by a king they had served with honor and in faith, they'd been accused of horrendous atrocities and, based on false witness drawn through unmerciful torture, sentenced to die.

Omont Montague stood near the back of the gathering, waiting for the perfect moment, praying for the Lord to give him both courage and guidance.

"Pa Pa, Fan." His small daughter turned in his arms, pointing her tiny finger toward another small child.

"No, Edeline, not Fran," Omont said, pulling the two-year-old tight against his chest, kissing the top of her head and breathing in her sweet smell. She was so young, so innocent. He prayed the fierce hatred burning wild in his soul would not somehow seep through to the purity which was hers.

As she cuddled against him, he studied the looming stone walls surrounding the fortress. Flanked with manned watch towers above narrow gates, they assured no one was getting in unannounced. Not that anyone would even try, as beyond the gates sat more of the king's army waiting to escort the prisoners to a readied field outside of Paris. The knights' fates were sealed. There would be no rescue. And although there was no true crime for the damned to bear shame, they would be shown no mercy.

Omont turned to the man at his right. "I need your word," he said, holding the man's somber gaze. "If I am taken, you will see it through."

Dressed like a merchant, his features well-hidden behind hood and muck, Federic nodded. "With God as my witness, I give you my word."

And there was no word Omont would grant more faith. He had fought beside the knight countless times and knew, without question, there was no braver or more righteous man than he.

The sound of opening doors groaned throughout the courtyard. The crowd, still mingling in multiple independent gatherings, quickly silenced and drew together. From the cylindrical tower sitting in the center of the fortress, eight men, bound by chains, were transferred from the keep to the first of seven barred carts.

"Be careful, my friend," Omont said to Federic, sensing his outrage and urge to respond. "If they realize who you are, you will burn beside the others."

"I would gladly burn in their place, if given the choice." The warrior's nostrils flared as his lips flattened and curled, but as suddenly as his fury had risen, despair stepped forward to dampen its fire. He took a calming breath. "I will be careful, but I will be sure they know their sacrifice was not in vain."

Omont nodded in understanding. It was a brave thing the knight would do, following the men to the field, standing close by so they might see his face and know the others survived. "Praise be to God," he said, placing one hand on the other man's shoulder. "May He bless them and take their souls quickly."

"Praise be to God," Federic said, momentarily covering Omont's hand with his own before breaking free and disappearing into the throng.

Now was the perfect time. Omont dare wait no longer. Sheltering the squirming Edeline in his arms, he pushed his way through the milling crowd and headed toward the tower.

The king's soldiers were everywhere, inside the keep and out. Omont stopped. He was not a man to cower, but he had everything to lose.

Standing to the side of the heavy tower doors, he waited as eight more men were brought out. Not one set of eyes looked up as they were marched single file toward the carts. They would face death as they had faced life, with honor, courage, and absolute faith in the Lord. These were remarkable men, a fact which had surely sealed their fate.

Nearly three years prior, while under service to the King, they had learned of his intent to arrest the Templars, charge them with heresy, and extract confessions from them using any means necessary. They sent warning. For the sake of their fellow knights and the secrets they guarded, they had held their posts at the castle, keeping up the pretense of normality while allowing their brothers to escape.

Few would ever know the sacrifice they had made, but their sufferings were plain for everyone to see. Their faces were beaten, and beneath their light covers, their bodies had, no doubt, suffered the same. Omont wanted to scream at the injustice, to curse the earthly powers who would allow such an atrocity. His hand itched for the sword not currently at his side. It would have done him no good. He was only one man, and to save them would take an army. But the only army that could save these men of honor, these soldiers of Christ, had, by the courageous cover of these now condemned men, made for the sea.

Their immense sacrifice renewed his faith. He moved inside.

Two guards, one on each side of the entry, drew their swords and stepped forward. His daughter's small fingers grasped hold of his tunic as she buried her face deep within its cover.

Omont pulled the letter from his pouch and held it out in front of him.

Taking the letter and carefully studying the seal, the guard to his left nodded to the other before breaking it open. Permission for passage was being granted by Louis d'Artois, a dignitary within the Ecumenical Council. It was written by Omont's cousin and was as fraudulent as the seal which had held it secure.

The first guard turned and called to yet another standing further in from the entrance.

Omont breathed a sigh of relief as the guard stepped forward, ready to escort him down the long narrow passage. The next thing he knew, he was being led through and up an uneven maze of brick and mortar. Flames from the burning candles lining the narrow walkway danced with the slight draft coming from behind. Their slender images, cast in long shadows, leaned forward like arrows pointing the way.

Cold and dreary, the passage housed several barred doors. Though no sound came from behind them, he knew they held the last of those to be taken. All were his friends, men he'd fought with countless times, men who shared his beliefs and who once had shared his dreams.

As they rounded another turn, the sounds of heavy chains echoed from an open chamber. A simple glance and he caught the hollow stare of Rupert Dupuy.

Guarded by two as one knelt at his feet, the once unstoppable warrior looked out through the door as though looking into a fog.

Edeline bounced in Omont's arms. "Oh," she gasped, enchanted by the dancing flames.

It was a second in time, yet it felt as though time stood still. Hopeless eyes caught sight of Omont and then moved, but for a moment, to the babe in his arms. Understanding flashed quickly across his face. In the very next instant, the expression cleared, and all evidence of their significance had vanished.

Theirs would be yet another secret the knight would carry to his grave.

At the end of the next corridor, they stopped. The guard unlocked the door and pushed it open. "There will be little time," he warned, stepping back and allowing them to pass into the chamber.

Omont moved inside and silently waited for the door to close behind him.

In a dimly lit corner of the small stone room, his feet chained to the bench where he sat, was the greatest man Omont had ever known, his brother by blood as well as spirit, a Templar priest and blessed man of visions, Nicolas Montague.

The priest raised his head. "Brother!" His drawn face lit with a mixture of joy and relief. He spread his arms, welcoming Omont into his embrace.

As the front of strength he'd held so tight shattered into a well of agony, Omont flew across the short distance and fell to his knees. Burying his face against his brother's starved chest, he wept with despair.

Edeline wiggled from his arms to the ground as Nicolas ran his hands comfortingly over Omont's bent head.

"We have not the time, dear brother," Nicolas said with a gentle voice both sure and unshaken.

Pushing himself away, Omont wiped the tears from under his eyes. With a weary sigh, he turned his head and kissed his daughter's troubled brow.

Wide blue eyes, so like her mother's, looked back at him uncertainly.

"It is all right, sweet child," he said, moving her to stand before her uncle.

Reaching inside his pouch, Omont pulled out the stone. Looking over his shoulder toward the door's peephole, he made certain no eyes watched. His hands shook as he placed the marble's chain around his brother's neck. It fell against the priest's chest, and a brilliant light instantly transformed the simple stone into an extraordinary gem.

Nicolas's frail hands wrapped around his, taking possession and hiding its glory. "We must move quickly."

Omont nodded and let go.

Running his hand lovingly down Edeline's soft cheek, the priest looked past the small child toward the chamber's door. He removed the necklace from around his neck, and the magnificent gem turned back to stone. With a heavy sigh, he lowered it over his young niece's head.

"A single stone shall guard men's souls. But only the purest of souls shall guard the stone."

Edeline smiled with delight as her tiny fingers lifted the marble. At two years of age, she had no idea the course of her days was now and forever changed.

The priest looked upon his brother with tired, sorrowful eyes. "I do not know if it be a blessing or a curse which I bestow."

"Nor do I," Omont replied, his own heart heavy with the weight of despair. "You are sure it was her in your vision?"

Edeline looked up. Bright eyes shined from a face destined for beauty as her fine blond curls captured the dim light from the small window above and turned to gold.

"I am sure," the priest said. "Already I see signs of the woman she will become — the same woman I have seen in my dreams. But the dreams are only guides, my brother. If their paths are not followed, nothing is certain."

Omont nodded and looked down to his daughter. "I wish I could be sure."

"You must have faith," said his brother, placing his hands on his shoulders and holding his troubled gaze. "For Edeline's sake and for the sake of everything we know to be holy, you must be stronger than your doubts."

The chamber door moaned.

"It is time," said the guard as he and another entered the small dimly lit room. Covered with plain gray surcoats and heavy black cloaks, their chain armor clattered as they stepped across the hard stone floor.

"I…" Omont began but lost his words to sorrow.

Nicolas pulled him abruptly into his arms, holding him tight and kissing the top of his bowed head. "We will meet again, my dearest brother. Now you must go."

As the guard knelt to release the chains which bound the priest to his chamber, Omont looked one last time upon the man he so loved. With a heart too heavy to do anything but obey, he pulled his daughter into his arms and turned to go.

In truth, he had little time to spare. It would not take long for the letter to travel and him to be found a fraud. The sooner he was away from the castle's damning walls, the better off he would be.

The guard met him outside the chamber's door. With a single nod, he instructed Omont to follow. Thankfully, the passage was clear all the way to the door. Soon he and Edeline were making their way back through the crowds and out the heavily guarded gates.

Right through his enemies' fingers slipped the most precious of stones. Years they had pillaged, hunted, and tormented in search of the very treasure they now let walk right out their gates. And for years they had sought the identity of the innocent soul who held its power. How ironic that they should have it all and right under their watch — the stone and the guardian — caged for a moment in time in their own godless prison.

With Edeline tucked securely in his arms, Omont rode hard and fast across the hills of France, eager for the distance from the horrors left behind and fearful of those which might still lie ahead.

For soon the beasts would know, as it all would unfold—the fraudulent letter, the incredible risk—inevitably leading them to the innocent child.

With the fury of the damned, they would come for her. They would do anything to gain her power, for Hell on Earth would be their prize.

The late afternoon sun filtered through the thinning tips of the tall beech trees, capturing odd sprouts and folds of branches, casting them down as eerie shadows throughout the northern forest. Anxious and leery—it was with no small measure of relief that Omont saw his dear cousin awaiting them near the path's second fork.

Lucas de Villeroir was a man of great compassion and still greater faith. It was uncommon, even in these troubled times, to see the knight in anything other than his white cloak adorned with its bold red cross. Now a simple gray cape served as his cover, paling his skin and emphasizing a long, jagged scar running across the right side of his face.

Today's journey was not just of faith, it was also of transport. They would be carrying with them two precious treasures, simple and pure and far too valuable to be risked in any way.

Lucas's interest fell almost immediately to the stone dangling from the chain which circled Edeline's neck. Taking a wary breath, he looked to Omont. "How was he, your brother?"

"Even in his weakest hour, he is the strongest man I know."

"And Federic?"

"He was there, and still determined to show his face."

Lucas looked down as though ashamed. "My heart could not take their agony."

"Nor mine," Omont confessed.

Both men rode silently through the rolling hills toward the woods near Brines Castle.

As they neared the road to Harfleur, Edeline leaned against Omont's chest and lifted the stone lying flat against her belly. She had no idea what power she held in her tiny hands, even less would she understand the enormous responsibility such power would bring.

If only there had been another way. But there was none. So many had already perished, so many more had fled, and those who remained behind grew bitter and uncertain. The only soul left unmarred by the evils of the times belonged to a child—his child. What could he do? Either way she'd be cursed, either to live in a world mastered by immorality or to be hunted by the men who would choose to see it rule.

There was for him no choice, for God was his master. And though the task seemed overwhelming, he would put his trust in the Lord.

Squealing with delight, Edeline pulled his attention back to the simple brown stone and the brilliant light now radiating from its surface. Her small fingers raised it high for her father to see. From one pure heart to another, the key to man's greatest treasure had been passed, and with it, the responsibility of countless souls.

Omont shook with grief.

The magic of the moment was lost to its meaning. His brother, a man he had loved with all his heart, was dead. And his daughter, as pure as the need, but far too young to bear its weight, would carry his burden to her death.

Removing the stone from around Edeline's neck, he watched as its brilliance faded. Leaning down, he kissed his daughter's precious face. "Please forgive me," he whispered, as her fingers softly moved against his lips.

"Omont," Lucas said, tapping his shoulder and pointing to the trail behind them.

Through his tears, he saw in the horizon a dense cloud of dust billowing down the path from which he had come.

It had not taken long for word of his visit to spread to the ears of his enemies. He had hoped to have more time, but time, once again, had not served in his favor.

His brother's words came back to haunt him.

"The dreams are only guides, my brother. If their paths are not followed, nothing is certain."

Omont slipped the stone inside Lucas's leather boot before handing him his most precious possession. "Federic will come for her. You must let her go."

Looking lovingly down toward his small bundle, Lucas's eyes began to mist with sorrow. "Are you sure there is no other way?"

"I am sure of but one thing. There is only one place she will ever again be safe."

As though sensing the heartbreak to come, Edeline cried, reaching out her tiny arms to her father, begging him to take her back.

Omont had always assumed it would be he who led his dear child down destiny's path. But it seemed his path was to take another direction. To protect her, he had no choice. He would have to lead the beast away.

"God give you speed, my cousin," Lucas said.

"And you, my dearest friend." Pulling on his reins, Omont turned his mount and headed back toward a fate destined to be his.

Brines Castle, Harfleur, France, One day forward

Federic's hurried steps echoed off the castle walls, with their high gothic arches and bright gold coatings. Despite the raging storm outside, the once lively castle was now uncomfortably quiet and hollow. Its long halls no longer captured the joy and prayers of its inhabitants. Instead, they sat as a silent reminder of their more recent cries of despair.

How had it come to such an end? So many good and honorable men rewarded by those they had served with such cruel and unjust deaths. It would be his fate as well if he were to be caught — not that destiny would be changed. His fate was set one way or the other, by duty, honor, and his belief in the cross. He was not afraid of what was to come, for he would gladly jump into the arms of the Lord and let Him choose his end.

He stopped just outside the chapel. The sound of loyal but disheartened servants weeping for those they had lost, for those they would lose, and for their own bleak and uncertain futures, slipped through the closed doors. His hand hovered momentarily against the massive wooden structure. If they were meeting in the chapel, then they already knew. At least he'd be spared the role of bearer. He took a deep breath and quietly stepped inside.

Three knights kneeled on bent knees, bowed in prayer before the altar. The castle's few remaining servants sat scattered amongst the small wooden benches, weeping and waiting to do their masters' biddings.

Federic watched the knights and wondered what would become of them. Three braver men he had never known.

Roncin, a natural born leader, was as noble as he was bold. He had taught his men to fight with honor and courage, only to have them destroyed by those who fought without.

Lucas, a man of great humility and spiritual devotion, had lived his whole life for a church which had now left him condemned.

Hemart, his dear friend, a giant of a man with a heart equal his size, would undoubtedly be lost outside the Templars' realm.

Bowing his head, Federic added his own silent prayers for his brothers who had passed and his brothers who remained.

The straightening of armor clattered throughout the small room as the three knights slowly stood, their long white mantles falling to the heels of their simple, unadorned shoes. Three solemn faces turned toward Federic.

"Is it true?" asked Lucas.

Federic nodded. "They captured him near Beaumont. He's been taken to Paris."

"And the others? Were any spared?" asked Roncin.

"None," Federic said sorrowfully. "They kept their faith till the end, dying with honor and blessed for their strength."

Roncin covered his face with his hands and raged against the men who had taken their brothers, their friends, their fellow Templars. "Monsters, not men — that is what they are!"

"They will be the ones to answer in the end," Federic said, offering the only comfort he himself had found. "The Lord has seen their deeds, as He has seen our brothers' sacrifices."

A little girl with curling gold hair and bright blue eyes peeked out from behind one of the long flowing draperies. She smiled at them all before dashing back behind the heavy cover.

"They will be looking for her," Federic said. "If we do not leave now, it could well be too late."

Looking back at the small lump behind the drapery, Roncin smiled at the tiny giggles. There was no laughter in his eyes, however, when they returned to Federic. "Are you sure this is the only way?"

"I am sure of very little these days, my friend. But I have never known the priest to be wrong."

"You are a braver man than I, Federic Depuis."

"I gave my word. It holds me bound."

Three silent nods spoke more than words. They were all men of honor, living by a code both sacred and trusted. None would break that trust, especially to a man as honorable as Omont Montague. Now jailed for his knowledge rather than any crime, he would be beaten without mercy. But for the sake of the righteous, he would keep his silence and, in the end, most likely, suffer the same fate as his brother. And because Omont was such a man, Federic would keep his word, regardless of its price.

"Federic is right. It is time for them to go," Lucas said, breaking the silence. "We cannot count on the storm lasting much longer." He stepped away from the group and toward the curtains.

"Come on, my precious Edeline." Reaching inside the draperies, he pulled out the giggling bundle. He kissed her long and lovingly on her forehead, burying his face in the soft warmth of her curls. Tears rolled unguarded down his scarred countenance as he handed her to Federic. "Perhaps we are the monsters," he suggested.

All four men stood silent. If the priest was wrong, and not one could deny some doubt, then they were sending the child to a premature end. But fate had forced their path through despair and into darkness. It would take a blind leap of faith to once again break through to light. So, Federic took the little girl into his arms and hid her within his large surcoat.

She cuddled tight against his chest.

He couldn't look at her. He wouldn't. It would make what he had to do impossible. His own fate, he could handle. Hers, he wanted no part of.

Lucas pulled the stone from his boot and placed it into Federic's hand. "If they catch you…"

"I will toss it into the sea. Now I must go," Federic rushed, knowing if he thought about it much longer he might just go back on his word. He turned swiftly, heading back the way he had come.

Hemart followed behind him. "Are you sure I can't accompany you to the banks," he asked in his abnormally deep baritone.

Federic stopped and turned toward his lifelong friend. He knew it would be the hardest on him. Laying his hand reassuringly on Hemart's shoulder, he emphasized his last wishes. "Do not follow me, my friend, for on this journey we must part. You belong with the others."

"Federic, you realize—"

"I know what it is I do, and I know what it is I protect. Is there any greater honor?"

Hemart bowed his head and admitted sadly, "There is not."

"Then stay, and pray it be the Lord's hands that capture us." With that, he turned and made his way through the long, silent halls and out into the storm.

The rain beat without mercy against his face as he dashed through the night.

Braguard, his loyal charger, ran as though he, too, understood the importance of their mission. Sweat mixing with rain saturated the stallion's black heavy coat. He, like his rider, was a warrior. Thick of body, but agile and swift, he was every bit as noble a sight as the man who sat proudly upon him.

As Federic flew across the rugged coastline, he barely noticed the raging waters below. White angry wisps of the ocean's brew lifted high above their stone barrier. The sky held its own battle as streaks of white fury cut through the thick, rolling, gray cover, lighting the darkness and then quickly vanishing behind the clouds.

By the grace of God or the will of angels, they made it to the bank without incident. Although he'd seen no one, he had not been able to shake the feeling he was being followed. If it were the king's soldiers, surely they'd have shown themselves by now. Perhaps they were waiting for him to round the jutting cliffs ahead. It would be their way—to ambush him when he was cornered.

Again thunder roared and lightning's veins lit the earth. That time he saw them—no more than a fleeting glimpse. Just like the lightning, they were there and then gone. He held tight to Edeline as he charged up the rising cliff.

She clung tightly to his middle, frightened, no doubt, by the violent thunder that rocked the dark sky.

From his lips, words of prayer rang into the night. They were captured by the wind, then lost in the storm. The heavens parted, and a bright white rod lit the sky as Braguard, ordered by his master, jumped from the cliffs of France into the raging sea.

Chapter Two

Realm: Los Angeles, California, Current Day

Grabbing the satin tie in his rough hands, Federic began loosening the knot. "It's suffocating," he grumbled.

Edeline had seen the scowl, watched him fidget and knew it wouldn't be long.

"No you don't," she said, swatting at her father's determined fingers. "This is a black-tie event. You are not going to embarrass Alison by showing up in an old cotton shirt, jeans, and those ratty old work boots."

Dodging her attempts to interfere, he swatted back at her punishing hands. "I look like a gorilla shoved into this suit. If she doesn't like me as I am, then—"

Edeline caught her father's hands in hers and held them still. "Quit acting like you don't have feelings for Alison. I've watched you watching her."

"I like her fine," he admitted, finally surrendering his satin foe into her capable hands.

"You like her plenty." Taking hold of the narrow end of the tie, Edeline slid the knot back up to the collar of his freshly pressed shirt.

Lifting his face slowly to hers, Federic grinned. "She's a fine woman."

"Yes, she is," Edeline agreed, laughing when her father turned and dashed away toward the hallway mirror.

Her father was more than slightly interested in the lovely Alison, but for some reason he was having a hard time admitting it. Edeline had a sneaking suspicion she was the reason why. He'd always been very protective of her, perhaps because for years it had been only the two of them.

They had moved to the states when Edeline was a toddler. Shortly after, Father Tom had offered Federic not only a job, but also a home. Living in the small cottage near the back of the parish for years, their lives were built almost entirely around the church and each other. But it couldn't stay that way forever. She was twenty-four years old. Someday she hoped to fall in love and marry. With all her heart, she hoped her father would do the same.

Afraid of leaving him alone too long with the tie, Edeline followed her father into the hall.

A quiet man by nature, tonight he was walking well outside his comfort zone to accompany Alison, the Event Coordinator for the parish, to a fundraiser for the local food bank. They were becoming good friends. With time, Edeline hoped it would grow into something more.

Puffing out his cheeks, Federic leaned forward to blow fog across his reflection. Slowly the image cleared. His shoulders slumped. "I don't know what she sees in me."

Edeline smiled as her reflection joined his. "She sees her knight in shining armor."

"A knight dressed liked a gorilla. I never thought I'd see the day." Taking one last long look into the mirror, he shook his head and sighed. "I'm old. When did I get so old?"

Lifting up on the tips of her toes, she kissed his freshly shaven cheek. "You're not old."

Federic took her into his arms and squeezed her tight. "Thanks for helping me polish up, Edeline."

"It's been my pleasure." Laying her head lovingly against his shoulder, she grinned. "You'll be the handsomest gorilla there."

Shining down through the tall, nineteenth-century brick buildings which made up LA's quaint district of Morrow's Haven, the sun hit against Edeline's back, warming her skin but never quite reaching the chill beneath the flesh. Typically she loved her early evening strolls past the many specialty shops lining the path to her favorite used bookstore, Paperback Adventures, but not tonight.

Despite seeing nothing which would validate her suspicions, she'd been unable to shake the feeling she was being watched. It trickled down her spine, pulling her attention away from the tiny shops and toward the shadowed doorways, distant corners, and countless tinted windows which covered the beautiful old buildings. Nothing was out of the ordinary, yet the feeling remained.

It was probably her overactive imagination fueled, no doubt, by the many mysteries she'd been reading as of late. Still it was unsettling, especially when in the back of her mind sat her father's endless warnings.

"Don't take chances, Edeline," he'd always say. "That sixth sense has more common sense than the rest of them put together."

He was probably right, but she saw no one, or at least no one who seemed to be paying her any notice. Spotting her destination, she quickened her steps into a near run. Distracted by the persistent unease, she nearly fell through the doors of her friends' store.

"Hey, Eda," Paul Dowen greeted her from his post behind the counter. He put down the wire and pliers he held in his hands. "Everything all right? You look a bit…frazzled."

"Phobic is more like it," she said with a laugh. "I've been reading too many suspense novels, I suspect. They've got me imagining hidden goons and invisible stalkers."

"Ah…" He grinned, his dark curls bouncing as he nodded his understanding. "That can do it to ya. There's nothing like a good suspense to bring about an irrational case of the 'heebie jeebies.' If you're looking for another hair-raising read, we just received in —"

"No." Holding out her hands, she waved away the suggestion. "This time I'm sticking to something a little less spooky — possibly a romance."

"Romance?" His brows lifted in mock terror. "Yikes, sounds scary to me."

"Your wife tells me you're very romantic."

"My wife has an amazing imagination." Grinning from ear to ear, he turned to open the stairwell door behind him. "Speaking of my wife, I better let her know you're here, or I'll never hear the end of it. Amanda," he yelled up the narrow passage, "Eda's here."

A moment later, a petite brunette wearing an excessively large pair of glasses and a warm, welcoming smile emerged from the nearly hidden door. "Where have you been?" she demanded, approaching Edeline for a hug.

"Helping Dad get ready for his date." Wrinkling her nose at the huge, black-rimmed monsters nearly engulfing her friend's face, she snickered. "What are you wearing?"

A bright pair of magnified brown eyes moved back and forth toward the black frames sitting across the bridge of her dainty little nose. Amanda chuckled as she pulled the large glasses from her face. Handing them back to her husband, she explained, "They're Paul's magnifying glasses he uses for beading. I borrowed them to pull a sliver from my heel."

"They're very attractive."

"You're one to talk," Amanda said, nodding her head toward the old, battered, khaki-green, bucket-style fishing hat sitting atop Edeline's head. "I really wish you'd reconsider the hat."

Edeline had won the hat off Father Tom almost fifteen years prior.

"Fair and square," he'd said with a grin as he pulled off his favorite fishing hat only to pull it down over her nine-year-old face. "Hope it brings you better luck than it did me." Glancing down toward his scrawny little trout, he'd released a sorrowful sigh.

Edeline had simply adjusted the too-large hat the best she could before picking up her winning trout. "You can win it back next trip, Father Tom."

But he never had, and she'd realized some time back he never intended to. The hat was just one of the priceless treasures she had collected through the years.

"What's wrong with my hat?"

Batting her lids in disbelief, Amanda laughed. "What's right with it? If I had hair like yours, I'd wear it proudly for the world to see." Her gaze progressed down over Edeline's one-size-fits-all T-shirt and seriously worn jeans. "And if I had your body—"

"Your body's beautiful, honey," Paul said, peeking over the rim of his huge black glasses and giving her an exaggerated "once over."

Shaking her head at his antics, Amanda smiled. "Thanks for the ogling, dear."

"My pleasure." His dark brows waggled roguishly as his fingers continued to weave.

A flash of silver drew Edeline's attention to the intricately beaded bookmark Paul was making. His work was the best she had ever seen, finely detailed masterpieces built to mark one's place in whatever wonderful world they might be reading. Edeline's admiration was easily reflected in the numerous bookmarks lining her shelves and dangling from her various reads. She watched him work.

Looping black and red cord, he added another silver bead. It was nearly finished and absolutely stunning. "I want that one," she told him when, on his final loop, he added a tiny silver rose.

"Nope." His now-magnified green eyes sparked with mischief. "I promised you I wouldn't let you buy another. Don't you remember?" He grinned so wide his dimples emerged through his closely cut, black beard.

"Paul," he mimicked her, putting his hands on his hips and his nose in the air, "no matter what I say, no matter how much I beg, do not—*do not* let me buy another bookmark." He batted his lids and pursed his lips. "I'm going to Paris. I need to save my money."

"I do not talk like that," Edeline protested, rolling her eyes. "But you're right—I do need to save my money."

"That a girl," said Amanda, laying out her hand for the book Edeline brought in to trade. "This is a good way to start." She waved the book in the air. "I'm proud of you for letting one go."

"It wasn't easy." In truth, it had been close to impossible. Edeline treasured her books like many treasured jewels. Through them she had traveled the world, experienced history, and fallen in love over and over again. She wanted to keep them all. But by giving up one, she saved half on another.

Amanda placed the book on the counter. "Think of it this way—you're now two dollars closer to France."

It was a good point, Edeline realized as she walked through the store's narrow aisles searching for her next great romance or adventure. Every cent saved brought her that much closer to her dream. She was born in France, and in France lay her history. It was a history her father was oddly reluctant to speak of, but one she desperately wanted to know.

At the moment, all she knew for sure was that she was born in a small village in France, and that her mother had died in childbirth. Although her father had assured her they had no living relatives, Edeline was still determined to at least return and stand once more upon its soil. Of course, she hadn't told her father yet. Something told her he'd be less than pleased.

"Having any luck?" Amanda yelled back from the front of the store.

"Still looking."

Spotting a title that caught her interest, Edeline reached up to pull it down.

Suddenly her eyes began to blur as the books began to spin. A loud and heavy moan roared in her ears. Her stomach turned, and her body felt instantly drained of energy. Grabbing hold of the shelf, she waited anxiously for it to end.

It had been years since she'd experienced the feeling, and she'd really hoped it was gone for good.

The bright lights beamed down upon the dance floor, their reflection bouncing off Federic's recently polished shoes.

"You're doing wonderfully, Federic," Alison reassured his bent head as he concentrated fully on the placement of his feet. "You needn't worry so. Really, you're doing fine."

"You say that now because your toes are in one piece. You won't be singing my praises when I bulldoze them over." He stopped. "I've lost count."

Alison smiled. "Don't count. Just dance." With a gentle pull, she encouraged him to move.

Unable to do anything but follow, Federic stepped back into the dance. As the music beat rhythm into the crowded room, he and Alison waltzed around the large dance floor.

The music ended, and they slowly made their way back to their table.

Her arm linked with his. "I've had a lovely time. Thank you, so much, for accompanying me."

Pulling out her chair, Federic helped her take her seat. "I wouldn't have missed it." Moving closer to the table, he waited as the waiter walked by, pushing a loaded cart of cakes and pastries. The rattling of the wheels merged with the voices around him into one solid, loud moan. His stomach turned, and his limbs weakened as the world around him began to spin.

"Federic, Federic!" Alison's voice rang from a distance.

Soon the voices cleared, the room quit turning, and Alison was right at his side, holding tight to his hand while her eyes searched his face. "Oh, Federic, are you all right?"

Nodding slowly, he moistened his lips. "Would you mind if we called it an evening?"

An hour later, he was hurrying to Edeline's room.

Sitting up in bed with her blue comforter tucked safely around her, she held what looked to be a new adventure tight in her hands. As he stepped into her room, she dropped the book against her chest and smiled. "You're home early."

"I…yes." He sighed with relief.

She appeared completely unaffected by the breach, but he knew it wasn't so. Like his, Edeline's senses had always become a bit muddled when a piece of the present passed through the barrier into the past. They could feel the invasion where those who were born of the present could not. Of course she'd never known what it was. She'd always written the experience off to a weak stomach, and he'd played along. He'd seen no benefit in confusing her world with that of the past. But the time was coming, perhaps sooner than later, when he'd have no choice but to tell her.

Her eyes fell to the open collar of his shirt, noting, no doubt, the missing tie. "Did you have a good time?"

"A very nice time. And you?"

She waved her new book in the air. "Stopped by Paul and Amanda's."

"Anything exciting happen?" he asked, hoping she'd tell him about the spell.

"Saved two bucks on my purchase."

"Good for you, Edeline." Just as he suspected, she didn't want to worry him. Stepping across her floor, he stopped beside her bed and bent to plant a kiss upon her forehead. "I'm going to bed. Love you."

"I love you too, Dad. I'm glad you had a good time."

Leaving her room, he headed straight to his.

The beautifully etched, wooden heirloom box sat atop his dresser. Opening the lid, he pulled out the general's number and sat down at his desk. He was torn for what to do, but in the end, he reached for the phone.

"General Matthews," answered an unhappy and groggy voice.

"General Matthews, Federic Depuis here. I'm sorry to be calling so late, but I thought you'd want to know. I believe there's been a breach."

The hot Texas sun pounded without mercy against Dane's back as he scooted forward through the brush. His movements, swift and smooth, were invisible to those who stood guarding the compound below. Camel-colored camouflage along with a brush-covered helmet helped him blend naturally into his surroundings. He reached into his pocket, pulled out his binoculars, and then scanned the heavily guarded zone.

There were three massive metal buildings side by side about a quarter of a mile from the makeshift airstrip. Several large field trucks sat in various clumps around the buildings, a couple of them loaded high with stacks of illegal cargo. Others looked ready to go, most likely awaiting their next wild ride into the rugged terrain. Several men walked back and forth in front of the isolated warehouses, while others ran scurrying around, preparing for their next assignments.

When the large sliding door to the first warehouse opened, another cluster of men moved outside. Two jumped into the loaded trucks while the others waited just outside the warehouse doors, boisterously waiving them in.

A tall Hispanic man in his late forties, dressed in military attire and sporting a lifetime of scars across his hardened face, walked out from the warehouse. He smoked a large cigar as he spoke intermittently into his two-way radio. Dane watched as the man took his own binoculars and searched the afternoon sky. He turned toward the other men, then started shouting orders unheard from Dane's position.

It soon became clear they were expecting company as the two loaded trucks disappeared into the warehouse, and at least a dozen heavily armed men hopped into various vehicles and headed toward the airfield.

The man, Casimiro Rios, threw his cigar to the ground and took a long hard look toward the hills. Dane lowered the binoculars to hide any glare. Rios was no fool. He knew there was no place on earth truly safe from his enemies, especially when his enemies included nations of great power and wealth.

The hum of a small engine turned into a near roar as it drew closer. Dane stayed low as the craft passed directly overhead. Yips and hollers exploded from the airfield as the men jumped from their vehicles and waited for the small private craft to land. He knew the plane as well as the reason for the men's excitement. Payroll had arrived.

Once again, Dane dared a glance toward the compound. Rios had evidently decided the coast was clear. He stood, with his binoculars dangling at his side, speaking to one of his guards.

"Prepare to move," Dane whispered into the thin microphone dangling down from his earpiece. He watched the plane come to a rocky stop. Moments later, the craft doors opened and two distinguished-looking gentlemen stepped out.

"Full house," he reported as the new arrivals greeted their men. Slowly he slithered through the brush toward the compound. This was one raid he would not miss.

A quiet static played across his radio before a familiar voice directed, "Abort."

Dane froze. *Abort?* He must have heard wrong.

"Again," he asked for clarification.

"Abort."

"Damn it!" What possible reason could there be in aborting a mission which had been planned for months? This was the chance of a lifetime. What the hell were they waiting for? The sound of choppers flying overhead a few moments later made him realize the obvious. The mission wasn't aborted, merely his portion. He was furious. What could be so all-fired important it couldn't wait for him to participate in one of the largest and most successful raids of his career?

Easing away from the compound, he headed back toward his rendezvous. The sound of artillery erupted with the cries of battle from the opposite direction. He was missing it all. Clenching his fists, he once more cursed the final order. "This better be worth it."

Chapter Three

The long, mostly flat road leading to the base produced the perfect boilerplate for the hot Southern Nevada sun. Still, Dane left the jeep uncovered. The constant breeze held back the sun's most powerful punch, and the open view it provided the military escort he'd picked up two miles back assured no misconceptions would lead to any mishaps.

This wasn't exactly the place to take chances as any fool could see. If one was too daft to pay attention to the countless signs warning against trespassing, the low-flying chopper scouting their tail and well-armed, multipurpose vehicles following their path from the opposite side of the barbed-wire fence should certainly give clues.

He slowed as he approached the checkpoint, a tin shack manned by half a dozen armed guards and a simple enough looking steel arm blocking the entrance.

"Lieutenant Colonel," greeted one of the guards as he approached the jeep.

Dane handed him his papers. They wouldn't tell the man any more than he already knew. Anyone making it this close to the checkpoint was already expected and thoroughly investigated.

The man studied the forms nonetheless, then handed them back to Dane, giving the interior of the jeep an obvious once over. Assured no danger lay within, the guard stepped back away from the jeep, saluted Dane, and then motioned to a new set of escorts, who'd just arrived out of seemingly nowhere, that the visitor had been awarded admittance.

In something similar to a funeral procession, Dane rode the center of his new entourage all the way to the base — a base which didn't look much different from any other secured military facility, but it was. This secured fortress housed the answer to one of the most contemplated and debated scientific questions of all time.

In the early eighties, after numerous reports by local civilians of odd sightings and weather patterns in the area, the military began running tests and found the area was high in unusual atmospheric and electrical activity. Various experiments were conducted using aerial devices, crafts which were later either explained away as aircraft or simply denied. When it became clear exactly what they had, the base was blocked off, securing it from public curiosity. Of course, this only intrigued the public, leading to stories of close encounters and alien invasions.

The truth was no less spectacular. Within its secured borders lay one end of a miraculous funnel, a conduit within the time-space continuum linking two distinctively different worlds.

The funnel was actually a small tear in the fabric of the universe — a universe where its embodiments were constantly in motion. The planets spun, the galaxies shrank and expanded. The tear between times had not moved, but the Earth had, linking one end of the funnel to a narrow time span around the year 1310, where the portal opened along the northern shores of France. On the other side, opening inside the Nevada desert, was a wider time span believed to cover approximately 1955 to sometime just after the turn of the twenty-first century.

After years of trial and error and countless investment dollars, the world's most respected scientists and scholars had found a way to somewhat manage and manipulate the most dangerous portal ever encountered by man. Thanks to modern-day science, they could pick and choose the exact date within the time span their travelers would land in 1310 France. And thanks to small date-stamping devices implanted within the travelers' arms, the portal was able to detect their return and place them back safely in their appropriate time.

It was an amazing opportunity and one they all had eagerly embraced.

For years, they'd breached the barrier of time, exploring the past for the benefit of science. But the danger of such travel became more and more apparent. Finally, five years earlier, travel through the portal had been completely banned by military command, and it all had come to an end. That is, until nine forty-five two nights earlier, when one small bleep from a sleeping system brought a room full of leading scientists out of their chairs and on full alert.

The small caravan made their way through yet another checkpoint, this time to emerge right outside the heart of the facility, a large concrete building surrounded by heavily armed guards, few windows, and odd antennas and wires sprouting from every which direction.

The lab — the door to the portal and the past.

Its doors opened, and General John Matthews, a tall, salt-and-pepper-haired man, stepped out.

"You're a sight for worried eyes," said the general, meeting Dane as he stepped from his vehicle. "I hear we pulled you from the Pallet raid. That had to hurt."

"It did."

"Sorry, Dane, it was unavoidable." He nodded for him to follow as he turned and headed back toward the building. "It was quite a success I hear."

"So I'm told." Dane followed the older man through the doors and down the long narrow hall toward the elevators, their hurried steps echoing off the near empty walls.

They stepped inside the open lift.

The general selected the lower level, and the doors closed. He turned to Dane. "How much do you know?"

"I know we have a breach. I know it came from the future. What I don't know, is why we care. The future's a large, unknown field. They could have countless reasons for going back."

Matthews nodded only slightly before taking a weary breath. "Actually, the field's not so large. The lab is scheduled to be permanently decommissioned in twenty-one days. But it's doubtful the portal will hold that long."

"It's closing?" Dane's stomach performed a nauseating flip as he recognized a whole new set of dangers.

"Yes, it's weakening by the day. We're assuming nine forty-five p.m. Saturday was a time where its fabric had grown particularly weak.

That's why our sensors were allowed to pick up the surge as those from the future passed through our time, and it's also why Federic was able to sense it so easily."

"Shit."

"I'd say that sums it up pretty accurately." Leaning forward, the general pushed the button to stop the cart mid-flight.

"Look, Dane, I'm not going to lie to you and tell you there isn't risk. There's risk and plenty. What I will tell you is we have no choice. Our travelers had to have come from a time very close to ours. I'm guessing within the next ten days. It's safe to say we would not have sent them."

Dane ran his hand roughly through his hair. The more he learned, the worse it got. "It has to have been someone from the inside."

"Yes, someone who knows the portal's closing and knows the risks. They're acting out of desperation, and they'll be every bit as desperate to get back. You know what that means."

"They'll take risks. They'll be careless."

"Chances are good."

"Damn fools."

"They're worse," said Matthews. "They're greedy fools. They can be after only one thing, and they're not likely to leave without it."

"The treasure?"

The general nodded. "Fail or succeed, it doesn't matter. We can't afford to wait for them to make it back. We need everyone and everything not of the past back where they belong, and the sooner the better. Every second they remain in the past, the risk to our world grows. We have to send someone to bring them back. Our chances of success improve tremendously if that someone is you."

"Any idea who or how many?"

"They wouldn't risk an army. I'm guessing two or three. As far as whom, I truly have no idea. There isn't one of those with access I wouldn't have trusted with my life." Saddened gray eyes looked away for a moment before returning to Dane. "If they believe in the treasure, then they also believe in the story surrounding it. That means they've taken two things with them—Edeline and the stone."

"I take it we now have both adequately covered?"

"Of course, but that doesn't solve the problem. It's simply too late. That part of the future has already been moved out of our reach into the past. Yes, we can change the future, but so can they. And *they* now sit behind us."

"Making the advantage theirs."

"That's right. Ignoring that fact could very well be a death sentence to us all. We have to even the playing field. We have no choice but to send someone back."

"You truly believe one man alone can bring them back?"

"All you have to do is bring back the girl. Without her, the stone is useless. Bring her back, and the rest will soon follow. They'll have no reason to stay."

Leaning forward past Dane's shoulder, the general pushed the button to start the lift moving. Once the elevator stopped and the doors opened, he nodded further down the hall. "Go ahead and see your way to the lab. I'll grab your things and be right there."

Lights flashed from behind the glass as the lab and its instruments were brought back to life. Men in military gear ran around the room checking monitors and testing voltage. It was all so familiar. Federic could still remember the terror of that night twenty-two years prior, when he'd landed behind the glass wall in front of him.

Now, just as he had that night, Professor Blaine stared back at him through the glass, only now they stood on opposite sides.

Holding up a finger, the professor indicated he'd be a moment.

A moment—life could change drastically in that small split second. A lesson Federic had learned the hard way. First, when the King's graces had turned in a second through an unbelievable and unforgivable act of selfishness. And later, when a single leap had led him into a life he would never have imagined.

When he'd taken Edeline into his arms and fled that night, it was with a heavy heart bare of all hope but one. He had hoped his faith was not in vain. And yes, he had questioned it, Lord forgive him, all the way to the shore.

Leaping off the towering cliffs, he had braced himself for anything, but still not been prepared. A ferocious wind had pulled them into its grip, flinging them around and around against invisible walls.

Peculiar shadows and tortured cries had run with them through the darkness until they landed in the light, a light like he had never seen, an artificial light made by man.

It was a world both foreign and unimaginable. It was not Heaven nor was it Hell, but it was as shocking as either could have been. It was the future. And it, thereafter, became their home—his, Edeline's, Braguard's.

Just as the priest had predicted, the Lord had taken them into his arms and carried them to safety. He'd placed them in the hands of modern day warriors, warriors who fought for honor and justice, warriors who fought in His holy name. It was one of those warriors who put them in contact with Father Tom. Perhaps that had always been the Lord's plan. For the good father was truly God sent.

He, and those who stood silently behind him, had provided Federic and Edeline everything they would need to survive in their new world: not just shelter and food, but a home, a job, and documentation to validate their existence. It wasn't easy, and at times it was frightening. He thought he'd never learn their language or their ways. But now they were his and thankfully hers.

From behind the glass, a young scientist handed the professor a clipboard and words were exchanged. Though Federic could hear none of it, the bottom line was written clearly within the lines now lying heavy across the professor's forehead. The portal continued to weaken. Time was running out.

"Miracles were never meant to be caged," the professor had once said.

He was right, and Federic was certain this miracle had served its purpose. It wasn't all coincidence—the priest's visions, the bridge through time, nor was it coincidence the men who stood at each end. The scientists could call it what they willed, but Federic knew what the portal really was. It was a means to an end. It had provided him and Edeline sanctuary in a world far away from their time, far away from those who would stop at nothing to obtain her power.

Though now, in light of what has happened, he had to wonder if there truly was such a place. Past, present, future—none were as secure as man would like to believe.

Federic took a weary breath.

He would have to tell her. There remained no time in which to wait. If their efforts proved unsuccessful, somewhere within the next ten to fifteen days, his daughter would vanish into the past.

Perhaps he should have told her years ago—the truth of her birth, of her heritage, of her role. But for many years, she had been too young and the truth too complicated. Then it had simply been too hard. He had raised her as his own, and he could love her no more even if it were his own blood which ran through her veins. And like any father, he wanted her to have it all—a happy childhood, a normal life.

But some things were not his to give and others not his to take back.

Behind him the door opened, and a young soldier walked in. Stepping forward to the observation window, he stopped beside Federic and stared through the glass.

Federic quickly sized the young man up. In any century, he'd be recognized as a warrior. Large, well-defined muscles spread across his torso. He carried the kind of confidence and ego that had to be earned. It could never simply be portrayed.

Piercing dark eyes turned toward Federic. He was sized up and judged under the same harsh appraisal as he'd bestowed on the young man. The soldier nodded, but his verdict was unclear. "Federic Depuis?"

"I am," he replied, offering the young man his hand.

"Dane Walker, sir." The soldier took his hand and held it firm.

First impressions could be deceiving, but the soldier struck Federic as one of high caliber. With what the young man was in for, he certainly hoped it was true.

On the other side of the glass, Professor Blaine ran his hands through his already ruffled hair, then handed his clipboard to the man at his side. He walked outside the lab and a couple seconds later walked into the glass-paneled room behind General Matthews.

"I see you two have already met," said the general, dropping an armload of ancient-style apparel onto the table at Dane's side. Looking at Federic, he nodded toward Dane. "He's the best there is. He'll see everything gets put back in its appropriate place."

Federic grunted. One of the "everythings" getting put back in place would be his daughter—or her future self, that is. Those who took Edeline couldn't have gotten her into the portal without the dating device. That device would ensure her return back to the future, a future which will have been altered, a future where she hopefully will have never been taken.

The same would be true for the stone and the men responsible for the abduction. Once they realized Edeline had been brought back, they'd have no reason to stay. They'd return, and like Edeline, at a certain point merely vanish from the portal into their new realities.

If all went as planned, the only one returning from the past would be Dane.

One of the lab technicians tapped on the glass from inside the lab, then raised three fingers when the general looked his way.

"Professor Blaine?"

"It will do," the Professor said, looking anything but certain.

"I'd ask for a translation," Dane said with a scowl, "but I'm not sure I want it."

The professor nodded in understanding. "In layman's terms, the bars represent the strength of the connection between the two ends of the portal. It tracks a number of factors but mainly the movement of the particles which make up the walls within the portal."

"And strong walls have what kind of reading?"

"Better than three." Taking in and releasing a long breath, the professor's typically confident stance seemed to waver. "It's likely to be a rougher trip than you're used to, but it will get you there."

"And back?"

The professor exchanged an uncertain look with the general.

"Never mind," Dane said. "No choice. I get it."

"Just make it quick," General Matthews said.

"We know approximately when they landed and, of course, where," added the professor, changing the subject. "They won't expect to be followed, so that should give you the advantage."

"Sounds easy enough," Dane said.

Smiling at the young man's confidence, the general picked up the pile of clothes lying on the table and handed them, along with a photo, to Dane. He pointed toward the dressing area.

Dane hurried and dressed, then took a quick moment to study the photo. Soft blond curls surrounded a perfectly etched face. She was without a doubt beautiful, her blue eyes as soft and beckoning as her luscious red lips.

He placed the picture down on the bench atop his discarded fatigues.

The photo would have to remain behind, but it didn't matter. The face was one he would never forget.

Chapter Four

Her lids felt heavy, burdened by the weight of an internal fog. But Edeline was determined to see a world which had lost all clarity. Where was she, and how did she get there?

A cooling breeze blew softly across her skin, carrying the unusual scents of fresh earth, musk, and forest. It was enticing, comforting… strange. Managing to pull apart her lids, she caught a glimpse of clear blue sky.

Bright!

She flinched, and her eyes once again closed. With her head already aching, the light only served to intensify the pain. As the pain slightly dulled, the oddity of her circumstance emerged. What would she be doing outside? Where was her father? Why was her head so muddled and unclear?

Attempting to turn away from the blinding light, she was surprised by the heaviness of her limbs. It seemed unlikely she'd be able to move, but she knew she had to try. Though exhaustion called her back to slumber, something else called to her very soul—an odd sense of belonging, an irrational sense of home. It was a feeling she desperately wanted to understand. For this place, wherever it was, seemed nothing like home.

"Edeline?" A low whisper came as though in a dream. It tumbled in through her ears, but rumbled through her spirit. Like a physical touch, it warmed her inside and out. "Edeline, can you hear me?"

Instinctively she smiled. Something about the deep, hushed voice simply pleased her. She wanted to see him, but her lids refused this time to open.

"They're coming back," he said just as she picked up the sound of muffled voices and breaking twigs. "You're going to be all right. I won't let anything happen to you."

There was a rustling of brush, then she sensed he was gone.

This was crazy. It couldn't be real.

Comforted by the certainty it was no more than a dream and too tired to fight the exhaustion any longer, Edeline allowed herself to drift back into the darkness, awakening some time later to the sound of a distant battle. No doubt, her father was watching one of those horrible medieval dramas he loved so much.

"Dad, turn it down," she tried to yell, but the words came out muffled.

The sounds continued.

With great effort, she opened her eyes. "Dad?"

"She's waking up," said an unfamiliar voice from the not-so-far distance.

Long blades of grass swayed gently in front of her. Through their cover she could barely make out three distorted figures. It all seemed impossible, but it played real enough. The grass was vividly green, the smells quite definable, and her body undoubtedly sore. Yet her mind could make sense of none of it.

One of the figures stood and headed her way.

It was a man. Reaching into his pocket, he pulled out what looked to be a syringe.

Edeline's head began to pound as her insides turned with fear. She forced her eyes to remain open.

The man tapped the needle's tip and lifted it high into the air to study its contents. He turned back toward the others. "This will keep her about six hours. Think that's too long?"

Fighting harder than ever to stay conscious, she cursed her helpless state. Panic pushed the loathsome taste of bile near the top of her throat. She had no idea what these strangers were planning, but none of this looked good.

As the man stood there waiting for a reply that never came, the once refreshing wind blew a retched smell past her nostrils. If she'd had the energy, she'd likely have heaved.

The world swirled and with it the man.

Moaning her refusal to succumb to slumber, she felt herself losing the battle all the same.

"Hey, darlin'," said the stranger, grabbing her arm and searching for a vein. "A bit woozy, are we?"

The sounds of anguished cries still rang somewhere in the background.

Searching the man's face in hopes of finding a memory, she found none. This had better be a dream, or she was in very serious trouble.

She closed her eyes.

The man chuckled. "That a girrr—"

His grip tightened then released, leaving her arm to fall back to the ground.

When she opened her eyes again, the man seemed to have changed forms. She blinked several times, but the figure did not clear. This was another person altogether.

Deep brown eyes bore into hers. She reached up her hand to touch the handsome face, but the figure blurred, and her hand fell to her side. Slumber once again pulled her into the dark.

Sitting atop a hill, high above and far out of sight from the battlefield below, Graham watched the bloody battle with undeniable fascination. They were like nothing he had ever seen, these Poor Fellow-Soldiers of Christ. Courageous, bold, fearless—no wonder they lived in infamy.

"Amazing," he said, unable to look away.

"Their skills?" Farrell asked as they watched another knight plant his sword through his attacker.

Graham shook his head. "Their audacity."

In the valley below, swords moved through the air with lightning speed as the warriors took one mighty blow after another. Their cries, along with those of their attackers, merged into one. The only way Graham was able to keep track of the victor was by the number of red crosses remaining on the battlefield. One by one the others fell until the field was clear of everyone but the three men in the boldly marked, white surcoats.

He had heard the stories and even studied the warriors' reign, but never would he have believed it if he hadn't seen it with his own eyes. These were the men of legends. These were the Knights Templar.

"They had to have been outnumbered four to one," Farrell said in disbelief. "I gave them no hope."

"They were the greatest warriors of all time. You'd be wise to never underestimate them. Isn't that so, Mitchell?" Graham turned toward his friend. "Mitchell?" Lying motionless in the tall grass was his friend's slim body. Graham's heart skipped more than a beat. The girl had vanished.

"She's gone!"

Pulling his gaze from the field below, Farrell looked back toward the small patch of green. "What the hell?"

Graham hurried back toward Mitchell. Kneeling down beside him, he felt for a pulse. Beating slow but steady, it emerged. He had clearly been drugged. Not far from his friend's unconscious body, Graham spotted the emptied syringe.

"She's jabbed him with his own needle," he said in astonishment. Moving to his feet, he looked frantically around the countryside. "How did she manage it?"

"Maybe her old man taught her a few tricks through the years."

It was a good guess. No doubt the aging warrior would be wary. The man had, after all, been charged with perhaps the greatest task of his time — perhaps of all time. They should have given that fact a bit more consideration, along with the fact that his charge was more than mere sugar and spice. The blood of a great warrior raged through her veins, not to mention the spirit and strength of a high priest.

"Come on," he said, motioning for Farrell's help, "let's move Mitchell into the bush and then go after her. She couldn't possibly have gotten far."

Lifting Mitchell's arms as Farrell grabbed his feet, Graham caught a flash of material falling toward the ground. "Hold up," he ordered, bending down to retrieve the damp linen cloth which had fallen from Mitchell's side. He pulled it toward him for a better look but dropped it immediately as a vile stench drifted past his airways. "It's some kind of homemade chloroform."

"Chloroform? Where the hell did that come from?"

"The Cavalry," he replied. "It seems our little captive may have had a little help."

Graham's gaze ran across the many surrounding hills. Behind them lay nothing but soft rolling hills; ahead, nothing but forest. Tall trees and deep chasms would provide plenty of places to hide. The game had taken a drastic turn.

He nodded toward the field below. "There will be a few unmanned horses down there. Let's see if we can catch a couple."

Chapter Five

Cuddling closer to the warmth, Edeline buried her face against its solid surface. The horrid odor had gone, and in its place was the pleasing scent of worn leather and musk. Pulling in another deep breath, she found even more — the fresh fragrances of forest, a rejuvenating blast of clean air. She smiled, enjoying the moment along with the gentle sway of a soft and steady gait.

Gait!

Her eyes flew open.

Green was everywhere — green in the foliage, green of moss, green in the tall, thin trees which went up much further than she could see.

Her stomach tightened. Her heart squeezed.

Oh, dear Lord, I really am in a forest.

She looked down.

No doubt about it. That was a horse.

What in the world is going on?

She snuck a peek to her right. A black cloak spread across broad shoulders to fall loosely over a solid sheet of male. She swallowed. One thing she knew for certain — that was *not* her father's chest.

This is wrong. Everything is wrong.

Pulling away from the wall of muscle, she stared in astonishment at the ruggedly handsome man before her. His face was square, with sharp lines defining a perfectly shaped nose and pleasantly masculine chin. Dark brows sat attractively above deep brown eyes wrapped in thick ebony lashes. A good day's growth shadowed his jaw, adding an alluring but dangerous aura. Typically she would have found the man nothing short of striking, but there was nothing typical about the moment, nothing typical about being in a stranger's arms.

Dark piercing eyes looked down to meet hers.

"Aaaah!" Her blood-curdling scream shattered the late afternoon's calm, startling the man and causing him to jump.

What had until then been an easygoing horse laid back its ears and began prancing around, snorting a warning it would soon leave them stranded.

Grabbing tight to the reins, the rider worked to refocus the mount's attention, quickly calming its troubled nerves. "Good girl," he praised, leaning forward to stroke her long neck.

Looking back toward Edeline, he caught her ready to let loose another cry.

"Enough!"

Stunned by his sharp command, she momentarily fell silent. Only her heart's heavy beats still rang in her ears.

"Enough," he had said, and enough was right. None of this made any kind of sense — a strange man, a strange world. If one thing did make sense, it had to be her fear. It was a rational, normal response to awakening in the arms of a stranger in the middle of an unfamiliar forest...*on a horse!*

"Aaaah..."

Lifting high into the timbers, her cries echoed through the hills. Birds flew from the trees, sending tiny leaves floating down to the forest's floor. The man stiffened as the mare once again began to toss her head and prance in nervous steps. A heavy hand landed firmly across Edeline's mouth as the stranger pulled her sharply back against his chest.

"Enough, Edeline. I'm not going to hurt you. I'm here to take you home." His light stubble scratching her cheek as his warm breath heated her skin. From the corner of her eye, she watched him scan the long beaten trail, first ahead, then behind. There was no one there, but still he seemed unconvinced.

The man was careful, conscious, normal-looking, in no way her vision of a villain, but if her father's many lectures had taught her nothing else, they'd certainly drilled in the lesson of not judging a book by its cover. It was quite possible this shiny cover held the story of a madman, possibly a psychopath or maybe even a serial killer.

Oh God, a serial killer!

Air became scarce. Her heart raced even faster.

What would he do if she attempted to run?

Images of her mutilated body ran through her head. Deciding it best to remain still, she held her screams momentarily inside, waiting anxiously for the next given opportunity. If he was that nervous about being heard, it had to mean there was help out there somewhere.

She followed his watchful gaze out into the distant hills, seeing no one, recognizing nothing. *Where in the hell are we?*

"I swear, lady, those lungs of yours could call in the dead." Shifting his position, he searched the hills to their right. "Are you trying to get us both caught?"

She stared at him in disbelief. *Ah…yeah.*

The man had to be a lunatic—certifiably deranged. Had he escaped from the nuthouse or was his breakdown more recent?

Threatening eyes, black with temper, met hers. "If I let loose, do you promise not to scream?"

Nodding her head, she prayed him such a fool.

His hand dropped back to the reins.

"Help! Help! H…e…l…p!"

Fury flashed with frustration across his face. Tightening his thighs against the mare, he ordered her up the hill and deep into the woods.

Curses rumbled past Edeline's ears as branch after branch swiped against his protecting flesh—scraping and gouging. The steep incline and the mount's determined charge had her full weight flush against the man's powerful chest.

She forced herself to look ahead, desperately hoping to recognize her surroundings. Tall, dense trees rose higher than her vision was allowed reign. Where she could see sky, it seemed blue and clear. She had no idea where they were, but she knew where they weren't. They were nowhere near LA.

They took a sudden and sharp decline down a steep, rather jagged gorge. She looked down at the shockingly deep chasm below. If there was an end to it, her somewhat impaired vision wasn't able to find it.

The horse's hooves slid.

Instinctively she wrapped her arms around the man's middle, burying herself into his chest as his arms tightened around her.

"Scream and you're likely to have us both tossed to the ravine's floor."

Scream? Not likely. She could barely think to breathe.

Masterfully, he took them down the hazardous slope, his body moving against hers, producing a fluid motion which both balanced and moved them with the beast. With a firm hold and fast actions, he gave the horse direction. Edeline knew horses well enough to know it took a special kind of confidence and self-control to ride a horse down a slope such as this. Both the man and the horse had to be well-trained. If the man was indeed mad, it hadn't always been true.

Finally, after what felt like an eternity, they came to a stop.

At first he didn't move. It had been a long and harrowing ride down. No doubt even the madman was feeling the stress of the venture. Slowly, she felt his body relax.

"Off," he commanded, his voice filled with anger but also unease. The man had been unnerved. Something told her that was rare.

For a moment she was afraid she'd be unable to move. Every appendage seemed oddly foreign and few were proving cooperative, but the urge to feel the ground was strong. She peeled herself off him and slid down the heated mare.

She fell as one ungraceful pile to the earth below.

Had he really believed this would be easy?

Releasing a weary sigh, Dane rose in his saddle and swung himself to the ground.

Typically his "rescued" knew his role as well as their own. He was the good guy. Hero, most would say. They'd cling to him and his commands like the desperate souls they were. It was never easy, but this...

Kneeling down beside her, he studied her disheveled appearance. Sticking sporadically throughout her long, curling, blond hair were varying bits of the surrounding foliage. She was nearly covered with leaves and needles from head to toe. Her lips, a bright, full raspberry-red, were the only thing left unmarked.

Enchanting blue eyes, still somewhat clouded from the drugs, narrowed and looked away.

"Would you like a hand?"

She moistened her lips, shook her head.

Leaving her where she lay, he stood back up to take a look around the deep gorge and surrounding forest walls.

There were always threats, but the location was actually ideal. The depth of the chasm and the trees would give them excellent cover. No one would expect them to lodge at the bottom of such a hazardous ravine. As long as he could keep his troublesome damsel from screaming, it would be a good place to hide.

"We'll wait here," he declared.

She finally looked up. "Where…" Biting into her bottom lip, she hesitated. "Where exactly is here?"

This time he hesitated. Usually he liked to shoot straight, but "straight" in the case would sound particularly bent.

A heavy scowl landed between her eyes as fear shifted toward annoyance. "Not sure? Not telling? Am I not allowed to know?" Catching sight of a twig dangling from her curls, she grunted and began brushing her fingers through her hair, dislodging the still-clinging foliage. "All right, fine. Don't tell me."

"I'm not sure it would ease your mind to know."

"Not knowing isn't exactly a comfort." Taking one last swipe at the clinging debris, she threw her hands into the air. "Can you at least tell me what it is we're waiting for? Maybe your name? Maybe why you've brought me here?"

Damn. He'd hoped she'd carry some memory, that she'd have some recollection of what had transpired and the predicament she was in. Obviously that wasn't the case. Her captors had kept her well drugged. She was as ignorant to her circumstance as she was to her history. Convincing her of any of it wouldn't be easy.

This was a situation they hadn't prepared him for. Time had simply been too crucial. His only instructions were to grab the target and bring her back. By the looks of the clear blue sky, that might require a little wait. The portal needed an abundance of energy to operate properly. Without the convenience of bottled electricity, that required a storm.

"Well?" she asked impatiently.

With no idea where to begin, he decided to start with the most basic of facts. Taking a deep breath, he then slowly let it out.

"*Here* is about twelve hours from our destination," he said. "I'm Lieutenant Colonel Dane Walker, a member of the United States Air Force and Special Operations Task Force. I'm here at the request of General John Matthews and your father, Federic Depuis. For reasons you wouldn't believe if I told you, you were kidnapped. I was sent here to find you and bring you home. Unfortunately, that will require we wait for a storm."

She stared at him dumbfounded.

Finally she blinked, shifting her position in preparation for standing. "I don't suppose you have proof," she asked, making it to her knees, "some kind of identification, maybe a letter from my father, perhaps a cell phone I could use to call and…verify the facts?"

Reluctantly, he shook his head. "No."

Now standing, she laughed and rubbed her fingers against her temples. "Do you really expect me to believe any of that?"

Not for a minute.

"It's the truth, Edeline. It's all I have to give you."

"I see."

She thought him mad, and that would likely prove a problem.

Stumbling sideways, she braced herself against a thick oak. Bent forward at the waist, she stared at the ground, by all appearances waiting for the world to quit spinning.

"They drugged you pretty heavily. It will take time for the effects to wear off. The best thing for you would be to sleep."

"Right," she said, pulling out her skirt and wrinkling her nose at the yards of fabric falling in the form of a dress clear to her feet. "What is this?"

Studying the foreign material, Dane realized, like his own ancient garments, it had to be both heavy and warm. He and Edeline were from a time when comfort outweighed modesty. They were, therefore, unaccustomed to the burdensome fashions of the fourteenth century.

"It's a dress," he replied, watching her take what must have been her first real look at the ridiculous attire.

Tight sleeves ran the length of her arms, swaddling her into what undoubtedly felt like a mobile sauna. To add to the weight, a sleeveless vest of some kind was thrown over the top.

"A dress?" she repeated in disgust. "It's an oven." Her dark blue pools shot to him. "Good grief, you look even more ridiculous than I do."

Looking down at his long linen shirt and simple black cloak, he grimaced as his eyes moved to the tight hosiery beneath. He couldn't argue.

"What kind of getup is this? How did I get into this horrid thing?" She gasped as her frown turned into a glare. "Did you dress me? Did you…undress me?"

His shoulders lifted and fell with a hopeless breath. "No."

The look she cast him couldn't have been more condemning. "I'm pretty certain I'd remember dressing in such laughable attire. For that matter, I'm certain I wouldn't." She huffed and turned toward the jagged stones lining the steep hillside. Letting her head fall back against her shoulders, she fisted her hands in the air and growled in frustration.

"I don't understand any of this. I don't. If you wanted me here, and now you've got me here, what's the harm in telling me why?" Her eyes grew wide. Her hands shot up to cover her heart. "Oh, God, this is some kind of ritual thing, isn't it? A sacrifice of some sort—the attire, the forest—it's all part of the ritual."

He blinked. That was a jump he hadn't expected.

She took several steps back, her eyes now wild. Spotting a large branch, she picked it up and held it out in front of her. "Stay back."

Holding out his hands as though approaching a spooked horse, he stepped slowly toward her. "It's nothing like that—no ritual, no sacrifice. I'm really just here to take you home." He took another step toward her only to have the branch thrust in his gut. "Ugh."

"Stay back. I mean it. Stay back or I'll…I'll…"

"Beat me with the stick?" he supplied.

With the branch still held out in front of her, she lifted her skirt and started backward up the hill. He could have intervened, but he figured it was best he let her realize the futility of her efforts now rather than try to convince her of it repeatedly.

The chasm was deep. Very little sun ever reached its depths to dry its foliage. The floor was slick and the climb steep. Her feet slipped and slid nearly every step, but she managed to make it up about five feet before she had no choice but to drop her skirt and reach for a boulder.

Dane stepped toward the hill. "I wouldn't—"

Her fingers slipped. Her feet moved out from under her. Dane watched with a mixture of appreciation and humor as she slid on her bottom back down to the base.

He moved to help her, but she waved the branch frantically in front of him.

"It's impossible in this getup," she said, getting back on her feet and glaring down at her skirt's heavy fabric. Grabbing a handful of the offensive material, she started to rip.

Dane rushed her, grabbing and sending the branch flying when she would have used it against him. Taking hold of the skirt, he lifted it up to inspect the damage. Seeing her mortified expression, he tried to explain. "You haven't got a replacement."

Looking down once more at the confining material, she lifted a sardonic brow. "I don't believe I want one."

"It's crucial to have the right attire."

"For the sacrifice?"

He dropped the fabric and cupped her frightened face. "I swear to you there is no sacrifice. I'm not going to hurt you. I'm going to take you home."

Her wide blue eyes now appeared more baffled than cloudy. "Then why do I need this getup?"

"To appear normal."

Her lips pursed. Her lids batted a couple times up and down before she took a shaky breath. "All right, Robin Hood," she said, pulling his hands away from her face. "I hate to be the one to break it to you, but tights hit their fashion peak a few hundred years ago and have since fallen to the category of feminine. And, hey," she added, lifting her hands out between them, "maybe that's your thing. I'm not going to judge. But this," she hesitated, looking down once again to her dress. "This isn't for me."

"Maybe not, but if you don't leave it be. I'll have no choice but to bind your hands."

She stared at him aghast.

It was obvious to him now there would be no reasoning with the woman. If he didn't get her under control, she'd end up getting them both killed, or worse yet, trapped in this merciless era.

"Look, Edeline," he said, backing away as he rested one hand casually in his belt and raked the other through his hair, "we both want the same thing."

Lifting her brows in mock surprise, she countered. "To see you safely back to the hospital from which you've escaped?"

She was doing much better if she'd now found her wits.

"Please, Dane, I don't know why you've taken me, but please let me go."

"I'm not the one who took you. I'm the one who took you from them, and for no other reason than to take you home."

"I'm to believe you're my hero?" She threw out her arms in exasperation. "Okay, then, fine, Colonel, Lieutenant or whatever you said you were, if you didn't take me, who did?"

"I don't know. I didn't recognize them."

"Did they have big heads, antennas, green skin?" She batted her lids, apparently unable to stop herself from poking fun at the lunatic. "Did they penetrate your aluminum cap and command you to take me prisoner?"

"No. They were very real, very much a danger."

"You mentioned a storm?"

"It's our passage — the only way back."

"You really are insane," she declared, turning back toward the trail from which they had come. "I've been kidnapped by a madman who's obsessed with the weather. Good grief, I'm in the middle of Lord only knows where…" She stopped, her shoulders slumping as she looked back up the steep path.

"You're in France, and I didn't kidnap you. I truly want only to take you home."

Looking back his way over her shoulder, she scoffed. "I can't decide which of those statements is more preposterous."

"They're both true. Edeline," he said, moving to stand beside her. "How much do you know of your birth?"

"I was born in France."

"Yes."

"We moved to America when I was a small child. I remember nothing of what came before that. I was only two."

"Your father never told you how you came to America?"

"No. He's told me very little." Her brows creased. "What are you getting at? Are you saying you know something of my past?"

He had no idea how much to tell her. He would have thought her father would have told her. It seemed foolish not to, and in addition unfair. But if he tried to tell her now, she'd never believe him. In fact, it would most likely only reinforce her belief that he was entirely mad.

"Why France? Of all the places you could have claimed, why did you choose France?"

"Because we are in France."

The afternoon sun beat down through the trees, catching the fear as well as the exhaustion in her downcast eyes. She put on a pretty good front—one of bravery and strength. Not that Dane doubted either. In fact, he was certain she possessed both. But beyond the strength was a young woman lost and uncertain, and beyond the courage was the knowledge of her own limitations. Without a doubt, she was outmatched. She couldn't fight against his strength, nor could she outrun him. She was at his mercy—a fact recognized, but still unspoken between them.

Purposefully keeping his voice soft and comforting, he delayed the inevitable. "I'm sure you're tired. There are probably things you should know, but I'm tired as well and not at all certain where to begin." He nodded back toward the mare. "I have bread if you're hungry and blankets for rest. Can we agree on a truce long enough to indulge in both and hopefully gain back our ability to reason?"

He could see on her tongue lay a sharp and most likely stinging retort, but she held it there carefully as she considered his offer. Suddenly her bottom lip nearly disappeared between gnawing teeth, only to reappear even more luscious and inviting than before.

"I *am* hungry."

He turned and headed back toward the mare.

Small, uncertain footsteps followed behind him.

He patted the mare before pulling the cloth satchel off her back.

"Really hungry," Edeline said as he pulled out the bread and tore off a chunk.

Grabbing her hand and turning it in his, he gently opened her fingers and rested the bread in her palm. "It's surprisingly good, but unfortunately dry."

Her eyes fell to the bread and his hands which now surrounded hers. A small growl rumbled on cue from her empty middle. She withdrew her hand from his and smiled somewhat reluctantly. "Thank you."

His dark eyes fell to her lips. There was something about the woman which simply drew him — like a moth to a scorching flame, no doubt. He would be wise to keep his distance. "Don't worry, Edeline. I won't let anything happen to you."

Startled blue eyes stared into his. The bread slipped from her fingertips and fell to the ground.

"Edeline?"

"I remember you," she said almost on a whisper. "I remember your voice. I couldn't see you, but I heard you."

It was exactly the break he'd been looking for. "I wanted you to know you'd be all right."

"He was going to drug me, but you stopped him."

He nodded, thrilled that she could remember. "That's right."

"You saved me."

It wasn't a question, so he didn't respond.

"I don't understand," she said, her brows pulling just above her nose. "Why?" She looked to him for answers. "Why would anyone take me? Why the clothes? Why here?" she asked, spreading her arms out to her sides. "And who are you, Dane? Why would you come for me?"

"I am who I said I was. I'm Lieutenant Colonel Dane Walker."

She looked away. The shock was wearing off, and the reality of her circumstance was setting in. She seemed lost, so very fragile. He thought about pulling her into his arms and comforting her, but quickly changed his mind. He wasn't the comfort she was looking for.

"It's complicated, and we're both tired," he said. "We should eat. We'll get some rest. Then we'll talk."

She shook her head. "I don't know. I—"

"I'll tell you. I promise."

Wrapping her arms around her middle, she appeared to be giving his words due consideration. Glancing down toward the bread lying on the ground, she lifted her shoulders and grimaced. "I'm sorry."

He reached inside the satchel and grabbed another piece. "It's all right," he said, handing it to her.

A tentative smile played across her lips. "Thank you."

She'd recovered quickly, yet another show of her strength. Good. There was every possibility strength would become vital. The road ahead was likely to be rough.

Dane was certain of two things. One, her captors would come for her. Two, even if they didn't know where they were now, they would know where they were headed. Which meant somewhere between here and there, he had to earn her trust.

"Her father?" guessed Farrell.

"No," said Graham, leaning down by the dirt where the tracks had disappeared. "It's one of Matthews' men." Raising his fist, he loosened his grip, slowly releasing the dirt back into the tracks. The soldier, whoever he was, had purposefully gone off the path and into the hills. Graham rubbed his jaw as he studied the hillside. He'd be damned if he'd follow him there.

"Just one?" Farrell snorted, apparently relieved or perhaps simply amused by the number.

"Just one," Graham acknowledged before standing and climbing back onto his horse. "One is all it takes." He'd served fifteen years under General John Matthews. The man only recruited the best. And under his guidance, they only got better. Though highly trained himself, Graham had no desire to spar with any of the newest elite. No one understood time better than he, and one thing time always allotted for was improvements. With a heavy sigh, he pulled his mount back the same direction as they had come.

Farrell grunted. "We're not just giving up?"

"No," he replied, undaunted by the anger in his comrade's voice, "but we *are* going home."

"Are you crazy?" Farrell raged. "I didn't take such a great risk only to quiver and give up."

Turning back to where Farrell sat still upon his horse, searching the surroundings for more clues to follow, Graham laughed. "You're a damn fool if you think you can take him alone."

"There aren't many men I can't handle," replied Farrell, throwing Graham a deadly glare. The bright sun beat red upon his receding hairline, making his large, rough features appear even fiercer. He was a huge man used to intimidating and having others cower.

But Graham wasn't a small man by any measure, and it took a whole lot more than one arrogant bastard to make him back down. "You know the dangers," he reminded. "We fight our enemies on our own ground, in our own time. We'll wait for LaFay to return, and then we're out of here."

"You really want to be the one to tell LaFay we've lost the girl? No thanks. I'd rather risk my fate with time." Farrell looked up toward the hill where the tracks disappeared and where Edeline and her rescuer, no doubt, hid. He nodded that direction. "I'd rather risk my luck with him."

Farrell had a point. Dealing with LaFay wasn't much better than dealing with the devil himself. Still, better an enemy you knew than one you knew not at all. They had no idea what awaited them in those hills.

The best thing to do would be to wait for LaFay. Hell, perhaps he'd actually bring back the army he so arrogantly said he would. Graham would put nothing past the man. He seemed to care very little about his own fate or the effects their trip might have on time. *The fool!*

"We haven't failed," he said. "The deal was we get the girl and the stone here. They're here. LaFay's quite capable of taking care of the rest."

"He'll have our heads."

"No." Graham shook his head and then added with disdain, "He'll enjoy the hunt."

Farrell's nostrils flared with temper. "I want my piece of the treasure."

"The treasure's not going anywhere, you fool." Lifting his arms, Graham swept them around the breathtaking panorama. Untouched by man, it stood in its purest splendor—evidence that this was not their world. He looked back toward Farrell. "Don't you get it? We're the only things here at risk of extinction."

Chapter Six

Edeline awoke to the sound of a light breeze blowing gently through the foliage. A pleasant and comfortable heat wrapped itself around her and cushioned her head. Against her back, she felt the even rise and fall of a chest, moving in perfect rhythm with the wisps of air blowing in and out over the top of her head.

She opened her eyes to find herself lying in Dane's arms. He'd been leaning against the tree behind her when she'd first lain down to rest. She had no idea when he'd moved to join her. Exhausted and still feeling somewhat beaten from the effects of the drugs, she must have fallen fast asleep.

The man smelled good. The alluring mix of leather and musk was now accompanied by the fresh scents of the forest. It pleased her — just as his voice had done earlier that day.

She was attracted to him.

How could she be attracted to a man she had every reason to believe was deluded? Sure, the man was gorgeous and at times seemingly sane. But those were merely facts distracting from a puzzle undoubtedly a touch irregular.

It was the circumstance. It had to be. She was scared, and he was…well, he was all she had. She didn't know where she was, why she was there or how in the world she was ever getting home. In an absolutely illogical way, he offered her hope.

She wanted to believe his crazy tales. As odd as they were, they still made her feel safe in this unfamiliar, mixed-up reality she found herself. And if her memory wasn't playing tricks on her, he *had* actually saved her. But from what and for what reason?

He had very few answers, and those he gave were utterly absurd.

France? Really? How ridiculous is that?

Though the man behind her might be real enough, the world he was living in certainly wasn't.

The day's events came tumbling back to mind with panic on their tail. Closing her eyes, she took a deep breath, trying once more to calm her scattered nerves. She needed to take inventory. It was possible things weren't as bad as they seemed.

Kidnapped, drugged, in some kind of forest supposedly in France.

The desire to laugh rose with hysteria.

Moving behind her, Dane's grip on her waist tightened. He pulled her close. Snuggling against her, his breathing once again took up a steady rhythm. As much as she wanted to lie there in his arms believing herself safe, she knew she couldn't.

Why, who, what, and where? She wasn't even sure which question needed answered first. What on Earth would anybody possibly want from her? If it was her body they wanted, she'd most likely already be dead. They'd had ample time to bestow their dastardly deeds and be done with her. They couldn't be after money. She, nor her father, had any. They lived very modest lives. No one would mistake them for wealthy. And how would such a scenario introduce Dane—a hero from out of the blue? Ridiculous! Unless…

Could he have been one of the men who took her but then, perhaps, gotten cold feet? Was he merely saving her from a path he himself had put her on? She closed her eyes and tried to remember. Her last memory was standing in the middle of her kitchen having just finished the dishes. She'd grabbed her popcorn and was stepping into the living room to watch a movie, and there they were—at least three of them. Someone, and someone very strong, grabbed her from behind and covered her face with a piece of cloth.

Edeline blew out a shaky breath and looked down toward Dane's powerful arms.

She never saw the man who grabbed her, only the cloth. It was exactly like the cloth Dane had been holding when she'd groggily opened her eyes in the tall grass earlier that day. Only that cloth had carried a wretched smell. There had been very little odor on the one that had been placed over her airways. Still—she sighed with regret—it was the same type of material, most likely intended to be used in the same manner and for the same purpose.

Disappointment hit with an undeniable thud. Despite wanting to believe otherwise, she simply couldn't. What other explanation could there be?

So where were the other two men, and who were they? She was certain the man she'd first seen upon waking was the same man she'd first seen in her living room. Edeline was also certain Dane was responsible for his disappearance. What about the third? Had Dane also taken care of him as well?

Her eyes widened as terror caught up with paranoia. She was sleeping in the arms of a killer—a fact which made the experience far less appealing. Lifting his arm, she did her best to move it without being caught. It didn't work.

"Not yet," Dane said. "We'll need our rest. It will be a long ride to the cliffs."

She swallowed. *Cliffs?*

She scanned the area. There was no way out but up. He'd have her caught and bound in less than thirty seconds. She'd have to outsmart him. And really—how hard could it be?

"I have to go to the bathroom," she lied. *Brilliant! Bravo! Old and overused, but totally believable.*

He grumbled unhappily, but eventually sat up. Those dark, mesmerizing eyes stared into hers. His hair was slightly ruffled, his face creased from the pouch he'd been using as a pillow.

"Don't go far," he said, rubbing his stubble-covered jaw while taking a watchful look around. "You need to stay where I can reach you in a hurry."

Yeah, right!

"I won't go far," she assured before rolling to her feet. She stood there a moment, trying to pick the best path.

The trees were dense everywhere she looked. There was plenty of cover for a getaway, but unfortunately most of it ran the steep slopes to the top. She wouldn't have a chance unless she could escape unseen.

Finally to the east, she saw where the woods stayed flat a good distance before disappearing behind a stone wall. *Perfect.* She smiled down toward his watchful eyes. "I'll call if I need you. I won't be long."

Taking his curt nod as permission to leave, she lifted the hem of her skirt and headed toward the thickest section of forest.

It was a rough trek through the dense gathering of thick oak and stately ash. Short bursts of light flickered through the tips of the heaven-bound trees, sporadically lighting the snapping assortment of rotting leaves, bark and twigs beneath her feet. She'd have to find a way to silence her steps or he'd realize what she was up to.

"That's far enough," he called, obviously already standing and most likely on his way.

Stopping on command, Edeline cursed her misfortune. *Dang, blasted twigs.*

Standing there like a rabbit caught in a trap, she was nothing but fair game. She had to start moving.

"There's a good spot up ahead," she called back, carefully picking up her feet and moving as fast as she could toward the towering stone wall. The sound of a not-too-distant waterfall sparked her next move. "I hear water," she called back over her shoulder. "I'm going to tidy up."

Her captor's approach could now be heard coming quickly from behind. Silence was no longer an option even if it were obtainable. No longer caring what clamor she made, she started to run, heading straight toward the sound of the falling water.

Finally she made it to the rocks. Lifting her skirt, she tied it into a large knot high on her right thigh and began making her way up the rock-covered slope. Thankfully, it was much easier than the slip-and-slide fiasco she'd tackled earlier that day.

"I'd better come with you."

Irritation ran as a tightened nerve up her spine, ending in the form of a scowl as she turned her frustration toward the sound of breaking foliage. Dane emerged from the trees. A glint of long silver drew her attention to his side.

A sword. *Great, just what every lunatic needs.*

"It's for our protection," he said, catching her look of dismay.

"Protection from what?"

"Protection from whatever."

After depositing an unwelcoming glare, she continued up the hill, mumbling her annoyance as she did her best to add to the distance between them.

"Those boulders could be loose. Test their endurance before trusting them with your weight."

Probably good advice. She'd take it and ignore him.

The next few steps would be rough ones. She decided to adjust the knot of material at her thigh. Modesty begged her to lower it. Common sense vetoed the plan for the sake of a quick escape.

"If you're worried about your skirt, you needn't be," assured Dane. "I won't look."

She shot him a disbelieving glance.

"You have my word," he said, bending his elbow and raising his hand into the air to display his palm and three raised fingers.

"Really," she drawled, raising her lip into a doubtful snarl, "you were a Boy Scout?"

He grinned.

Rolling her eyes, she turned back to the task at hand. "Swell, I have the word of a madman with a merit badge. I feel so reassured." She reached for her next handhold. "Bet your tracking skills are in top form."

"I could track a coyote through a hard and dry canyon," he admitted, already standing directly below her.

She jumped, scanned the impressive distance he'd so effortlessly covered, then scowled again. "Terrific. I'm thrilled."

"My hearing's pretty sharp, too," he added with a grin. "I can hear twigs snap and the pitter-patter of runaway feet from several yards away." His hands circled her waist as he helped her up the next steep incline.

"I'm perfectly capable of taking care of myself," she snapped, irritated by how easily he'd reached her and realizing her efforts would all most likely be in vain. Her feet hit the ground, and she promptly brushed off his hold.

"I'm sure that's true in Los Angeles, but you're not in the city any longer." He effortlessly swung himself up to her level. "Hmm," he grunted as they both eyed the rock's surface doubtfully.

Edeline took a deep breath, puffing out her cheeks and then releasing the air in exasperated puffs. She drummed her fingers against her hips. As hard as it was going to be to admit it, she was going to need his help.

She half smiled, half grimaced his way.

"Do you climb?" he asked.

"In and out of bed on a daily basis."

He sighed and eyed once more the rock's surface. "All right, here's the plan." He pointed out the crevices where she'd place her hands and feet once he lifted her.

A second later she was hanging on for dear life. Heights weren't typically one of her fears, but then she'd never before been left hanging on the steep side of a stone wall. She hesitated and looked down.

"You're all right," he assured. "Pull yourself up and wait for me at the top. If you drop, the furthest you're going to fall is into my arms."

She reached for the next small crevice and pulled herself up. In two relatively short moves, she found herself at the top of the rock's rough peak. "It's beautiful," she exclaimed as she caught sight of the tiny waterfall and gentle stream. Sunbeams fell through the trees and danced against the water like sparkling crystals. "Truly beautiful."

"Hold up. I'll help you down." Dane jumped toward the first crevice where he'd directed Edeline. He missed, tried again, and missed again. "Okay." He frowned and looked around for another.

"Problems?" She smirked from her safe vantage point.

His eyes narrowed, but still he grinned. "No problem," he assured and reached for his next target. The surface chipped, and the crevice disappeared. "Not good," he said, unable to find another crevice within reach. He jumped down a level and searched for another route.

Edeline turned her head to hide her amusement. It was then she spotted it. A path tucked just beyond the waterfall. The trail was vague, and the brush to its sides thick, but it definitely was a trail. *A trail has to lead somewhere, doesn't it?*

She looked back down toward Dane who had successfully found another path.

If she ran, she'd have no idea what she was running to or even from. And there was that part of her which wanted desperately to believe in Dane. There were times the man screamed reliable, honorable, and trustworthy. Perhaps he had been at one time.

He was the right age for the onslaught of schizophrenia. All of this, to him, could be very real. Perhaps he did see himself as her protector. But that still left the question—was he dangerous?

Years of her father's preaching the logic of paranoia won out. She swung her body over the rock's peak and made a run for it.

"Edeline, no!" Dane shouted from the distance, but she didn't stop.

What kind of lunatic dressed like an ancient warrior and helped kidnap a woman only to then turn around and help her break free? Sick or just deranged, the answer was simple—the kind you run from.

It was an easy descent down as the backside of the rock was far less steep. Her feet hit the ground beside the trail, and she took off on a sprint, or at least as much of a sprint as one could muster in such ridiculous shoes. They were made of soft leather, long and pointed, with soles thinner than pizza crust.

Branches slapped against her face as she charged up the trail, but thankfully they grew sparse as the trail widened further up the path. Looking ahead it seemed unending. Her breath was already labored, and her lungs ready to burst. Tears filled her eyes. She wouldn't make it, but she'd be damned if she'd give up now.

His arm circled her waist as he dove from behind. Together they fell to the hard surface below. She tried to crawl from his grip, but he held on tight, eventually forcing her onto her back.

She hit, kicked, and clawed, trying her best to break free. But in the end, her efforts proved to be in vain. He soon had her pinned motionless beneath him.

"Enough," he ordered, lowering his head to rest beside hers. "I'm not going to hurt you."

A shadow, cast from above, fell across Dane's shoulder.

"What be your plans, young warrior?" asked an incredibly deep baritone from somewhere above…*in French!*

As the sun blinded Edeline to the figure, a sharp blade appeared against Dane's neck, and shortly after, two more.

"Release her at once," demanded another stern voice.

Two strong sets of hands reached down and made sure Dane complied.

Edeline scrambled to sit up.

Still somewhat blinded by the light, she could barely make out three new players. They were all speaking back and forth between each other in French, and not the modern-day French Father Tom occasionally spouted, but rather the odd-style of French spoken by her father.

How could that possibly be?

"I mean her no harm. I'm here to take her home," Dane spat out in the same awkward French as he was pushed to his knees.

Edeline slowly looked up, blinked, and then vigorously rubbed her eyes.

Oh, frolicking forest of freaks, there were now four of them. Dressed in tights and wearing ridiculous cloaks. She turned and looked up the path ahead. She'd never make it. Her head fell into her hands. Sobs shook her body.

"You have been harmed?" asked a gentle voice. One of the men had knelt beside her. When she looked up, all she saw was warmth and compassion in his hazel eyes. He was, like the others, a large man. His long dark curls fell from a badly scarred but kind face. Oddly enough, it seemed somewhat familiar.

Tilting her head, she asked in the best French she could muster, "Have we met?"

He studied her slowly, his brows drawing together in confusion as first he studied her eyes, her nose, than her long flowing curls. "You do indeed look familiar. But I'm certain I'd remember such a lovely face."

"Lucas," another called, "has she been damaged?"

He looked toward her inquisitively. She shook her head as she untied her skirt and covered her legs.

"Nay, she is not damaged," he yelled back before offering her a hand and helping her to her feet.

"I have committed no crime against this woman or any other," Dane professed angrily. In one swift move, he ducked under his captors' hold, rolled, and flew to his feet. They'd taken his sword, so he stood before them unarmed. He eyed the dagger which hung from the closest knight's belt.

The man beside Edeline roared with laughter. "Best be watching yourself closely, Roncin, or he'll soon have your weapon as well as your pride."

Roncin snorted. "I welcome a challenge." Motioning toward the man standing closest to Dane, he ordered, "Hemart, throw him back his sword."

"I think not," Hemart said simply and held his guard. He was the largest of all the men by far. His fierce looks exaggerated plentifully by his thunderous vocal cords. Even without a weapon, he'd be a formidable opponent.

"On your knees, you fool," Roncin ordered of Dane.

"And find my head rolling forward? No thanks."

Roncin glared, raising his sword high above his head. "A strike easily made while you stand."

"No!" Edeline cried. She clumsily made her way down the hill to stand between Dane and the two men now guarding him.

"No? You wish to protect him?" Roncin asked, a confused scowl hanging between his brows.

"Yes…maybe…I don't know."

She looked behind her to Dane. "Why? Why did you take me from my home? What is this? Where are we?"

"Edeline," he said her name softly as he took a step toward her. "You have to believe me. I didn't take you from your home. I'm only here to take you back."

Her eyes narrowed with rage. Still he chose to lie to her. Sick or deranged, either way he was dangerous. She stepped away from his reach and behind the other men. "I withdraw my objection."

Roncin nodded and then raised his sword high in the air.

"No!" she cried again. "Wait."

The man actually seemed intent on taking Dane's head. "Are you all insane? I don't care what this is. You can't just go around flinging swords and taking lives."

The man looked back over his shoulder her way. "You certainly are confusing, my lady. Make your claim. Is the man foe or perhaps… lover?"

She looked toward Dane, but he seemed more interested in the men's cloaks than her declaration. His look of fear turned to one of hope. "I'm here at the request of her father, Federic Depuis, an honorable man and Templar Knight."

Edeline watched as the three men fell frighteningly silent.

Good heavens, do they actually believe him?

"He's lying," Edeline shouted. "He's delusional. He took me from my home, away from my father, who is no doubt worried sick. And believe me, though he is a prince, my father is not, nor has he ever been, a Knights Templar." She knew the legends of the Knights

Templar, and she recognized the symbols the three men wore across their cloaks. Was that the role these men were playing? Did they realize she was an unwilling participant?

"A prince?" Roncin repeated, his brows pulling together into one straight line.

"Edeline?" Lucas looked at Dane but moved her way. "I remember. You called her Edeline?"

She looked nervously back toward Dane. "Yes," she confirmed, "Edeline Depuis."

Lucas tilted his head and studied her eyes. He nodded his head as though agreeing to some unstated declaration. "Where are you from, Edeline Depuis?"

Dane shook his head in warning, his dark eyes once again filled with worry.

"Los…Los Angeles…California." She could see Dane's head drop as though handed a dreadful blow.

Three confused faces exchanged fleeting glances.

"And where were you born?" Roncin queried from behind.

She turned, surprised to find him so near. "A small villa in northern France."

"And the date of your birth?" Hemart put away his sword and walked to her side.

Suddenly Dane seemed like her safest option. She looked between the three hovering men toward the madman in back.

"No," Dane mouthed the word, shaking his head adamantly.

"Ah…I don't know," she said, still staring at Dane, "for sure." She wrung her hands together nervously as Roncin looked suspiciously behind him and then stepped to his right, successfully blocking Dane from her view.

"Open your mouth," Hemart insisted as he lifted her jaw.

She jerked her head away. "What for?" she demanded.

"Your years, of course."

"I'm twenty-four," she snapped and tried to step away, but they simply followed her.

Lucas smiled. "So that means you were born in the year…" He paused and waited.

"Nineteen —"

"Edeline!" Suddenly Dane was behind her, pulling her away from the small hovering circle.

Roncin looked to Dane in disbelief. "Six hundred years?"

What are they talking about?

Edeline followed Roncin's gaze to Dane. He looked sick, as though his world had recently come crashing down. "Dane?"

He ran his hands roughly across his face. With a heavy sigh, he dropped his hands and looked past her to the men. "Closer to seven, actually."

Chapter Seven

"I don't believe you." Edeline looked toward the three men standing several yards away near the stream. "I don't believe any of you."

"I can't say as though I blame you," Dane said wearily before hanging his head and shaking it in frustration. "It's the truth, Edeline. I don't know what else to tell you."

She could see he was thoroughly exhausted. Whatever this was, he was apparently unable to simply call its end. And no wonder. It was incredibly complicated. Every time she was given an answer, it only served to conjure up another dozen questions. For instance, if these men were all part of the same elaborate scheme, why wasn't there any sign of recognition between them and Dane? No one was that good of an actor—always on mark, always on cue. And they were so eager for word of her father; eager, actually, to know anything about their lives. If it hadn't been for Dane saying she'd had enough and pulling her away, she was certain the questions would still be coming.

Dane studied the men before looking back her way. "Look, Edeline, you're going to have to trust me. As difficult as I know it sounds, you're going to have to try. Ignorance in this case is deadly. You have to realize what we're up against. You have to realize the risks are real."

"I want to go home." Her lips quivered. She was beyond tired, hungry, and her feet throbbed thanks to the horrid things these men called shoes. To top it all off, her head was pounding with idiotic tales of knights, time travel, and magical storms. With a whimper of surrender, she slid down beside an old beech tree.

Dane followed. "I can get you home." Taking her hand in his, he gently held it as he looked toward the three knights. They were standing just beyond the falls deep in conversation. "But I'm no longer certain exactly what that will hold."

So much for the warm fuzzies. She pulled back her hand. "Are you trying to scare me, Dane? If you are, you can stop trying. I'm already bordering on hysteria." Unshed tears pooled in her eyes. She, too, looked toward the three men. None of them were the ones who'd taken her from her home. They were three new pieces to this already complicated and confusing puzzle.

"I'm scared myself, Edeline. But I believe it's a good sign that I'm still here. If too much had changed, I doubt that would be true. I have a feeling we're very lucky we stumbled onto these three men."

Babble, it was all babble. As real as it was all beginning to seem, she had to keep reminding herself it was all nonsense. People didn't simply fly through time, and there was nothing special about her. She was probably no more than a random, unlucky choice for this surreal disaster.

"Dane." Taking back his hand, she covered it with hers. "Why are you doing this to me? Why the elaborate game? What can I do to make it stop?"

His eyes held hers for some time; then suddenly he chuckled as though stumbling upon a discovery. "Oh, Edeline," he said, shaking his head and smiling. "I think I have an answer. I'm going to make you a deal, and you have my word, lunatic or not, I'll honor it."

Her brows pulled as she studied him warily. Perhaps this was the key to win the game. Take the key, and eventually it would let you out. "All right."

"Play along."

"What?" The gasp was real. The request seemed impossible.

"You heard me. If you want to make it home, you'll play along. You'll pretend it's all real. You'll do as I ask, and I'll make sure you're home within three days."

"But…"

"In the meantime, if you see even one person who fits your description of normal, feel free to ask for help. You have my word I won't interfere. In fact, I'll help you to them."

"I..." Looking toward the waterfall, she realized she really had little choice. The offer was the best she was likely to receive. And what, after all, could she do? She could try running, but where would she run? It was obvious to her now the woods were part of the game. The one hope she had, stirred by a belief quite strong if not rational, was that Dane wouldn't hurt her.

She watched the three men suspiciously. They seemed harmless as well. In fact, they seemed rather sweet. But they, like everything else, made no sense at all. She sighed. "You won't leave me alone with them, will you?"

"They would never hurt you."

The tears which had pooled started to fall. She was exhausted. Good choice or bad, she needed to believe in him. "Promise me."

His eyes softened as he reached forward and wiped away her tears. "You have my word."

Dane's jaw was beginning to throb. He tried to swallow but quickly gagged.

Hemart grunted and pushed his mouth even wider apart. "Hmm," he snorted, tilting his head for a better view. His brows pulled together as he reached inside Dane's mouth and tapped against the gold coating.

Jerking his head free, Dane snapped shut his mouth. "All right, that's enough," he said as the two men sitting across from them watched with great interest. What in the blazes had possessed him to mention the gold filling anyway?

"Teeth have always fascinated our dear friend," Lucas grinned. "And yours are especially eye-catching. How do you do it?"

"It's called good hygiene," Dane retorted as he rubbed his now aching jaw. The three men once again exchanged confused glances. Though he dreaded more questions, he decided to explain. "We have men who specialize in the care of teeth."

"And you are such a man?" Hemart asked, apparently fascinated with the idea.

"No," Dane said, shaking his head, "but I visit them."

A round of "ahs" and "mmhmms" were followed by poorly hidden smirks and snickers.

"I'm a soldier by trade," Dane added, suddenly finding himself on the defensive.

"And a fine one, I am sure," Roncin added right before he and the others threw out all pretense of good manners and simply laughed out loud.

Dane shot them a look of exasperation. So much for the belief Templar Knights were void of humor.

"I'm curious," Dane interrupted their chuckles. "You don't seem particularly surprised by the idea of time travel. I would have thought you'd find it disturbing."

Roncin's eyes lost their humor as they looked back toward Dane. "Nothing could be more disturbing than the atrocities which rule these days." He shot a weary glance toward the other two knights. "Very little could now surprise us."

"Roncin," Lucas said, anxiously scanning the surrounding trees, "there is no reason we cannot tell him."

Staring at his friend, Roncin quietly considered his words.

All three men were of extraordinary character—noble, honorable, determined—still Roncin was the one who seemed to emerge as the natural leader. It wasn't hard to see he took the role and all its responsibilities to heart. He was guarded. No doubt the times had made him so.

The Knights Templar was a remarkable group of men who had pledged their lives to a cause they held more valuable than life itself. And yet, seemingly without remorse, the men they had served, for the sake of their own selfish fortunes, had turned against them. Many knights had lost their lives for no more than their devotion, a devotion which had for hundreds of years served many kings and noblemen, including those who now sought to see them destroyed.

Respectful of Roncin's position, Dane remained silent.

Eventually the knight nodded his agreement. "You are right, of course. If Federic can trust him with Edeline, I imagine we can trust him with what little we know."

The knights all drew closer.

"The possibility of time travel is not new to us," Lucas said, surprising Dane.

The shock must have shown, as Roncin smiled and quickly added, "Yes, it is against our most fundamental beliefs, and there was a time we would have denied it vigorously. But how can we deny what we have seen with our own eyes?"

Once again, Dane was taken aback. "You've actually seen it?"

"We were not sure what we saw," replied Hemart, rubbing his eyes as if he were still trying to clear the vision. After a quick drink from his flask, he wiped his mouth against his arm and looked back toward Dane. "Against Federic's wishes, we followed him to the cliffs below Brines Castle."

"It was my decision," Lucas confessed, his sad glance moving toward Edeline. "I was torn. She was so precious, so innocent. I knew it had to be, but I…" Dropping his head, he released a heavy sigh. "I am not certain why I followed. As for the others, they followed me."

"And it is a good thing we did, or we would have thought him mad. What we witnessed was unimaginable. If I had not seen it with my own eyes, I would never have believed it true," Roncin said. "The skies held the white lightning rod still as it set the hills aglow. Odd shadows, not cast but still there and remarkably clear, danced across the cliff's tall walls. Air, rain, and sand swirled into what looked like a long, endless tunnel. As we watched, the shadows told a story, but not of our world."

"The white rod vanished into the frightful air from which it had come," Lucas added, his eyes suddenly wide with remembered disbelief. "The tunnel closed, and the shadows disappeared along with Federic and Edeline." His eyes lowered to the ground where Hemart had taken a stick and drawn what looked to Dane to be a tunnel into the earth. "We were unsure of what we had seen. But we knew, whatever it was, it was not of our world."

They had witnessed the portal, which even to Dane's more worldly eyes, was still a sight to behold.

"We searched the rocks below," Hemart said. "Even if they had made the water, it would have only thrashed them back against the cliffs. By the Lord or by His will, they had been taken."

"We assumed the priest's visions had come to pass," Roncin said.

Lucas nodded. "Nicolas Montague, Edeline's uncle and my cousin, served as a High Priest in the Knights Templar. He was the most honorable and God-loving man I ever knew. Blessed," he added. "Blessed in spirit, blessed with vision."

"It is true," Hemart added. "He knew about the shores and the tunnel."

"Yes," Lucas said. "It came to him in a dream. Of course, he thought it was Heaven's gate he was seeing. He saw visions only. Their meanings were not always clear. In his visions, he saw Edeline entering the tunnel a child, but later emerging as a woman.

"We were not sure what we had seen that night, but Heaven's gate seemed a logical answer. Of course, we assumed it would be years before she returned." Turning, he looked back toward the trees where Edeline slept. "It is hard to believe she is the child we held but two days prior. But having witnessed the priest's vision coming to pass and knowing what we know of the treasure, it is not so surprising."

"The treasure?" Dane asked, leaning closer. "You know about the treasure? Can you tell me what it is?"

There were countless theories surrounding the treasure linked to the Knights Templar. Many liked to believe they'd held and still possessed the Holy Grail and the Ark of the Covenant. Absurd it might seem, but it was hardly surprising—the myths, the mystery, the speculation. The world's fascination with the Knights Templar wasn't exactly a fluke. It was the result of a wealth in unusual facts all surrounding an order pledged to the highest power of all: God.

"We have known of the treasure for some time," Roncin said. "Only a few, mostly now gone, ever knew its location. But we have all seen a piece of it at one time or another. Some pieces have been used to barter, some in war; others were used often in our worship. But the greatest treasures have remained hidden. We have heard many tales, but there is very little we know for sure."

"Tales?"

"Tales of near mountains of gold and precious gems, riches beyond anyone's imagination," Hemart explained.

"The kind of riches that buy and sell men's souls," Lucas added sadly. "Put in the wrong hands, such wealth, such power, could destroy a kingdom."

"Put in the wrong hands, it could do far worse," Roncin said, exchanging a troubled glance with his men.

Dane closed his eyes, running his fingers roughly across them. He got the picture, and it explained a great deal. Put in the wrong hands, it could bring down a giant, perhaps even one as great as the church they served.

"Do you honestly believe Edeline is the key to this treasure?"

Roncin nodded. "Yes. We saw it with our own eyes. When she touches the stone, it changes forms, turning a brilliant brown and shining like the sun. Only the guardian has that kind of power."

"Guardian?" Dane repeated. "I've heard that term before but never understood exactly how it works. The guardian, the stone, the treasure — how do they all relate?"

"Legend has it that the stone works as a key to the treasure, but only in its empowered form."

Dane looked once more toward Edeline. Could she truly hold such power? It was all a bit farfetched. He wasn't one to believe in the supernatural. But then, he would have never believed in time travel if he hadn't seen it for himself. The world was not nearly as black and white as it seemed. He of all people should know it true, as here he was, in the middle of fourteenth-century France, speaking to men of legends.

"A magical stone? Where did it come from? How many know about it?"

The three knights exchanged uncertain glances. Roncin shook his head. "This is all new to us. We only learned of the stone ourselves when the knights were condemned and our help was needed. We were told the stone has been with the church for ages as is true with much of the treasure. How it came to be, we do not know.

"We do know there are those who seek it, not for the sake of the church or its people, but for purposes of their own — purposes both dark and troubling."

"The king?" asked Dane.

"The king seeks all the Templar wealth, but it is doubtful he knows of the stone. If he did, he would have turned over all of France looking for it. He would have demanded it."

Hemart snorted. "Which is likely the reason he was never told."

"I'm certain that's true," Lucas said. "The man's greed is notorious."

"Okay, so if it isn't the king, then who?"

"We know neither their faces nor their names," Roncin said. "We were told about them briefly in warning, that's all. You have to remember, this was only recently made known to us. We were told only what we needed to know."

"Certainly you have an idea?"

A branch snapped nearby. All four men moved swiftly to form a circle, their backs to each other and their hands hovering uncertainly over the handles of their swords.

The sound of the waterfall hitting the stream mixed with the hushed mutterings of a nocturnal world awakening to its realm. Within the dense trees, shadows from the day's end were quickly losing their form as the forest turned to darkness.

The scurrying away of an animal's quick steps could be heard in the snapping of more foliage. Relief escaped in the form of four sighs as the men holstered their swords and once again drew together, none of them taking their eyes off the woods for very long.

"There are many who seek the treasure," Roncin said. "But how many would know of the stone? That is the real question, and we do not know the answer."

"We couldn't possibly," Lucas said. "We know too little of the stone's past, which is where their identities lie. As for those who seek the treasure, Roncin is right. There are many. Our enemies alone count in the thousands, and they would stop at nothing to covet what is ours."

"Your enemies?"

"There have always been the two sides. Good and evil have always walked the earth beside man, using us as weapons in a war where the winner takes all."

Hemart's gaze never left the woods. "We do not always know who we are fighting. They are a varied group, often working for different masters."

"We, on the other hand, fight for what is right," Lucas said. "We fight for our Lord. Who we are is always clear. It is perhaps our greatest disadvantage."

"Yes," Roncin said, "but we fight as one and for one. That is our greatest strength. Our enemies might follow the same path, but they are there for their own selfish reasons. They may be united, but they are not one."

Dane took in a deep breath as he struggled to take it all in. It was all interesting history, but it was the threat to Edeline which concerned him. "You said earlier, as long as she lives, there is no access but through her?"

"Yes, that is true," Roncin said, "but you would also need the stone and the location of the treasure."

"The men who took Edeline most likely hold the stone," Dane said. "And with such limited time available to them, they either know the location or believe they can obtain it. The good news is we now have Edeline and they're left with very little time. They're likely to realize the risk isn't worth it. Hopefully they'll leave your world, taking with them all risk. Your enemies, whoever they are, won't know who Edeline is. Even if they know about the visit to her uncle, they will never connect the child to the woman."

"This is all true," agreed Roncin. "Those of our time would know nothing of Federic's journey or your journey here. As long as our enemies' paths do not meet as ours have, we should be safe."

It was an unlikely threat, but still an unbearable thought. Dane looked toward Edeline. "What happens if she dies?"

"I am uncertain. Though I imagine it is possible the treasure could be lost to all forever."

"I sure hope they realize that." Dane looked to the distant hills, feeling for the first time the weight of the world land squarely on his tired shoulders.

Chapter Eight

"Edeline."

Dane's deep chords worked their way pleasantly into her dreams. Too tired to face the dawn, Edeline merely buried her head deeper into the cloak she'd been using as a pillow.

Her shoulder was grabbed and lightly shaken. "Wake up, Edeline. We need to be going."

Funny, it didn't feel like morning, probably because she'd had such little actual sleep. Between the horribly hard ground, Hemart's bear-like snores, and fitful dreams of being stalked by four crazed men in tights, she hadn't probably slept more than a couple hours. Thoroughly exhausted, she was ready to sleep now.

Somewhere in the distance, the faint crackling of a fading fire played steady behind the rustling back and forth of busy feet. Perhaps the night really had come and gone.

"Edeline." This time his voice rang with a hint of impatience, and she found herself far less appreciative of its low melodic tone. Batting her hand blindly over her shoulder, she tried to shoo him away.

"Come on, Edeline, we need to be moving."

Slowly she began pushing away the blanket, but quickly reconsidered as the cool and somewhat damp morning air sank through her clothing to nip at her flesh. She shivered and drew the cover back up around her neck. Cuddling deep into the blanket's warmth, she prayed he'd have pity and leave her be.

With a determined tug, the wool cover was grabbed from under her fingers and abruptly pulled away. The brisk air assaulted her full length in one unwelcomed blow.

"Hey!" she yelled her displeasure as she battled to open her eyes. Finally they opened, but offered her no light. There were still stars in the sky and not a single sign of dawn. "It's dark." Wrinkling her nose, she sat up to offer him the full extent of her glare. "It's still hours until daylight. Have you gone mad?" The words slipped out before intelligent thought slipped in. Covering her mouth with her hands, she giggled. "Sorry, I forgot who I was talking to."

He smiled. "You seem to be doing better this morning. Get a good night's sleep?"

"Not at all. You?"

He leaned closer and whispered. "I kept thinking we were getting attacked by grizzlies. I've never heard a man snore like that."

She couldn't help but smile back. "My father does. That's the only reason it didn't have me running into the woods."

Though the night hadn't brought her much rest, it had at least brought her some peace of mind. These men, whoever they were, whatever nonsense it was they were up to, didn't seem to want to hurt her. In fact it was exactly the opposite. They seemed genuinely concerned for her well-being. It wasn't that all doubts were gone. She still had doubts and plenty, but the dark cloud of pending doom had dissipated into something more like a fog of mystery.

She had hope.

Hope that eventually normality would find her. Either that or Dane would prove true to his promise and simply take her home.

"We need to get moving," he said.

Running her hands through her hair like a comb, she looked all around their campsite. "It's still dark. Wouldn't it be better if we could see where we were going?"

"Dark is what we're after, but if you continue to dawdle, we're going to lose it to the light." Lifting one of her long blond curls, he unexpectedly grinned. "Come on, Goldilocks, the porridge is warm and ready to be eaten, this bed's about to move, and your chair's sitting atop my horse, waiting to be warmed." He looked back over his shoulder at the three men packing their few but scattered belongings. "They've offered to accompany us to Harfleur. All things considered, we'd be fools to turn them down."

Edeline peeked around his shoulder toward the three men. Still in tights and wearing their ridiculous capes, they gave her about as much comfort as an airborne plane without a pilot. Biting nervously into her bottom lip, she looked back to Dane. "Are you certain that's such a good idea? I mean, they may even be crazier than you." She grinned. "No insult intended."

"Mm," he grunted and began rolling her blanket.

She watched his bent head. He was very focused for a mad man…and handsome. Her glance fell to his tights, reminding her that the one was more pertinent than the other. She grimaced. "Your tights, though truly a fashion faux pas, are one thing. But your new playmates are not only running around in tights, they're also wearing long capes and pretending to be Knights Templar." Placing her hand over Dane's, she looked deep into his eyes and whispered, "I think they believe it's true."

"It is," he whispered back before rising to his feet and leaning down and pulling her to hers. "We're very lucky to have them," he said as though in reprimand. "Now behave yourself and get moving."

"Knights Templar." She snorted in disbelief as she brushed away the foliage still clinging to her skirt. Wouldn't her father get a kick out of that one? Taking a step toward Laur, Dane's horse, she suddenly stopped.

"Wait," she said, walking a small circle, searching the ground as she turned.

"Have you lost something?" Dane asked as he too began to search.

"I seem to have misplaced my fairy wings and magic dust." Raising her brows high in animated terror, she covered her cheeks with her hands and gasped. "What will I do without them?"

"Very funny," he drawled sarcastically, but his smile was real. Pointing toward Laur, he nodded his head for Edeline to move.

"What about my porridge?" she complained.

"Hungry?" Lucas asked as he approached with what did indeed look like a small bowl of porridge. His eyes caught hers and held them with what struck her as true affection. "It was your favorite. I hope you still like it. It will fill your belly and last until dawn."

"Ah," she said, taking the warm bowl in her hands. "Thank you."

"You're welcome, Edeline." His hazel eyes sparkled as his smile warmed his rough, scarred features.

A vision, vivid and sharp, played from her memory. Edeline took a deep breath and stared at him in astonishment. She was certain it was him. Same face, same scar, same kind eyes, and, shockingly, the same age. But the memory wasn't recent. Belonging to a time long passed, the memory was from her childhood. She was but a child reaching for a treat as he held it out in offering. "I remember you," she muttered in disbelief. "How can that be?"

Lucas looked toward Dane uncertainly.

Dane shrugged his shoulders. "She'll never believe a word. Let her come to it on her own."

"We need to be leaving while we still have the darkness," Roncin called.

"Finish up." Dane nodded toward her bowl before stepping past her to Laur.

Edeline slowly took her first bite of the mush, testing it hesitantly on her tongue. She smiled. "It's good. Thank you, Lucas."

His smile broadened. "All is well, my Edeline," he said before bowing and turning back toward the other men.

It was all so confusing. She'd known him, and he'd cared for her—she was certain. And when he and the others had spoken of her father the previous afternoon, it had been with true affection and respect. Looking around the ravine at the tall trees and peaceful surroundings, she could find no point in any of it—the charade, the games. What did they have to gain, and why in the world was she here? She had a feeling nothing was as it had first seemed. Could it be real? Could they be telling the truth?

Impossible.

She took in a deep breath of the fresh earth smell. No manufactured odors, no exhaust or smog. Wherever she was, it was a long way from Los Angeles. She never thought in a million years she would yearn for the smells of the city.

This wasn't real. She'd have to keep reminding herself of the fact, or she'd soon be flying as crooked as the rest of these loony birds. And the striking man, who now felt so familiar, was really but a stranger. She would take him up on his offer and scream for help at the very first glimpse of sanity.

The men were miraculously quiet as they led the horses up the steep incline. Small nocturnal creatures, well hidden by the dense forest, were by far louder as they rummaged through the foliage. Not one man so much as whispered a word. They spoke through silent gestures and nods. Dane, every bit as instinctively as the others, knew when to move and when to pause. Taken in by the sheer intrigue of it all, Edeline sat quietly atop Laur and watched with appreciation as the men moved carefully forward.

A simple world made beautiful by the touch of God, everywhere she looked nature's art had produced yet another breathtaking scene. Trees, young and old, wide and narrow, towered into the black abyss of the pre-dawn sky. Their arms, yielding leaves both broad and plentiful, stretched across the horizon, forming canopies of green. As they moved further up the steep slope, the sun began to shine across the magnificent peaks of distant hills. Its soft golden light found its way through the gaping holes of nature's cover, capturing its brilliance in the moist drops of morning dew. The damp, moss-tangled foliage glistened from the forest floor like a bed of diamonds.

What an odd place to find herself. A mystic forest untouched by the hands of man, men dressed as knights from an era long buried, and she in the middle of it all. It was surreal. But long having given up the notion of it all being a dream, it was indeed real. And there would be an explanation, perhaps bizarre, but it would come. Then everything would make perfectly good sense. Well, maybe not everything. It wouldn't explain the reason her eyes always searched for her captor, or why her heart seemed to race whenever he was near.

She watched him. Though covered in layers, nothing could hide the broad shoulders and strong, muscular frame of the athlete beneath. But he wasn't just physically fit, he was agile. The way he had moved across the rocks took skill. The way he had moved away from under the other men's swords took training. His confidence and ease could only have come from experience. He had declared himself a soldier, and by all appearances the title fit. In truth, the man seemed better than normal; he seemed bright, courageous, and toward her — protective.

Edeline pushed away the irrational thought.

Roncin suddenly stopped and looked back toward the others. Silently motioning toward a distant trail, he lifted his arm indicating the path would be steep but faster. The three other men looked and then nodded. Silence, signals, mysterious trails — a part of her wanted to laugh. Like Robin Hood and his merry men, they made their way through the enchanted forest ever fearful of the corrupt king and his army. She should probably be afraid, not of the imaginary villains, of course, but definitely of her interesting escorts. But she wasn't afraid — not anymore. In an odd and unexplainable way, she was actually starting to like the peculiar crew and maybe even slightly beginning to enjoy the unsolicited adventure.

They were halfway up the hillside when the path became almost unbearable. Dane stopped and reached up to help her down. Longing to feel the ground under her feet, she didn't hesitate to slide down into his arms.

Perhaps it was her wayward thoughts or merely the enchantment of the mystic forest, but in that unexpected moment, everything seemed significant — the warmth of his hands as they caught her and moved her to her feet, the way his eyes never turned from hers. Like a seductive touch, it all seemed to draw her in. And though she tried, she couldn't look away.

Neither, it appeared, could he.

They grew very still as the air around them charged with awareness. Between them, silence settled as loud as any roar. A muscle twitched along his jaw, drawing her attention to the curve of his lips. They were nice lips, lips she wouldn't mind kissing…if only the words they uttered made any kind of sense.

Raising Laur's reins over her head, Dane smiled and moved directly behind her.

Their small party, once again, began to move.

Despite the unsettling reaction she was having to his hands against her back and sometimes gently cupping her sides, she was still glad Dane was behind her. Not only was the support greatly appreciated, but from the back, he couldn't see how her face burned with embarrassment or how her lips still trembled with the very idea of a kiss.

Taking hold of her waist, Dane redirected her around a deep burrow. "Careful," he whispered, his breath moving across her flesh like a tender caress.

She reminded herself once more he was not her hero…but she could no longer deny she wanted him to be.

It felt like an eternity before they finally emerged out of the woods. Her feet hurt horribly and so did her calves, thanks to the hill's steep incline.

"Does this mean we can now ride?" she asked, staring out over what was yet another entirely unrecognizable location. Fields of grass, green and lush, lay for miles before them. They were surrounded by hillsides as breathtaking as the clear blue sky.

"It's pretty open," Dane said with what sounded like concern from directly behind her shoulder.

"It's beautiful," she said, turning to face him. "Where are we?"

One very sexy brow lifted comically.

"Oh, right…France." She rolled her eyes and shook her head.

"You're catching on," he said with a chuckle, his dark brown eyes sparking with humor as his face lit with a heart-stopping smile.

He portrayed such a normal picture. Weren't crazy people supposed to look crazy? In her limited experience it was so. In fact, she'd always assumed it was nature's way of warning those around them.

Looking ahead toward the others now carefully scanning the fields before them, she realized it was the same for all of them. Not only did they, for the most part, appear entirely sane, but they also had an air of integrity and strength — very much like her father.

It didn't make sense, none of it, and that was the most frustrating part of all. She liked things to make sense. It was one of the reasons she so longed to return to France in the first place. She longed for explanations.

Roncin looked back their way and motioned them forward.

"It's so open," Dane remarked again, a great deal louder. "Shouldn't we stay to the trees?"

Roncin shook his head and then mounted his horse. "They'll see us, but we'll also see them."

"Them?" repeated Edeline.

They were most likely speaking of their imaginary foes, but, oh, how she hoped the "them" they were speaking of wore jeans and spoke English. French was a language she knew well, thanks to her father. But still she longed for the familiarity of the English tongue, not to mention the taste of sanity it would bring.

The other men mounted their horses as Dane helped her atop Laur and then pulled himself up behind her.

Lucas moved forward into the field. "If we're to make Harfleur by nightfall, we'll have to leave the woods," he explained as he carefully eyed their surroundings. "Besides, it's always better to meet a marksman in the field as opposed to the forest when one is traveling."

"What about an army?" Dane mumbled, moving ahead slowly.

Hemart laughed. "That depends on their numbers, my friend."

They road quietly for some time, each of the men watching carefully the trail ahead, the hills to their sides, and the path from which they'd come.

Edeline simply leaned back against her escort, enjoying the openness of the field and the illusion of safety the warm arms around her provided.

An uncontrollable smile tilted her lips.

He'd wanted to kiss her. The thought should horrify or at least trouble her, but it didn't. It pleased her. Right or wrong, crazy or… well, crazy, but maybe she was falling for her counterfeit knight in shining armor. How could she not? In this world, this insanely unrealistic world of peculiar rhetoric, ancient dress, and unfamiliar lands, he really was her greatest hope.

Deciding it best to refocus her thoughts, she set her sights on their remarkable surroundings. Wherever she looked, a new, equally as picturesque, scene emerged. Ahead, lush green fields sprinkled with colorful wildflowers in both white and varying shades of pink rolled leisurely across the land, twisting and turning with the hills at their sides.

In the distance, mountains soared like mighty towers clear into the heavens. The hills surrounding them rose from deep hues of green to majestic peaks of gray. Unlike the pine and fir-covered forests near Los Angeles, these hills were covered with oak and beech. Though every bit as beautiful as the dense, gigantic pines, the trees covering these unfamiliar hills were vastly different. Their branches grew wider, both dense and thin, twirling and bowing an elaborate dance through-out the forest. They were enchanting—magnificent—and still not enough to keep her mind diverted from the man behind her.

She shifted uncomfortably.

He shifted his weight behind her.

"Am I making you uncomfortable?" she asked, looking up and over her shoulder.

A devilish grin lifted playfully his lips. "You could say that," he said, a heavy dose of amusement accentuating his words.

She stared at him dumbfounded. "Sorry," she finally replied for lack of a better response before turning back around.

A deep chuckle rumbled past her ear.

Hemart slowed his horse and waited for them to catch up while the other two knights road on ahead. "Tell me about Federic, Edeline. Has he fared well?"

Never had she been so grateful for a distraction.

"Father? He's doing well. He's met a nice woman he's quite fond of. They've been spending a lot of time together as of late, visiting museums, going for walks. She's even managed to drag him to a social."

Hemart's brows pulled uncertainly.

"A dance, a gathering," Edeline explained. "When he's not with Alison, his job at the church keeps him busy. He enjoys what he does. It's sometimes hard to pull him away."

"What he does?"

"Father works maintenance—fixing things." Her father was a resilient man. Originally hired as janitor at Saint Paul's, through dedication and hard work, he had moved up to maintenance. Federic could fix anything. His fascination with technology was unmatched by any other. He loved learning how things worked, the more in-tricate the better.

"Federic always was very good at fixing things." Hemart nodded. "He has a sharp mind for such work. Never could leave anything untouched. He wanted to know how it worked and how it could work better. I have often watched him throw his hands in the air and declare a task 'impossible.' But I have never actually seen Federic give up. He never gives up."

Edeline laughed. "That sounds like my father. How do you know him?"

"I have known Federic all my life. We lived in the same village. Our fathers were friends. We fished together, hunted together, clashed swords more than once. He is my oldest and dearest friend, and my oldest and most troublesome ally." Hemart grinned. "He has led me into more trouble than I can remember. Though, I do remember once, he talked me into putting on a cape and jumping with him off a hillside and into the wind. We did indeed fly, straight to the ground. We were seven. I broke my right leg. Federic broke his left."

"You're Mart!" She recognized immediately the story her father had been telling for years. "But how…I mean…you're much younger than my father."

"Three days older, actually." Hemart chuckled. "We had many good times, Federic and I, always coming up with one bad idea or another, always competing to outdo the other. He always shamed me with the sword, but I always got the better of him in a battle of might. It never did set well with him."

Edeline's mouth dropped. No, it hadn't. She remembered the many times her father had told her stories about their young adventures and hilarious mishaps. But this man couldn't possibly be Mart, the boy who had stolen her father's clothes as he skinny dipped in the lake, and then left him to make his way unseen back into their villa. That boy would be much, much older. But how…

"Riders," Lucas called back over his shoulder.

Still some ways in the distance, their features in no way discernible, emerged the six horsemen.

The smile on Hemart's face immediately faded.

She sensed Dane ready to bolt.

"No," Hemart warned, apparently sensing the same. "It is best we stay together. In these parts, they could be friends as easily as foe."

As the riders neared, the two men exchanged nervous glances.

"They wear no markings," noted Hemart, squinting toward the arrivals. "Keep Edeline back," he ordered as he shook his reins and moved forward to ride beside Roncin and Lucas.

Dane slowed Laur. Edeline could feel his body tensing noticeably behind her.

"Dane, what is it?" She turned, but instantly wished she hadn't as she caught sight of his troubled face. "Dane?"

"It may be nothing," he said as he pulled Laur to a stop. Carefully watching the scene before them, he raised himself up and quickly dismounted. "Take these," he said, handing her the reins.

Up ahead, the three knights spoke casually with the six men sitting nonchalantly upon their mounts. They, like her self-appointed guardians, wore similar attire, but their cloaks were plain, without markings of any kind.

There was a quick exchange, smiles, laughter.

"Thank goodness." Edeline allowed herself to breathe. "I was getting worried."

One of the new arrivals pointed back toward Dane and Edeline.

"Can you ride?" Dane asked.

"What?"

"Can you ride?" was his abrasive response.

"I—"

Without warning, the new arrivals threw back their cloaks and drew their swords. Edeline's three escorts instantly backed away. A sick churning hit her middle. She shook her head in denial. It was a charade, an enactment. They were playing a game.

"Edeline, can you ride?" Dane's voice rose to grasp her attention.

Fear nearly choked her as she turned her gaze to his. "You promised you wouldn't leave me."

He squeezed her hand. "I'll do my best to keep that promise, Edeline." He glanced toward the others as they all dismounted and the first sword was raised in battle. "I want you to ride into the hills and hide well. If we don't make it, stay hidden. When you're certain it's safe, find help and do whatever it takes to make your way back to the cliffs below Brines Castle. They'll come for you."

"Who? Who'll come for me?"

"Your father," he said before turning toward the others and taking off on a run.

She watched in stunned silence as he ran toward the battle where swords were now flying through the air, their silver blades catching light from the sun and tossing it back as sparks from the huddle.

With no small degree of dread, she watched as Dane charged straight into its midst.

"Dane!" His name ripped from her throat, a desperate plea to go unheard.

Grunts and cries rang from the cluster as anguished faces flashed sporadically into view, tortured, determined, and raw with conviction. As horrifying as it was, she found she could neither leave nor look away. It was like a haunting dance, dreadful, shocking, and entirely enthralling. Their grunts and roars were its gloomy melody, their thrusts and turns its peculiar steps. An odd yearning began to move deep inside her, creating an unexplainable desire to join the ball.

But then clarity emerged in the form of reality.

Watching as the tip of a blade emerged through the back of one of the new arrivals, she realized instantly the strike was real. This was not an enactment. The fight was real, and men were dying.

Real.

The men, the fight, the emotions…the slaughter—it was what it was, and there was no pretense. Gruesome, sickening, and *real*, death danced within their circle, choosing its victims one strike at a time.

Real.

Blood turned the cluster to red, the warm liquid falling to the earth below, softening the soil at their feet and sending it flying into the air. The sound of metal hitting metal rang across the distance. One by one the cluster shrank. One, two, three—she counted their coats and thanked the Lord the knights were all still standing. And every time Dane's dark head moved into her sights, she was so grateful she practically sobbed.

Real.

Her heart beat heavy in her chest. She could feel her blood pumping wildly through her veins, carrying oxygen to breathe life into a spirit she knew was hers, but could hardly recognize. If she'd had a sword, it would have been in her hands.

Real.

"God, please don't let anything happen to him…to any of them," she whispered, realizing their tales were indeed truths. Everything Dane had told her was true. This was not the world she had known. Los Angeles was more than a distance away. These men were who they said they were. And none of this was of her time.

It was real. And she, most likely, was in fourteenth-century France.

Finally, when she felt she could take it no more, it was over. The only men standing were the ones who professed to be her guardians. Without even realizing she had moved, she was suddenly upon them. Jumping down from Laur, her eyes never left Dane's blood splattered face.

Tears finally came. Deep, jarring sobs wrenched her body and lodged in her throat. She moved toward him—relieved, mortified, and more frightened than she'd ever been in her life. Her arms wrapped around his neck as she clung to him as though he was her only foundation. And in an odd and still unimaginable way, it seemed he now was.

Chapter Nine

Tears fell unguarded down cheeks flushed clear of color. Deeper than sorrow, her pain stood visible inside eyes which had seen too much. Her world had been turned upside down, and everything she'd believed in poured out onto a field of battle. Her dreams and trust lay trampled beneath its bloodied soil, lost, as was her history, inside this world she didn't understand.

Lifting her into his arms, Dane stepped over the fallen warriors and away from the horror he hadn't wanted her to see. It was a harsh awakening into a reality which had been, until now, impossible to fathom. But, without any doubt, his beautiful ward had seen enough to be convinced.

"Edeline," he whispered, setting her down on her feet several yards away from the carnage, "it's all right. It's over. You're safe."

She trembled in his arms, still holding on tight.

He had wondered how it would come to her, but never imagined such a scene. From a protected existence to one of insanity, her entire world had been pushed over an unforeseen edge. Of course she'd be shaken, reaching, looking for something to hold on to. It made sense that something was him.

Resting his head atop hers, he took a moment to calm his own frenzied senses and simply breathe. After all the ugliness, the fear, the killing, she was a sweetness he badly needed. Soft and warm in his arms, she reminded him that behind it all there was a purpose.

Eventually she dropped her hold and stepped back. Her lips quivered. Shock, fear, anger—they altered the lines of her face as she moved through a series of emotions on her way to acceptance.

With a choked sob, she hit her fists against his chest. Her expression more resembling despair than anger. One by one her fingers unraveled, moving like a gentle caress across the bloodstains on his tunic, eventually gripping the fabric in her hands and pulling it away from his flesh as though unable to bear seeing it against him.

He took her hands in his.

She closed her eyes, squeezing them tight as she stepped back against his warmth. He kissed her cheek and nuzzled against her. More than anything he wanted to take away the pain, to be her strength and her reassurance. And that wasn't all. He wanted more—her smile, her laugh, her happiness.

Somewhere along their journey she had become more than his charge; she had become someone he admired, someone he cared for more than he should. When had she come to mean this much to him? Perhaps he had felt it from that very first look. He closed his eyes, remembering the photo. It wasn't hard. Her image had haunted him with a feeling of inevitability, as though they were always meant to meet. Ridiculous of course, but the feeling was real nonetheless.

"Hemart, check the satchels," Roncin ordered, still standing with the others inside the field of battle.

Dane looked back toward the knights as they searched the fallen men. No doubt they were looking for clues as to who they were and why they were there. A question which Dane would very much like answered.

As Dane watched Hemart step across the fallen bodies toward the horses, an uncomfortable realization hit him.

He'd done the unthinkable. He'd stepped directly into fate's path and quite possibly altered history. Were the men now lying dead upon the ground meant to see their end? How about the soldiers standing?

His sword had ripped through the flesh of more than one man. He had caught and held a strike destined for Lucas. In short, he had broken a cardinal rule; he had, eyes wide open, charged into a battle never meant to be his. His gaze once more swept the scene. But then again, perhaps it was not meant to be theirs either.

He couldn't deny it. The mission had shifted forms and become a lot more complicated. New players had emerged and, he feared, not yet revealed their strengths.

Damned if he did. Damned if he didn't. He had an uncomfortable feeling fate was destined for a turn the moment Edeline Depuis was brought back through the portal. Perhaps he had not so much stumbled into destiny's path, but rather been pulled.

"Edeline." He moved his hands to cup her face. Her lovely blue eyes opened to stare uncertainly into his.

"We're in France," she acknowledged.

He nodded. "We are."

"What year?"

"Thirteen-ten," he said as his fingers caressed away her tears.

"And you're here to take me home?" she asked, her eyes never leaving his.

"Yes, I'm here to take you home."

"We need to be moving," Roncin said, suddenly standing at their side. He handed Dane Laur's reins. "I'm certain they weren't alone, only sent ahead."

Dane nodded and waited for him to step away.

Turning back to Edeline, he wiped away another tear and then bent to kiss her forehead. "He's right. We need to go now."

Edeline covered his hands with hers and held them still against her dampened flesh. "Don't ever leave me again," she said, her lips once again slightly trembling. Then dropping her hold, she stepped past him toward Laur.

Silently they followed behind the others — past the fallen soldiers and their wandering horses, toward the distant hills. Only this time he pulled her close and held her in something more resembling an embrace, telling himself she needed him.

Heavy lids closed to rest as he kissed the top of her head again.

It was a new feeling for him, but he recognized it for what it was. More than mere attraction and deeper than affection — his feelings for her were growing. And from her reaction on the field, he suspected those feelings were shared. But he hadn't forgotten what lay ahead. He would take her back, and he would lose her. For the first time in his career, he was contemplating throwing an assignment. "What ifs" played over and over in his head. What if he didn't take her back? What if things stayed just as they were?

He looked around at the men who were now escorting them back into the hills. Already the past had been changed simply by their meeting. But he hadn't disappeared. He was still as he had been. If their meeting had changed the course of history, certainly he'd have seen the signs. Perhaps the intrusions weren't so damaging after all. Perhaps he and she could…

No! It couldn't happen. As much as he didn't want to lose her, he knew the risks were real—to both of them and to everyone. In addition to that, she wanted to go home, and he had promised to take her there. The only way to see that promise through was to take her back, and by doing so, erase all they had shared. The portal would send him back to his time, and unfortunately, her back to hers. She'd forget all of this. Her reality would consist only of the life she was now living with her father back in the present and the new future which would be built once Dane put all back into place.

He was going to lose her, and there wasn't a thing he could do about it.

Edeline watched the men before her—courageous men who lived their lives with honor and for purpose. They rode with confidence, fought with valor, and despite their trials, carried an undying faith. And they knew her father, respected him even.

"Why?" she asked. "Why did we leave? What did my father have to do with the treasure?"

Three uncertain faces turned to look her way, or were they looking over her?

She leaned back and turned her head to Dane. "What? Why shouldn't I know?"

He didn't immediately respond. But finally, after a brief glance toward Roncin, he replied. "Maybe it's not our place."

"Don't be ridiculous," she said, holding his uncertain stare. "I have a right to know."

"You should ask your father when you return," advised Roncin.

"I'm asking you now," she persisted. "Dane said my father was a Templar Knight. Is that true?"

"Yes," answered Lucas from up ahead. Turning to look toward the others, he shrugged his shoulders. "She's right. It has been brought to rest on her shoulders. She deserves to know as much as we can tell her." Then looking back toward Edeline, he continued. "Federic Depuis was a fellow knight. He is our brother as much as our friend."

Edeline swallowed. She'd been through so much already, little could surprise her now.

"All right, very good, so my father was a Templar Knight. That's not something I expected…certainly not an everyday discovery." She took a deep breath and tried to imagine her father as one of the men before her. Her father was every kind of honorable man, but still it was hard to fathom. She forced a bright smile. "I'm quite capable of handling the truth. Now tell me how that's possible? I thought Templar Knights didn't have families."

A heavy sigh sounded from behind her. "Can't this wait?" said Dane. "No one knows your father's motives better than he. Give him the chance to explain."

Looking back his way, she could tell by the lines deeply etched across his brow, he was worried. He was doing what he always did—protecting her. But after seeing what she'd seen, she knew their journey would not be without risk. This might be it, her one chance to learn the truth of her past.

"Please, I want to know. I've accepted silence far too long. I want to know who my mother is. Who am I? Why, out of all the people in the world, has this happened to me? I mean, really, here I am in this…unbelievable position. Not just miles from home, but centuries. *Centuries!* Care for me enough to trust me with the truth."

"You're right, of course," Dane said. "The story is yours. Perhaps the more you know of it, the safer you'll be."

Edeline turned to the others. "So, my father ran with legends. That's…well, weird."

"Legends?" the three knights chorused.

Both Edeline and Dane laughed. The men before them would never understand why they'd be remembered or held in such regard. They were modest men living one purpose, which was serving the

Lord. They had no time for, or interest in, the egos of modern man. And that, perhaps, was the very reason their legend lived on.

"If my father was a Knights Templar, then explain to me how? I thought Templar's weren't allowed to wed or have children?"

"There were knights who had families," assured Hemart. "Many of our brothers joined the order after they'd been married and had children. They'd often join after the death of a spouse. Of course, their children were already grown or wards to another."

"My father joined after my mother's death?"

Clearing his throat, Hemart shifted uncomfortably. "Uh…no."

Confused more than ever, she stared at him blankly.

Lucas slowed to ride beside her and Dane. "Edeline, are you sure you want to know this? It will change nothing."

"I…" She leaned closer to Dane. "Yes."

"You love your father, yes?"

"More than words can say."

He smiled. "Very well…"

She listened silently to their words as they shared a story she would have, on any other day, never believed.

Federic was not her birth father. She had another, Omont Montague, and he had sacrificed his life to protect her.

A soft breeze blew through the branches above as Dane stood beneath the sturdy oak watching the surroundings for any unwanted guests. But try as he may for vigilance, his attention kept wandering to the crystal clear stream and the reflection of Edeline.

It was a lot for her to take in, but she was doing a remarkable job. She was a brave and resilient woman.

Collecting handfuls of water and letting it run over her dust-covered flesh, she glanced his way and smiled. Lovelier than he'd ever imagined possible, at that moment she looked more like a dream than actual flesh and blood.

Footsteps sounded behind him.

"They were not the king's men," Roncin said, walking up beside him and motioning for him to follow.

"I was afraid as much," Dane said, turning to walk beside him and away from the stream. The men's interest had not been in the three knights. That would not be so if they were the king's soldiers. "Do you know who they were?"

"No, they were new to me, and I've fought beside the king's men enough times to know their faces as well as their skills. These men were not the king's. They belong to another. Their clothes bore no markings, but the way they fought…" he said, hesitating a moment as his thoughts seemed to drift to the memory of that afternoon. "They've been trained together and fought together more than once."

"Yes," Dane said, raking his fingers through his hair, realizing his worst fears were most likely coming true. "I sensed it as well."

Roncin came to a stop beside his horse. Pulling out his flask from its well-weathered holster, he took a quick drink and then roughly ran his arm across his lips. Slowly his eyes searched the hills.

"What's bothering you?" Dane hadn't known Roncin long, but already he felt he knew him well. The knight was afraid, and *that* alone was terrifying.

Placing his flask back into its holster, Roncin gently ran his hand down the horse's long neck. Whatever he had to say, he wasn't finding it easy. Finally, after a sorrowful glance back toward the stream, he replied, "Their interests lay in Edeline."

Dane remembered the men's reactions when they'd first seen her. They hadn't taken their eyes off her for more than a moment's time. "She's a beautiful woman. Maybe they were interested in something other than her power, maybe a brazen attempt at abduction? They happen, right?"

"They happen, but I do not believe that was their intent. I think they were hunting. And I believe they found their prey."

"They were looking for her? You think they know who she is?"

"I do," Roncin said.

"But how? They weren't her abductors. I would have recognized them. Certainly you're mistaken." Rubbing his hand nervously along his jaw, he glanced back toward Edeline. Her long blond curls flowed free over her shoulders and down her enticingly curved back. She was twirling a wet rag around and around, watching the water drip into multiple circles to dance together in the stream below.

He knew what Roncin was saying was true. He'd sensed it all along. Admitting it, however, meant facing a possibility he hadn't yet accepted. He might not be able to protect her.

It wasn't like him to cower from the facts. Always a soldier first, typically he would assess a situation, recognize a course of action and execute. That was that, simple and clear. But there was nothing simple about Edeline, and nothing simple about his feelings for her. She was no longer merely a mission, and protecting her wasn't only a job.

But if Roncin was right—and somewhere in the denied recesses of his mind, Dane knew he was—protecting her was not going to be easy. To the beasts that followed, she was not human. She was merely a tool. They would use her in any way they pleased and then most likely discard of her. The thought ripped at his heart.

She had asked for none of this, but that didn't mean she wouldn't pay a great price for what destiny had deemed hers.

Roncin stood beside him, watching Edeline sit down beneath the oak where earlier Dane had stood. Seemingly without a care in the world, she dried her feet and then began putting back on the shoes she so vocally detested. He looked to Dane. "I know it seems unlikely, but, yes, I think they know. I am not sure who *they* are or *how* they would know, but I think it would be foolish to ignore what could be ahead."

"You're sure it's not the king? I realize it's not his army, but perhaps he's hired someone outside his service—mercenaries perhaps?"

"No, it's not the king. If the king knew of Nicolas's connection to the treasure, he'd never have let Nicolas die, nor would he have let Omont leave the chamber that first day with Edeline." With obvious frustration, Roncin shook his head and looked past Dane to the woods. "It makes no sense at all. How would they know?"

No longer willing to deny the facts, Dane sighed. "Regardless of how, we both know there is only one reason they would be after her. And if they know about her, then they know they need the stone. They most likely think she has it."

Roncin nodded. "I doubt they would believe otherwise."

Chapter Ten

Words failed her. It was beyond magnificent. Ancient stone buildings merged together on each side of the narrow pathway, twisting and turning like a maze to form a complex community of homes, church, and commerce. Overhead and appearing sporadically throughout the quaint villa were stone archways linking one side of the street to the other, establishing an undeniable sense of unity.

"What's its name again?" she asked Lucas.

"She is the village Vanac."

"Vanac," Edeline repeated while doing her best to take in every inch and every detail of the deserted city. It was unlike anything she had ever seen. Built in a time when reliance upon one's neighbors built more than community, Vanac spoke of trust.

The *clickety-clack* of hooves pulled her attention down.

Stunning.

Emerging from the cracks in the stone pathway leading them through the city, grass peeked and wildflowers grew, adding to the beauty already laid with brick and stone. Such fine work, such precision—had those who had built it proudly walked its path every day?

The horses swayed left around an abandoned cart. Lying one wheel shy along the path's side, it told a tale of a long forgotten misfortune while leaving behind a mystery. Had it been taking goods to market or was it there to take goods home?

Edeline imagined the streets filled with people. Merchants with long wooden tables would be lining the streets while their patrons wandered in and out between their individual stalls. What would be their goods—fruit, silk, wool, wine?

What would it have been like to live here?

She pictured children playing, women hanging laundry, and men scurrying back and forth between the buildings. What would be their day? She wanted desperately to know, for this mystic wonderland of old would have been her home.

She looked to her right. Small windows cleverly designed in a multitude of shapes and sizes lined the tall walls, making each building unique and recognizable.

"How did they think of this? So much character built from mere brick and stone. I never would have imagined," she said, looking anxiously around. "It's all so clever. I'd love to experience it. I'd love to live in a place such as this."

"There are still villages standing today with similar design," Dane said. "They've been restored and somewhat renovated through the years, but the idea is the same if not the era."

Looking up over her shoulder, she caught him vigilantly scanning the narrow streets and tall stone structures. Always a soldier, this man she now admired. She wondered how she could have ever doubted his sanity. Everything about him screamed reliable, trustworthy. He was what she had always oddly sensed: remarkable.

"How similar?" she asked.

He looked down and smiled. "It's actually amazing how much of the early culture has been preserved."

"It should be preserved," Edeline said, thrilled to hear such simplistic splendor still existed in the world. "It's so warm and inviting. It feels like we've walked into her arms and been embraced."

Dane's smile softened to a look of appreciation as his gaze momentarily moved to her lips. "I believe that captures it nicely."

"It is so different from the world in which you live?" asked Hemart, pulling his horse to a stop and quickly dismounting behind Lucas.

"Much different from my world," Edeline said. "Though our buildings are still close together, the sense of unity is no longer as strong. Everything about my world is new, built for convenience and ease. We're no longer as dependent on each other."

She took another long look around at the brick and stone buildings. "Detail and design are still very important to us, but so is space. We like to build up. Thanks to modern-day materials, our buildings can now soar high into the clouds."

The knights exchanged incredulous glances.

She laughed. "It's really quite remarkable…but so is this," she added, her voice growing soulful as she took in their surroundings. "It captures the beauty of nature as well as the artistic vision of man."

"Beautiful and brilliant," Dane acknowledged, pulling Laur to a stop before moving to the ground.

Roncin laughed. "Edeline or the village?"

Dane's eyes met hers as he reached up his arms to help her down. "Both," he said simply, his eyes never leaving hers.

She slid into his arms, where he held her longer than really necessary, not that she minded. The warmth of his hands was something she now looked quite forward to.

"Are you sure no one remains?" he asked Lucas when the knight motioned them to follow.

"I assure you it is deserted." Lucas turned to walk down a small opening within the stone wall behind him.

While Hemart and Roncin stayed behind to keep guard, Dane and Edeline followed Lucas.

"The land never did take well to harvesting," Lucas said, "though the villagers managed somehow for near a hundred years. But the weather has been vicious over the last few. The ground here can no longer reap. What little hope they had of perseverance completely disappeared. The village has been vacant now for nearly two years."

"Where did they all go?" asked Edeline, now following Lucas down the thin walkway.

"Most scattered to the larger villages; others found work as laborers closer to Paris." He stopped outside a simple stone dwelling and tried the door. It easily opened to a small, now-vacant dwelling. He looked inside before smiling back at Edeline. "Brun and Agnes le Picart moved to Paris. I believe he serves as a butcher, as was his calling here."

"Brun and Agnes le Picart?" Edeline queried, stepping into the quaint dwelling.

"Yes, Edeline. Their daughter was Jaquette le Picart, your mother."

Her fingers flew to her parted lips.

A flutter of excitement soared from her heart on a wave of emotion, taking her breath and sending her stumbling backward. If it hadn't been for Dane's strong arms, she surely would have met the ground.

My mother? Could it be true?

"You knew my mother?" she asked, her voice slightly shaking.

Lucas nodded, a soft smile on his lips. "Only for a short time, but I knew her parents well. They frequented the parish. They sought solace there after your mother's death."

Slowly Edeline's balance returned. She patted Dane's steadying hands, then moved away from his hold.

So this was her past. How amazing it was.

Anticipation bubbled in her belly.

Stepping further into the room, a warm and comforting sense of belonging overtook her. She slowly walked through the dwelling. "My mother—she, too, lived here?"

"Until the day she married your father."

The dwelling was near bare but a few remnants from its occupants remained. Edeline ran her hands lovingly across a well-worn table, picking up and squeezing an old forgotten cloth which lay haphazardly across the table's end. "My grandmother held this, perhaps my mother." She lifted it to her cheek and the first tear fell.

Dane moved to comfort her, but she lifted her hand keeping him back.

"I'm all right," she said, looking away, already searching for more treasures. She was overwhelmed. She'd long ago given up hope of knowing anything of her mother. This was a treasure to which none could compare. She would breathe it in and hold precious every second.

Slowly she moved to the back of the dwelling where two small rooms were sectioned off. Stripped completely bare of everything but an old chair which had seen better days, the first room was blessed with the light from the afternoon sun. She closed her eyes and tried to imagine it furnished and filled with warm personal touches. She walked toward the lone chair, bent down on her knees, and leaned her head against the hard wood.

Dane stood at the entrance. "Edeline?"

"I'm not sad," she said as tears ran down her face.

He smiled. "I know."

"I'm really," she hesitated and sat up, wiping her tear-covered face with her sleeve, "happy."

"I know." He walked across the room to the chair where he bent to his knees.

"Are your parents still living?" she asked.

He nodded. "They are."

"Do you have brothers and sisters?"

"A younger brother." He reached out and pushed back a stray curl from her tear-dampened face.

"I always wanted a brother or sister," she said reflectively. Her eyes closed. "But I would have given anything to know my mother."

"I'm sorry, Edeline."

"This is," she said, opening her eyes again and taking a long look around the room, "the greatest gift I have ever received. My grandparents' home. I never imagined…" A sob caught in her throat.

He offered her his embrace.

She moved into his outstretched arms and allowed him to comfort her. He kissed her forehead, his hands comforting and cradling her as the tears fell.

"I can't meet them, can I?" Her voice was full of hope as she looked up into his handsome face. "My grandparents. Lucas mentioned them. They're still alive here in this time."

His eyes held regret as he slowly shook his head. "The risks are too great. We need to get home."

She leaned into his chest and held on tight. "I know," she whispered. And she did. If anything went wrong, they both had everything to lose. The world she and Federic entered into twenty-two-years ago could very well be gone and all of history changed. But what frightened her most was what, and more importantly to her heart, *who* might never be. She looked up into Dane's eyes. She would do nothing to risk him. "We should go."

His dark eyes met hers in silent understanding.

There was something between them. Strong and persistent, it was born in the trenches of the doubt, raised in the midst of uncertainty, and now thrived in this world of acceptance. There was something…

His gaze dropped to her lips—lips which then trembled. The slightest smile wavered across his face.

She didn't move, didn't smile, only breathed.

Warm hands cupped her face as slowly he lowered his lips to hers.

He kissed her. With lips both warm and pleasing, he set her heart racing.

There was passion and plenty, but there was also something more, something stronger than passion and more nourishing to the soul. There was a bond now between them which could not be broken. In a very real way, in this extraordinary world, they were one.

"Edeline!" Lucas called from the other room, the excitement in his voice unmistakable.

Slowly Dane released her, kissing her briefly once more as they turned to leave.

Hand in hand they walked around the small partition.

Lucas was on his knees holding a small metallic brooch adorned with colorful pastes and embossed with a heart crossed with a sword. Looking up, he smiled and held it out for her to take. "It was sitting on the ledge between the rooms. I must have knocked it loose when I brushed the corner. I remember it. Your father had it made for your mother."

Her heart fluttered and then soared as though it had wings. She smiled, wanting to believe it but fearing it too good to be true. "My mother's?"

"Your mother's," Lucas assured, lifting it up higher in offering.

She stepped across the room and bent to his side. Her own hands shaking, she accepted the brooch. It didn't actually glisten, but in her eyes it shined. It was the only thing she'd ever seen of her mother's, not to mention owned.

"Thank you. Oh, Lucas, thank you so much. My mother's." She studied the brooch several moments longer before wrapping her arms around him. "Thank you for everything, Lucas, but especially for bringing me here. It means more to me than you'll ever know."

He held her close and kissed her cheek. "You are welcome, my precious Edeline."

"We should go," Dane reminded, holding out his hand.

Pinning the brooch to her dress, Edeline smiled and moved back to her feet. "I'm ready," she said placing her hand in Dane's.

"Well, it's true," Edeline said, laughing as she leaned with him to avoid a low hanging branch.

The light scent of the fresh wildflowers she'd placed throughout her curls filled Dane's airways. He purposefully leaned in closer, taking a deep breath and simply enjoying the feel of her in his arms.

"She's teasing you again, Hemart," Roncin said. "You should really try and be less gullible. Why, she almost had you convinced men could fly. 'All over the skies,' she said, and you nearly believed her. You are a silly man to believe such tales."

Edeline gasped in indignation. "Don't listen to them, Hemart. I'm telling you the truth. We do fly, all the time and all over the world."

"Yes, in metal holders built with wings and tails." Roncin chuckled. "Next she'll be telling us they can fly to the moon." He shook his head. "Lucas is right, my friend, you are far too trusting."

Dane felt her prepare to respond and whispered in her ear. "I wouldn't bother."

"Believe me or not, but I'm telling the truth. Men do fly. Perhaps not like the birds, but in airplanes, which are not so dissimilar." She sighed and sat back up as they passed another obtrusive branch. "And is it really so hard to believe that we choose to indulge ourselves in luxuries? It's certainly not a new concept."

Hemart scowled as he scratched the back of his head. "Adding length to one's fingernails?" He stretched his arms out in front of him, studying his nails. "What would be the purpose?"

"Image," Edeline said. "And creativity. You should see how they can decorate nails in our time. It's really quite remarkable. In fact, it's art."

"Art?" All three knights turned on their mounts and looked back her way.

"Yes, art. They actually create artwork right on the nail—pictures, words, diamonds and other gems. You'd be amazed."

Hemart snorted. "It is hard to believe a man would allow his wife to so foolishly spend his earnings."

"Who said they were his earnings? Besides, even men have their nails done. Tell them, Dane," she said, turning his way for needed support.

"Edeline…" He moaned as he reluctantly looked up to see the others' reactions.

Hemart stared suspiciously back at the two of them and then pulled back on his reins. "Let me see your hands," he insisted.

"My hands are not manicured," Dane said, internally noting he'd have to have a private word with the beautiful woman he held in his arms. "Nor are they painted. And they certainly do not have, and never will have, extensions. But she's right. There are men in certain professions who choose to have it done, but not in mine." He shook his head and added, "Certainly not in mine."

"There's nothing wrong with keeping oneself groomed," Edeline said to the three now-snickering knights. "It's a concept alive even in these ancient days."

Glancing suspiciously toward Dane's hands, Hemart's gaze narrowed. "I'd like to see them."

Lucas and Roncin turned their heads back to the path, but it was obvious from their rolling shoulders, they found the whole conversation extremely amusing. And Dane had little doubt a good share of their amusement was directed at him.

"Let me see them," Hemart persisted as he held out his hand, determination sitting solidly across his face.

"This is ridiculous," Dane grumbled as he laid his hands out for inspection.

"Humph," Hemart grunted and showed his own much more weathered and battered hands. He studied his and then Dane's. "They're not as pretty as his teeth," he announced. "And I suppose they're not completely soft."

"Soft!" Moving his hands back to the reins, Dane looked toward his tormenter in disbelief. "There is nothing 'soft' about my hands. And just for the record, let me say, tights are for pansies in my day."

"Pansies?" Hemart tilted his head.

"They're much more common for the women…the manicures, I mean," Edeline jumped in to the suddenly heated debate. "I polish mine myself." She stretched out her hands. They still appeared neatly trimmed, but the polish had been completely removed. Letting out an irritated huff, she dropped her hands back into her lap. "Well, they *were* a lovely pinkish-pearl."

"What other odd practices have you?" Hemart asked. He was fascinated by their world, more so than the others.

"We also tan, you know, color our skin. People actually pay to have themselves painted the color of, mm…say…Dane."

In unison, the other two knights turned once again to look at Dane, their mouths—along with Hemart's—dropping in astonishment.

"I do not color my skin," Dane declared defensively, "nor do I tan, at least not intentionally."

"Oh no. No!" Edeline waived her hands out in front of her. "I didn't mean Dane. His is natural. Right?" she asked uncertainly, looking his way and receiving an irritated scowl in return.

"Right," he assured between clenched teeth.

Looking Dane over skeptically, the three knights exchanged unreadable glances before turning back around in their saddles. Hemart grunted again and moved forward once more to join the others.

"I would really appreciate you not giving them any more fuel for the fire," Dane whispered in her ear. "They already find me foolish enough."

Undaunted, Edeline grinned. "They like you."

"They enjoy taunting me."

"No," she said, her adorable smile still firmly planted on her lips, "they like you. How could they not?" Covering his hands with hers, she leaned back against his chest and looked up.

Leaning down once more, he stole another kiss.

With a pleased sigh, she looked back to the trail. "I adore our new friends, but I must admit I'm looking forward to some time alone, just you and I."

"Yes," he agreed, realizing with a shock how much he meant it. He couldn't wait to get her all to himself, to kiss her lips without restraint and to feel her body pressed to his. She had, quite surprisingly, become a strong desire of his. Having her so near, but forced to maintain his passions, was a grueling test of self-control. He leaned down once more, and her hand reached up as though to guide his lips to hers.

He heard the pull of the bow before the whistle of the arrow. "Archer," he yelled, bending over Edeline and sliding them both to the ground. The arrow whizzed just overhead before barreling into a tree. Right behind it, three other arrows flew through the air toward various destinations—destinations where luckily the knights had left.

Dane huddled with Edeline behind Laur, then moved her to a large old oak. Pulling her behind the thick cover, he shielded her body with his.

Twigs snapped, branches popped, and another round of arrows were launched in their direction. The dull whine of their force breaking air hummed through the trees. If they were still shooting, they had targets, which told Dane the knights were already on the move. Though it was against his every instinct, he stayed perfectly still. To get an idea of what was happening, he'd have to leave her, and that he wouldn't do.

The nervous snorts and prancing of the horses was the only sound he heard for several long seconds.

"To your right," he heard Roncin warn another as the breaking of a twig was followed by the sound of a charge, the *chings* of metal and the grunts of battle. Inevitably, there was the fall, but Dane could not see to tell the victor.

The sound of scurrying feet echoed from seemingly every direction. He could no longer tell who was where or who was who. If he were on his own, he'd take his chances and charge into the unknown. But he wasn't alone, and that wasn't an option.

"There are at least seven," Hemart said, suddenly appearing behind the tree next to theirs. "They are coming from the east and trying to flank us. We cannot stay here. We have to somehow draw them into the open. You need to take Edeline and try to find a better place to hide."

"Point me the right direction," Dane said.

Hemart pointed directly behind him. "I'd go now," he said, before ducking low and running back into the dense trees.

"Good advice," Dane said. Standing back up, he carefully looked out from behind the tree. The sun was moving from the south, casting shadows into the already unreadable battlefield. He'd rarely in his days felt himself at a disadvantage. He did now. Whoever these men were, they were well trained, and they most likely knew the grounds a great deal better than he. Not to mention, he was the one acting as protector—rarely, if ever, an advantage.

"We need to move," he said, taking Edeline's hands and helping her to her feet.

Her eyes wildly took in their surroundings. She was scared, and she had every reason to be.

He cupped her face in his hands. "We have no choice. We have to move. Are you ready?" he asked and received a courageous nod.

Holding tight to her hand, he forged their way through the trees, hoping for signs of their friends, watchful for signs of their enemy. They'd made it no more than a few yards into the denser woods when a branch swayed unnaturally at their side.

Dane stopped.

Fierce green eyes peeked through the leaves.

Pushing Edeline behind him, Dane raised his sword and prepared for battle. The man's eyes widened with shock, his lips parted, but no cry emerged as he fell forward across the branch to land on the ground at their feet. A quick glimpse caught a red cross disappearing back into the trees.

"Dane?" Edeline's blue eyes looked up to him for reassurance.

"It's going to be all right," he said, his words coming out much more confident than he felt. He had to find a place to hide her. If the knights failed, he would be her only hope, and their odds improved considerably if he could move alone as he did his job.

"Hold on to my tunic," he instructed. Then raising his sword, he looked back over his shoulder. "Pull. I want to know you're behind me." Feeling the cloth tighten around his middle, he moved on.

The thrashing and grunts from two unseen battles could be heard in the distance. Damn, he felt useless, but he would not leave her. He'd fought with the knights, and he gave them much faith. But no man or army was undefeatable, and he couldn't deny these opponents had strengths.

The distant battles soon ended. Once again there was silence. He pulled Edeline to a stop.

They both eyed their surroundings nervously.

"Wait," he said when he sensed she would move. They waited and listened.

The faint brushing of limbs was now somewhere behind them. The knights could be as silent as still water when they chose. It wasn't them. "Let's move this way," he said, pointing away from the snapping twigs.

Staying as low as they could, they moved deeper into the woods. Every step they took seemed amplified to his ears. Yet they could be no quieter. Their luck would not hold. If they were to survive, he needed a plan.

"Edeline, we can't keep running. I need to stop them. I need you to hide." He scanned the area. A dead trunk with heavy brush offered the best coverage. "Here," he said, motioning for her to follow.

"Dane." Her eyes begged him to stay.

"I won't be far," he promised as her hand slid from his.

She curled into the shelter. Bright blue eyes, strained with worry, watched as he gathered twigs and debris from around the forest's floor to give her sufficient coverage. It was with a heavy heart he covered their beauty.

He said a quick prayer for them both. Then he did what he did best; he became invisible.

Chapter Eleven

Shaking violently, she prayed she made no noise, for certainly it would be heard. In the eerie silence, everything sounded louder—the quaking of the leaves, the normal settling of foliage, even the silence. The knights must have all moved on to battle or to run. Either way, if they survived, they'd come back for her…for Dane.

She closed her eyes, searching the silence for any clue as to his whereabouts. Why hadn't he come back? Why had she heard nothing? Quiet or not, knowing he was there, shouldn't she have heard something?

Minutes passed slowly, feeling like hours. Where was Dane? Was he fighting alongside the others, chasing their attackers away? Was he hiding? Was he hurt? Was he even alive?

She couldn't take it any longer. Pushing away the brush, she rose from the trunk.

Death be the fate of fools.

Across the small clearing, heading back into the trees, a dark and unfamiliar figure stopped and turned.

How had she not heard him?

From a face as cold as it was striking, black eyes bore into her very soul, touching it, squeezing it, whispering her future in words felt but never spoken. She couldn't breathe. She couldn't move. Chilled far beneath flesh and deep into the bone, she realized instantly the man was cursed with darkness.

Though slight to the point of question, his lips turned with a smile. Sparks of wicked delight flashed from eyes she'd swear were bare of soul. Though not held, she found she couldn't move. It was as though the very roots of evil had broken through the ground and wrapped their spiraling arms around her, holding her captive.

From under his shirt he pulled out a long chain. At its end, dangled what appeared to be a simple stone. Resembling brown marble, it was not unique from others she had seen. Could it possibly be the stone of which the knights spoke?

Cold and baleful, he seemed somehow pleased by her uncertainty.

Reaching to his side, he pulled from his quiver an arrow.

Watching in an odd sort of fog, she found herself powerless. Somehow he'd stolen it all—her breath, her voice, her ability to think beyond the blinding wall of terror.

If this man was Death, she was not surprised.

Lifting his bow, he aimed straight at her heart, his dark, hollow eyes never leaving hers. They held her prisoner—imprisoned without chains. He could let go the string, and she'd stand still to take the arrow.

What kind of beast held such power?

"Edeline." Her name fell from the monster's lips as though it had been lying there teetering for centuries. Then, quickly redirecting his aim, he let loose the string.

Ringing with a deep and powerful whine, the arrow flew up toward the boulders behind her, missing Dane by a fraction of an inch as he jumped from the rocks, pushing her back and breaking whatever spell had held her bound.

Like a shield, he fell on top of her, protecting her while leaving himself exposed.

Over his shoulder, Edeline watched the black knight toss his bow and draw a long sword.

"Dane!"

Rolling to his feet, Dane drew his sword, blocking a direct plunge meant for his heart. Metal clashed with a resounding ring, the grunts of the warriors echoing the force. Planting his foot solid behind him, Dane heaved forward, pushing his opponent's sword away from his own.

Though the sword swung to his side, the beast didn't miss a step. With a sure and fluid motion, he twirled the sword back into another powerful strike.

Dane blocked the blade but was thrown off guard by the strength of the blow. He stumbled back toward Edeline—armed but unguarded.

In the stranger's dark, soulless eyes, Edeline saw victory flash. Raising his sword, he charged.

Her heart stopped, yet her blood pumped savagely. From the blind depths of a spirit she hadn't realized slumbered, courage arose, and with it a strength she'd never imagined she possessed. Grabbing from beneath the foliage a handful of earth, she sprang from the ground. An angry cry roaring from her lips as fury, stronger than her greatest fear, drove her directly toward the beast.

"Edeline, no!"

She heard Dane's cry as her hand flew through the air, flinging the dirt into the eyes of their attacker.

Stunned by the charge and perhaps torn between reactions, the black knight's sword lost direction as he turned in an attempt to avoid a direct hit.

"Stay low," Dane yelled as he gained his footing and moved between Edeline and the now furious man.

Swords clashed back and forth as strikes flew steady, both men moving as though in a dance, one step matched perfectly by another. They'd learned fast each other's strengths and weaknesses, making it hard to better their opponent.

Finally the swords collided and held as might confronted might. Edeline could do nothing but watch as Dane fought for his life and hers.

The sound of rushing warriors echoed from the forest behind her. With great relief, she watched her guardians emerge.

The black knight lifted his leg and kicked out toward Dane.

Dane stepped back, and the swords broke free. Within the blink of an eye, their attacker turned and ran into the trees, Dane instantly moving to follow.

"No!" Edeline cried, but he had already disappeared, Hemart and Roncin following right at his heels.

"Are you all right?" Lucas asked, offering her his hand.

"I will be," she replied, her eyes never leaving the woods, "as soon as they return."

Several minutes later they did, but they had found nothing. The black knight had simply vanished as quickly as he'd appeared.

Dane searched the last pouch but found nothing. Looking up toward the others, he shook his head. No one blinked an eye. It was what they were expecting—nothing, not a clue. Whoever sent these men had sent them as blank slates—untraceable, undefined.

"I've seen them before," Roncin said, running his hand across his jaw as he studied the lifeless body at his feet. It was one of seven now scattered throughout the woods. "Their coats, their armor—they were on the battlefields near the ruins of Raud."

"I remember. They fought against us," Lucas said as he studied the man's sword. "I remember the snake." He lifted the slain man's sword for the others to see. Burned into the handle was a small image of a cobra wrapped around a sword, its mouth wide open, its fangs bared.

"I, too, remember the symbol," Roncin said. "I wondered its purpose then. I wonder it even more now."

"Think they're part of the same group we met this morning?" Hemart asked.

Roncin nodded. "I'm certain of it. The way they move. The way they fight. They're together if not one."

"Not hired men?" Dane asked.

Roncin shook his head. "Too much conviction. Their battle was about more than mere wages."

Suddenly a vivid image of the same coiled snake flashed through Dane's memory. Moving to his feet, he reached for the sword. "I've seen this before," he said, pulling the sword closer, his stomach knotting with a heavy dose of unease. "I'm sure of it. Not the sword, but the emblem. I can't recall where, but I'm certain it was in my day, and it was identical down to the last detail."

Strange.

He looked back toward Edeline. What would be the odds that the exact emblem would survive seven centuries? Did it still carry the same meaning? Did it represent the same cause?

It *was* strange, and it troubled him more than he dared let on. But it was by no means the only thing troubling him.

The dark warrior had called her by name. There was no doubt but that she was their target. Who were these men who would go to such lengths to take Edeline? They were not her abductors, so how did they know she was the same small child who had left from their world only days prior? And how did they know of her importance and the power of the stone? But most disturbing of all—what in the world did they have to do with the twenty-first century?

"Did you…" Edeline hesitated, her eyes lifting to search theirs. "Did you see his eyes?"

The men stood silent. How could they answer and not say what was on all their minds. She had stared into the eyes of something touched by darkness and hollowed of soul. Their glimpse had been fleeting, but, yes, they had seen his eyes.

Wrapping his arms around her shoulders, Dane pulled her near and kissed her tenderly. "We should be going. Are you all right to travel?"

"I'm fine," she assured, accepting his embrace and leaning against him.

She might still need him, but she'd proven that day she was stronger than even she had imagined. When he'd needed her the most, she'd dug down deep and pulled forth a courage that had likely saved them both.

Dane smiled, but the smile quickly faded.

He'd almost lost her. The reality of it hit him solid, and it had nothing to do with it being a nearly failed mission or the resulting consequences which would have followed. The pain came from near loss—personal and more devastating than anything he could have imagined.

The beast, the army—they would have taken her, used her to get what they wanted, and then who knew what would be her final fate.

"These men are a threat," he said to the three knights, "in both your world and mine. I need to know who they are."

"I know someone who might know," Lucas said, "but it would mean another day's travel."

Looking toward the sky, Dane could see it held the promise of a coming storm. Did he dare miss it? If he waited too long, there would be no going back. Still, he had no choice. If the evil that hunted her in this world was bound to hunt her in the next, he had to search for answers, and he had to search now. He simply couldn't risk them being buried in time.

The tall beech trees rose high above the low hanging mist. Branches, long and colorful, drooped down from the occasional oak. Small drops of dew broke free from their leaves as the small party passed. The moisture softened the foliage beneath, helping them move quietly over the carpet of broken limbs, leaves, and other sorted debris.

From the lush green trees, a roe deer suddenly wandered into their path. Instinctively the men reached for their swords. Large, unblinking eyes studied them suspiciously. The men relaxed their stance as their hands returned to the reins. Cocking its ears their way as the hair on its back stood on ends, the deer prepared itself for flight. With a single bound, it disappeared back into the woods.

They continued on, alert, watchful.

To Edeline it was like a magical forest—beautiful but mystic, full of known but unfamiliar creatures—deer, foxes, hares. Birds, as glorious as any picture, would occasionally appear from nowhere, their wings an array of bright majestic color, their soft chirps as delightful as a young babe's laugh. She leaned back against Dane and breathed in the smells of the forest. It was her very own fairy tale filled with knights, mystery, and a dashingly handsome warrior. She smiled as she lifted her head to admire her escort.

Dane looked down, raising a curious brow.

"I'm happy," Edeline whispered, lifting her hand to brush a light caress across his cheek.

He captured her hand to lay his lips gently across her fingers. "You amaze me," he said. "After everything you've been through, you can still find happiness."

"I think, perhaps, happiness has found me," she said, holding his gaze.

Pulling her palm to his lips, he held it there for a long kiss.

She closed her eyes and snuggled against him, enjoying his warmth. She liked him, was attracted to him. He made her feel tingly and oddly happy, even in this era so polluted with peril. How stupid was that? After everything they'd been through, her thoughts were still mostly on Dane, fantasizing about being alone with him, about kissing him, about being held in his arms.

She snuggled even closer.

One would think her in…

Her eyes flew open as her heart performed a funny little flutter. *Oh, God, is that what this is?* Such a silly feeling. Such unusual desires.

Was she?

She was. She was falling in love.

Did he know? Could he tell? Did he feel at all the same?

Hesitantly pushing away from his chest, Edeline looked up and into his eyes. He smiled, his eyes warm with affection.

The flutter in her heart returned with a touch more flare.

Maybe he did.

After what felt like hours, they emerged into a small clearing. A peaceful little cottage sat within its center. It was simple but charming and completely isolated.

"This is it," Lucas said, urging his horse forward.

Smoke rolled from the stone chimney, disappearing into the mist. Signaling warmth, it was a welcomed sight to the weary travelers.

The cottage, the yards—they were simply enchanting. There was a small woodshed in back and to the right of the cottage, its aging back leaning heavily against a somewhat weathered barn. To the left was a charming garden with a jumbled array of colorful flowers and high-rising stalks. Only its ever-evolving stone pathways gave any indication of orderliness. It was filled to its rims and overflowing with shows of produce.

Lifting his nose into the air, Hemart sniffed. "I smell supper."

"Pray there will be enough," Lucas said, casting his fellow knight a hopeful grin before dismounting.

The others followed suit, moving to the ground and tying their horses to the right-side railing.

It was exactly as Edeline had always pictured the countrysides of France—green, peaceful, and full of promise.

The door opened, and an elderly priest, stooped with age, squinted into the mist as he looked their direction. A broad smile lit his face as recognition emerged. "Lucas!"

"Father Michael," Lucas said, heading for the door and the open arms which waited.

"What a marvelous sight for long-worried eyes," the priest said, wrapping the knight tight within his embrace.

"It has been too long," agreed Lucas, taking a step back and studying his friend. "You look well."

"As do you," acknowledge the priest somewhat sadly. "You're a mighty welcomed sight in these troubled times. I fear your name each time I hear…news."

"These are, indeed, troubled times," agreed Lucas.

The smell of cooking venison rolled from the open door along with a sudden burst of welcomed warmth. It passed quickly by, and then was gone. Edeline, now standing outside the doorway with the others, shivered. Once again, the old priest squinted, taking a long hard look her way. An odd expression crossed his face. He chuckled to himself and then glanced back inside the door. "Please come in," he invited them all.

One by one they were introduced as they headed into the cottage. "I am so glad you have come," he said, closing the door behind them. "There is a fire burning and blankets to the side." He pointed to a stack sitting on a small bench nearby. "Please, make yourselves comfortable. I will throw some more dinner on to boil."

But before he stepped toward the fire and large boiling kettle, he stepped to the back of the room to look around its corner. "It is safe," he said to another.

All four of her escorts promptly stood to full attention.

From around the corner emerged a tall, regal-looking man with blond curling hair and bright gray eyes.

A chorus of three shocked gasps sounded from the knights.

"Omont!"

Chapter Twelve

"Omont?" Edeline repeated, staring at the man as though in a daze. Could this be her father? It seemed unlikely. He was so young. But the hair, a golden-blond mass of curls, was identical to hers.

Lucas hurried to him, pulling him forward into a warm embrace. "My cousin, I had given up all hope."

Omont squeezed him tight. "God blessed me, my cousin." He patted Lucas's back and then pulled away to look at Edeline. "God has blessed me much this day."

"I thought you mad," the priest said apologetically to Omont, shuffling past him toward the brewing stew.

"I'm sure you did." The man chuckled before walking to Edeline and drawing her hands into his. Looking her over from head to toe, he smiled. "My dear sweet Edeline, what a beautiful woman you have become."

She looked down to where their hands joined. It was all so very odd; until a day prior, she hadn't even known he existed. He was a stranger, but yet she could here in his voice, see in his eyes, that he cherished her beyond words. "Ah…thank you," she offered awkwardly. She had no idea how to respond to this man who was her father.

"How did you manage it?" Roncin asked. "How did you get away?"

Still holding Edeline's hands in his, Omont turned to the knight. "They let me go. I am sure they hoped to be led to the treasure, but instead I lost them just outside of Paris." He turned back to Edeline. "I knew you would be here. I knew you would return. My brother saw it in a vision. Through the Lord's gates you would find sanctuary, and two moons later, through the Lord's gates you would return a beautiful woman. And you would be found here, in the forest of mist and amongst men of men."

"You knew?" asked Lucas standing behind him. "Why did you not say something?"

"I hoped," Omont replied, never taking his eyes off Edeline. "I had first assumed it would be I to walk the journey with her. I gave little heed to the 'two moons' until later. My brother's visions were often marked with symbols. The 'two moons' had me baffled. It wasn't until after my arrest that I gave them serious thought, and even then, I only hoped they be precise."

Looking toward the priest, he smiled. "He thought me a mad fool, our dear priest. But I knew," he said, his gaze returning to Edeline. "I felt you in my heart. I knew you were near." He studied her, taking in every feature as though burning it into his memory. Grabbing a lock of her hair, he held it gently in his hands only to let it slip through his fingers. A barely discernible smile touched his lips. "It was the only thing which ever marked you as mine." He touched her cheeks. "You look so much like Jaquette, your mother. She, too, had eyes so deep, so blue." The smile spread across his face. "You are, indeed, the image of my beautiful Jaquette."

His gaze slid to the brooch. He blinked, smiled, then circled it with his finger. "Where did you get this?"

"We found it at my grandparents' in Vanac."

His thoughts seemed to drift for a moment to a distant memory. Nodding his head, he let go of the brooch. "I had it made for your mother. She was heartbroken when she lost it. I know she would be glad of where it sits. Your mother was a remarkable woman, Edeline. Smart, determined, as magnificent as any the Good Lord ever put on this earth. She would have very much liked to have known you."

"I always wished I'd known her," Edeline said sadly. "I never understood why my father…" She stopped, uncertain how to refer to Federic. He was the only father she had ever known. In her heart, he remained her father. It was the man before her who was hard to place. "I mean…" How could she word it? She had no wish to hurt him.

"Federic?" Omont asked, lifting his brow as though confused by her dilemma.

She finally nodded.

He smiled. "Federic is a good man. I would have trusted no other with my child. What he did, he did at my request. He is an honorable man…your father."

Edeline fought the tears which so desperately wanted to fall. "He's very good to me. I've had a good life, a happy life. You can be assured your faith in him was well placed."

Pulling her into his arms, Omont kissed the top of her forehead. "It was not easy, Edeline, not one of the choices I made, but ultimately they were all made out of my love for you. You mean everything to me. You and your mother have been the best parts of my life."

"I have so many questions," she said, leaning against him.

Pulling back to look her in the eye, he answered solemnly, "I will do my best to answer them."

A short while later they all sat quietly around the fire, enjoying its warmth and filling their bellies with bowls of stew. They listened carefully to Father Michael as he shared with them what he knew.

"The treasure has been ours to guard for centuries, but it is not what you think. It is not the many treasures collected throughout time and placed within its walls that are its greatest value, but rather the walls themselves."

"The walls?" repeated Roncin. "How could the walls be more valuable than the treasures of the crusades and the riches of our labors?"

"Diamonds are just diamonds, my friend, and gold just gold. There are many treasures more valuable."

"Like the stone?" asked Edeline.

The priest nodded. "Yes, like the stone. It holds no value on its own, but in the hands of its guardian, it offers the treasure of knowledge through the eyes of time."

Edeline leaned forward. "Tell me about the stone? Was it found during the Crusades?"

"The stone has been passed down from generation to generation for hundreds of years, long before the crusades and the rise of the

Knights Templar. It has passed through those both pure enough to be worthy and strong enough to bear the immense responsibility."

"Until now," Edeline said with a sorrowful sigh.

Taking her hand in his, Omont squeezed it tenderly. "Even now. You are stronger than you think. When strength was needed, you rose above your fear and did a very courageous thing. It took courage to stand against such a fierce opponent."

Edeline glanced at Dane. He smiled and nodded his agreement, but she knew it had been something even stronger than courage which had given her such strength.

The priest continued. "The treasure sits within a cavern deep beneath the cliffs of France. Though within the cavern's walls are many treasures gathered through the years, it is indeed the walls which hold the true fortune. They tell stories of the righteous — past, present, and future. The stories are guides as well as premonitions of what will be. For centuries we have given our lives to protect it. For centuries they have given theirs to try and make it their own."

"Who are they?" asked Dane.

"They call themselves the Dark Army, for they are the devil's guards," said Father Michael. "But we call them the Dogs, for although they are merely men, there are amongst them beasts — men without souls, men without conscience, and yet they have fierce loyalty to their master. Whether they were born as men or born as demons, we are not certain, but many have seen them. I have seen them twice. Though our meetings were in passing, both times I have known, with utmost certainty, I was in the presence of pure evil. I believe it was one of them you met in the field today."

"But they are not all creatures of the damned," added Omont. "Most are simply men — men, who when given the choice, for whatever the reason, have chosen the path of darkness. It is hard to know just who they are. They are everywhere — men of power, men of might. One could stand beside you in battle, only to stab you in the back when it was done."

"How do they know about Edeline?" Dane asked.

"My brother, Nicolas, wore the stone for years. He was a remarkable man — strong and faithful and gifted like no other. When he was condemned, we knew we had to move the stone and secure our access to the cavern. We were not sure what would happen if the stone was not passed. Would it bar everyone from its treasures throughout eternity, or would it simply remain unprotected? It was a gamble we could not take. Not only could the riches of the treasure bring the Dogs frightening power, the knowledge held on its walls could do much worse."

"What kind of knowledge?" Roncin asked.

"The cavern walls speak of a final conflict, one we must win. And the means to its victory are to be found on the cavern's floors."

"How do you know this?" Dane asked.

"My brother saw it in a vision, and I believe we can all agree that his visions should be heeded."

Every head nodded.

Omont continued. "With very little choice, we passed the gift to Edeline. Someone must have become suspicious of my visit and questioned my passage. When they realized it was fraudulent, they ordered my arrest. They weren't looking for Edeline when they first found me, so I'm assuming it's my knowledge of the treasure they were after. They probably never imagined I might actually hold the key to their entry. I doubt they even realized such a key was required.

"When they returned me to the prison, the guard who had led me in and out recognized me and asked about Edeline. One of the men who had brought me back instantly began questioning the guard in such a way, I am certain he knew about the stone and suspected what we had done. I have to assume he is a member of the Dark Army and that he passed on the information. But apparently not soon enough or I would not be here now. Treasure or no treasure, if they believed I could get for them the stone, they would have seen to it that I was never let go."

"Or perhaps it wasn't the treasure they were hoping you'd lead them to," Dane said, looking toward Edeline.

"I never considered…" Dropping his head, Omont closed his eyes and rubbed against his temples. "I am certain I lost them. I was very careful."

Lucas patted his shoulders. "If they had followed you here, we would have seen signs. We were very careful on our journey."

"If they were here, we would have never made the cabin," Roncin said, standing and moving closer to the fire. He held out his hands to the flames, then looked back their way. "Even if they realized the child had been used. That still doesn't explain how they'd know the child had become a woman, the one we now protect."

"The cavern walls tell of warriors from the future who come back to visit our day," the priest said. "Some who worship the cross, some who wear the mark of our enemy. Is there a chance the men who took Edeline have been here before?"

"A very good chance," Dane said. "Those I serve believe it is one of our own."

"Then that is how they know who you are. The enemies of our future have somehow connected with those of our time," the priest said, taking Edeline's hands in his. "We must get you home as quickly as possible. You are not safe in either world as long as the power is yours. But in this world they have the advantage of authority as well as numbers."

"You said as long as she has the power? Will she not have the power until death?" Omont asked.

"There are two ways the power can be passed. One is as Nicolas passed it to Edeline—which is upon a guardian's death. But there is another way. The guardian can pass the power to another whose heart is pure, but only if their hands sit together upon the cradle."

"The cradle?" Edeline blinked. "What does that mean?"

"It means there is hope," Dane said, taking her hand in his.

The priest quickly shook his head in warning. "She can pass the gift, but it isn't simple, and the responsibility of it is great. The heart of the recipient must be sound and solid. They must understand the enormity of what it is they take. Their ability to stay vigilant, strong, and faithful is crucial. It will not be easy to find such a soul. And do not forget, you will need the stone."

"The stone!" Edeline sat forward remembering a very important part of the day's events. "The dark knight—he wore a brown stone around his neck. He pulled it forward for me to see. It seemed… significant."

There was a moment of complete silence. Finally Omont took her hand in his. "As much as I don't want to let you go, we have to get you home, back to your time."

Standing just outside the cottage doors, Dane stood with Edeline in his arms, watching as the distant storm slowly approached. He closed his eyes and took a deep breath. The morrow was something he both feared and mourned. They would be only a few against many. Their only hope of survival would depend on luck and trickery.

It wouldn't be easy. Nothing about the day would be easy, not even the jump itself. This time when he left, he'd be leaving so very much behind. It wouldn't be like times prior when he'd jumped so willingly through the portal toward home. This time the jump would cost him and cost him dearly.

"It's lovely here," Edeline said, leaning her head back against his chest and pulling his attention back to the moment. She breathed in the pleasant scents of the nearby garden. "I believe I would have been happy here in France."

"It's certainly beautiful," he agreed, looking back out into the distant skies. Not for the first time he wondered how much to tell her. "Aren't you happy in Los Angeles, in our day?"

She touched his face softly as though sensing his sorrow. "Yes, of course. My father is there and my friends. It's a very happy life. But I'd have been happy here too, perhaps not in this day, but another."

He covered her hand with his as he looked down into her beautiful eyes, so warm and welcoming. Pulling her palm to his lips, he kissed it tenderly. "It may sound selfish…and perhaps foolish, but I'm glad you came to my world. Chances are I'd never have met you in yours."

She smiled. "It may be both, but I feel the same. I'm thankful every second it was you who came for me."

His gaze dropped to her lips. He smiled. "I'm going to kiss you."

"I know."

"Your father may not like it."

"My father's inside."

He bent low and claimed her lips. Soft and tender, his hands cupped her face as he drew from her lips a passionate response. Her arms wrapped around him as she turned, her fingers teasing the nape of his neck as she melted against him.

"Careful," he warned. "I know it seems we're alone, but believe me we're not. They would be fools not to guard, and they're not fools."

Sighing with disappointment, she buried her face into his chest. "I can't wait until we're finally alone — really, truly alone. Isn't there somewhere we can go? Somewhere we can hide?"

Dane laughed. "Not in this century, I'm afraid." Running his hand lovingly down her face, he glanced back toward the cottage where behind the window Hemart's startled face quickly turned to look away.

The knights, her father — they were right to worry. What the priest had said was true. This world, even more than the future, was a great danger to her. These precious days borrowed from the past could not last. He had to get her home. Then he'd have to find a way to win her heart again. "We'll be together, Edeline. I promise you. I'll find a way."

"So," she said slowly, her disappointment seeming to mount with the weight of that one simple word, "we'll watch the coming storm?"

"Yes," he said, reaching for her hand and looking up toward the dark rolling clouds, "tonight we'll watch her fury. Tomorrow we'll jump into her arms."

Looking back toward the cottage, she sighed. "I'll miss them. All of them."

The sadness in her eyes nearly broke his heart in two. Wrapping his arm around her shoulders, Dane pulled her against him.

How could he possibly tell her the truth? She wouldn't even remember them.

Later that evening, as he and the priest walked across the small yard toward the woodshed, Dane expressed his concerns. "Perhaps I should tell her? Not telling her is beginning to feel more and more like deception. It's becoming harder and harder to bear."

Father Michael shook his head. "I wouldn't tell her. In this case, the truth can do nothing but bring her pain. When you leave, take with you her memories. When the time is right, you will give them back to her."

"It feels so deceitful. She trusts me." It was nearly eating him alive, making her promises he wasn't certain he could keep and listening to her speak of their time here as though it was all a wonderful gift she would forever treasure. If he could grant her this time, he would. He'd do anything for Edeline.

Catching his troubled expression, the priest pulled him to a stop. "Yes, she does trust you. She trusts you to do what is in her best interest. That just happens to be a little complicated, but nonetheless clear. She has to go back. There really is no other option. Have you considered that telling her might make her wish to stay?"

"I have," Dane said, taking a long look around the peaceful forest Edeline had so adored. "Perhaps the choice should be hers."

"And perhaps it is a choice you would like as well," the priest said. His look was one of compassion as he patted Dane's back. "This world holds nothing for her. Everything she is, every dream she's held, lies in another." Once again he began walking toward the makeshift shed. "I can see you have feelings for her. It's important you make sure those *feelings* don't overshadow your good judgment."

The warning took him by surprise. He'd never let emotion lead him on a mission. He was always a soldier first…always, until now.

The priest was right. His feelings for Edeline had left him distracted, driven a few decisions, caused him to loss focus…blinded him to what should have been obvious and should have been avoided.

He was falling in love with her—a dangerous truth he never would have imagined. They'd barely known each other two days. If he'd been asked before if it were possible, he'd have thought the notion ridiculous. Perhaps that's why he had never put up his guard.

But the truth was it had happened that quickly.

Whether it was the fierce attraction between them, their circumstance, or fate, it really didn't matter. It was foolish. No matter if they stayed or returned home, destiny was waiting to take her.

He stumbled as he mindlessly moved toward the woodshed.

The priest was right. He knew what he had to do, and it might be the hardest thing he'd ever done. He had to take her home. He had to let her go.

"I'll get the wood," Dane said, hurrying to catch up with the priest.

A few minutes later, his arms loaded to full capacity, they headed back toward the cottage.

"There's something else," Dane said hesitantly. It was the thought which had been haunting him since they'd met up with the three knights the day before. "I'm not even certain what my world holds anymore. Without a doubt, I've pricked the fabric of time. I have no idea if it has changed the look of the future."

The priest smiled and once more came to a stop. "You give yourself far too much credit, young man. Destiny is the path which leads to the future. It is made of much stronger material than you give it credit. The roads may curve, twist, and fork, but they all lead the same direction."

"But—"

"Trust me, nothing is as random as it seems."

"Then why worry?" Dane asked as he shifted the heavy pile in his arms. "If destiny is so powerful, why bother to hide the treasure? Why bother to fight?"

The priest's eyes grew somber. "Like man, destiny cannot see her way in the dark."

"Which means?"

The priest smiled. "It is not the fabric of time which leads destiny. It is the fabric of man." He pointed toward the cabin. "As long as there are men such as those inside…" He turned back, placing his hand over Dane's heart, "as long as there are soldiers of courage and conviction. Destiny will always see her way." He patted Dane's chest, then again started walking. "We fight the fight of the ages. We fight for the light."

Dane looked toward the cottage where inside Edeline now sat beside her father, listening to stories she would not carry past the morrow. "I'm falling in love with her," he confessed.

"As I believe she is with you," the priest said. Looking up into the heavens, he smiled. "Have faith, young man. I have a feeling your paths will never again veer far."

Chapter Thirteen

They left early the next morning, traveling under the thick blanket of darkness and mist. They would be there, the Dogs, waiting, watching. Their numbers would be great, their advantage immeasurable. The only hope for Edeline and Dane was that their wits would be the wiser and their cause blessed.

For the most part, they traveled under the cover of forest. By now their foes would have gathered enough reinforcement that their own much smaller party wouldn't stand a chance in an open field. But still there were times their only choice of paths took them straight through the long, flat plains. It was then they'd say their prayers, put their faith in God, and move carefully across the valleys.

By nightfall they arrived high upon the cliffs of Harfleur. The wind had just begun to whip with the promise of another upcoming storm, and rain fell steady from the sky. Wrapping her arms around her father, Edeline begged. "Come with us."

Squeezing her tight, Omont bent to place a kiss atop her head. "This is my world, Edeline. I must stay. There are things I must do, things I must see are done so that your world never changes." His eyes watering, he ran his hand lovingly across her cheek before fisting the hand and placing it over his heart. "Know you are here, with me, forever. I love you, Edeline, more than you could possibly know."

From the stories she'd been told, she knew her father was an honorable and brave warrior, but on his face tonight sat only worry and sorrow.

Tears mixed with rain to fall like a stream down her face. "I love you, too." Like he had done, she ran her hand across his wet cheek, fisted it, and placed it over her heart. "Forever."

"You'll wait for the signal?" Lucas asked Dane for assurance.

"We'll wait. When I'm sure it's safe, we'll run toward the cliffs and hide within its shadows." Looking to the sky, he noted the fierce clouds in the distance. "It shouldn't be long before the storm takes its shape. Can you keep them running long enough?"

"We can," Lucas said with confidence, "as long as it takes."

Taking Lucas's hand in his, Dane patted his arm in farewell before looking toward the others. "I'll never be able to thank you. But believe me when I say I will never forget you. None of you."

"Nor we you," assured Lucas, stepping away from Dane to take Edeline into his arms.

"Take care of my Edeline," Omont said, stepping forward to take Dane's hand. "That will be thanks plenty."

"I will, that I promise you. I will guard her with my life, with everything I have."

Hemart's eyes filled with tears as he approached Edeline. "I will miss you, Edeline, as I miss your father."

"And I you, Hemart." Finding the goodbyes every bit as hard as she'd imagined, she closed her eyes tight and embraced the giant of a man. "My father speaks of you so fondly. I know he misses you terribly."

Hemart held her a moment longer, obviously reluctant to let her go, but then, with a heavy sigh, he released her and moved forward to Dane. "You are the finest of soldiers, my friend. It has been my honor."

"The honor has been mine." The truth of Dane's words sat apparent in his solemn expression as he took the knight's hand in his.

Taking Edeline into his arms, Roncin looked to Dane. "You take with you the real treasure. Make no mistake its value."

Dane glanced her way and nodded. "Its value is unmistakable."

"We can wait no longer," warned Father Michael, covering his head with a long draping veil. Dressed in Edeline's skirts, he had to lift them high as he pulled himself atop the waiting mare.

"I pray this works," Omont said. Now dressed in Dane's attire, he mounted the mare behind the priest.

Roncin glanced their way. "It is convincing enough from a distance. We will let them get no closer."

The hope was that their enemies would fall for the mirage and follow them away from the high cliffs to the cliffs which lay below.

Watching the three knights move back toward their mounts, Edeline's heart nearly crumbled. They had come to mean so much to her in such a short period of time. She would miss them. She would miss Omont. She would even, in a strange way, miss this world that would have been hers, if only things would have been different.

A comforting hand gently took hers. As the men mounted their horses, she turned to find Dane's eyes full of compassion as well as their own personal sorrow.

"Let the Lord bless you and keep you safe," called the priest before he and the others waved their goodbyes and shortly after disappeared into the hills.

Escaping from somewhere deep within her soul, a painful sob burst into the night. She wavered, the pain of it nearly taking her to her knees. She loved them—all of them. And they were about to risk their lives so that she might live.

Wrapping his arms around her, Dane pulled her tight to his chest, offering her the support and comfort she so badly needed.

"It hurts," she said. And it did, more than she could have imagined.

"I know." He kissed her gently. "I know."

Above the anguished cries of the brewing storm, shouts rang from the hills above.

Staying hidden, Edeline and Dane watched as the forest came to life. The clamoring of metal echoed through the trees as the army of Dogs moved swiftly out of hiding. Out of the shadows, they burst forward into the night, the hooves of their horses pounding against the forest's floor, causing the ground to shake and the earth to rumble like a violent rolling thunder making a break from a tortured sky.

Grunts and cries echoed all around them as the army of the fallen swarmed down the hillside in pursuit of their prey.

They were everywhere—the Dark Army—countless in number, fierce in might. The knights had warned her of their numbers, but still she was amazed.

"Dane." Looking his way for reassurance, she saw her own disbelief reflected in his eyes.

"They'll be all right," he reassured, but it was too late. She'd seen the fear on his face and knew he was every bit as worried as she.

"We must go," he said, taking her hand and leading her forward.

Up the steep hillside they hurried, straight past the shadows which had housed the damned. Dressed in nothing but black, they blended with the night, their steps nothing more than another secret lost in the dark.

It felt to Edeline as though they'd been running uphill for hours by the time they reached the mountain's top.

"We're nearly there, Edeline," Dane said, gently moving his hand against her cheek. "Are you all right to go on?"

Tired and beat, still she nodded. The exhaustion helped distract from her fears, while the aches helped dull her sorrow.

Once more Dane took her hand in his. Down the darkest paths of the forest they moved until finally they reached the forest's edge. There, before them, lay a wide open field of grass and beyond that, jagged cliffs and a turbulent sea.

It was a gloomy yet breathtaking kind of beauty. An endless and amazing pool of dark blue lay topped with tumultuous waves turning to white at their crests before diving back into the ocean. The glory of the sea was echoed in the sky above, as black, thick clouds of the approaching storm rolled toward them, creating a blanket which covered the light from the moon and stars above. Darker, more ominous clouds, rolling as though fisted, followed closely behind, seemingly pushing forward the blanket as they made their way across the night's canvas.

Looking up and down the rock face which separated the forest from the sea below, they saw no one.

"We'll need to move fast and stay as low as we can," Dane said, studying the path ahead.

Edeline glanced out toward the long field of grass, its tall, thick blades, pushed by the growing wind, leaned toward them up the hill. It was high, but it wouldn't entirely cover them.

"We'll be all right," Dane assured, looking back and recognizing her concern. Then, ducking low, he pulled her out of the woods and into the open.

Running faster than she would have imagined possible, they made their way across the open field. She wasn't certain if it was the fear or exertion which raced her heart and stole her breath. Either way, she was relieved when they finally reached the cliffs.

Looking past her toward the field behind them, Dane made sure they weren't followed. Satisfied with what he found, he turned to study the rock barrier before them.

"Stay close against the wall," he said, letting loose her hand and motioning for her to follow.

The wind, having picked up speed, beat against the rock's surface, its frightful moans bellowing through the deep crevices which ran throughout the large, towering, granite walls. Heavy gray clouds now rolled in clusters over the protruding stone edges of Harfleur, as the piercing roars of thunder rumbled from its turbulent sky.

She and Dane moved slowly across the rugged terrain, leery of the many hazards which could be lining the steep path. As they pushed forward toward the rock's towering front, violent bursts of wind whistled in from the coast, winding around the earth's hard, jagged edges and slapping cold wisps of moistened air against their faces.

Slowly they made their way around the enormous wall. Dane pulled her close beside him, leading her around the corner and straight into the storm.

Thin, narrow crannies lined the rock's face. Peeking inside each, Dane finally turned toward Edeline and nodded. Stepping into the opening, he pulled her in behind him. Two steps forward and the path took a sharp right and suddenly stopped.

A small hollow nook, barely big enough for two, would be their shelter.

"We'll be safe in here until it's time to go," he said, leaning back against the rock and pulling her into the warmth of his arms.

She shivered, neither from the cold which sat heavy all around them nor from the damp which now weighted down their clothes, but rather from the fear for those she loved who were still out there.

"I can't believe what they did for us." Laying her head against his chest, she closed her eyes and absorbed the comfort. "Do you think they're all right?"

"My money's on our friends. They know what they're doing. They're clever men and incredible warriors. Don't underestimate them."

"There were so many," she fretted, remembering the enormous army. She'd never forget the haunting sounds of their pursuit or the vision of her father and the knights as they bravely lured them away.

Tears filled her eyes as reality struck—she would never know what happened to them.

"God is with them. He's greater than any army, regardless of their number."

"They are such amazing men. It's hard to believe my father was one of them. It's not that he isn't noble. He is. But I've simply only known him as a peaceful man." Still clinging to his tunic, she leaned away from the warmth of his chest to look into his eyes. "Dane, why do you think he never told me?"

"I'm sure he was merely protecting you. Nothing he could have said or done would have changed what was or what had passed. Whatever he did or didn't do, he did it based on his love for you." Dane cupped her face, holding her still to look into her eyes. "I met him before I left. His only concern was for you. He loves you. He is and always will be your father."

"I know," she said, leaning back against his chest. "I'm ready to go home."

The wind was picking up speed and whipping viciously into the crevice, its harsh chilling fingers nipping at their flesh. But as of yet, the clouds had not unleashed the electric storm they held inside.

Dane moved her behind him and then peeked out around the stone wall.

"Is it time?" she asked, not sure what answer she was hoping for.

"Soon, Edeline, very soon," he assured, stepping back around the corner to draw her back into his arms.

She nuzzled against him as he bent to kiss her cheek.

"What is it like—the portal?"

"It's loud and…hard to describe. Perhaps a bit nauseating. But don't worry, we'll pass through quickly."

"We have to jump?"

"Yes, and there can be no hesitation. It would probably be best if you close your eyes and put your trust in me."

"I will. I believe I'll have to. I don't think I could do it on my own." She cuddled against him. "I'm so glad it was you they sent for me. Do you think, perhaps, it was always meant to be?"

He smiled, leaning down so that their heads touched. "I'm beginning to think destiny played a heavy hand in it all." Gently brushing his lips across hers, he seemed to drift away. "I hope it has. I hope…" Lifting himself away, he stared into the darkness.

"Dane?" Reaching up, she took his face into her hands. "What is it?"

Dark troubled eyes looked down into hers. "You mean a great deal to me, Edeline. I want you to know that. I know we've only known each other a short time, but I feel I know you well. You're kind, honest, strong. It would be impossible not to have feelings for you."

They were beautiful words, words she'd longed for. They were also holding something back.

"What aren't you telling me?"

It took a lot to trouble her soldier, and that's what worried her the most. After having her world turned upside down, her beliefs shattered near to the wind, after everything they'd been through, what could be so terrible he couldn't tell her?

Leaning forward, she kissed his lips, kissed his cheeks. "I feel the same way about you, but I also trust you. Now trust me. Tell me what's wrong."

She kissed his lips once more, this time longer, taking her time to enjoy what they hadn't before had time to. If the worst happened and she only had this one night, she wanted it to be in the arms of the man she loved. And she loved him, this soldier who had risked his life over and over to protect hers. She loved him not just for his courage and his strength, but for his very spirit. He was a good and honorable man, just like her fathers.

Pulling her tight against him, he returned her kiss with passion, kissing her as though he adored her, kissing her as though he might never have the chance again.

That's when it hit her—that was exactly his fear.

Dropping her hold, she stepped back into what little space she had. "No!"

"Edeline?"

"Why would you leave me?"

Staring at her as if struck, he blinked, then reached for her. "I would never willingly leave you. I couldn't. You mean too much to me."

It wasn't what he was saying. It was what he wasn't, those words that held his tongue but floated in the torment of his eyes.

Her world was collapsing, and it had nothing to do with the storm, the portal, nor Heaven or Hell. There was much he was not saying. She knew it. She felt it. Things for them would never be the same.

"Why are you leaving me?"

"I will be there for you. I swear."

"But? There's more, I know it. I want you to tell me." She had been wandering through this ancient world in a bit of daze. Nothing seemed real, yet everything seemed possible, including love and happily-ever-after. But they were heading toward home, and reality was starting to reappear through clearer more focused eyes. They'd only known each other three short days. In truth, she knew very little about him. He might care for her. In fact, she was certain he did. But he could very well be tied to another.

Stupid! The thought had never crossed her mind. Had they ever discussed it? No…no, there hadn't been the time. She should have asked. She should have at least considered the possibility. But she hadn't. Her inexperience and emotional dependency had blinded her to the possibility.

The damp stone behind her suddenly grew uncomfortable. A single sharp sob broke free as she lowered her eyes away from his and moved to step past him. "I never thought to ask if you were taken. You should have told me. You should have said…something."

He reached for her hands, but she pulled them away.

"Edeline, it's not what you think." His face was troubled and uncertain. "There's something I need to tell you. I just…God, I just don't know how."

She bit into her trembling lips, certain he was about to tell her he belonged to another.

"It will be hard to understand, but I need you to—" Dane suddenly stopped and stepped back to look out into the storm, undoubtedly eager to escape the discomfort of the moment and plunge back into the portal. He stood silently for a moment studying the dark, his forehead wrinkling into a frown.

"It's all right. You don't have to expla—"

He moved his finger to his mouth in a shushing motion before quickly looking back out into the dark.

The pain was too much. Her heart ached, and being so close only made it worse.

"If it's time to go, let's just do this," she blurted, slipping past him into the short and narrow exit.

"Edeline, no!" Dane reached for her arm, but she pulled away and ran out into the storm.

The wind whipped her hair violently out of its loose hold, sending it flying in a mad array around her head. The roar of the wind was as loud as the raging howls from the sea. Unprepared for its brutality, she was pushed back against the stone wall. Steadying herself, she looked into the threatening sky. Still there was no lightning—no key to passage.

Only moments ago she'd preyed the storm would be patient and allow her as much time as possible to be alone with Dane. But now, uncertain and torn, she was more than ready to return. She needed away. She needed time alone to pick up the pieces of her shattered dream.

She was about to turn back toward the crevice when her arm was taken in a cruel grip. Startled, she turned abruptly into the arms of a stranger. His face was brutal and cold, his expression determined and merciless. Whatever his intent, it wasn't to her favor.

She screamed, but her fright was lost in the rumble of the storm. In the very next instant, she was lifted up and over the man's shoulder. She kicked and struggled for her freedom, but it did her no good.

Slung over his shoulder, she watched as he moved back through the grass fields toward the hills, the cliffs where Dane hid, slowly disappearing into the distance. Built like a giant, the man moved effortlessly over the rough terrain and through the grass.

A smaller man, slender in build and with what looked to be a hint of Asian ancestry, emerged from nowhere. She recognized his face even before she saw the needle. He was hurrying to keep up with her captor. Stumbling over the rocks, he carefully held the needle out in front of him, preparing it for use. "Slow down!" he hollered after nearly taking a fall.

The giant stopped and yelled over his shoulder. "We haven't got all day, you incompetent fool. Hurry up, and do it right this time."

Catching up with them, the man reached for her arm.

Determined to never again be left unconscious, she swung her arms up and against his, sending the needle flying into the air.

"Damn it," he swore and instantly began searching the ground. But the force of her hit and the lift of the wind had blown the small instrument far away into the grass. "I'll never find it in this," he said before moving back to his feet and searching his pockets. Finally throwing his hands up into the air, he admitted, "I don't have another."

"We'll head back to the horses. If she causes a fuss, I'll knock her out myself," was the gruff reply of the giant. He turned and began walking back toward the woods, the other man following close behind him.

Edeline dangled helplessly from her captor's shoulder, watching the man behind them fight against the strength of the wind. That's when she saw Dane. Like a silent leopard he flew out of nowhere, wrapping his arms around the other man's neck and pulling it back like the twist of a cap. In an instant, the man lay lifeless on the ground.

Her captor, unaware of the attack, stormed out of the grass and up the steep hillside into the trees.

Dane disappeared from sight.

The howling of the wind was replaced by the swishing of the branches and the snapping of foliage beneath her captor's feet. She tried desperately to spot Dane, but he was well hidden within the trees.

They came to a sudden stop.

"You're a damn lucky fool, Farrell," said another from behind. "Where's Mitchell?"

Her captor, Farrell, turned, bringing her face to face with another. He, like Dane, was built like a warrior. Older than Dane by at least two decades, he was still every bit as solid. Unlike Dane, his eyes were cold—not ruthless like the giant's, but void of life, hopeless and uncaring. They looked past her with disinterest as they searched the path below.

"He was right behind me," said Farrell in disbelief. "Oh, the idiot! He's probably tripped over his own feet. The man's a fool."

"You're the fool," the other man snarled. "Where's the soldier?"

"She was alone." Farrell turned back toward the other, and once again Edeline was facing their trail. The dark, heavy clouds were now rolling angrily across the sky. In the distance she could hear the sounds of the troubled sea lifting and spraying over the stone walls of the cliffs. And in the not so far distance, the first menacing strike of lightning lit the banks.

The man behind her let out a frustrated groan. "I guarantee you, she was not alone. And you can bet your last dollar she's not alone now."

Her surroundings swirled as Farrell turned back and forth, scanning their surroundings. "I don't see anyone."

"Yeah," said the other with disdain, "and that includes Mitchell."

"Let's get to the horses and get the hell out of here," Farrell said, turning and starting back through the woods. "We need to get her to LaFay and get back to the portal before the storm ends."

"Watch your back," yelled the other, now behind them and heading down the trail they'd just come. "I'm getting Mitchell."

"He's useless," hollered back her captor. "Leave the damn fool be." Then, grunting and mumbling to himself, he continued up the hill.

Edeline frantically searched the shadows.

His cohort was right; she wasn't alone. Dane was out there somewhere. He wouldn't leave her.

With every ounce of strength she could muster, she lifted herself up straight and jabbed her fingers directly into her captor's eyes.

"Bitch!" He stumbled back, loosening his hold but not letting her go.

Edeline squirmed and twisted, falling down but not out of his arms.

Fighting was new to her. All she knew was not to give up. Digging her fingers deep into his face, she clawed as hard as she could.

The man howled, trying to pull away from her hold.

She refused to let go.

Lifting her up and out of his reach, he tossed her roughly to the ground.

The thick foliage beneath scratched but gave cushion as she landed.

"You bitch! I'll teach you to mess with me," Farrell said, leaning down to grab her from the dirt, an ugly scowl turning his already fierce looks to frightening.

She kicked out, landing her foot directly into his groin. A furious cry rumbled through the forest trees as Dane landed square in the middle of the giant's back.

The man, already bent toward the ground, fell flat against the earth.

Grabbing a fistful of the man's hair, Dane lifted his head and wrapped his other arm around the man's neck. Then just as quickly as he had the other, Dane put to rest her captor.

Shock and horror froze her only momentarily to the ground. There was still the other attacker out there, and though his size had not quite matched the man now lying still on the forest's floor, she had an uncomfortable feeling this one would be far less manageable.

Accepting the hand Dane offered, she moved to her feet. Together they stood scanning their surroundings, searching for the man who had disappeared down the trail.

"Think he's still down there?" she asked.

"I don't know, but we're not taking the chance," Dane said, grabbing her hand and pulling her off the trail into the thick cover of woods.

The next thing she knew, they were back on the cliffs. And, by all appearances, they were alone.

"Will he come for us?" she asked, clinging to Dane's arm.

Dane eyed the field behind the towering rock walls. "I don't think he'll risk it," he said, looking back down into her frightened eyes. "He won't risk you…and neither will I. Edeline, we can't wait. We have to go now."

She nodded and looked away.

Cupping her chin, he pulled her back to face him. "I love you, Edeline. There is no other, not in my heart nor in my life. There's only you." Yet, the pain in his eyes told her all was not well.

"But we won't be together, will we, Dane?"

Lightning struck directly above, lighting the ridge and the hills around them. Dane searched the hills quickly; then his eyes turned back to her. "Believe me when I say, if there is any way, I will never leave your side."

Deep in her heart, she knew it was true, but she also sensed the secret he kept was big enough to tear them apart. Reaching inside her black cover, she pulled off the brooch hidden inside. "Find a way," she said, placing it in his hands and squeezing his fingers around it. Lifting up on her toes, she kissed him. "Find a way. Whatever it takes, don't ever leave me."

She knew, by the torment on his face and the dropping of his head, it wouldn't be easy. But suddenly those deep brown eyes, which had only hours ago stolen her heart, looked deep into hers. "As God is my witness, I won't leave you, Edeline. Now do me a favor. Close your eyes."

As the clouds raged battle with the sky, and the waters below fought valiantly against the wind, he lifted her into his arms and ran toward the sea.

Lightning flashed and held as the earth and sky joined forces to build a bridge through time. They were lifted with a jolt and thrown into the sky. A fierce pull caught hold of their flailing bodies. It felt as though she were being suctioned into a tube.

Unable to resist the temptation, she opened her eyes.

Shadows of past and future played against the stone walls behind them. Moans and laughter mixed into a roaring collage of what was and what was to be. Wrapping her arms tight around Dane, she watched as everything around them blurred into an indecipherable whirl, and she was carried, once again, from her past into her future.

Graham looked down at Farrell's lifeless body. He should leave the oaf. It would serve him right.

Behind him, lights blazed and lit the earth as the roar of time echoed into the surrounding darkness.

They had gone.

He sighed. What a bloody wasted endeavor. Reaching down, he grabbed the motionless form of his associate and lifted him up and onto the back of his horse. He'd take the fool along with the other to drop at the feet of his employer. Hadn't he warned him? Neither ego nor ignorance had any place on such a mission. Although, he had to admit, the two idiots weren't the only thing royally messed up.

He wondered, not for the first time, what misfortune had transpired to allow the soldier access to the portal. When he and the others had left, the lab had been completely under his employer's control. Whatever it was, he hoped like hell his employer had taken back the reins. If not, he hated to think what might await him.

Making his way down to the cliffs, he cursed the storm as he searched again for Mitchell's body. He finally found it lying between two large stones. With another huge heave, it landed beside Farrell's. His boss wouldn't be pleased with their loss or their failure, but maybe next time he'd smarten up and let Graham pick his own crew.

Eyeing the hills behind him, he wondered how long it would take LaFay and his fourteenth-century recruits to realize they were chasing an illusion. If he was lucky, it would take days. He wasn't particularly fond of the man and wouldn't mind one bit leaving him to rot in time. As far as Graham was concerned, the man would blend nicely into the era of malevolence. And what more harm could he possibly do? He'd already led a number of his army off fate's course, but yet nothing seemed to be affected.

What exactly would it take to rock destiny off course? He'd hate to think it was all predetermined. If it was, he'd been dealt a pretty rotten hand. *Thanks for the ride, but I'd just as soon skip the next damn round.*

Something metal glistened from under the grass, catching his attention. He reached down and picked up the syringe. Looking back over his shoulder to the two limp forms, he scowled. *Damn bloody fools.* It appeared they could do nothing right. He shoved the syringe into his pouch before continuing down to the rocks.

Sitting atop the cliff, he waited for the lightning. It was odd to think that in less than a second's time, from this end of the portal, he would most likely be returning to this very spot. His employer wasn't one to give up. There was little to no chance that he wouldn't be sent back. The Dogs wanted their precious treasure. They were mad for the power it would bring.

Graham snorted his contempt. *Like the world isn't messed up enough as it is.*

"They got away?" The deep, emotionless voice slapped like a bullwhip across his back.

Graham jumped. He hadn't heard the man approach. "Is that a question, or are you simply stating the obvious?"

It was a brave tone to take with such a man — monster — whatever the hell his unwanted companion was. Or perhaps it was simply stupid. Truth be told, he didn't much care. He was finding little to value in his own or others' characters these days.

LaFay's dark, emotionless eyes studied him. Their sinister, soulless gulf had always chilled Graham. Tonight was no exception. The beast shifted his weight as he looked past Graham toward the sea. "I saw the lightning, heard the roar. They played us all for fools."

Graham nodded. It wasn't just LaFay's eyes which made him uncomfortable. The man was one scary-ass dude.

LaFay looked toward the two dead bodies slung across the mount. He nodded his head, apparently less than surprised. "Saves me the trouble," was all he said.

Graham said nothing, but he wondered if his own last breath would be coming soon. LaFay had already made his thoughts on the bungled mission painfully clear. He blamed them all, especially Graham.

The wind whipped wildly around them, pushing toward the tall stone walls behind them, then whistling through their long shallow crevices. LaFay turned toward the sound. "I won't be sad to see the last of this place."

Graham's gaze snapped back to him in surprise.

LaFay had managed the impossible. He'd established contact with the Dark Army of the fourteenth century and managed to convince them the girl with the golden curls was also the one who guarded the stone. Thanks to twenty-first-century knowledge and trickery, he had also convinced them he was something more than he was. He had an entire army at his disposal. Graham couldn't believe the man would simply walk away from such an advantage to never return.

"You don't think they'll send us back?" asked Graham. "They're certainly not going to just give up, especially after you've made such a valuable connection."

"Valuable connection?" LaFay raised a sardonic brow. "We've just seen how valuable they are. A whole army against a handful of men — who would you say won?"

"Their luck won't hold."

"Neither will the portal walls. And, I, for one, have no intention of risking my hide once more through that dilapidating tunnel."

"Not even for the location of the treasure?"

LaFay motioned toward the hills where, no doubt, lay his army-in-waiting. "Think if they had the location or access to it, I wouldn't already have it? You underestimate me."

Arrogant bastard.

"Perhaps."

Those dark, hollow eyes seemed to dig straight into Graham's chest and squeeze.

"And I overestimated you," LaFay said. "It seems we are both capable of error."

The sky rumbled overhead.

"All aboard," LaFay said, stepping forward to grab Farrell's lifeless body off the back of the beast and tossing it over the edge.

A white bolt of lightning reached out her ends toward the dark clouds above and the earth below, accepting LaFay's gift as she held her steady grip.

Graham picked up Mitchell and would have tossed him over the edge, but having received a less-than-helpful shove from behind, he instead found himself falling with his lifeless companion into the arms of time's taxi.

A swift swirling funnel emerged from the storm's scattered debris, holding in its center a dark, endless chasm.

Lightning flashed once again and held as LaFay followed.

A second later, all traces of the future were wiped from the past—all but some clothing and a horse by the name of Laur, who stormed with its riders through the hills of France toward its Southern border.

Chapter Fourteen

Dane tried to hold on to her, even though he knew it was in vain. Time and destiny ruled the portal, and they would take from him what he had no choice but to surrender.

Wide blue eyes stared in disbelief from a face torn with fright. She reached for him. "Dane," she sobbed as hope withered and died. Her hand never quite touched his, but her despair hit him hard.

Oh, God, but it hurt. Deep in his soul he felt the wretched pain. "Edeline," he called as she drifted further away, fading with every inch into the realm of what would never be. The force of the portal grabbed hold of him, pulling him toward his time.

"Edeline!" The cry ripped from his heart and landed along with him on a cold, tile floor. He was back in the lab, the fierce wind of the transporter whipping from all sides, holding him caged behind its powerful walls.

He'd lost her.

From that moment forward, he would carry the memory — the look on her face as she drifted away — betrayal, pure and simple. *God, I should have told her.*

Was he right? Was he wrong? Was there a choice to be had?

Trying to stand, he fell back to the floor. He'd never fought the tug of the portal before and was surprised by its brutality. His muscles burned. His ribs felt hammered. The portal had taken the last blow, striking him hard as the woman he loved slipped through his hands. He closed his eyes, trying to manage the pain, not just the physical ache from what had been an abnormally brutal pull, but also the internal one which weighed down his heart, collapsing his will.

He struggled to his knees as the wind began to calm, and the scene around him came into a hazy view. Generators roared as lights flashed and changed colors. Machines whined. Voices boomed. Feet scurried. A firm hand took hold of his shoulder.

"Dane! Dane, are you all right?" The general's troubled voice was, oddly enough, his first reassurance not a lot had changed. "Dane?"

"I'm all right." The words sounded gruff and strained even to his own mottled hearing. He struggled to clear his vision. Slowly it all came into view — the machines, the transporter, the people — they were all as they had been the day he left. Thank God.

"You did it, Dane," said the general, slapping his shoulder before reaching down to offer him a hand. "All is as it were, so I'm assuming the girl is now back where she belongs?"

She belongs with me.

"Yes," he replied, still struggling to get his bearings as he made it to his feet. The lights were doing very little to relieve his pounding headache, which was in turn doing very little to relieve his nauseous state. He narrowed his eyes and looked to the floor.

A new pair of boots landed beside the general's. "You all right, Dane?" asked Professor Blaine.

"Will be once my stomach lands."

"Rough ride back, was it? It must be the portal. It's weakened substantially. You're probably lucky you managed to make it back when you did."

"Dane, where's Laur?" the general asked.

"Safe. It's all right. She's in trustworthy hands."

"What? Shit, Dane. What do you mean 'trustworthy hands'?"

He knew there'd be numerous questions, but he had only one. "How's Edeline?"

"Edeline's fine, Dane. What do you mean by 'trustworthy hands'?"

"Are you sure? Who's watching her? Where is she?"

"She's fine, Dane. See for yourself." The general pointed to the room behind the glass pane.

Dane followed the finger toward the room, his breath catching as his heart once again expanded with life.

Edeline.

Eyes he knew to be a beautiful blue stared directly his way—bold, curious, and void of any recognition.

It was true. How could she now deny it? The proof stood right before her. Her whole life was a lie, her world a sham. The stranger on the other side of the glass knew more of her world than she. He turned her way, his eyes seeming to almost search her out. Meeting his stare, she couldn't look away. He was handsome, shockingly so, but it wasn't his looks that caught her attention as much as the way he looked at her.

What had they lived? What had they shared? She had to know. She had to speak with him. Was that her name upon his lips?

He was far enough away she couldn't tell, but she'd bet her last nickel those piercing eyes were the darkest of brown. Unshaven, haggard, and covered with soot, he was still a magnificent sight. A soldier, without question—he was tall, his shoulders broad, and beneath his cover undoubtedly lay a wall of might. Beyond the beaten exterior of his impressive frame, she sensed strength like no other, a fierce honor and determination working as a backbone to a man who would not be broken.

Yes, she wanted to meet this warrior—her rescuer. With any luck, he held the answers she needed, the sanity she hoped for. How could so many believe something so foolish? Perhaps she and her father had jumped the invisible barriers of time, but *her*—special, blessed, some kind of gatekeeper? Really, how could they believe such ludicrous nonsense? It was folklore, mythology, all coming from a time when absurdity ruled. Sure, she understood it made the situation no less dangerous. Still, she'd love to hear even one person speak some sense, echo her reason.

The man, Dane Walker was his name, had lived the truth of her time for days. Certainly he'd see reality and stand on her side.

The general pulled the soldier's attention away, motioning toward the door. As the small group made their way out of the lab, Dane once again looked back her way. No one had ever looked at her with such intensity. It was as though he believed she could read his mind, and he wanted her to. She wanted to, but all she could sense was pain.

"He's hurt," she said, looking to her father for explanation once the group disappeared.

Federic's attention had followed the men. He seemed almost surprised to find her still standing at his side, which was odd considering he hadn't let her leave it the last few days. "It could be the portal," he replied, nodding through the glass toward the raised platform. It was surrounded by dozens of metal panels holding complicated circuit boards with tall oblong blades in the center.

"It's not as strong as it used to be," he explained. "I know they've been somewhat worried about his return." He took a deep breath and looked back her way. "It wasn't that way for us. It was jolting, of course, but not brutal. Even Braguard came through unscathed." He halfheartedly chuckled. "He wasn't happy by any means, but he wasn't hurt. I believe our greatest danger was perhaps his reaction to having landed in the lab. It frightened him, and he let it be known. He'd had no problem jumping from the edge of a cliff into a monstrous storm, but he wanted no part of this unfamiliar world."

She smiled. "I miss him."

To what had been the best of her knowledge, Braguard had belonged to a good friend of Father Tom's who owned a ranch near the top ridge of the Santa Monica Mountains. They had gone there often for years, to visit the horse her father called his friend. As a child, she'd never thought it odd, her father's devotion to the animal. Looking back, it should have raised some questions. At the time, she was too thrilled to be taken to her favorite pastime. She was thirteen when their dear friend passed.

"He was a fine horse, a true friend," Federic said, rubbing his eyes as his brows pulled with obvious exhaustion. The last few days had been rough ones for her father, and he was no longer a young man.

It was the first time in her life she could recall her father seeming less than sturdy. "Perhaps now you can rest," she suggested, looking back through the glass.

"I'll sleep better anyhow." He wrapped his arm around her shoulders, his gaze following hers to the lab. "It's really something, isn't it?"

One electrical board after another stretched nearly the entire length of the room. Large panels, hanging high above the boards and displaying one odd mathematical equation after another, were scattered throughout. A handful of technicians still stood carefully watching various monitors as at least a dozen soldiers stood guard over the room.

"It's…odd," she said, with a shrug of her shoulders. "Everything is simply…odd. It's a lot to grasp."

Looking down, Federic's face grew solemn. "I'm sorry, Edeline, for not telling you sooner. The best course was never clear to me. I knew only that I wanted you to be happy."

"I am happy. I have always been happy." She squeezed him tight. "You're a good father—the best. We'll be all right. We always get by. You and me, remember?"

Hugging her back, he chuckled. "Yes, you and me."

"With plenty of room for Alison," she added, looking up and grinning.

"You are relentless," her father said with a quick flick to the end of her upturned nose.

"And you are in love."

He stared at her a moment before shaking his head. "It's complicated. We're complicated, Edeline. And I have much in my past, much she may not understand. If I ask her into my world, I will first have to tell her it all. I will never again betray one I so love."

The pain in his eyes nearly ripped her apart. "Daddy, you didn't betray me. You protected me. I see the difference." She took his downcast face in her hands. "I love you. You're my father. You always will be."

Covering her hands with his, he patted them affectionately. "How can one man be so blessed?"

Bright lights suddenly flashed from inside the lab. They both turned to see the men hurrying back to their individual machines as a siren rang through the halls behind them, echoing with the pounding of hurried feet.

Through the window they saw the general and the professor emerge, each running to two individual machines.

"What's happening?"

"I'm not certain," he said, stepping closer to the window.

The men scurried back and forth between the machines, entering data and diligently watching the boards. Finally the room seemed to calm. The professor visibly sighed as the general appeared to commend the men around him.

"Problem solved apparently," Federic said, still watching carefully the room. He looked back over his shoulder her way. "I'd give a pretty penny to get my hands on one of those machines."

"What for?"

He looked at her as though surprised. "Well, to see how they work of course."

She smiled. "Of course."

General Matthews walked into the room. "The day's travels seem to have worn the portal thin. It's rapidly declining." He looked past them into the lab. "I imagine that last surge belonged to our anonymous friends." He scratched the back of his neck. "I'm guessing their journey ended shortly after this port."

Federic's brows rose in question. "Sorry?"

"We've changed the future. Once they hit that curve in time, they simply would have disappeared into the here and now. The past few days for them will have never even happened. Good news for a couple of them."

"Why do you say that?" she asked.

"Two were put down, a state that, sadly, won't cross the borders of time. In this day, the two are very much alive and very much a threat. Our altering the future will inadvertently offer them a second chance."

Put down. The words sat like a chill along her spine. "They were… killed?" Her gaze drifted past the general to the door behind him. "He killed them?"

It was hard for her to believe. Men had actually died in this ridiculous affair? What had happened? A part of her wanted more than ever to talk with the soldier, Lieutenant Colonel Walker. Another part was starting to think distance might be wise.

"They left him no choice," the general said, as though no further explanation was required. Looking her way, he sighed. "Are you still having doubts?"

"They've all been replaced with questions. Can I see him?"

"Sorry, Edeline, no. He's in debriefing."

"Debriefing?" Federic suddenly perked up. "I'd like to be there. I'd like to know what happened."

"I know you would," the general said with a humored smile. "Just…give us some time with him. It's easy to forget the little details when you've been through something like this. But sometimes it's the little details that give the clearest picture. Our experts know what they're doing, but they need this time alone."

"I understand." Her father looked as disappointed as she felt. "Have you found out anything you *can* tell us?"

"There were at least three, but he heard them mention a fourth. He said it sounded as though the man was actually there. If he was, Dane never saw him."

"Did he know any of her captors?"

The general hesitated.

"What?" Federic asked.

"We possibly have an ID on one, but…"

"But?"

"But I doubt he turns out to be our man."

"Because?"

"Because the guy's a good guy, not particularly materialistic and not fond enough of the past to willingly go back."

"Go back?" Federic scowled. "You mean he's been there before?"

"As I said, I don't believe we're talking about the same man, but yes. The description does somewhat match a former time traveler. But the description's pretty general and most likely a coincidence. We'll have Dane look through some photos. If it is him, we'll know soon enough.

"Look, I'm really sorry. I know you both have questions you want answered, but right now I have to find some answers of my own. I've arranged for you a place to stay here on the base. It's not much, but it will have to do." His gaze darted back toward the lab. "It's probably good that you're here. Things are about to change for all of us. We'll need to make plans."

Edeline exchanged a curious look with her father before they both turned back to the general. "Change?"

"The base was created to manage the portal. If the portal closes…" He shrugged his shoulders. "Well, I'm not exactly sure what will happen." Shifting his weight, he looked back toward the door. "I need to go. They're waiting for me. I promise, as soon as I can, I'll see you get your answers. Now, if you'll both come with me." Turning, he motioned for them to follow.

Leading them out the door, he then escorted them down the long hallway to the elevators where two armed guards waited.

It was a strange world—the lab, the base, even the ride to the base had been bizarre. The road toward her past had been lined with nothing but the peculiar—long, deserted desert roads; eerie signs warning of extraterrestrials; military restrictions and low flying, unidentified objects; guarded gates; and well-armed escorts with strictly no-nonsense demeanors.

All of it seemed as surreal as the knowledge that she was somewhere else living another reality in another time. She wanted it to end. She wanted to wake up and find it had all been a dream, a ridiculous fantasy. But she'd long ago realized she was wide awake, and the only dream she'd been living had been her life up until that point.

She needed answers, and she wasn't at all happy about being left in the dark. Yes, she got that the risks were a matter of national security. But this was her life. She wasn't just another pawn in this bizarre game of past and present. She was the prize and would therefore stand at the mercy of the strongest hand. She had every right to know the risks. She had every right to know the game.

The general stopped and passed them forward to the guards. "I'll be in touch soon," he promised, then turning on his perfectly polished heels, headed directly into the room behind them. It opened only a brief moment as he hurried inside, but it was enough time for her eyes to land squarely on the face of the soldier.

Once again his eyes locked with hers. And there it was—that look, the one that would continue to haunt her. The one that said clearly he believed her to be his.

Curiosity etched with skepticism—he'd seen the look before. But this time the anger and frustration were gone. This time there was no other emotion there at all. She neither feared him nor trusted him. He was simply a link to her past. It was a truth he'd have to accept, but it was hard. No, it was impossible not to hope, search, long for recognition.

"Sorry I kept you waiting," the general said, stepping inside the room and pushing the door closed behind him.

The connection was broken. As weak as it was, Dane still missed it when it was gone. Any connection, any at all, instantly gave him hope. He stared at the entrance, tempted to run after her, tempted to…

There was nothing he could do. *They* were no more.

He looked back toward the men sitting around the debriefing table, they'd all been with the base for years—General Matthews; Professor Blaine; Lieutenant General Corbin, second in base command right under General Matthews; General Thompson, Head of Special Intelligence; and Dr. Hatcher, Lead Psychiatrist for the Special Ops Division.

Moving to the head of the table, the general stood behind his seat but never actually sat down. He looked Dane's direction and then down to the manila folder lying on the table underneath his arms. "Well?"

Dane opened the folder and tapped his finger against the photo inside. "It's him."

Shock played across the general's face. It was the same reaction he'd gotten from every other man in the room upon first confirmation.

"Are you sure?" General Matthews asked, his brows pulling with doubt.

"I'm sure."

Releasing a long, troubled breath, the general bent his head and sighed. "Sorry, Dane, of course you're sure." He tapped his fingers against the back of his chair and then turned to pace the floor. "You'll have to forgive me my reluctance. I worked with the man for several years and would never have questioned his character. Shit!" he said, looking away as he raked his hand roughly through his hair. "I can't even begin to tell you how disappointed I am."

"I knew something wasn't right when he left," Dr. Hatcher said, regret apparent on his face. "But as hard as I tried, he wouldn't let me inside that head of his to do any good. I figured he was burned out, ready to make a clean break. I should've known better. I have a feeling whatever it is he's gotten himself into, he feels it's out of his control…and maybe it is."

"Look." General Thompson leaned forward. "I think it would be best if we kept this knowledge under wraps for a while. It's the only lead we have, and it might end up being our lucky break. I'd certainly hate to lose the advantage by having it leaked to the wrong ears."

"He's right," Dr. Hatcher agreed. "If the wrong people were to find out we know about Graham, he'd disappear just like those who wired the security cameras. This should stay between us and us alone for now."

"What a mess." The general sighed. "Who can we trust? We have someone from inside rigging our security. In fact, for all we know, it could be countless someones. Now there's a former traveler gone rogue, walking around with enough knowledge to bring this base to the ground. And somewhere out there is an army of mercenaries with the balls and backing to storm the nation's most highly-secured base. I feel like a damn sitting duck floating in a pond surrounded by shotguns."

"You're going to have to catch me up," Dane said. "I have no idea what you're talking about."

The professor looked his way. "We know how they did it, or at least most of it. They accessed our tunnels and came in from underneath the base."

"How in the world would they have managed that?"

The tunnels, built more than a mile underground, had been drilled by an enormous machine nicknamed Bulldog which cost well over a billion dollars and, if ever inquired upon, didn't exist. It dug burrows through the earth, melting rock in the process and then distributing it back into the walls of the newly constructed channels. Tougher than steel, the passages were believed to be impenetrable.

"That's the part we're not sure of," the general said. "There are two entrances from here to Los Angeles — one in LA and one just outside of Las Vegas. We've investigated both and come up empty. Of course, it's a little difficult to investigate a crime that hasn't yet happened."

"But you're certain they used the tunnels?"

"We're certain. When we learned of the breech, we called in Colonel Martin to help us figure out what could have happened. It was Martin who figured it out."

Colonel Martin was Lead Security Advisor for the base. According to General Matthews, the man was a genius.

"While looking through security tapes, Martin found a glitch so small I'm certain none of us would have even noticed it. A door, only slightly ajar in one sector, was shut solid in one scene and then barely ajar again in the next. It was a miracle he spotted it, and thank goodness he did. It led us to the tunnels."

General Corbin filled in the rest. "The cameras inside the tunnels were all rigged. With a simple flip of a switch, they'd show an empty passageway, regardless of what was actually there."

"Switch?"

"Well, in this case, a remote signal. The trigger and the bypass were brilliantly wired into the power cords—power cords we had put in as replacements throughout the tunnels nearly a year ago. They could literally switch the screen as they moved from one sector into the next, producing a near flawless vision of inactivity on our monitors."

"The men who supplied the cords as well as the enlisted we used to service them, have all disappeared," the general said. "Most likely they're all dead. They were the labor not the brains of the operation. The people behind this had more knowledge of this base and its operations than any mere service crew. They were able to skip right by our security and censors by using our own technology. That takes some high-level clearance."

"Not to mention intelligence," added the professor. "It was genius, really. If Federic hadn't been so certain and the portal so weak, they'd have been successful."

The general sighed, finally sitting down in his chair. "I hate to even think what could have been the outcome. It was nothing more than dumb luck that we were able to figure it out and thankfully reverse the damage. I doubt we'd be so lucky again. The professor is right. I'm not willing to take any risk with anybody. From here on out, all information is on a need to know basis."

"It's necessary," the professor agreed. "The success of their mission was reliant upon one thing—the element of surprise. Unfortunately for them, surprise has a short shelf life and can be dealt as well as played. If we work this right, Graham may very well be our ace in the hole. I say we leave this amongst those of us here."

"Agreed," the general said in the form of an order.

"So that's how they did it," General Corbin said. "What we don't know for sure is how they got into the tunnels, accessed the stone and managed to work the lab."

"Well, we have a pretty good idea on the latter and a likely scenario on the first," General Thompson replied. "They probably had a great deal of help getting in. And most likely they stormed the lab and took hostages to accomplish the rest, though we may never know for sure."

General Matthews reached across the table to take the file from in front of Dane. "And now we know how they planned to maneuver the past. All that's left is to figure out who *they* are and what they'll do next."

Chapter Fifteen

"It's a rock," Edeline said. Lifting the simple brown stone from around her neck, she glared at its plainness. It was hard to believe the military had kept the thing locked in a vault for twenty-two years, even harder to believe that somewhere in the would-have-been-future men had actually risked their lives to steal it. Then again, it was equally hard to believe they'd taken her along.

She nearly snorted out loud. A *treasure*—this rock? It was as stupid a notion as her being somehow magical.

"I don't understand," the general said, staring at the not-so-extraordinary stone. "Maybe it needs to sit directly against your skin. Perhaps you should try rubbing it?"

She laughed. "Oh…you're serious," she said, seeing his somber expression.

"It's worth a try," he explained.

Pulling the necklace off, she placed the stone between her hands and rubbed vigorously.

Footsteps came to a stop outside the lab's open door. Cleaned and freshly shaven, her so-called hero stood there looking anything but haggard. He looked hot, so hot the word nearly flew right out of her mouth.

She couldn't believe she'd actually spent time alone with him. Lucky her!

Arresting dark eyes stared her way. Confident enough not to care how his boldness would be perceived, he didn't bother to look away when her eyes met his.

"Edeline." Her father's impatient voice brought her back to her task.

"Sorry," she said, looking apologetically around the room. She uncovered the stone to find it every bit as dull and unimpressive as before. "Nope, nothing," she said, lifting the stone for all to see.

"It can't be," Federic said, looking toward Father Tom, who had been asked to join them along with Colonel Martin. "I saw it with my own eyes, right here in this room. It wasn't quite what I had expected, granted, but it did glow."

Edeline shook the chain. Nothing happened.

"Perhaps it was a fluke," the general suggested, looking toward the professor. "Some weird twist of science which made the stone react to heat, maybe it only appeared to shine?"

"We all three held it," Federic reminded, glancing from the general to the professor. "It only lit when Edeline put it on."

"True." The general bent his head, tapping his joined fingers back and forth against his chin before stopping to address the priest. "Could it be the loss of innocence?"

"Hey!" Glaring at the general, Edeline felt her face heat with embarrassment. "I'm still…innocent."

Father Tom took her arm and patted it reassuringly. "No one's questioning your virtue, Edeline. He's speaking of a different sort of innocence, and the answer is no. Once the power has been passed, it belongs to the recipient until death, or that's the legend anyway."

The handsome young soldier looked toward the priest as if about to dispute the rumor, but then he seemed to think better of it and looked away.

"Dane?" Professor Blaine queried, having apparently caught the motion.

"I heard it told a little differently," the soldier explained.

Martin's head swung his way. "By whom?"

"His name was Father Michael. He was a very wise man, trusted by the Knights Templar and one of the few loyal to them at the end."

Martin seemed more than a little taken aback. "You met this man during your travels to the past? You actually spoke to him?"

"I did." Dane looked once more toward Edeline. "Actually, we both did."

Intrigued beyond words, she instinctively smiled and took a step toward him. "We met them—those of the past? We actually spoke to them?"

Martin scowled, his gaze running the room. "Isn't that against the rules?"

"Rules lost priority on this mission relatively fast," Dane said, never looking away from her.

Quickly stepping forward and clearing his throat, the general intervened. "Their interactions with those of the past have been determined to be non-detrimental."

"But interesting," Martin said, obviously hesitant to let it slide.

Edeline lifted the necklace once again for all to see. "Did they tell us the stone was bogus? Because I have to say, I've seen marbles with more personality."

The soldier's mesmerizing eyes moved to the stone.

"You say it lit?" he asked, turning back to her father. "That sounds much less extraordinary than the way I heard it described."

Oh no, certainly he isn't a believer!

Lowering the chain, Edeline placed it and the stone back into her fist. She had an uncomfortable feeling all hopes of a reasonable voice were about to get blown. "How was it described, Lieutenant Colonel?"

"They said it turned into a gem that glowed like a star from the heavens."

"They?" Federic, Martin, and Father Tom all chorused.

"The knights—Knight Templars. They had actually seen it with their own eyes."

"Were they sober eyes?" Edeline snorted, now more convinced than ever the whole thing was the result of overactive imaginations... or inebriation.

Yeah, it could definitely be a drunkard's tale.

"You spoke with the Knights Templar?" Martin asked.

Her father moved toward Dane. "Where did you see these knights?"

General Matthews hung his head. "Gentleman, please, we need to focus on the stone for now. Dane brings up a valid point. Though it definitely glowed, the knights' description does seem a bit…off. And if the stone's radiance was overstated, maybe a lot of things were."

"Perhaps it was merely flamboyant speech?" Martin suggested. "I'm not a real history buff, but wasn't speech rather exaggerated back in the day?"

Federic snorted.

Dane shook his head. "That wouldn't describe the men I met."

"I'd like to hear about the men you met," she mumbled.

Dark, tired eyes looked her way. "I promise you, Edeline, soon."

Looking once more toward the lifeless stone, she sighed. "Am I alone in thinking it's all a bunch of embellished folklore? I realize men believe it, but it certainly wouldn't be the first time men have been led astray. For goodness' sake, they're still chasing Big Foot and the Loch Ness Monster." With a shrug of her shoulders, she handed the necklace back to the general. "I think the stone says it all: it's not real."

Holding up the stone, the general studied it against the light. "I have to admit, I've always found it a bit farfetched. But real or not real, I do remember the stone having a distinctive glow."

Her father rubbed at his temples. "I find it hard to believe so many men, so many remarkable men, could have been so wrong."

Father Tom took Edeline's hand in his and patted it gently. "Real or not, Edeline, the belief alone holds its own set of dangers."

"The biggest danger has just closed its doors," Martin said. "They'll never get close to the portal again. Believe me, I'll see to it."

"I doubt it would matter if they did," the Professor replied. "The walls have weakened substantially. It's unlikely the transporter will ever again make contact with the portal and even less likely, if it did, that the portal would transport anyone anywhere. It's probably less than a matter of days. The portal is closing. We won't even have to shut her down. I believe she's going to 'logoff' all on her own."

"Portal or no portal, we still have a threat." General Matthews held the necklace up by its chain. "Perhaps it *has* lost its shine, but that doesn't necessarily mean it's lost its spark. If there's any truth to the tales, this could still be a very powerful tool. There isn't anything they went back for that isn't still here. Granted, they'll have a harder time getting to it, but still…" He dropped the stone and chain into his free hand and then squeezed it within a tight fist. "Father Tom is right. The threat's real even if the tale isn't. The stone will remain in the safe."

"Mountains of treasure, walls of prophesy? I'm with Edeline. I just don't buy it," Martin said. He laughed and shook his head. "It's a lot of ado about nothing, is my opinion."

"We don't know that yet," Federic warned.

"And more importantly," Dane added, "neither do they. You didn't see what I saw on the other side of the portal. Those men, the ones that protected us as well as those who followed, they believed the stone was real. They believed Edeline had the power to make it work. And there were men there, men I have great faith in, who had actually seen the cavern."

"They saw a cavern with treasures on its floors and stories upon its walls," the professor said. "No one denies the Knights Templar had their treasures, and as for the drawings on its walls…well, cavemen drew on walls. It's impossible to say what they saw. They may have described it as a final war between good and evil, but it could have been nothing more than a story.

"And if it really was a prophesy they saw, then you might want to consider you've just described World War One and Two as well as several other notable skirmishes. Those men didn't know our world. They wouldn't recognize the warfare of today. In their eyes, it could easily look like black magic."

Martin threw his hands up in frustration. "He's right, gentlemen, we can't keep pointing fingers at some unknown bogeyman. For all we know, we are the bogeyman. It could have been us they saw on those walls."

"Valid points," the general agreed. "With those in mind and with all that's happened, I believe it's time we take another look at the situation as well as what direction we will take. If the portal closes down, and it looks as though it will and soon, our choices will be few. With the doors closed and the past safely tucked on the other side, this national threat becomes obsolete and so, I assure you, will the funding."

Sitting inside a large rectangular conference room amongst a large group of scientists and military brass, Edeline looked toward her father. Lines of worry etched his forehead as he listened attentively to those around him. As her gaze moved down the table, she saw the same look of concern sitting heavy on the face of Lieutenant Colonel Dane Walker.

He was a striking man, her so-called hero. Not for the first time, she wondered exactly what had transpired during their travels into the past. The way he looked at her made her think there had been a particularly strong bond…an intimate bond. Without question she would have found him attractive. What role would that have played?

They weren't there long, and a portion of the time she would have been held by her captives—a truly alarming thought. As eager as she was to know what happened in France, there was a part of her which feared what she would find. Would he tell her everything, or would he continue to play her protector?

He looked her way. Yes, there it was again—affection, warmth, and maybe something more? Too quickly his attention was pulled away when General Thompson asked him another question.

She continued to watch him. His dark hair, not too short but definitely military, went perfect with his regal good looks—squared jaw, an average but perfectly symmetrical nose, nicely shadowed cheekbones, and wonderfully masculine lips.

Had she kissed those lips? Surely she would have wanted to. It would be hard to resist their perfectly bowed form and the way one side tended to raise slightly higher than the other. They were truly mesmerizing just like his eyes. No one, at least no woman, could ignore those dark, penetrating eyes. Surrounded by thick black lashes and incredibly arresting brows, they would have intrigued her.

Yes, she would have found the Lieutenant Colonel quite hard to resist.

Her inspection moved to his hands. Had they touched her? And if so, how had they touched her? A vision of those hands against her flesh flashed into her mind. She could almost feel their warmth caressing her, so very masculine, powerful…deadly.

She looked away.

It was hard to reconcile the breathtaking male with such a fearsome act. Of course he was trained to kill; he was a soldier and quite obviously a good one. She looked back his way, and he was looking right back at her.

Her breath caught. She literally trembled. The vision of those powerful hands holding her tight rushed back into her head. But this time it wasn't only his hands touching her flesh, but his lips taking hers. Her heart pounded back to life with deep heavy thuds. Her face warmed as she shifted uncomfortably.

In profound embarrassment, she took a sharp breath and looked away, cursing her inability to hide her attraction. And she couldn't, not for her life. It was too strong. Was it because he looked at her so that her thoughts were so shocking?

Determined to stop her runaway musings, she turned back to safety.

"It's an odd feeling," her father was saying. "I know I've lived in this world for nearly as many years as the other, but there's definitely a part of me which feels the loss. As long as the portal was open, I still had a connection. To know it will likely vanish by the morrow…" He bowed his head and shrugged his shoulders. "I find myself mourning."

Dr. Hatcher nodded with understanding. "It's only natural, Federic. Your past, though plagued by the hardships of its time, was still your foundation. The closing of the portal won't change that fact. The past is still very much alive and living in your memory, in your ideals and in your heart. It's all right to mourn it. But while you do, also take the time to embrace and cherish the world that is now yours."

Federic's gaze landed on Edeline. "God knows I do." He looked around the room at the many high ranking officials. "I pray these men understand how fragile this world is. By underestimating my world, they could easily put theirs at enormous risk."

"There may be little they can do." Dr. Hatcher looked apologetically toward Edeline then back to her father. "General Matthews is right. It was never the stone or Edeline the military was protecting. It was the past. Now with the past tucked securely in its realm, there will be little funding, if any, to guard and protect."

The conference room door opened and the general and Professor Blaine walked in.

"Gentleman. Edeline," the general greeted them as he took his place at the head of the table. "I have news."

The room grew quiet.

"At six thirty-seven this evening, all readings surrounding the portal failed to register activity."

"Which means what exactly? Has it closed?" Martin asked.

Looking around the room, the professor nodded. "The window to the past is now officially closed."

All around the table, conversations broke out. Laughter, sadness and relief filled the air.

Closed.

It was exactly what she'd wanted to hear and still it hit her hard. It was just like her father had described it. "Closed" broke the link—a link which still held her past, a past she couldn't remember and now would never know. She looked Federic's way, wondering if it had hit him equally as hard, but all she saw on his face was worry.

The general stood and paced the floor behind them. "It's hard to believe it has all come to an end. This has been my life for many years."

"And mine," the professor said. "As much as I'm relieved to see its end, I can assure you, I wouldn't have missed this ride for all the money in the world."

"Nor I," General Corbin admitted somewhat sadly. "With the lab bound to close, I may actually have to consider retirement."

"You won't last a day," General Matthews said, slapping the man's shoulder. "You're too much like me. You can't stand idle."

"What does this mean for Edeline?" her father asked, looking back and forth between General Matthews and Professor Blaine. "The door to the past may have closed, but the threat remains on this side. Everything they need is right here." He looked to the general. "You said it yourself."

The general's eyes held compassion as they turned toward her father. "I'm not sure yet what it means, but I imagine we will very soon. I know no one is denying danger still lurks. We're simply no longer certain to what degree. It seems to be dwindling with every turn of the hour—first the stone, now the portal. If the news has passed as quickly as we believe it may, then those who were behind the abduction must now be having doubts similar to ours."

"That could be a costly assumption," Federic said.

"Think about it, Federic," Martin countered. "Whether the stone is real or not, Edeline is only valuable to them if they have it and can access the treasure. Considering the odds of them getting to the stone or the treasure are next to nil, I believe Edeline is safe."

"He makes a good point, Federic," Dr. Hatcher agreed.

Martin nodded. "And it's been mentioned more than once that the caves where the treasure is believed to have been hidden have eroded past recognition, and that the actual cavern may no longer be there at all. If it's true, then any attempt would be futile, which is probably why they took Edeline and the stone to the past in the first place."

"I don't know," Federic said, shaking his head. "Something's wrong. I know it is. I feel it in my heart."

"Daddy." Edeline reached for his hand. "You worry too much. What they're saying makes sense." And she was more than willing to accept it as fact and get on with her life. Her father would, of course, have difficulty with it. He was a champion worrier. After all, he had had twenty-two years' worth of pretty intense practice.

She smiled toward the others. "Believe me, I can never tell you how much I appreciate what all of you've done for me, but I'm ready to have my life back."

"It wouldn't hurt to keep surveillance on her a little longer," Dane said, ignoring her look of irritation. "I'm with Federic on this one; something doesn't feel right."

The general looked around the room to the other men in uniform and then back to the Lieutenant Colonel. "Sorry, Dane. I understand your and Federic's concerns, but there really isn't a lot we can do. With the lab closing and the portal gone, our superiors will be making new plans for the base, and they won't include us. Very soon we will no longer have the money or the men to run any kind of surveillance, and they'll never allow it, not when we can no longer justify it."

Dane retraced the general's gaze to the other officials. "Do your superiors realize who they're dealing with? Do they understand these people are willing to do just about anything?" His turned back to the general. "We've all seen what they're capable of. How badly they want this. I find it hard to believe they're going to simply give up."

"They saw a good plan, and they took a gamble," Martin said. "Without question they're risk takers, but they've also proven themselves to be far from idiots. They're going to know they're beaten. Sorry, Dane. Sorry, Federic. I believe General Matthews has it right. There's no longer a plausible threat."

General Matthews sighed as he walked to the window and looked out toward the airfield. "There's nothing I can do. We can hardly go to our superiors and tell them we're battling the beasts of hell. They won't buy it, and they're certainly not going to fund it."

Running his hand roughly through his hair, Dane stood and followed the general to the window. "Look, I understood the argument, but I'm also pretty clear on the risks. You didn't see what I saw back in time. You may not understand their conviction, but I do. They're not just interested in the treasure. Their goals are much darker than that."

"Which still leaves me with the same argument, and it's not one I can sell. Our hands are tied, Dane. I'll do my best to provide coverage the best I can for as long as I can, but I can give you no guarantees."

"I might be able to help," Martin said. "I'm owed a favor here and there. I'll see what I can do."

"I'd appreciate any help you can give us," Federic said to Martin.

Edeline cringed. The idea of being watched like a monkey in a cage had never set well with her. It appealed even less with the need having literally vanished into thin air. "It's a gracious offer, Colonel Martin, but I really doubt it's necessary."

He nodded his understanding. "I have my doubts as well, Edeline, but it would do no harm to take some precautions. It won't last forever, and it would help us all rest a little easier."

Leaning forward in her seat, she swallowed. "To be clear, we're talking weeks not months, right?"

Martin grinned. "I'll try for months and most likely get weeks."

She smiled with relief as she sat back in her seat, her glance shifting back toward the window and the unhappy soldier now staring her way.

Dane fought hard to control his temper, angry with the turn of events which had led to the military reconsidering their role in Edeline's protection, and particularly angry with the beautiful blonde sitting at the end of the table, acting as though she hadn't a care in the world.

He loved her, God help him, every stubborn ounce of her, but at the moment he'd also love to shake some sense into her.

Looking his way, she caught his unhappy glare. She flinched, swallowed, and then shook back her hair and squared her shoulders.

Stubborn.

"I'd like to know what happened in France," she said. "I believe I have a right to know."

"Of course," the general said, interjecting before Dane could respond. "We know you're very anxious, but for now you'll have to wait. There's still information we need to go over before anything's released."

"Released? General, I'm not a reporter. This is my life. I'd like to know what I lived."

Studying her determined demeanor, Dane knew whatever he told her, she'd hear it through the filter of her own preconceived doubts. "I'm not so sure you're ready to hear it," he replied honestly.

An adorable scowl landed between her brows. "I can take it, whatever it is. I'll admit I'm a bit nervous, but even more than that, I'm eager."

"Eager enough to listen with an open mind?" he asked.

The scowl deepened. She shifted in her seat. "Look, if this is about the stone—"

"You're not taking any of it seriously enough, Edeline."

She batted her lids. "It's just a stone, Lieutenant Colonel, and I'm just a woman. There's no magic or power in either of us. You saw it with your own eyes. I don't know what everyone saw back then, but…" Throwing her hands into the air, she shrugged her shoulders as though it all should be obvious. "It's just a rock, polished but plain."

"You don't know that for sure."

"But I do. I feel it in my heart," she said, sitting up and leaning forward in her seat. "Or maybe I should say I don't feel it in my heart. And wouldn't I? Wouldn't I feel something? If I held this extraordinary power, this…gift, wouldn't I sense it?" Shaking her head, she once again leaned back. "There is nothing special about me, only the oddity of being from another time."

Dropping back his head to rest momentarily on his shoulders, he sighed with exasperation. How could he convince this woman she might actually be more than her imaginings?

He understood her hesitation, and he had to agree, everything everyone said made a whole lot of sense—until he took a look back at his time in fourteenth century France, when men were willing to risk everything to possess the stone and the woman who could make it come to life.

"Look, I can't explain it, not even to myself. But despite all the arguments against it and circumstances which question its validity, I still believe there's truth in what those men believed back then. They were truly remarkable men, not the type easily played a fool. And I'm sorry to say, though I despise the men who are behind all this, I still believe in their ability to decipher the truth. There is a darkness which surrounds them. I felt it when we fought them in France. It's neither blind nor naïve, but careful and shrewd. As much as I believe in the greatness of the Knights Templar, I also believe in the ruthlessness and cunning of their opponents. They would not act with such fierce determination unless they had reason to believe you held the power you deny."

"You fought them in France?" Curious blue eyes held his mesmerized.

"Dane," the general warned.

He'd released too much, something he never did. The woman simply had him tied in so many knots he couldn't see past their binding.

She shook her head. "Look, regardless of what happened in France, the men who are here know only what they learn from us. Isn't that what I've been hearing? They know what they know because of their connections, whatever they may be."

"Edeline." Her father sighed. "What's your point?"

"If they're so bright, so well informed, then I believe Colonel Martin's right. I'm sure they already know that they've lost. They'll have no reason to come for me."

Dane stormed to the table, slamming his hands down on its hard wood. Leaning forward, he glared across the distance into her startled blue eyes. "That kind of thinking could very well get you killed."

"What would you have me do, Colonel? Lock myself behind safe doors, surrendering my life for the risk of losing it?" Slamming her own hands down against the table, she stood, glaring across the table right back at him. "I'm telling you now, I won't do it."

"No matter what you think, no matter what *they* think," Dane said, nudging his head toward the others, "you're by no means out of danger."

She hung her head and shook it wearily before standing up straight and looking back into his eyes. "Will you please tell me what happened back there? Please. Perhaps then I'll understand what makes you so willing to believe what to me is unbelievable."

He wanted so badly to reach out and touch her that his fingers actually ached with the desire. But he knew he dare not. For it would surely be impossible to ever again let her go.

Pushing himself away from the table, he turned to General Matthews. They'd taken his information and were now weighing its value. What he could and couldn't release had yet to be determined.

"Sorry, Edeline," the general said. "It's going to have to wait."

Chapter Sixteen

oping to beat the light, Edeline wrapped her arms tight around the overstuffed, black, trash bag and sprinted toward the crosswalk. Two steps from *made it*, the signal flashed an orange hand telling her to stop. She glared at the light and dropped the bag to the ground.

Rubbing her hands up and down her aching arms, she watched as up ahead the black Suburban pulled in parallel to the curb.

Her babysitters. Nice to see they weren't overburdened.

She'd had half a mind five blocks back to ignore the rules and storm their vehicle, depositing a large black bag they could much easier carry.

More than she wanted their help, what she really wanted was them gone.

After two weeks of being "shadowed," she was ready to pull the blinds and stand in the dark. It was eerie being the center of so many strangers' worlds. Luckily, it was coming to an end. Two more days and it would all be over. The military would officially withdraw from the picture and life could return to normal.

A little electrical man appeared on the sign across the walk. The crowd around her moved forward as she gathered the bag back into her arms and hurried to join them. Ignoring the Suburban with the dark tinted windows, she hurried down the street to reach the next crosswalk. Once again she barely missed the light.

"You've got to be kidding me!" The bag dropped to her feet.

"You almost made it," said a masculine voice coming up from directly behind her.

As more pedestrians gathered near, she turned toward the stranger now at her side.

He was a handsome man. She'd guess him in his late forties, possibly early fifties, tall, broad, looked like he hit the gym on a regular basis. His eyes were a nice green—open, friendly. He seemed safe, not that it mattered—*Brute* and *Force* were a mere sprint away.

She smiled. "I've managed to hit every corner just in time to miss the signal. That's a lot of waiting when you've walked near ten blocks with a garbage bag full of paperbacks."

The man glanced down toward the bag and grimaced. Reaching down, he lifted it up, testing its weight. His right brow rose as he looked toward her small arms. "You've walked these ten blocks? They weigh more than you."

"Not really, but I must admit it feels that way. I've had to take a couple breaks." She pointed toward the next block where Paperback Adventures sat midway down the walk. "I'm just about there."

Shaking his head, the man lifted the bag into his arms. "I'm heading that way. I'll give you a hand."

"Oh." Edeline blinked, surprised by the offer and not so sure how her chaperones would take it. "You don't have to do that. I'm fine."

"It will be my pleasure." The man's grin lit his face to charming.

She couldn't refuse, and was pretty certain it would do her no good anyway. So instead she nodded. "I thank you, and my arms thank you as well."

The man chuckled and looked up into the clear afternoon sky. "It's a lovely day."

It was. There wasn't a trace of smog in the air, only soft pastel blue wherever one looked. Through the splendid canvas, the sun beamed down, bouncing off the many windows adorning the old brick and concrete buildings, adding a little extra brilliance to the already glorious day.

The light changed and they, along with a small herd of various other characters, moved into the street.

He patted the bag. "You're an avid reader I take it?"

"Yes, but they're not all mine."

"I would hope not. Such a beautiful young woman shouldn't spend all her days hidden behind books." He nodded toward the bag curiously. "You're selling them?"

"Not exactly. They're donations from members of my church toward a charity book sale my friends are sponsoring for the local children's shelter."

"Very nice," he said, peeking into the bag. "I'm an avid reader myself. Perhaps I'll stop by. When is it?"

"From noon to seven." She stopped outside the bookstore where Paul stood atop a ladder hanging the sign she and Amanda had made a week prior.

Turning to her new friend, she smiled. "Thank you again. It's really very kind of you."

The man placed the bag beside the door. "My pleasure, Miss…?"

"Edeline," she said, offering him her hand, "but my friends call me Eda."

"It's been a pleasure meeting you, Eda. Good luck with your fundraiser." He patted her hand and turned to leave.

"Wait," she said, taking a step to follow. "I didn't get your name?"

"Hunter," he said, turning back with a smile. "Everyone calls me Hunter." With a quick wave, he turned again and merged with the rest of the sidewalk traffic.

"Hunter," Edeline repeated his name as she watched him walk away. "I've always liked the name, but I don't hear it very often."

Looking down from the top of his ladder, Paul grinned. "Seems like a nice guy."

"Yeah, certainly does," she agreed, scowling at his careless footing. "You're going to fall and break your neck."

Paul ignored her concern, the twinkle in his eyes telling her he wasn't about to miss the opportunity to tease. "He's a little old for you."

Placing her hands on her hips, she shook her head. "He was simply giving me a hand." She pointed her finger and twirled it toward his feet. "Will you please turn around and put both feet on that ladder?"

"Paul Dowen, show me you have better sense," Amanda said, stepping out the door behind Edeline. "Turn around and pay attention before I end up having to rush you to the emergency room."

"Yes, dear." Paul grimaced and turned back to his task.

"Wow!" Amanda's eyes grew wide as she glimpsed the huge black bag. "Another full bag. Those ladies always come through for us, don't they?"

"They sure do." Edeline lifted the bag. "Where do you want these?"

Amanda nodded toward the shop and led the way inside. "Why didn't you call me? I would have met you and helped you pack them." She took the bag from Edeline, frowning as she lifted it up and down. "This thing weighs a ton. You should've called."

Edeline glanced across the many piles of books scattered on the store's floor. "You're busy enough."

Amanda shook her head as she dug into the bag and started looking through the books. "You know, it hasn't been that bad. Father Tom stopped by this morning with the new carpenter." Pausing in her rummaging, she looked up to shoot Edeline an accusing scowl. "I *can't believe* you never mentioned him, by the way."

Plunging back into the bag, she quickly emerged with an armful of mysteries. She held them up in the air. "Good, these always do well." Placing the books in the pile furthest from the door, she looked back toward Edeline.

"Anyway, by the time they left, they'd helped Paul put together all the racks and bring down all the boxes from the attic. I didn't have to lift a finger. It was really nice. I was able to stay downstairs and sort through all of this." She nodded her head, indicating the multiple piles which were taking up most the empty space in their already tiny shop.

"The new carpenter?" Edeline pursed her lips and gave it some thought. "I didn't know there was one." Leaning forward and over her friend, she picked up one of the books from the pile of mysteries. "You'll have three of these," she said, waving the book under Amanda's nose. "I noticed them as I was stuffing the bag." Lifting the book, she quickly scanned the back cover. "Hmm, sounds like a good one. Maybe I'll take one off your hands."

She lowered the book to find Amanda staring at her, her mouth gaping wide open.

Edeline giggled. "What?"

"The carpenter—you haven't met him—the very definition of a hunk, stud-muffin extraordinaire, tall, dark and likely to send your hormones into overdrive?"

"Why, thank you, darlin'," Paul said, stepping into the store behind them and flexing his muscles in the form of a pose.

Both women laughed.

Hanging his head theatrically, he placed his hammer on the counter, turned and walked back toward the door.

"Oh, honey, you're a stud-muffin," Amanda assured, adding a whistle for good measure.

"The studliest," Edeline agreed with an exaggerated wink.

"Give it up." He nodded his head toward the front window. "I know exactly who you're talking about."

Both Edeline and Amanda hurried to the window.

Edeline's heart nearly stopped. There he was—a simple T-shirt, nice fitting jeans and the same "tall, dark and handsome" he'd been wearing at the base—the soldier who had brought her home, Lieutenant Colonel Dane Walker.

She'd done little else but think about him over the last two weeks. His rugged good looks, the way he'd looked at her as though they shared a secret, and then, of course, there were all the answers he held, answers to questions which had plagued her night and day.

Now suddenly, right as she was giving up all hope of ever seeing him again, here he is.

"Dane." She played his name across her lips. What in the world was he doing here of all places?

"Yes, Dane." Amanda grinned, oblivious to the enormity of the moment. "Have you met him?"

Leaning over their shoulders as they peered through the window, Paul knocked on the glass just above them.

Dane peeked over the rack he was adjusting and smiled their way.

Both women smiled back before turning to glare at the man behind them.

"Paul!" Amanda reprimanded, her hands flying to her hips.

"Yeah, right, like you didn't deserve it," he said, playfully swatting her backside before heading out the door.

Amanda turned back toward Edeline. "He's perfect for you."

"Paul?" Edeline raised her brows in mock surprise. "I hear rumors he's already taken."

Amanda giggled. "Yep, that hunk of lovin' is already mine."

Wagging her finger toward Edeline, she turned back to look out the window to where Paul and Dane were rearranging racks. "Don't tell me you don't think he's hot. I watched your eyes light up when you saw him. He's perfect for you, admit it."

"How do you know?" In truth, she really was curious exactly what Amanda did know. She had a sneaking suspicion it was actually very little.

"I quizzed Father Tom." Amanda turned from the window and grabbed the pricing stickers sitting on the front counter. "He's single, stable, employed." She searched the counter, moving papers and lifting books. "Ah, there it is," she said, grabbing a pen which rolled out from one of the multiple messes. Waving the pen in the air triumphantly, she added, "And he's straight."

Edeline stared at her friend in disbelief. "You asked Father Tom if the man was gay?"

"I was tactful."

"I can only imagine." Edeline rolled her eyes and then looked back out the window. Dane was staring right at her. She could say one thing for the guy. He was blazingly forward. Now the question begged to be answered—why was he here? It wasn't that she wasn't glad. She was tremendously pleased, but…Paperback Adventures?

"I know what you're thinking," Amanda said. "I thought Paul was too good to be true, too. Now look at us." She looked out the window and blew her husband a kiss. "Love happens all the time," she said, moving away from the window and toward the piles of books lying on the floor. "There's a Prince Charming out there for everyone. Of course, they're not all as good looking as Dane and Paul," she added with a sheepish grin.

"Did it ever cross your mind Prince Charming might already have a Cinderella?" It had most definitely crossed Edeline's.

"Asked. He doesn't. The position's still available."

Of course she'd asked. Her friend was bound and determined to find her a man.

"Just because there's a vacancy, it doesn't mean he's looking to fill the position."

"When did you become such a pessimist?" Amanda scoured the floor. "You know, the piles are already sorted by genre except for this first one. I'll sort it, and then I say we take them outside and worry about alphabetizing them out there?"

"That will work," she agreed absentmindedly. "Did you say Father Tom brought him here?" The oddity of it suddenly hit her. Why would Dane go to the priest and not her or her father?

"Yes." Amanda bent down to her knees in front of the first pile and started categorizing the unsorted books into their appropriate piles. "Father Tom thought we could use his help setting up. He was right. Dane's been a great help."

"Amanda, do me a favor and don't…" Edeline shook her head and groaned. She knew her friend well. It was pointless to even ask.

"Don't what?"

"Don't try setting me up. We know nothing about this guy."

"I just gave you his whole spiel. I don't work blind you know. I check them out before I nudge them your way."

Edeline groaned.

"He seems like a nice guy, Eda."

"Even nice guys have their demons." She knew Dane had his. Necessary or not, he'd killed at least two men. How could anyone take a life and not be haunted?

Grabbing the pile of books at her feet, Amanda stood up. "I imagine they do," she said before heading outside.

Edeline quickly grabbed her own pile and headed out behind her.

"Science fiction?" Amanda called.

"Over there," Paul answered, pointing toward the back rack.

Edeline looked at her pile. "Westerns?"

"Here." Dane patted the rack right in front of him.

Perfect. She took a deep, deep breath. This was the moment she'd been dreaming of, her chance to have the warrior somewhat to herself. She headed his way, eager for the meeting. And it had nothing to do with his dark piercing eyes, which yes, they were to die for—dark, watchful, completely unforgettable. No, it wasn't that at all. She wanted only one thing from this so-called carpenter. She wanted answers—long overdue answers.

Once again those eyes watched her, looking at her as if she was the whole of the universe. It made it very difficult to remember he was but a stranger. Without question he was a stranger to her. Regardless of what they had shared in another world, she didn't know the man at all.

Of course, he might see things differently.

Edeline shook off the thought as she neared the rack. She was not about to get sidetracked by this man, regardless of how sexy were the thick lashes which framed his deep brown eyes—a fact she'd noted that day in the conference room. And it didn't matter how delectably his lips curved more to one side than the other when he smiled—a fact she'd noted when he'd walked into the lab and seen her shaking the stone. No, it didn't matter at—

"I'll take those from you," he said, reaching out and taking the books from her hands. "Louis L'Amour," he read, lifting one of the books after placing the pile on the shelf. "I thought I recognized the cover." He glanced her way. "My father was a big fan. He's read every book the man ever wrote." He placed the book back with the others and began sorting them by author and title.

Casual conversation? Not what I expected.

"What are you doing here?" she whispered.

He nodded back toward her friends. "Not now, Edeline."

Looking over her shoulder to see how focused was their audience; she found both sets of eyes were directly upon them.

Wonderful, Mr. and Mrs. Happily-Married had found her a prospect.

It appeared she'd be forced to play along. As strangers they would be expected to maintain a certain degree of casual banter. Moving behind him, she began placing pricing stickers on each of the books.

"My father enjoys him as well," she began. "But then, my father enjoys all things historical. He's a fanatic like Paul. When the two get together, it's nearly impossible to pull them from the past."

"Well, there's a lot to talk about. I understand perfectly their interest," he said, his words spoken so matter-of-factly she would have missed their meaning if not for his manner—the quick meaningful glance, the somber expression.

"Yes." She swallowed. "There's so much to be learned, so many questions."

They moved on to the lower shelf, both bending out of sight.

As she reached for the next book, his hand covered hers.

She nearly gasped. The man affected her in the strangest of ways. Lifting her eyes to his, she whispered. "Why here? Why now after all these days?"

"I'm your watch."

She shifted uncomfortable. "I have a watch. They drive a black Suburban, shadow my every move and haunt my yards. They couldn't be more annoying if they tried."

"They're going to be gone in a couple days."

"A fact I embrace with every passing hour."

"You can't go without coverage, Edeline. Not yet. Not until the power is passed and any personal threat to you is gone."

"There is no power to pass, Lieutenant Colonel, and I don't need more coverage. What I need is answers."

"I'll answer any question you have—later, with your father."

He undoubtedly caught her immense irritation. It seemed to amuse him. Watching her quietly a moment, then continuing on with the task at hand, he added, "You need to quit calling me Lieutenant Colonel. The name is Dane."

She glared at him. "You've certainly kept me waiting long enough… *Dane*."

He chuckled. "That's my girl."

The *possessive* caught her by surprise. She wondered exactly what the comment meant. Had they bickered? Based on what had been their circumstance, it would surprise her. Though he certainly seemed the argumentative type, she definitely wasn't…or didn't consider herself to be.

Dane finished the row and stood.

"So, Dane," Amanda said from a couple rows back, "how is it you know Father Tom?"

No! Panic struck Edeline direct as a pang inside her chest. Already kneeling on all fours at the bottom row, she crawled to rack's end and peeked back toward the menace.

Amanda leaned casually over her rack, Dane direct in her sights.

Nausea swam the surface of Edeline's stomach. She knew exactly where this was going. Amanda had an agenda, and Amanda with an agenda was a little like a cat on the prowl. There simply wasn't a lot going to stop her.

She'd try all the same. Drawing her hand across her neck cutthroat style, she glared at her friend, who chose to ignore her.

Dane tilted his head to look down to where she knelt. The same amused expression from before shifted his good looks into downright sexy. He looked back to Amanda. "Father Tom and I share a mutual friend."

Edeline jumped to her feet. "Done," she declared. "Amanda, why don't you follow me inside? You can help me pick the next load."

"Nope, not quite done marking this one," she replied, pulling a sticker from the sheet and placing it on the next paperback for show. "You go ahead and run inside. I'm chatting with Dane."

Gritting her teeth and snarling her displeasure, she fought the urge to grab Amanda by the ear and yank her inside. When it became obvious the little matchmaker wasn't going to budge, Edeline shot her one last warning look and then reluctantly headed into the shop.

If she were smart, she'd sneak out the back door and head for home.

Why, after twenty-four years of doing just fine on her own, was everyone so determined to take over her life? If her father had his druthers, she'd be imprisoned in their cottage. If the general had his way, she'd be hooked to a pole and dangled through the streets for all the lunatics to find. If Amanda had her way…well, that was nothing new. Amanda was always trying to hook her up with someone. Blissfully married women couldn't tolerate their friends' single status.

What Edeline wanted was answers and to know it was all going to end. She wanted the whys, whens and hows. After that, she simply wanted her life back.

One glance around at the seemingly endless piles of books assured her running was out of the question. She'd have to help and keep her friend on track if they were going to open by noon. At least the work would be a stack of *normal* she could both handle and use. Reaching down, she grabbed another armload.

Romance.

She glanced back out the window. Dane was still standing by the westerns and getting drilled by Amanda.

Hmm. Romance was several rows back.

She couldn't deny it—she was more than slightly attracted to the man. Who wouldn't be? He was built to appeal to a woman's basic desires. What nature hadn't blessed him with, iron and discipline had graciously supplied.

What had it been like for her, getting rescued by such a man? Certainly there would have been gratitude, but had there also been adoration? They were gone three days. How many of those days had she been with him? What had they talked about? What had she shared? She wondered exactly how much she had revealed and how well he knew her.

It was a little unnerving not knowing.

The way he looked at her—the way he spoke as if…well, as if there had been some level of intimacy between them, made her wonder how big of a fool she had been.

Edeline put down the pile in her arms and scanned the floor for more westerns. She wouldn't examine her reasons.

Loaded with another armful, she headed back outside.

"Eda." Amanda looked her way. "Did you know Mr. Hasenbrook hired Dane to help Father Tom finish the west addition? That's why he's here. He's actually staying with Father Tom until the renovations are done. Isn't that great? Fortunately for us, he heard about the fundraiser and volunteered to help." She snapped her fingers. "Just like that, now he's ours. It's like it was meant to be. Don't you agree, honey?" Amanda glanced toward Paul, who was now watching her through narrowed lids.

"I'm always glad to lend a hand to a worthy cause," Dane said, holding out his hands once again as Edeline approached. "This is a great cause, and I have to admit, I don't much mind the company either."

He'd looked right at her. There would be no denying the statement was meant for her.

Edeline felt herself blush from the top of her head clear down to her toes as she handed him the books. "Thank…you," she said awkwardly, meaning for the help, but frazzled by the compliment—a compliment which was sure to do nothing but encourage her obstinate friend.

Soon all four were working in a familiar pattern in and out of the shop, until all the outside shelves were full.

"I do believe we're ready," Amanda declared, taking one last look around.

"Good job, team," Paul said, hitting them all with a high-five. "If you ladies want to grab the cookie trays, Dane and I will open things up."

"Sounds like a plan." Amanda gave her husband a kiss and turned toward the store, motioning for Edeline to follow.

Once the door closed, the matchmaking began.

"Round two of the grilling revealed nothing off-kilter." She beamed. "Just hot and handy. *Hot and handy,*" she repeated with a snort and a slap across her leg. "I crack myself up."

"You should've been a comedian," Edeline said dryly. "Now, put down your bow and arrow, Cupid. The man's probably not even interested."

"Oh, he's interested." Amanda bit into her lip and wiggled her brows humorously.

"Stop," Edeline warned.

"Can't help myself."

"Try." Lifting the first tray of cookies, she shot her friend one last warning glare—a wasted moment if ever there was one.

Dane watched as she bagged the customer's purchases.

"Thanks for stopping by, Mrs. Levitt," she said with a smile as she handed the woman her bag. "We certainly appreciate the support."

The elderly woman's face lit with affection as she took the bag into her arms. "Oh, Eda, you know I would never miss it. You kids are so good to do all this." She adjusted the bag to her hip and then reached out and squeezed Edeline's hand. "May the Lord bless you, dear."

"And you, Mrs. Levitt."

Everyone loved her. But then, how could they not? She was nothing if not lovable. God knew he loved her. Being so close to her and being bound by the restraints of a stranger was nearly killing him. She wasn't a stranger. She was the woman he loved, even if he was having a time getting use to the modern version of the woman.

Eda was definitely the typical twenty-first century lady. Oh, she was, of course, still his Edeline. Her enchanting curls still fell unruly in every which direction, her smile was still bright and genuine and impossible to forget, and her blue eyes were still as vibrant and alive as ever. But there were additions. The touches of makeup, though light, slightly changed the final picture, emphasizing the long length of her lashes, the allure of her lips.

It was definitely a different look from the unadorned look she'd carried in the past. Not one was more appealing than the next, both were simply captivating.

As a modern day woman, she wore modern day clothes. A simple T-shirt, though modest, emphasized nicely her feminine physique, and her jeans, worn and beaten, could stop traffic with how well they fit her hard-not-to-follow curves. They couldn't have been more eye-catching if they'd been spun of fine gold.

He could barely keep his eyes off her, though he really should try perhaps a little bit harder.

"Do you read?" she asked, sitting back down in her seat beside him and bringing him out of his musings.

"Yes, mostly thrillers, war stories, occasionally a western. To be honest, I'm usually too busy."

Looking around, she made sure no one was listening and then leaned forward. "What do you do, Dane, when you're not rescuing damsels and traveling through time?" She was nothing short of adorable when she teased.

Leaning in closer, he whispered, "I tackle dragons and fight giants."

She laughed, the soft familiar sound filling his heart as well as their surroundings. "A regular David bettering Goliath."

"Only Goliath's strength isn't so much in his physical size as it is in the size of his army or, in many cases, cartel."

She quit laughing. "That must be very frightening?"

"It can be. They have a lot of loyalty. Not just from those who work for them, but from those who fear them as well."

"That would be very difficult to work with."

He couldn't help but smile. "Not nearly as difficult as a rebellious damsel."

She blinked, obviously taken by surprise. "Certainly you're not speaking of me."

He chose not to answer.

"You're teasing me."

It amused him how certain she was of the fact.

A soft floral fragrance tinted with an alluring mix of exotic accents—not quite musk, but every bit as sensual—drifted slowly his way. Beneath the perfume, he could still pick out her natural scent. He'd missed it. He'd missed her. In a sense, he was still missing her. Having her so near without holding her close was its own kind of loneliness.

Her bright blue eyes sparkled against the intense sun. She looked down to hide a nervous smile. He'd been staring.

"Sorry," He shook his head. "It's hard to remember you don't know me."

"It's all right." That time she smiled openly. "It's hard for me to remember you do know me. How long were we together?"

"I found you the first day. They hadn't expected company, so they'd done very little to hide you or cover their tracks. They were on foot, with passenger—finding you was easy. Taking you was easier yet. You're very cooperative when you're unconscious."

"What? I was unconscious?"

"You were drugged," he said as he fiddled with the various knick-knacks scattered across the table. For the life of him, he couldn't quit grinning. Visions of her first reaction were still clear in his mind.

"I was drugged?" She frowned as though perplexed. "Why is that funny?"

"It's not, not at all. It's just…you weren't always the most cooperative."

Her lips parted as though about to argue the point. Dear Lord, he wanted to kiss her.

"I find that hard to believe," she said, crossing her arms and sitting back in her seat, transforming instantly into the stubborn, headstrong woman he remembered from France.

He couldn't help himself, he laughed out loud.

"Rude," she chided, "and completely unfair. For all I know you could be fabricating the whole thing."

"And I'd do that why?"

She looked away. "I don't know. I don't know you. It's hard, harder than I think you realize—not knowing."

"Sorry, Edeline. I would *never* purposely hurt you, and I give you my word—I will not lie to you."

Their eyes met and held. Just as they had done so many times during their journey toward the portal, they seemed to connect on a much deeper level. In this world, just as they had in the other, they would share an unusual bond.

But that wasn't the only connection which survived.

Whatever they had between them, whatever it was which pulled them together and made it so difficult to part, had made it through the centuries. She was his, and somewhere deep inside her, he hoped that she sensed it.

Big green eyes looked up at her from behind the tin box holding the cash.

"Can I help you?" Edeline asked, looking down at the small red-headed boy.

He took the last bite of his cookie and chewed—a concerned scowl sitting heavy between his young brows. Swallowing big, he placed the book he had tucked beneath his arm onto the table. A big goldfish swam across the cover. The boy squared his shoulders and pinned Edeline with a no-nonsense stare. "I know the book says a dollar, but I'm hoping you'll be reasonable."

The smile escaped, but she quickly reeled it in.

"Uh oh, Eda," Paul said from behind, "I believe you have yourself an experienced bargainer."

"Reasonable, huh?" She picked up the book and eyed it carefully. "Let's see." Flipping the book from side to side, she raised it against the sun as though inspecting a flaw. "The cover does seem a bit worn. I imagine that's worth a slight discount. How does fifty cents sound?"

He uncurled his fist and counted the change in his hands. His big green eyes saddened. "Not reasonable enough."

"Of course, I haven't yet inspected the interior. We all know we can't judge a book by its cover, now don't we?"

"Yes, ma'am. My mom says it all the time." He bit into his bottom lip. As his one hand fisted around the two dimes and one nickel held in its palm, he crossed two fingers on his other.

The look of hope on the child's face was priceless, worth much more than twenty-five cents.

The pages were spotless. "Well, it could be better," she said, shutting the book and placing it back in front of him. "Why don't we say..."

The boy's shoulders tensed and lifted as he squeezed his crossed fingers tighter.

"Twenty-five cents. Does that sound more reasonable?"

A bright smile emerged along with two dimes and a nickel. "Thank you," he said with an ear-to-ear grin.

"Nice doing business with you," she said as his mother approached carrying a small redheaded girl in her arms.

"Did you find something, Billy?"

He raised his book proudly for her inspection. She noted the sticker and looked curiously Edeline's way. "Should I—"

"We're good," Edeline assured. She'd slip in an extra dollar of her own at the end of the day.

"Cute kid," Paul said with a chuckle as the boy and his mother continued to browse.

"How's the sale coming?" asked a familiar voice from somewhere down the sidewalk.

She turned and smiled that way. "Hunter, hello, I'm glad you could stop by."

"Hey, it's a great cause—wouldn't miss it." A friendly smile spread across his face as he neared the stands.

She waved him over to her table. "These are my friends, Paul and Amanda Dowen." She nodded their way. "They own Paperback Adventures." She gestured toward Hunter. "This is Hunter. He was kind enough to pack the books for me this morning."

"Half a block," he said with a roguish grin, "not quite as gallant as it might sound."

"Still very thoughtful," Edeline assured. She smiled toward Dane as he approached the table. "And this is Dane. Dane this is Hunter."

Dane's eyes noticeably narrowed. At first it seemed as though neither man would make an acknowledgment past the point of sizing the other up. Finally Dane stuck out his hand. "Nice to meet you, Hunter."

Hunter took his hand and shook it slowly. "You look familiar. Have we met?"

"It's always possible. I do a lot of contract work. I'm a carpenter."

"Hmm." Hunter looked doubtful. "Maybe."

The two men weren't going to be friends, that much was obvious. Edeline wasn't certain if she'd ever felt so much tension between two strangers. "Can I help you find anything," she asked, anxious to get the two apart.

"I'm a big history buff. Got anything in that genre?"

Edeline and Amanda both laughed. Paul's contribution to the cause was a full rack alone of history.

"I'm a big fan myself," Paul confessed. "Let me show you what we've got."

The two men disappeared.

Amanda stood from her seat. "I better go replenish the cookie trays. Mrs. Taylor's looking none too pleased about their current empty status."

Edeline would have thought it a tactic to leave her and Dane alone, but she'd seen Mrs. Taylor's sour expression and realized it was true.

"People take the 'free punch and cookies' thing seriously," Dane said, taking the seat Amanda had vacated.

She laughed. "Yeah, well, no one likes false advertising."

Dane didn't respond. She couldn't help but notice how he kept looking back toward Hunter. "You do know him, don't you?"

"Vaguely," he confessed — his expression grim. "Are you walking home after this?"

There was a great deal of concern lingering behind the question. She was certain his concerns stemmed from Hunter. He didn't like the man nor, it seemed, did he trust him.

"Yes, after we get everything put away."

"I'll walk you home." A kind gesture, but it came across more like a command.

"It's really not necessary. I walk back and forth all the time. It's safe. Besides it might take us a few hours to get it all put away." She looked across the street at the black Suburban. "And don't forget, I've got Rambo and Rocky ready to take action."

He grinned. "I'm walking you home."

Her gaze drifted back to where Hunter and Paul stood conversing over an open book. "Are you worried about Hunter? You really needn't be. He seems like an okay guy."

"Look," he said, moving closer, "you don't know the man, Edeline. He's taken an interest. You need to be careful."

"I hardly know you better. Perhaps I should be leery of you as well."

The hurt in his eyes was unmistakable. She instantly regretted her words. "All right," she said, "thank you. I'd love for you to walk me home. Besides, I've been looking forward to getting you alone."

"Really?" he replied with a sheepish grin.

She couldn't help herself. She batted her lids. "Oh, yes. I've been tossing and turning and dreaming of it for days."

He laughed out loud. "I'd love to read more into that, but I have a feeling we're talking less a seduction and more an interrogation."

"Afraid so," she said, before looking down. "I know I'll never live it, but it makes it no less my life."

A warm hand ran gently across her face. "I understand that more than you know."

Chapter Seventeen

Dane secured the last box with a good round of masking tape.

"That should do it." Paul patted him on the back. "Thanks for your help today. I'm not sure how we would have managed without you."

"I'm sure you'd have managed, although I was surprised at how busy it stayed. Is it always like this?"

"When we have our charity sales it is." Paul secured the deposit bag and shut the till. "We beat last year's fundraiser by near two hundred. Father Tom will be thrilled." He handed the bag to Edeline.

"You're a peach," she said, throwing her arms around him and giving him a big hug.

"What about me?" Amanda complained.

Laughing, Edeline turned to hug her friend. "*You* are the cherry on top. Thank you both so much."

"We enjoy doing it. Besides, you were right here with us, pal." Amanda smiled. "So was Dane. Give Dane a hug too." The smile widened.

Dane couldn't help but grin as Edeline threw a bewildered glance toward her friend. Amanda was many things. Subtle wasn't one of them.

"I won't bite," he assured.

An all-too-familiar crimson covered her cheeks. Pulling in her bottom lip and dragging her feet, she approached him tentatively, moving slowly into his arms. "Thank you, Dane. You were a huge help. Please don't judge me by my friends."

He realized he should have thought it through the moment she embraced him. Instinctively his arms wrapped around her. God, he loved the way she felt in his arms.

"Your friends define you perfectly," he said, finally letting her go. "They're kind and caring and as real as a person can ask for."

Beautiful blue eyes stared at him silently.

"*Ohhh…*" Amanda sighed.

"Ah, thanks." Paul chuckled. "I have to agree," he added with a wink toward his wife.

"We should be going," Edeline said, grabbing her purse and avoiding all eye contact.

The bell above the door jingled as they stepped out into the night. They walked silently to the next block, the black Suburban never far away.

He looked her way. "Did I embarrass you?"

"No," she said too quickly before sighing and looking boldly into his eyes. "It's just…you barely know me, yet you sounded so sincere."

"I know you better than you realize."

She moistened her lips. "You made a comment earlier that made me believe we didn't get along."

"We argued a time or two. It was your fault." He grinned at her look of indignation. "Hey, I told you I'd never lie."

"Please! Your nose is growing right in front of my eyes."

He laughed. "I didn't mean to embarrass you back there."

"It's all right." She glanced up into the clear evening sky. "Don't be sorry. It was a nice thing to say and very observant. Paul and Amanda are two of the kindest, most caring people I've ever met."

They walked the next block in silence. The night had cooled nicely the heat of the day. Many of the windows lining the tall brick buildings along their walk were opened wide. Various aromas, laughter and song drifted out into the darkness, adding a peaceful background to their slightly less than comfortable silence.

Then, inevitably, the questions began. "So, tell me." She tilted her head his way. "How is it you know Hunter?"

There was no "right way" to break the news, so he said it like it was. "His name's not Hunter. His name's Phillip Graham. He's one of the men who kidnapped you."

She stopped dead in her tracks, her eyes wide and incredulous. "What!"

He smiled and shrugged his shoulders. "That's why I couldn't tell you earlier. He can't know that you know. You have to remain approachable."

Edeline continued to stare at him, her mouth still agape.

"You're having a hard time with it, and that's perfectly understandable," he assured.

She shook her head as though trying to reorganize her thoughts. "He…you…I…"

He laughed. "Okay, now you've lost me."

Her eyes searched his. "Hunter was one of them?"

"Graham," he corrected with a nod.

"Are you certain? He seems so nice. I mean I—I can't imagine." Doubt played like a drama across her lovely face. "Certainly you're mistaken."

He shook his head, his eyes never leaving hers. "I'm not mistaken. His name is Graham, and he's one of the men I saw. There's very little, if anything, I don't remember and still see vividly. Every face. Every word." He took a deep breath, the memories every bit as vivid as he claimed. "Every moment is etched deep into my memory. You can believe me, Edeline. Graham was there."

Disbelief turned to worry. "Dane, he recognized you."

"No. He only thought he did."

How was he going to explain it? Graham hadn't actually recognized him. They'd never met before their excursion in France. And the Graham whom Dane met in France wasn't the same Graham he met today. Like Edeline, that Graham had been from the future. Dane was the only one from the present who had actually been there.

"What Graham recognized was the look, the stance, the soldier. He simply recognized his own kind."

"His own kind? Are you saying he's a soldier?"

"*Was.* Like me, he was a time traveler. For thirteen years he worked directly under General Matthews. No one's made more trips through the portal than he. The man's practically a legend within our small group."

"Why would a legend do such a thing?"

He shook his head. It was a question he'd been asking himself over and over. "Sorry, Edeline. That's a question you'll have to save for Graham."

She shifted her weight uncomfortably before turning toward the black Suburban. "They should arrest him."

"For what? He hasn't done anything. Not yet."

Sighing in frustration, her shoulders lifted and fell. "Something has to be done. I can't live caged like this forever. I'll go insane."

Lowering his gaze, Dane stared down to where their feet now met nearly toe to toe, so close to actually touching. He looked back up. "We have to do this right. There's too much at stake not to—you for example, and you're not something I'm willing to risk."

Taking her hand in his, he gently pulled her back into a stroll. "Graham wasn't alone in this endeavor by any means. And the men we suspect backed him are very dangerous men—men we need faces and names for."

She shook her head, looking off into the distance. "It's all so silly. How can so many believe such a ridiculous tale—a magical stone, a mystical treasure and one extraordinarily unextraordinary girl?"

"Unextraordinary?" He squeezed her hand and chuckled. "That word belongs nowhere near you."

Long curling strands of gold cascaded across her shoulder as she turned her head to look his way. "Tell me about it. What happened in France?"

"How much do you know?"

"I know as much as my father."

Dane hesitated, looking away.

"I know he's not my birth-father, if that's what's worrying you."

It was. He stopped. "There's so much to tell you, but…I'd rather your father be there. I believe he needs to hear it as much as you."

She moaned her displeasure.

He squeezed her one hand as he took her other. "Please, Edeline."

"I've already waited so long. You really want me to wait longer?"

"I will tell you, if I must, but I'd really rather wait for your father."

He could see she longed to insist. Her brows drew together to form a pained expression. "I won't let you get away with it forever, you know."

He chuckled. "Believe me. I know."

"So what do I get for my patience, which, by the way, will run out in exactly twenty-four hours?"

"It will run out before then, I'll wager." He laughed. "I'll tell you what—ask me another question. Any question. I'll tell you the truth and nothing but the truth."

"How about three questions?" She smiled. "It seems a better trade."

"Mm," he groaned. "All right, but then I get one question…the last question."

"Deal."

They began once more to walk.

"How long are you planning to stay?" she began.

"Until the job is done," he said, and then quickly added before she could ask, "No, I have no idea how long that will be."

"Are you from Los Angeles?"

"No." He shook his head but didn't elaborate.

She waited.

He smiled.

"I am way more curious than that," she said, gesturing for him to continue.

"My, my, you're certainly pushy."

She shrugged her shoulders. "I like to know about people. For all of my life I can remember, I've lived here. I enjoy living vicariously through others."

"Makes sense," he said, turning his head and looking up ahead. "I'm an army brat. I was born in Colorado, but I've lived all over the world. Now I just travel wherever my job takes me."

"It sounds lonely."

"It is sometimes." They crossed the street and stopped in front of the church. "I'll see you to your door," he said, motioning toward the walk which led back to the cottage she shared with her father.

"I get one more question," she reminded as they moved down the small cobblestone path.

"Shoot."

"Are you really as nice as you seem?"

"How nice do I seem?"

They stopped just outside her cottage door. Deep blue eyes studied his. "Very nice," she said, looking down at their joined hands.

"I'm not sure how to answer," he said honestly. His past was full of both good and bad. Most of the bad being for the sake of a greater good, but still he couldn't answer. "Decide for yourself, Edeline. Come out with me tomorrow night."

Her lips twitched. After biting nervously down into the lower one, she asked, "Is that your one question?"

"It is if the answer's right." He grinned, knowing her well enough to know she was fighting a smile. "Say yes."

Their eyes locked and held. She was going to say yes. He could see it in the playful glint of her eyes, in the way she held his hands and in the way she leaned, ever so slightly, closer. But she, like he, was savoring the moment.

"Yes," she said, smiling wide as she pulled away. "Good night, Lieutenant Colonel Walker."

He took a deep breath, savoring the moment, one moment longer. "Good night, Edeline."

He waited for her to get safely inside, waving to her father when he met her at the door. Federic stared at him a moment, undoubtedly as eager as his daughter to have answers. But instead of stepping out into the night, he simply nodded, shut the door and turned the locks. The questions would wait for the morrow.

It had been a full day, watching Edeline every moment, making sure she was safe, fighting hard the pain their separation brought. Far worse, was watching Graham approach her, not once, but twice. The first time, when he'd trailed her to the bookstore. Graham had appeared from almost out of the blue.

Dane had been too far back to get to her before Graham actually reached her. It was a lesson he wouldn't have to be taught twice. From that moment forward, he vowed she'd never be more than a few quick steps from his or her father's side.

Graham. It was still hard to believe. Phillip Graham, former commander of the Transport Troop assigned to brave the portal. He'd retired before Dane had joined the squad. The man was legendary. A brilliant soldier, both skilled and courageous, there was hardly an example Dane was ever given that didn't carry the man's name.

When Dane had described to General Matthews the men who'd taken Edeline, the general had first mentioned Graham. But then he'd shaken his head and denied the option. It wasn't until Dane positively identified the soldier's photo that the general began to even consider the possibility. There was no denying it now. Phillip Graham was most definitely involved. Now the question was—who was he working with and what were their plans?

The large brick mansion stood as proud as any castle in the middle of its endless sprawling grounds. White flowers blossomed through the ivy which crawled up the towering walls and wrapped its sturdy vines around the railings of the second and third floor balconies. Such breathtaking beauty was but a façade to the ugliness which walked the halls within.

Graham hated them, and he hated even more what they had made of him.

Standing at the bottom of the wide sweeping steps leading to the mansion's grand entrance, he contemplated throwing a match. If there was even an ounce of justice in the world, fate would do the rest.

Justice…Ha!

He wouldn't bet his hide on that.

There was no turning back. He'd bartered his soul long ago to buy his freedom—his life. What a joke! Yes, he'd lived, but he was still very much a prisoner. And the life he had bartered for was gone. If only he'd been the man he'd thought he was, he'd have died that night and at least found redemption. But instead he'd sold his secrets to the hounds of hell and ever since lived his days with them at his heels.

His breath met the chilled night air, the moisture from his lungs condensing into rising clouds of fog which slowly evaporated before his eyes. He was procrastinating. The large wooden doors stared down at him, ordering him to hurry. *They* would be waiting.

Slowly he ascended the concrete steps to present himself at Hell's front door.

The bell chimed from within announcing his arrival. Seconds later the heavy door opened, and an immaculately dressed butler stared expressionless his way. Taking a step back, he motioned for Graham to enter.

The moment his feet were in, the door was closed and locked with a heavy bolt. With the sound still ringing, the butler lifted the swinging cover of the peephole and looked out. Satisfied with what he saw, or didn't see, he let the metal cover drop back into place.

"This way," he said, passing by Graham to head down the long hallway.

The mansion's tall walls were decorated from top to bottom with dark wall coverings. The same dark texture was captured beneath his feet in the rich wooden flooring. Paintings from years gone by adorned the walls throughout. No doubt, they were originals, their value immeasurable and to Graham unimpressive. Unlike so many, wealth had never been his enticement.

His escort led him through the backdoors and down a long breezeway, which passed through the magnificent grounds manicured to perfection and decorated with bountiful gardens and miniature stone waterfalls. They entered into what looked like a large pantry. The butler opened the cellar door and nodded for Graham to enter.

Graham eyed the man for any show of emotion. There was none. The man was as dead and tired as he, bought and sold, no doubt, at the same heavy price. Graham wondered what they'd used against him. Was it pride, wealth or fear? They had so many of which to choose. It was no wonder they were so abundant and overwhelmingly successful.

"Thank you," he said as he started down the long narrow stairs to the cellar below.

Fear — who'd have thought it would be his weakness? But when they'd taken him from his home all those years ago, tortured him without mercy and then made him watch as they murdered another, only to show him what would be his fate, he had crumbled. Not wanting to die, and without the faith which had given strength to so many through the years, he had surrendered to their will.

His tormentors already knew about the child and the knight who had passed through the portal, and they already knew about the stone. What they wanted from him was a single trip back in time. It was a trade he'd made to keep himself alive.

And so it was, six months after that horrifying encounter, he made his last trip into the past. He and his men landed one day prior to Edeline and Federic's legendary jump. Their mission was simple. They were to study the portal's activity on and around that fateful night.

Trusted by his men, he had easily disappeared into the darkness, sneaking into Brine's Castle and replacing the stone with a replica. It was a replica that, when placed around the child's neck and left to dangle, would take on a magical glow—nothing blessed or divine, just simple mechanics of the twenty-first century—magic not even the scientists in the lab would have yet discovered or would be able to recognize.

And it obviously worked, at least long enough to do its job. For the fraudulent stone had sat decades inside the vault, undisturbed and undetected, its so-called power fading over time as the man-made magic of an incredibly small battery wore off.

The past had been changed and nobody even knew it, nobody but the monsters who held the stone and waited for the day they could safely ride back into the past and steal from it, not only its fortunes, but also its secrets.

It was the perfect plan with Graham's soul as the only casualty.

But all the planning in the world couldn't overcome the hands of time. The portal had weakened and fate had stepped in, robbing from the Dogs their best chance at success.

The portal had closed. They'd lost their golden opportunity. Now, to accomplish their goal, they'd have to take on what they had worked so hard to avoid—the guardians of the cavern, the soldiers of Christ, the phenomenal force of the mighty Knights Templar.

Though secret, they still survived and had come to once again thrive through the centuries. No one knew it better than those Graham served, for the knights had been standing in their way for hundreds of years.

But that didn't mean the Dogs would surrender. They were simply too close. They had the stone. They knew the location. The only thing they needed was the girl.

"Edeline," Graham whispered her name as he lifted a bottle from the tall wine rack lining the wall of the cellar. The wall moaned and slowly began to move. He wasn't proud of what he would do, but then, neither was he proud of what he had done. If he wanted to survive, he would do whatever they asked. And anymore, survival was all he had, though these days he certainly wondered its value.

Chapter Eighteen

Dane stared down at the plans. His familiarity with blueprints came from an entirely strategic point of view—finding the best point of entry, potential hot spots, target and exit. It was rare he looked at plans simply for their admirable qualities.

"They're very nice," he said. It seemed a rather weak offering, but he could think of nothing better. His attention kept wandering to the back of the room, where Edeline boxed old hymn books, fought with masking tape and grunted in frustration as it failed to cooperate.

Father Tom chuckled, his gaze following Dane's. "She's a blessing, our Edeline—such a kind and generous spirit."

"Augh." The blue-eyed beauty groaned as the tape she'd rolled out so neatly twisted and bunched. Trying to salvage the strip, she managed only to get it coiled and stuck around her fingers. Irritably, she pulled her fingers free, wadded the mess into one small ball and shot it across the aisle toward the wastebasket.

It missed.

"Really?" she said, looking into the air and questioning fate before walking to the wad and depositing it into its targeted destination.

"Place the end of the tape on the crease and then slowly roll it out," Dane instructed, mimicking the action with his hands.

"I've tried that, but it keeps lifting."

"That's because you were trying to go too fast and pulling too hard."

Her brows wrinkled at the top of her dainty nose. "I did not."

"You did. Try a little more patience."

The nasty look she gave him made both men laugh.

Dane looked to the priest. "You forgot to mention patient and compliant."

Father Tom chuckled. "I didn't forget them. I merely didn't apply them."

They watched Edeline try once more Dane's simple technique, slowing it down as was suggested. It worked. She looked their way, her lips twitching as though she was finding what she had to say distasteful. "Better," she admitted, looking away when Dane grinned.

Stubborn, but adorable—that was the Edeline Dane knew and loved.

Lowering his voice, he turned to the Father. "Have you heard anything back yet? Have they made their selection?"

"I should hear something today. It's not an easy choice. The Knights Templar is full of men with great courage and faith, but it takes more than that for the transfer to be successful. He who takes Edeline's place as guardian must also possess purity, a quality not so common in man."

"Not even in such men?"

Father Tom shook his head regretfully. "Not in any man, especially of this world where temptation is so abundant."

"Every day we wait, she is at risk."

"I realize this and so do they. No one is standing idle, son. Now that we know there is an option, we are all eager to make the exchange. But we can't afford to err. The cost would be too high." He let out a long troubled breath, his eyes turning toward Edeline. "The Dark Army is stronger in their region. It's one of the reasons we've left her here. Before we are called back, there are other preparations which must be made—preparations for her safety. As much as we want this, our enemies do not. Believe me—they would rather see her dead than us successful."

The muscles in Dane's shoulders and across his back tensed. "They'll have to get through me to get to her."

The priest's expression grew somber. "It must have been very hard for you to let her go."

The question took Dane by surprise. He hadn't told anyone of his feelings for Edeline or the love they'd shared.

Father Tom smiled. "Don't look so surprised. It's not an easy thing to hide. I see it in your eyes when you look at her. I hear it in your voice when you say her name. You love her, and I suspect strongly she loved you."

Dane looked down. "She'll love me again?"

A comforting hand landed on his shoulder. "Yes, I imagine she will."

"I promised her I would never leave her, and I never will."

The priest nodded. "She would be a hard one to leave."

A roll of masking tape came undulating their way, Edeline following close on its tail.

Dane picked up the runaway roll and handed it back to her. "I'm hoping you're better with utensils, or tonight could be embarrassing."

"Thank you." She laughed as she took back the tape. "I promise I am better with fork and spoon."

"How about I meet with you and your father around noon? Think he can make it?"

"He will. He's quite anxious. If you want to meet sooner, I'm sure that would be fine as well."

"But not later?" he teased.

"Not a second." Pursing her lips, she shook the masking tape his direction.

Dane held up his hands in mock surrender. "Careful, you're not a real good driver of that thing."

Laughing again, her blue eyes captured the light from the windows above and shined like gems before his eyes. "I'll see you at noon."

"Noon," he promised.

The priest was grinning from ear to ear when Dane turned back around.

"What?"

Continuing to smile, Father Tom shrugged his shoulders. "I knew the day would come."

"What day is that?"

"The day my Edeline would find her future." Father Tom sighed and looked back toward the lovely woman now humming happily between the pews as though she hadn't a care in the world. She had surrendered to the masking tape and switched her efforts to distributing new hymn books. The priest looked back to Dane. "I just never imagined her future would carry with him her past."

"Eda was only two when she and Federic left their world for ours," Father Tom said as he, Federic and Dane moved through the basement which lay beneath the church. "It was Professor Blaine who contacted me. I was living in Italy at the time."

The priest stopped outside a large ironclad entrance. Pulling a key from his robe, he unlocked the door. "The professor and I had met three years prior at a conference in Rome," he said, looking back over his shoulder. "We shared a great interest in history and a special attraction for the Knights Templar. His interest stemmed from science, mine from my father."

"Your father?" Dane asked.

"My father was an archeologist. He'd made some amazing discoveries in his day, but nothing compared to his work in France. It was there he uncovered some truly astounding artifacts which led to a great deal of research on the era and the men who called themselves the Knights Templar."

Father Tom pushed open the door, the hinges squealing in protest at its heavy weight. "I was probably twelve when I first realized my father had a secret life. When I say I remember it as though it were yesterday, I really mean it. The memories of that night are as vivid as this day's. My mother had ushered us all to bed early, insisting we put aside our books for the evening and try to catch up on rest, which was not needed or missing. I knew something was up. For hours I lay there unable to sleep. I could hear my parents whispering and moving around downstairs. My mother was fretting, worried about something I never could make out."

Dane and Federic followed the priest into the small, poorly lit room.

"We should put some better lighting down here," Federic said, already eying what was there.

"Perhaps we should," the priest said, bending down in front of a small stack of boxes near the back corner of the room.

Dane quickly followed his intent and ran to take his place. "Here, let me get those for you, Father." Bending down, he started lifting the boxes, moving them to the side.

"There it is." Father Tom pointed to a large chest in the back.

Dane pulled it out into the middle of the small room.

Kneeling beside the chest, Father Tom ran his hands slowly over its top. "I heard men start to arrive sometime well after I should have been sleeping. One right after the other they came. I had to see who they were. Although we'd been warned to stay in our rooms, and I knew I'd be whipped if caught, I still snuck out. I was a young boy fascinated by mystery. Nothing could have kept me in that bed."

He glanced toward Dane. "There were dozens of them — regal looking men all dressed in plain clothing. They disappeared into the basement with my father, and later my father disappeared into the night with them. I watched them drive away and knew with absolute certainty, wherever it was they went, I would someday follow."

The priest's face lit with excited remembrance. "My father became one of them that evening. I didn't realize it, of course, until years later, but my father had stumbled upon a secret society still very much alive, and still very much dedicated to the cross it had always served."

"The Knights Templar," Dane said. He'd been more than a little relieved and excited when he'd learned the order had never truly seen its end. "There was always speculation, but I honestly assumed it was merely wishful thinking. It's hard to believe they've existed for so many years and never been found out."

"They are humble men," the priest said. "Not the sort to boast proudly. It would never even occur to them. For centuries they have worked in secrecy, credit for their work going to others or to fate." Father Tom opened the chest and started pulling out old news clippings and journals. "But it has been their hands and their swords which have guarded the innocent and fought back those, who would, for their own benefit, destroy what good still survives in our world."

Dane looked slowly through the years of atrocities and turmoil plastered across the pages before him. "Who are they fighting…and how? What are their weapons in this day and age?"

"Their strongest weapons have not changed — faith, honor and courage. But as always, we must fight with what we are given. Both sides have riches and power. Both sides have determination. Our enemies have not changed. They are those who turn their backs on Christ, who care not about their brothers or their sisters, but rather their own selfish desires. They are those who worship power and riches above the souls of men. They are many and varied. But the ones we watch the closest are those who fight for something far darker than greed or vengeance. The Dogs are still our greatest threat. They are heartless, cunning and cruel. And they serve their master direct. Ah, here it is," the priest said, pulling out a beaten photo album.

Accepting the album, Dane began browsing through the photographs of ancient relics found and articles covering bizarre disappearances, happenings and frightening claims of conspiracy and cover-ups. "If the knights knew these Dogs were a threat, why weren't they already protecting Edeline? I would have thought they'd want her near them."

Federic moved to stand beside him. "We had no reason to believe they'd have any clue about Edeline, the stone or our jump into the future."

The priest nodded, his glance dropping with apparent regret. "With so many years having gone by without incident, perhaps we did become careless."

Federic placed his hand on the priest's shoulder. "There was no reason to suspect, even I realize this."

"I've often wondered why they took her back to the past. It seems an unnecessary risk," Dane said.

"Edeline and the stone mean nothing without access," the priest said. "The general was right, that would have been much easier back then."

"And now?"

"Not easy at all. That's one thing we've done right. We don't know exactly where in the cavern the treasures lie, but we have a good idea, and we keep the entire area well-guarded. Of course, it helps that there is but one entry."

"I never did know where the cavern was," Federic said. He then pointed toward a photo of old coins bearing the Knights Templar symbol. "It's been a long time since I've seen one of those."

"They were probably in much better shape back then," the priest said.

Federic nodded, but his attention was elsewhere. "I'm confused. How would these men have hoped to find the treasure? Very few ever knew where the treasure lied. How her abductors hoped to find it going back in time, is beyond me. If the Dogs held such knowledge, their actions didn't suggest it."

"Omont knew where the treasure was," Dane said. "That's most likely why he was let go. They hoped to follow him."

"Omont was let go?" asked Federic.

"Yes. Luckily, he knew what they were up to and lost them just outside of Paris."

"How do you know all this?"

"He mentioned it."

Federic stared at him in disbelief.

He'd already decided, long before he'd even been granted leave from his post, that he would tell these men everything. In truth, no one knew who could be trusted anymore. These were now the only two men alive he knew with absolute certainty were on Edeline's side. They were her greatest chance of survival. He'd already told the priest most of it. He couldn't wait. He'd needed to know how much help could be expected and when. And much to his relief, the priest had assured him, that when tomorrow came and her security was pulled, the knights would be there to take their place.

"Please," Federic said, "I need to know what you lived, what you saw. It haunts me, and it has for years—what happened to the knights I left behind? So little is written. So little is known."

"I will tell you everything, but I promised Edeline I'd tell you together. She needs to hear it as well. It's important she understand the threat, and right now, she doesn't." Which is exactly why he'd made her wait, he'd wanted these men's support. He'd wanted proof—the kind of proof she'd hopefully find within the articles.

The priest closed the chest. "Edeline is so eager to have her life back the way it was, she's taking everything said in the lab that day as truth. But I fear the general and his men were wrong. I believed the cavern walls speak of a war to come, not one that has already passed. And my guess is the risks those men took in going back in time were never about the treasure as much as they were about the walls."

"If there's an advantage to be had, they want to make sure it's theirs," Dane said.

Closing his eyes, Federic took in and let out a slow breath. "And if that's impossible…"

Father Tom grimaced. "Then they'll want to make sure it's not ours."

Finishing the last of a long stack of thank you notes, Edeline set them down to rummage her drawers. "Hmm," she said, pulling out a handful of envelopes and her last three stamps, "this won't do."

Looking out her window toward the now parked Suburban, she wondered if the Blues Brothers would object to giving her a ride to the post office. Public transportation, she was told, was completely out of the question.

A light knock sounded against her office door. She looked up to see a cute little redhead peeking around its corner.

"I hear you have a date," Alison said, entering the room with her typical warm smile.

"Ah, you've seen Dad." She'd told her father earlier that morning about her and Dane's plans. He'd been suspiciously unsuspicious.

"Yes. I stopped by to see him earlier when he was working in the new addition. It's coming along so nicely." Her smile contorted into a know-it-all grin.

Edeline bounced the stack of envelopes against the stack of notes. "And?"

Alison raised her brows comically as she stepped into the room. "*And*…he is very handsome, our new carpenter."

"Agreed," she said, unable to hide her smile.

Alison pulled out the chair in front of Edeline's desk and sat down. "Tall, dark and handsome—seems a pretty good match for gorgeous, blue-eyed blonde."

It was Edeline's turn to raise her brows. "You're thinking of introducing Dane to Nate Porter?"

Alison laughed as she flicked the envelopes in Edeline's hands. "You're terrible and far too humble."

"I like him, Alison, actually. A great deal."

Scooting up in her seat, Alison leaned forward as though about to tell a secret. "Then I have good news for you, dear. Your father likes him as well. I can tell. I saw the two of them and Father Tom chatting away on their way down the hall."

Edeline once more bounced the envelopes. "Yeah?"

"Yeah, something about France. I can't even get Federic to talk about it for more than a quick nod or a mumble. But they were chatting away about it like they were only there yesterday."

Dropping the envelopes, Edeline jumped from her seat. Her chair rolled back a few inches to teeter at the edge of the vinyl floor mat. Certainly they wouldn't begin without her? "Any idea where they were headed?"

"Ah…" Staring at the chair, the pretty redhead blinked in surprise. "Well, no, honey. Is something wrong?"

"No, nothing's wrong," she said, tripping over the wastebasket as she scurried around the desk and made for the door.

"Are you sure? You seem…agitated," Alison said, moving from her seat as Edeline rebalanced her steps and continued toward the door.

"I'm fine," she said quickly, reaching for the doorknob. "I just—"

"You just what?" she heard Alison ask right before she slipped out the door and headed toward the chapel.

She was *just* going to have a few choice words with a certain good looking Lieutenant Colonel and her impatient father. She couldn't believe Dane would start telling the story of their time in France without her, especially after making her wait. But even if he hadn't started out to tell the tale, she could easily see her father getting it out of him. He'd let his curiosity get the better of him, start with one innocent question. Dane would have a much harder time putting off her father. Soon the whole story would be told, and she'd once again be left in the dark.

She hurried her steps.

The door to the chapel squeaked as she opened it up into the massive room. *Empty.*

She ran down the hall and through all the hanging plastic to the new addition. A few workers were scattered throughout, some hanging drywall, a few following behind them taping the walls. "Dad?" she called, hoping she merely wasn't seeing him. "Father Tom?"

"Father Tom was headed toward his office last I saw him," said one of the men from the ladder across the room. "Your dad stepped out with the new carpenter a few minutes ago, but he didn't say where to. Should I have him find you when he returns?"

"Please, Jamie, thank you."

Ducking back through the plastic, she headed straight for the priest's office, but no one was there. She peeked inside the rest of the rooms along the hallway, but other than the one where Alison was now addressing the last of the envelopes, they were all as empty as the first.

The only place left for her to search was the upstairs. Five minutes later she'd checked the entire top floor and was headed back down the stairs.

Alison stood at the bottom shoving the thank you notes into a small tote. "Find what you were looking for?" she asked.

Reaching the last step, Edeline paused. "No, actually, everyone seems to have disappeared?"

Alison pulled closed the tote. "Have you tried the addition?"

"Yeah, they weren't there."

"I'll bet they're all out back working on the broken sprinkler. I heard your dad threatening to take a hammer to it earlier."

Edeline laughed, picturing easily her father's declaration. "Mystery solved. I'll bet you're right."

"Well, I'm off to the post office," said Alison, giving her a quick hug and then heading for the door. "Do you need me to pick you up anything?"

"No, I'm good. Are you walking?"

"Just down to the library. I'll catch the bus from there. It's a more direct route. You're welcome to come along."

"I'd love to, but I can't. I've still got plenty to do here."

"All right, then. I'll see you when I get back," said Alison, disappearing out the front door.

Edeline headed straight for the backyard. Her father had been trying to fix the stubborn sprinkler-head for near a week. He'd be thrilled to have help.

Stepping out the back door, she looked around the lawns. They appeared empty. "Dad?"

No response.

"Dad?"

Still no response.

"Hey, boys, have you seen my dad?" she called to the agents she knew would be lurking. They, not surprisingly, remained silent. "Thanks," she yelled out sarcastically.

Through the cottage's back window, she caught a glimpse of dark hair. Most likely her father had found another project which Dane and Father Tom could help him with. She headed that way.

Letting the screen door slam behind her, she hurried inside. "Hey, you guys aren't starting without me, are you?"

The only response was a round of muffled whispers from the front room.

"Really?" She grunted, heading that direction. "Think you're going to get away with—"

She spotted the two strangers only a second before she was grabbed from behind and pulled back into a solid wall of muscle. Terror ripped through her so fierce it was impossible to register anything but the shock itself.

The next thing she knew, a white cloth was lifted and placed over her airways. Grabbing against her assailant's hands, she pulled, digging her nails into his flesh as deep as she could manage. Still the hand didn't budge. Lifting her leg, she prepared to kick, but the world suddenly tilted, throwing her into a black bottomless pit.

Waiting in the chapel while Federic headed to the office to collect Edeline, Dane flipped through the multiple articles in the album, while the priest stood behind his podium, reviewing Sunday's sermon. It was incredible all the world events the Knights Templar had had their hands in through the years. Dane couldn't help but wonder how many would have turned out differently if the incredible force hadn't been there guarding destiny's path.

One thing was for certain. He'd feel a whole lot more comfortable once tomorrow came and the knights arrived.

He looked back toward the chapel doors. "It's taking him too long." He shut the book. "I'm going to go look for them."

Just as Dane stood, the doors flew open.

Federic stood in their frame, his face as white as the walls around him. "I can't find her."

Can't find her! The words seemed to physically crash into Dane. The hairs on the back of his neck stood on ends as his body chilled. His feelings for her had driven him straight to panic. Luckily years of training were there to drive him back to reason.

If ever there was time to think like a soldier, that time was now.

Putting down the album, he started with the obvious. "Isn't she in the office?"

"No, nor is she in the new addition or anywhere else on this floor."

"She has to be here somewhere. I told her repeatedly not to leave the church without you or me. And even if she didn't listen, every single door is guarded."

Federic ran his hands nervously over his head. "I can check the upstairs if you want to check with the guards."

Father Tom was already headed toward the doors. "I'll make one last sweep of this floor while you do."

All three men met outside the chapel and then split to go their own directions.

Stepping out the massive front doors and into the late morning sun, Dane hollered, "Roberts! Tellen!"

A rugged looking street bum corrected his posture and moved from his stakeout near the west corner of the building to head Dane's way. From the bus kiosk across the street, a well-dressed business-man put down his newspaper, hid again his sidearm and then ran across the street.

"What's up, Colonel?" Tellen asked, pushing back his battered cap to adjust his earpiece.

"We're looking for Edeline. You haven't seen her have you?"

"No one's left the building at all outside of the redhead," Roberts said. He looked down toward his watch. "That was a little over an hour ago."

"Here she comes now," Tellen said, nodding his head toward the sidewalk where halfway down Alison approached. "Should we keep our cover?"

"Yes," Dane said, reaching inside his pocket and pulling out change to hand to Tellen. Roberts followed suit.

Tellen thanked them both and then turned to leave just as Alison made her way up the walk.

"Wait," she said, grabbing Tellen's filth-covered arm and bringing him to a stop. "Have you eaten? We have a kitchen inside. I could make you a sandwich and bring it to you. There's some literature inside as well that I'd like to share with you and information on locations where you can find help."

"Ah…" Tellen glanced toward Dane.

"That's a great plan, Alison," Dane said. "Why don't you head inside and put it all together? I'll run it out to him when you're done."

"Sure thing." She stepped past all three to make her way up the stairs.

"Alison," Dane stopped her.

She turned and looked his way. "Yes?"

"You haven't seen Edeline recently, have you?"

"Last time I saw her, she was headed out back looking for you and Federic."

"How long ago was that?"

She leaned against the door, giving it some thought. "Maybe an hour…maybe a little longer. It was right as I was leaving."

"Thanks, Alison."

"Sure," she replied, slipping inside the building.

Tellen instantly radioed the men in back.

"Cramer?"

They all waited, but all that played back was static.

"Cramer, this is Tellen, do you read me?"

More static.

"Patten? Patten, are you there?"

"Shit!" Dane pointed to the east corner. "Tellen, head around the rose garden and check on Patten. Roberts, take the west side and radio for help."

As both men drew their weapons and headed their separate directions, Dane ran back inside the building and straight into Father Tom and Federic.

"She's not in —" Federic stopped as he got a good look at Dane's face. "What's happened?"

"Not sure yet. Follow me."

They landed in the backyard just as Tellen and Roberts arrived.

"Cramer's alive," Roberts said, "but he's down. He was hit pretty hard from behind. I've already called for help."

"I can't find Patten," Tellen said, still eyeing carefully their surroundings.

Federic instantly moved toward the cottage, terror and fury riding double across his face.

"Federic, wait," Dane called, he and the others following directly on the older man's heels.

But there was no stopping him. The back door of the cottage flew open, and Federic stormed inside completely unarmed.

Dane followed Federic's path straight into the unknown, but all they found was an empty cottage.

Federic turned to him as they stepped from the kitchen steps onto the lawn. "How could I have let this happen? Why did I take my eyes off her?"

"This isn't your fault," Dane said, even as he cursed himself for the very same thing.

"Patten," Roberts hollered from behind them as the sound of steps over gravel sounded from the side of the cottage.

Patten came wobbling out from behind the house, rubbing his head. His glance fell instantly to Dane. "Dane, I'm sorry," he said, his manner displaying both pain and regret. "They hit me from behind. I never even heard them coming. When I came to, there was commotion coming from the front of the cottage. I ran that way, but got there just in time to see them drive off."

"Did you get a license?"

Patten shook his head. "No. I took a hard hit to the head. My vision was a bit blurred. I know they were California plates and it was a black Suburban like ours."

"How many?"

"There were at least three."

"Anything about them that sticks out?"

"No," Patten said, roughly rubbing his hands up and down over his face. "I'd better call Martin and let him know what's happened. I'll see if he can't get us some help." Reaching into his pocket, he pulled out his cell and dialed as he made his way back toward the parish.

Turning to Tellen, Dane instructed him to call Matthews. He then turned back around. Federic and the priest were both heading back to the cottage. "Federic?"

The knight grabbed a ladder from the side of the small house and carried it to the back steps of the cottage. Father Tom stood at the base of the steps as Federic moved up and pulled a decorative decal from the overhang.

Sighing a breath of relief, Dane asked, "Tell me, that's what I think it is?"

Father Tom nodded. "There are a total of six hidden all around the yard and inside the cottage. We planted them here the first day we realized Edeline could be taken."

Cameras.

Brilliant.

"I think I love you two," Dane said, turning back toward the parish, intent on having a word with Martin as soon as Patten was through. But something about the look on Patten's face stopped him dead in his tracks. He was watching the priest and Federic not with a look of relief, but rather a look of apprehension.

"We have a problem." From the distance his words were silent, but Dane had run reconnaissance long enough to easily read words so simple. The soldier turned away from Dane's view as he continued his conversation with his employer. His head was bent as his free hand massaged his neck. Beneath his hand, his flesh was painted.

A violent chill ran the course of Dane's spine.

The soldier's hand dropped to his side, leaving exposed the cobra's head tattooed into his flesh — angry, defensive, its body wrapped tight around the blade of a sword as its mouth opened wide to reveal its poisonous fangs.

Chapter Nineteen

At some point she realized she was dreaming, but she didn't want to wake. Perhaps it was the soft whisper which played over and over in her head, soothing her, comforting her, providing her with a false sense of security. It was as real as the chants which filled the room, ringing like a dark melody—rhythmic, deep and haunting.

At first she thought the chants had come from her dream, but she realized now it was the other way around. They had slithered into her subconscious, pulling her into a forest where the trees where unlike any she'd ever seen. Spindly and old, their branches swayed in the wind, their round, flat leaves quivering as though chilled. They seemed to watch her, not hindering her way or holding her back, but rather pointing their thin, twisted limbs, directing her forward as the eerie chants continued to push at her heels.

As she neared the forest's end, the sun's warmth hitched a ride on the breeze and blew, as its rays did fall, in between the thinning trees and onto the foliage covered floor. The chants seemed to pause, holding back as she ventured out of the forest and down toward the sun-kissed cliffs. Turning to look behind her, she could see no one.

"Edeline." The whispers began, encouraging her to move on.

Then suddenly she was standing at the cliff's edge, looking out into a sea both welcoming and oddly familiar.

"Come with me," the voice encouraged from the sea.

The wind picked up.

The chants began again, this time closer, more persistent.

"Come with me." Suddenly there was a woman. She looked much like her but the woman's face was framed with long brown hair and there was a whitish glow about her.

Is this an angel?

The ground shook as the chants landed at her back. She froze with terror.

"Edeline." The woman touched her face, startling her out of her dream and landing her back in an unfamiliar bed.

She opened her eyes and the same woman sat at the edge of the bed. Edeline blinked, and the image was gone.

"Don't leave me," she whispered.

Exhausted, terrified and hating the dark, she didn't care if the woman was a ghost or a figment of her imagination. She didn't want to be alone. But alone she was. The woman, whoever…whatever she was, had vanished.

But the chants remained. Ringing in an unfamiliar tongue, they chilled her through and through, making her feel as though she'd slipped through the hands of the mortal world into a deep, blackened chasm of an ungodly empire?

Maybe she had.

Bound and gagged, she'd originally gained consciousness in the backseat of a car. Carefully she'd peeked through her heavy lids to see two men sitting quietly in the front seat. They'd taken her to a breathtaking mansion sitting high in the hills overlooking the bay. Then they'd lifted her from the cool leather seat of a Mercedes and carried her inside the mansion only to throw her into a dark room and leave her there, her mouth covered and her hands still tied behind her back. It was a simple room with a bed and a mattress which had immediately lulled her to sleep, as it would lull her again now if she let it.

Is that what they wanted, to have her sleep? A silent prisoner until…what exactly? She started to shake as a sob formed low in her throat threatening to choke her. She had to get out.

Swinging her legs to the floor beneath, she tried to remember the layout of the room. She'd only seen it lit for a few short seconds as the light from the hall had rolled in as they brought her inside. Small, mostly unfurnished, nothing to cut the tape holding her bound. What could she use when all she had was a mattress, box spring and frame?

Of course, her frame at home had sharp edges.

Moving to the floor and scooting back against the bed, she found the corners of the frame not only sharp, but also easily accessible. Scraping her bindings back and forth against the sharp edge, it did nothing at first, but when she tried raising her wrists up under the angle, the tape punctured and began to tear. In a second her hands were free. Ripping off the tape covering her mouth, she nearly yelped from the pain.

Her head felt heavy, her limbs weak. Sleep had never sounded more inviting, but she couldn't shake the feeling the woman in her dream had been there to save her, waking her and encouraging her to move when every other part of her screamed for her to surrender.

And then there were the chants. They continued to slide into the room from underneath the door — black, ambient murmurings that clawed at her sanity. They were close, but it didn't sound as though they were directly outside it. Turning onto her knees, she made it to her feet, the throbbing in her head never subsiding.

She searched the room for windows, but if they were there, they were blocked. Her only way out was through the door, which she feared would be guarded. Pressing her ear against its solid surface, she listened for sound, but there was nothing outside of the heathens' eerie mantra. Carefully she placed her hand on the knob and turned, sighing with disappointment as it didn't move at all.

Of course, it was locked. She should have known.

She felt the knob. It was exactly like the ones in the church. That, she could handle. Numerous times little girls and boys had left the restrooms and pulled the still locked doors shut behind them. Edeline had become a bit of a pro over the years at picking locks. This one would be simple…if she had a hanger. There wasn't much to the room, but she could remember a closet. Making her way across the dark space, she prayed it wasn't empty.

She reached inside and found a full wardrobe, or more accurately — a full closet of robes. Grabbing a metal hanger, she allowed the garment it held to fall to the floor. Untwisting its neck, she made her way back to the door.

The metal end fit snug but still managed to push through. Twisting and turning the rod, she finally felt it slide into the narrow whole which held the needed lever. Lifting the rod, she heard the lock turn.

Dane spotted the slight rise in the leaves near the aging Oak. If he was right, the tripwire should be right around…here. Taking the stick he'd grabbed a few feet down the hill, he carefully scooted around the surface debris. There it was, thin and well hidden.

He had to hand it to Martin. He knew his craft.

Luckily for Dane, he knew it even better. Kneeling down, he carefully clipped the tight wire.

Now he understood why his superiors had found it so hard to believe Graham was involved. He never would have suspected Martin. If he hadn't asked for Patten's phone, spoken to Martin himself and verified it was he the soldier was warning, he probably still wouldn't believe it, though it all made sense now.

Martin was in the perfect position to lead such a rebellion. He had the knowledge, the money and everyone's trust. No wonder the man had been so fast to cast doubt and yet so eager to supply protection.

If Dane managed to get his hands on him, he'd rip him apart.

Taking the end of the now broken line, he lifted it carefully and followed its path back to a plank covered with sharp blades. Not exactly the typical protection one would expect from a modern-day security expert. But then it wasn't the common thief Martin wished to deter. That much was made obvious by the intricate and assorted devises covering the hillside leading to the mansion.

Today's security was all about system sensitivity, civility and law enforcement—nothing scary enough to put off one trained in the jungles of actual warfare, where humanity took backseat to "survive and conquer."

Dane had to hand the man one thing, he knew them all—security measures as well as tactics both old and new. The entire property was monitored by the most advanced closed-circuit video system available to man—well, the wealthy man anyway. Of course, no alarms rang to any police station or neighborhood watch. No, the only rapid response unit Martin would have alerted would be his own. And their response measures would be no more civilized than the guerilla-style booby-traps planted throughout the steep slope.

Not for the first time, Dane wondered just who his enemies were and more importantly, who were his friends? General Matthews had brought Martin into the fold. Did he know who the man really was? Dane's stomach turned. He could only hope the general was as blind as he had been, but he couldn't be certain. So from that point forward, he'd have to do it alone. There could be no asking for help.

Black muck covered his hands and face as he carefully moved through the cover of brush, dodging one trap after another. "Damn, the man's paranoid," muttered Dane as he stopped at the edge of the brush and stared at the tall, high-voltage fence, watched over at every angle by well-armed guards.

Dane was good, but no one was that good.

Edeline hurried down the hall, moving quietly along on the tips of her toes.

Where was the exit anyway? It felt as though she'd already been from one end of the massive mansion to the other, and still she'd found no way out. Her luck wouldn't hold much longer. If she didn't get out of there soon, she was bound to get caught. She should have paid better attention when they were bringing her in, but she'd simply been too groggy and more than a little afraid.

And where was everyone? The chanting, which had been her only source of direction telling her where *not* to go, had faded several turns back. Is that where they all were? Were they all together? Somehow she doubted it. Though she had no desire to see any of them, knowing where they were and avoiding them would make her a lot more comfortable than the ghostlike silence which now echoed through the dark, foreboding hall.

Deep resonant chimes danced off the walls where she stood. Following their rings down the next turn, she reached the end of the west hall just outside the foyer.

The door was only a few steps away.

She sighed with frustration as she spotted a well-dressed butler stepping forward from a side room to answer it.

Searching the hall for a place to hide, not one option seemed better than the other. She chose the closest door. Praying safety lay behind, she carefully snuck inside.

The room, a study, stood bare of all life. Odd—she couldn't explain it, but it didn't feel empty once inside. Something about it made her feel watched…edgy.

It wasn't that anything seemed unusual. Everything seemed in place. It was clean, elegantly furnished and simple in design. The walls of shelves were full of richly covered hardbacks, dusted and well preserved. The paintings on the walls were pleasing and…Stepping closer to the picture hanging on the wall to her right, she realized the feeling was stemming from there.

A high-rising cliff overlooked the sea. Peaceful and calm, it should have been soothing, but instead it haunted her, and not just because it was the cliff from her dream. She touched its frame, longing to touch the canvas, to walk into the scene and feel the breeze from the sea against her skin. Her hand hovered in front of the image, desperately wanting to touch it, but for some reason afraid.

"Edeline."

She jumped back when she heard it—the same voice from her dream. But the voice hadn't come from a dream. It had come from the painting.

Certainly she'd imagined it. It had to be the residual effect of whatever drug they had used on her.

The feeling of being watched intensified and started to swarm, coming at her from all angles of the room. She whirled around, but the room was still bare—bare but not silent. At first she thought it the shelves which rumbled, but she soon realized it was the books which shook and drummed against the wood. From the midst of the thunder, a book plummeted to the floor, bouncing onto its back and opening its cover.

Like the painting it called, not with words so much as a fascination. Stepping across the room, she bent down to her knees.

Odd words, undecipherable, jumped from the page, holding her prisoner with an uncomfortable allure. Suddenly the chants she had heard earlier, started again, rolling down the halls from some unseen chamber and filling the room with their dark, cadenced beat.

"Edeline."

She turned back toward the painting and once again it seemed to call. It was easy to imagine herself there—the sea calm, the breeze refreshing. She instinctive raised her face as though lifting it to the wind—and a wind did reply. From the canvas it blew picking up the ocean scent and carrying it to the floor where she knelt. Somewhere in the back of her mind she knew it was impossible, but it seemed so real.

The pages of the book began to turn—only a few until they stopped, revealing a hole cut out of the book's center. And in it was a necklace—a long chain with a simple stone. The wind picked up and danced around her, taking her hair and boldly slapping it back against her face.

She reached inside the hole and lifted the chain. The stone dangled in the air, whipping wildly with the wind.

Could this be the stone, the same one from the lab? She moved the chain over her head and allowed the stone to drop.

No. This was another.

It fell against the flesh of her chest and instantly her body warmed as a bright illuminating glow transformed the stone into a breathtaking gem.

Staring at it in awe, she had a hard time believing her own eyes. *What? How? Why?*

It made no sense at all.

The marvelous light spread from the small brown stone and shot across the room, illuminating every corner and nock with an indescribable radiance.

The voices came next, at first soft and few, then loud and many. The chants outside the room were completely buried beneath the voices of millions which now rang in her head. Everything became muted as the sounds became one and were picked up and carried into the room's whipping wind—swirling and flying and moving away.

"No," she reached out for them and found herself pulled, into the wind which whipped into a tunnel. Just like the others, she flew through the air at incredible speed. It was dark, damp and musty. From one stone passage to another she moved, led by no one but guided all the same.

Suddenly the stone walls turned into fields, and the voices emerged as riders storming the ground to an unseen battle. The earth shook beneath them. The land and its possessions knelt at their feet. Determination and tenacity defining them, they wore no metal armor, no helmets, no guns, only long silver swords and chains holding silver crosses.

Oh, how it consumed her — the beauty of courage, the power of belief, the need to be a part of their magnificent journey. Who were these men and where were they going?

The wind began to calm, the army to fade. She reached out her arms, grasping at air, hoping to catch hold of the moment and hold it in her arms. The fields disappeared behind tunnels and the tunnels behind walls. Edeline emerged back on the study's floor.

No!

She mourned it. She wanted to go back. She didn't care what it was or whether or not she belonged. It had fulfilled her in a way she could never describe.

But there'd be no going back. Whatever magic the room had released, it had reined back in. Not even the odd feelings remained… nor the chants outside the door. They had been replaced by voices — voices which were not all that far away.

She had to get the stone and get out of there. But how was she going to do it and not be seen? One thing was certain, the stone could come nowhere near her or it alone would give her away. Pulling the chain off from around her neck, the stone transformed to plain.

Looking around the office for something in which to carry it, she spotted a small can of paper clips sitting on the desk. Opening the desk drawer, she emptied the can's contents inside before dropping the stone into the can and shoving it into her pocket. It seemed to do the trick.

Her glance fell to the open book still lying on the floor. It would be a dead giveaway. She picked it up and placed it back on the shelf.

Now to get out.

The front door seemed a bad bet, all things considered. It would have to be the window. Moving the long flowing drapes aside, she unhooked the latch. Much to her relief, the window moved easily. Much to her horror, it set off an alarm.

With no time for careful, she kicked out the window's screen and took a leap of faith.

Her feet hit the ground, and she instantly started running. Luckily from that point, she could see which way was out.

When she first hit the graveled drive, it appeared to be deserted. She could make for the hedges or trust her luck would hold and make for the car. The black Mercedes, which had been her transport, was still sitting where they'd left it. Having no idea what waited behind the bush, she opted for the car.

Three armed guards rushed forward from behind the main gate. Thankfully she reached the car and found it unlocked and the keys still dangling from the ignition. Shaking near uncontrollably, her hands circled the keys and turned the ignition.

The motor roared to life just as the mansion doors swung open and at least a dozen men with long black capes and silver masks stormed out. Panic swept through her like a raging inferno. *Run,* was her only clear thought.

Throwing the gear into drive, Edeline stomped her foot heavily on the gas. The car heaved forward, fishtailing until the rear wheels found traction. Whatever it took, she was getting the hell out. There wasn't a one of them she wouldn't mow down to get there.

A second later, she was storming down the drive and straight for the gate where even more guards had emerged.

"Don't shoot!" She heard hollered as the guards took aim.

Black capes flew down the drive behind her, and out of nowhere a man flung himself upon the hood of the car. The swaying of the vehicle was more shock than intent, but it rolled the man back and forth as he hung on tight to the hood. A silver mask did nothing to hide the frightening black eyes which stared through the windshield.

"Hollow of soul," she'd always wondered the phrase. But here it was before her, chilling and ugly and horrifyingly real. She couldn't see his face, yet she'd swear he smiled.

A second later fate stepped on the brakes as she collided with the closing gate. The demon from the hood rolled off the Mercedes onto the ground below.

Jumping from the car, she ran for her life.

Gravel popped and ground under the man's heavy weight as he moved to his feet and took off after her. She hadn't made it far before he flew at her from behind and sent them both tumbling into the brush.

Turn after turn she rolled across the rough earth, the man's ridiculous cape wrapping itself around her with every toss and roll.

Finally they came to a stop. She fought him for all she was worth, but the beast was too strong. The duel ended when a heavy backhand landed hard across her cheek.

The sting of it penetrated clear down to the bone.

Pulling her arms way over her head, he trapped her still beneath him. "Keep that passion for later," he said. "When they're done with you, I'll drain every ounce of it from what's left of your useless frame."

"Enough!" A familiar voice commanded from the top of the slope.

Edeline pulled her gaze from the monster on top of her to the top of the hill.

Colonel Martin stood at the edge of the drive, his mask dangling at his side.

Betrayed.

It was hard to take in. She had trusted the man and he'd brutally betrayed her.

"That's enough, LaFay," he commanded. "Pick her up and take her straight to the temple. I see no reason to drag this out any longer."

Her insides turned. She wanted to scream but fear had left her muted.

The man Martin called LaFay snorted and pulled off his silver disguise. The picture behind the façade was one more disturbing than the mask itself. The man wore evil like a veil. His features, though in an odd way striking, appeared ruthless and cold, creating a face as frightening and poignant as the dark eyes it held.

Moving to his knees, he then lifted her into his arms and packed her up the hill, mumbling as he passed Martin. "When it's over —"

"When it's over, you'll do your job and be done with it. The quicker we do this, the safer we'll be. We've waited hundreds of years for this moment. If you screw this up, I'll kill you myself. Understood?"

Stopping dead in his tracks, LaFay turned to face Martin. The deadly look in his eyes sending shivers all the way down Edeline's spine. "Have you forgotten who you're talking to, or are you just that stupid?"

Martin searched the masks now surrounding them as though weighing his support. Apparently unconvinced, he looked back to LaFay. "We've a lot to lose."

"I'm well aware of what's at stake," LaFay replied, his frightening gaze turning back to her, running longingly down her body, telling her clearly he'd do as he pleased.

Watching with pure disgust, Graham could have easily vomited. The beast would take her, have his way with her and then happily cut her throat. She didn't deserve it. She was an innocent victim in the battles which raged between Heaven and Hell, but still she would pay the ultimate price.

Not wanting to have any part of it or their heathen ceremony, he fell back, pretending to be concerned with the car.

"Leave it," Martin hollered from up the drive.

"I'll just see if it will start," Graham yelled back.

Martin scowled and threw his hands in the air. "You're a damn pain in my ass, Graham. Move the piece of shit and get inside. We won't wait for you."

"Oh, the pity," mumbled Graham, opening the door and crawling behind the wheel. The sound of plastic breaking was followed by an uncomfortable poking against his backside. He reached beneath him and pulled out a tin can. The small plastic window built into the can's top was now destroyed. Inside the can lay a plain brown stone.

He stared at it in stunned silence.

Sure it was just an ordinary brown stone, but this one he knew exceptionally well. He'd stared at the thing for hours before actually handing it over to the demons. She must have found it. How'd she manage that?

She was really something — Edeline Depuis.

Damn it. Damn them!

The key turned and the motor roared. Looking down the road, he thought about how nice the ocean would feel. A burst of speed and a straight path on the winding road would have him there in practically no time. The temptation was stronger than it had ever been before. Laughing an empty laugh, the irony of it hit him dead on. To leave this hell, he would take his own life, when it was for his life he had entered it.

Tapping his fingers against the wheel, he realized he truly didn't care if he lived or died. So what the hell was he doing? The answer came to him so clearly he almost choked on its starkness. He would end his misery, but first he would end hers.

He looked down at the stone. Maybe, just maybe, he could right a few of his wrongs.

Moving the gear into reverse, he threw his arm across the back of the seat and turned to look behind him.

A hammer pulled and the cold touch of steel landed between his eyes.

Silver masks filled the benches on each side of the darkened chamber. Red candles in black sconces hung on the temple walls, their flames licking high as their shadows danced against the tapestry. An odd scent filled the air. Cypress and musk mixed with some unknown aroma which turned the combination into a heavy, not quite pleasant scent. It seemed to mess with her mind, making the pagan statues guarding the entries seem to come alive. The same dark feelings she'd first felt in the study were here but compounded. Nothing but ugliness breathed in the room.

The masked audience bent their heads and chanted as the man named LaFay dragged her down the wide carpeted path toward the steps of their altar.

His touch turned her stomach, sickening her to the point of physical illness. But it was the look in his black merciless eyes which haunted her soul. His desire for her was without emotion, it was derived of a cruel and revolting lust. Without speaking a word he'd made his intentions clear. If she survived this ordeal, she would only live to die in his unmerciful arms.

She wouldn't allow that to happen. Whatever it took, she would escape or see it ended here.

He threw her to the base of the steps where four tall figures stood waiting. Their faces masked or not she couldn't tell, were hidden somewhere deep within their capes' oversized hoods.

Instantly turning to move, two sets of hands took hold of her arms and held her where she'd fallen. A puppet in their play of worship, she felt utterly helpless to do anything but obey the cords.

The low steady hum of their dark rhythmic chant rose like an invisible wall from the back of the room, chilling and foreboding in its hollow, soulless beat. Between it and Edeline lay nothing but masks.

More troubling than any of it, however, was the cry of a child which emerged from somewhere deep inside the sea of silver faces.

What was a child doing in such a nightmare?

The answer came to her directly on the heels of the question—a horrifying truth she'd give anything to be wrong. It was heartless, the epitome of appalling—but as the damned cared neither for the beauty nor value of innocence, reason led her to the obvious conclusion. The child was her replacement.

The reality of her situation was now abundantly clear. Things were so much worse than she'd ever imagined. She wasn't going to be killed because she wasn't anything special. She was about to be killed because the power she held was.

Edeline fought once more against the hands holding her still.

"Enough," Martin said, making his way through the crowd to stand before her. A snide smile crossed his lips as he caught her unbridled look of contempt. "Realizing you may have played the Devil's advocate, are you?"

It was true enough. She'd been so certain it was all a farce; she'd chorused his fraudulent doubts as though they were gospel. She'd been careless, almost taunting in her certainty that all concerns were needless and even ridiculous.

He laughed at her look of remorse. "Even science speaks of magic, my dear girl. They may label and definite it, but it makes it no less spectacular. You of all people should realize it's so."

She looked past him to the man now standing behind him with a little girl in his hands. Looking back toward Martin, she pleaded, "I'll do whatever you ask. Please don't do this."

Following her gaze, he turned. "Where's the stone?" he asked the man, taking from him the small child.

"It wasn't there," said the man, shifting his glance hesitantly from Martin to LaFay.

Martin's lip twitched in annoyance. "What do you mean it wasn't there?"

Edeline tried hard to hide her relief. They hadn't found it.

The man continued to squirm, glancing once again to LaFay and then back to the Colonel. "The book was there but it was empty."

"Empty," Martin repeated the word as though testing it for taste. Closing his eyes, his mouth visibly tightened over gritted teeth. "Where is it?" he asked, turning to face Edeline.

"Where's what?"

The palm of his hand landed across her face, stinging as the crack of the blow echoed throughout the room.

The little girl whimpered and then began to cry.

"I haven't the patience to play with you, Edeline. I'll ask you one more time, and then I'll hand you to LaFay."

It wasn't a matter of courage. She simply knew that even if she told him, it would not change her fate or the child's. "I have no idea what you're talking about."

"I'm hardly that big a fool, Edeline."

"No, you're a monster—a horrible, loathsome excuse for a man."

He pulled a long face. "Now that hurts, Edeline." The next slap came just as fast and just as hard. "I warned you, didn't I?" Looking toward LaFay, he nodded her way.

LaFay smiled, pulling her into his arms and back against his chest. Roughly grasping her jaw, he pushed her head up and back, forcing her to stare into his black, cold eyes. "If you don't care to talk, I see no use for your tongue."

Edeline shook. The man hardly seemed the type for idle threats.

He let loose her neck, and her glance fell back on the child. It wasn't just her own life hanging in the balance; it was the young girl's as well. But there was a difference between surviving and living.

One of the few things her father had been able to tell her about her past was how she'd obtained the power. Though she'd thought it a sad and twisted tale at the time, she could see clearly its implications now.

She'd hand the child—an easily manipulated carrier—the stone. Edeline would then be killed, and the power would pass to the child. She'd survive, but for what?

"There's no point in playing the hero," Martin said. "Sooner or later you're going to tell me. You may as well leave this place in one piece."

She wouldn't tell him, but sooner or later they'd retrace her steps and most likely find the stone.

"You'll free yourself from the burden, Edeline. Just do it," he said.

"Free myself for what—to be slaughtered. I know how it works. I'm not a fool, nor am I so cruel as to curse an innocent child with the likes of you."

"How very noble of you," he drawled, a slow grin crossing his ruthless face. "But then, nobility runs in your blood, does it not?" Pulling a gun from inside his cape, he pointed it at the back of the little girl's head. "Let's try another route."

"Don't!" Edeline cried, jerking against LaFay's hold.

"Let her go," Martin ordered LaFay, moving the child closer to her.

The girl's wide eyes met Edeline's. A trail of tears ran down her small face as she reached out her tiny hands, begging to be taken.

"All right," Edeline said, pulling against her restraints.

"Let her go, I said!"

The hands reluctantly fell away.

Edeline reached for the small child who fell willingly into her arms. She squeezed her tight and comforted her.

"Oh, that's very sweet, Edeline, very sweet," Martin said. "Now tell me. Where's the stone?"

She kissed the top of the little girl's head and wondered what kind of world she'd be cursing her with.

Martin pressed the gun once more against the child's head. "Last chance, Edeline. I can go get another innocent. We can do this again and again and again. How many have to die?"

She closed her eyes as though the darkness might find her peace.

It didn't.

"It was in my back pocket. It's probably in the car or perhaps somewhere on the hill."

"Watch her," Martin said to LaFay before nodding toward the four grim reapers still standing behind her. "Follow me," he said and headed out the chamber.

The sound of their steps faded into the distance, leaving her and the child alone with LaFay and a room full of masked servants.

He watched her silently a moment, no doubt pleased by her discomfort. He stepped toward her, and those behind them began once more to chant.

Pulling the child as close to her as she could, she stepped back and up the stairs.

His eyes flashed with something akin to amusement. "Eager?" he asked, looking pointedly past her and up toward a metal table sitting in the center of the altar. It was bare, but to its side, on a table well lit with candles, lay a knife. Its long silver blade, picking up the reflection of the flames, seemed to burn as though on fire.

It was hard to look and equally as hard to look away. Though the thought of the knife plunging through her heart made her nauseous, she still couldn't believe that this would be her end.

"Such a shame," said LaFay, his tone contradicting his words. "I'd like to say I'm sorry, but that would be a—"

Raised voices and scuffling were heard just outside the chamber.

The haunting chants of their audience were replaced with the sounds of bodies turning.

Through the open chamber door, a man was thrown unceremoniously into the room and onto the floor. Wearing camouflage and covered in dirt, he hit the ground hard, then lay there a moment, seemingly injured.

Graham, the man she now knew to be a traitor, followed him in to hover over his helpless form.

Slowly the injured man looked up.

"Dane!"

Horror ripped through her, sending her bolting forward to be by his side. But halfway to the floor, her arm was caught and she was ruthlessly jerked back by what was surely of the devil's own blood.

"What do we have here? A want-to-be hero?" said LaFay, laughing as he pulled Edeline and the child closer to his side. "Ignorant man, unless there's a cavalry behind you, I'd say your journey's done."

"Get your hands off her," Dane said, struggling to get to his feet. He made it to his knees, but was pushed back to the ground by Graham's booted foot.

"Your fate is sealed, soldier. I'd tell you to say your prayers, but I doubt seriously they'd be heard from in here." Looking to Graham, LaFay nodded toward Dane. "Kill him."

Graham aimed his gun at Dane's head.

"No!" Bolting against LaFay's hold with the child still tucked in her arms, Edeline fought wildly to break free. "Please, oh please, don't do this."

LaFay only tightened his hold, turning an angry glare Graham's direction. "Damn it, I said kill him!"

Hatred sparked from Graham's eyes. Pulling back the lever, he positioned himself to fire, lifted the barrel and pulled the trigger.

Stunned silence filled the room.

Staring back at Graham with a look of disbelief, LaFay stood a full second, blood streaming in a steady line from the hole now planted between his eyes.

As Dane burst from the floor, the monster's body plummeted to the ground.

Grabbing hold of Edeline's free hand, Dane rushed her and the child out of the altar and into the cellar.

"Make one move and you're dead," yelled Graham to the worshipers as he swung his gun wildly and backed out of the altar behind them. Stopping outside the chamber's door, he reached into one of the wine racks and pushed up a bottle.

The door to the altar turned out to be a wall. It moaned its burden as it sealed the room in. "They won't wait long," said Graham, moving from the lever to the stairway. "We'll need to move fast."

Edeline held on tight to the little girl as she and Dane hurried to follow, her eyes never leaving Graham.

What role, exactly, is the man playing?

Stopping at the top of the cellar stairs, Graham quickly poked his head out the door, then back in. "It's clear."

Dane nodded toward the child. "Can you handle her and fast?" he asked.

"Yes." And she could. She could handle anything if it meant getting them out and away from this man-made hell.

They followed Graham out into a long breezeway that ran the length of a well-manicured lawn. Back inside the mansion, they followed the same long hall where she'd made her escape earlier that day. Four lifeless forms dressed in hooded capes appeared along the way. Guessing them the same men from the altar, she looked for their master but found him missing.

"Where's Martin?"

"Martin?" Dane repeated, looking back her way over his shoulder as he headed around the next corner. "He wasn't with —"

"Dane!" Edeline screamed just as Graham reached out and grabbed his shoulder, stopping him from walking directly into Martin's gun.

With the barrel still pointing squarely between Dane's brows, Martin threw Graham an angry snarl. "I should have known," he said dryly. "Drop the guns."

Neither man moved to follow his instructions.

The barrel's nose shifted to Edeline. "I said drop 'em."

Without further hesitation, both men dropped their weapons.

"Fools," Martin said just before a shot fired from further down the hall.

Jolting forward, their captor's face twisted into an ugly collage of pain and surprise.

The barrel flayed from its mark as the gun, slipping from his grip, bounced along the edge of his fingers. Finally sliding off their tips, it crashed to the ground, clattering only a moment before Martin's dead weight silenced its jangle.

With her face buried deep in Edeline's curls, the little girl whimpered.

"It's going to be all right," Edeline said, her gaze like the two men's at her sides, moved from Martin's now motionless form down the hallway to its end.

Looking somewhere between haggard and dead, the butler stood near the door, his hollow stare focused on the body lying at their feet. Dangling from his right hand was the smoking gun.

Graham knelt down beside Martin, checking for a pulse before looking back to the butler. "Why?"

The man turned, opening the door behind him. "You should hurry," was his only reply, not a show of remorse anywhere on his face.

None of them waited for a second invitation.

Outside in the courtyard, the Mercedes sat idling.

Dane ushered her inside and hurried around to the driver's seat.

The back door swung open and slammed closed. "They're coming," said Graham, immediately turning to face the mansion, his gun still drawn.

With gravel spitting behind their wheels, they bolted forward down the drive. Reaching across the leather seat, Dane pulled her and the child down across the seat. "Stay low."

Behind them shots fired, shattering the rear glass and rocking the car as it continued to fly down the drive.

"Hang on," Dane said, punching down further on the accelerator. This time the car flew straight through the gates, sending the iron barriers flying and setting off a new string of alarms. Gunfire seemed to explode from every direction, thankfully echoing from an ever growing distance.

Hesitantly handing the little girl back to Graham, Edeline once more cast doubtful eyes Dane's direction.

"She's safer back there," he assured, sensing her discomfort, though never actually taking his eyes off the road.

The child stared wide-eyed at Graham as he secured her the best he could into the oversized seat. He turned off his cell, handed it to her to play with and then promptly went back to his role as lookout.

Edeline couldn't help but stare at him, wondering what bizarre happenings had transpired to bring the man to their side. Not that she was entirely shocked. She'd caught his expression outside the mansion earlier that day when LaFay had shared with Martin his vile intent. The look read like an open book. Without a doubt, he hated LaFay. In fact, it seemed as though he loathed them all. Was that why he was helping her and Dane now, or had he ulterior motives?

Her thoughts ran back to the stone.

Glancing down to the floorboards at Dane's feet, she saw no trace of the stone or the tin can. If the stone wasn't in the car, then it undoubtedly was lying somewhere upon the devil's hill. The thought made her sick, but she couldn't deny it. There was every possibility the monsters had already found it?

Shoving her fingers beneath the seat's cushions, she searched their unseen crevices.

"It's not there," said Graham.

"You found it?" she asked, looking tentatively back over the seat.

"Yes," he said, not bothering to elaborate or look her way.

"Where is it?"

"Safe."

"It's all right, Edeline," Dane said. "It's in the trunk, hidden inside the rim of the spare tire."

Breathing a sigh of relief, she situated herself back in her seat. A hundred questions swarmed in her head, but she couldn't see past the terror of the last few hours to form a single one.

Staring at Dane's profile, she was overwhelmed by the memory of him lying flat across the chamber's floor, a gun pointed directly at his head. Her stomach curling, she flinched and looked away.

He shot her a curious glance. "Are you all right?"

She avoided the question with one of her own. "How'd you find me?"

"Once I figured out Martin was behind it, finding you was easy." He motioned back toward the manor. "The mansion's his." He slowed the Mercedes and took the next turn. "Reaching you is what took a little skill…and luck. You're attempt at escape actually served me well. It was the cover I needed to get in through the gates."

"I can't believe they didn't see you."

He nodded toward the backseat. "I hitched a ride from our friend. Edeline, you remember Graham don't you?"

"I…yes." She didn't know quite what to say. The man was merely another bizarre piece to a plenty bizarre day. Her mind was simply too muddled. Along with her hundred questions, she had a hundred concerns…and a nervous breakdown was long overdue.

Opting for silence, she stared out the window.

Rich, decorative lawns sprawled on both sides of the winding road. Huge, gorgeous homes adorned the hills. Edeline looked back to Dane. "How'd Martin afford such an extravagant lifestyle?"

"He was born into a great deal of money. I always wondered why he didn't just retire. I assumed it was passion for his country." Dane shook his head as though angry with himself. "I read the man completely wrong."

"He fooled everyone," said Graham. "Matthews, Blaine, the entire unit. Me," he added on a note of self-disgust. "I should have killed him years ago. To be honest, I don't know why I didn't. I don't know why I didn't do a lot of things."

Dane looked back at the man through the rearview mirror. "Have you told me everything?"

"Everything I know."

"Matthews and Blaine — neither are involved?"

"Not in any way or form. They're both good men. They have no idea what Martin was up to, and I imagine they'll both find it hard to believe. Their faith in him is one of the reasons I never went to either."

Looking once more into the rearview mirror, Dane pulled his cell from his pocket and began dialing. "I can't promise you what will happen," he said to Graham, "but I'll do what I can."

The general picked up instantly, his voice blasting through the earpiece to sound throughout the car. "Where in the hell are you?"

Pulling the phone further away from his ear, Dane replied, "We're about twenty minutes away. Look, I need you to—"

"We? You and who else?"

"Edeline and Graham. I need you to listen—"

"Edeline and Graham! What are you talking about—Edeline and Graham?"

Slowing the car, Dane merged right, taking them onto the connector which would lead them to the freeway.

"It's a long story," he continued. "I'm going to need you to accept the short version." He moved onto the on-ramp. "I need you to take Patten into custody. Martin's the one behind Edeline's kidnapping, and Patten was in on it. I also need you to put in place a wide sweep near Martin's mansion. I need the whole damn thing closed down and—"

A loud explosion boomed from behind.

The road rocked as the earth rumbled.

Rolling into the sky behind them was a huge ball of fire.

"What was that?" The general's voice cut across the echo of the blast.

Still watching the rearview mirror, Dane visibly cringed. "That *was* evidence—a whole mountain full."

Chapter Twenty

A long row of identical black SUVs lined the streets outside the parish. Armed soldiers stood on every corner. No longer were they hiding in bushes or stalking from cars. The yard looked like a warzone. Men dressed in high-ranking military uniforms walked back and forth in and out of the church.

All of it did a nice job of putting an exclamation mark on the last few hours lived.

Nothing was as it had been.

Edeline looked sorrowfully toward Dane.

Smiling reassurance, he reached across to take her hand. "It's all right, Edeline. It won't be forever."

There wasn't a bare spot along the curb. Dead center in the middle of the road, Dane pulled the SUV to a stop right in front of the church.

The car's doors were instantly opened.

Both she and Graham were grabbed and pulled from the vehicle. But while she was taken gently into concerned arms and pulled under a protective cover, Graham was pulled from the rear seat and taken immediately to the ground.

"Wait," she cried, trying to capture sight of Dane and the child. But no one stopped. They simply hustled her into the church and quickly closed the door.

The cover was removed and the soldiers all stepped back.

Both her father and Father Tom came around the corner as though they were racing a speedway.

"Dad!"

"Edeline," he said, his arms wrapping around her. Burying his face into her shoulder, he shook with the depths of his emotions.

"It's all right, Dad. I'm safe."

Tears pooled in his relieved but angry eyes as he pushed her back to look at her. "Edeline Depuis, don't you ever leave my side again. From this day forward. Not ever. Dear God," he said, pulling her back into his embrace, "I thought I'd lost you."

"I'm sorry, Dad. I'm so sorry." Holding her father tight, she looked over his shoulder to Father Tom.

The priest ran his hand lovingly over her head. "All is well, Edeline. You're back," he said, looking around the well-guarded parish. "And you are safe."

"For now," a deep voice said from behind her.

Edeline turned to find General Matthews. Dane stood right beside him, holding the little girl protectively in his arms. Behind them, Graham stood between two heavily armed guards.

"I'll be right in," said General Matthews, motioning for the soldiers to take their prisoner into the room at their left.

Following orders, the men disappeared with Graham inside the room, then shut the door behind them.

Looking to Dane, the general's expression was one of uncertainty. "What do you think?" he said, nodding back toward the room.

"I think the man's been living in hell and is ready to get out."

General Matthews looked down, sorrow and disappointment evident in his stance. "I can't just let him go."

Dane nodded. "He's made some serious mistakes, and he'll be the first one to admit it. But he did save Edeline's life and mine today. He didn't have to do it, but he did and with plenty of risk to himself."

"He's not innocent."

"No," Dane said, "but that might actually work in our favor. You should have seen him. He knows how they think and how they'll respond. He's quick, precise and fearless. I wouldn't mind having him at my back."

Federic shook his head, obviously uncomfortable with the direction the conversation was going. "We can't trust him."

"I think we can," Dane said. "The kind of rage I saw in his eyes can't be feigned. He hates them—almost as much as he hates himself."

"I don't know, son," Father Tom said. "The type of anger you describe can easily backfire."

Dane looked toward the closed door. "I know," he said, running his free hand uncertainly through his already disheveled hair. "He was a soldier once," he said, looking back to the general, "and a very good one. He'll know how to handle the anger, and more importantly, he'll know how to handle them."

General Matthews closed his eyes and rubbed a soothing finger atop the crease between his brows. "Let me talk to him. Maybe then I'll know what to do."

Turning on his heels, he headed for the room, but stopped halfway there and turned back.

"I let you down," he said to Edeline and Federic. "I'm sorry. I'm afraid I was a bit of a nonbeliever. I could stretch my imagination only as far as my eyes could see. They could see the portal and understand its risks, but demons and angels were a little out of my vision."

"I can hardly blame you," Edeline said. "I had the same problem."

"Had, but not now?"

"No, not now."

Having only that day stood beneath the altar of the damned and flown under the wings of an angel, she could hardly deny their existence.

Dane opened the door to the chapel and stood momentarily just inside its walls, studying the lovely blonde waiting patiently in the pew at the front of the church.

It was still hard to remember the past they'd shared belonged only to him. He'd give anything to have her know what they'd shared, but to simply blurt it out didn't really seem an option. The last thing he wanted to do was to scare her away. He'd have to choose his words carefully, telling the story without what was to him the most important part. They'd fallen in love.

"Is there a reason you hesitate?" she asked, turning in the pew to look his way.

He grinned, knowing her well enough to feel her annoyance. She'd been kept waiting long enough.

Stepping forward into the aisle, he made his first step toward a moment he had both dreaded and longed for. As much as she wanted to know what they had lived, he wanted to tell her. He only hoped he could do the truth justice.

Her lovely curls cascaded across her shoulder as she tilted her head to look past him toward the door. "Is my father coming?"

"No," he said, entering the row where she sat and sitting down on the bench beside her. He sighed, fearing she'd be none too happy with the why. "He's already heard a good share of it."

Edeline watched him silently a long moment, her beautiful blues showing no sign of either anger or disappointment. "I knew he'd pull it out of you. My father has his ways."

Dane laughed, certain of its truth. "In this case, he didn't have to pull too hard. It came up in conversation. I felt it was necessary at the time. I'm sorry, Edeline."

She fidgeted, looking up toward the altar. "I forgive you. I imagine you had a good reason."

"I did," he assured, following her gaze. "I'm not sure where to begin."

"From the beginning," she said. "I want to hear it all, every detail."

He let his thoughts slip back in time — back to the first day of his mission. "I didn't know what I was stepping into that day. There was very little time for explanations." He looked back to the same beautiful face that had stared at him from the photo that day in the lab.

Leaning back against the bench, Edeline turned to face him, her eyes widening with excitement as an eager smile touched her lips.

"I had been told very little about you or the stone, only that you were my mission." Looking down momentarily, he chuckled and shook his head. "Arrogantly, I thought it would be that easy. I'd go back, find you and bring you home. I had no idea I was about to be tested more thoroughly than I had ever been tested in my life. And it wasn't only my skills which were tried. It was also my beliefs, my honor."

It was too early to mention his heart.

He told her about how he'd found her and rescued her and about her rather unappreciative response.

"I actually said that?"

"You did. You thought I was completely crazy."

"How horribly ungrateful." She laughed, looking a far cry from repentant.

"You think that's funny do you?"

"Perhaps a little, though I'm sure at the time, I was actually quite frightened." She allowed her head to rest against her arm. "Obviously, somewhere along the line, you managed to charm me."

"Charm you?" It was his turn to laugh. "No, I simply became the less frightening of your choices."

Her sparkling blue eyes danced with amusement. "So in a world of undesirables, you became the desirable?"

"Something like that." His eyes dropped to her grinning lips. The urge to kiss her was nearly unmanageable. For the life of him, he couldn't imagine what had made him sit so close. He should have known it would be difficult. He couldn't be anywhere near her without instinctually wanting to pull her into his arms.

"We became a team, you and I. Like I said, you hadn't really much of a choice. Everything and everyone which came our way was strange to you. I simply became the most familiar."

She lifted her head, watching him as he struggled with how much to tell her. "It was more than that. Is there a reason you won't tell me?"

He hesitated. He could tell her everything that happened, but how could he tell her what was in her heart?

Her expression grew somber. She looked down toward the bench. "I would have found you attractive. That alone would have swayed my actions."

Bold. Just one of her many traits he so admired.

"The attraction was mutual. You were the most…you are the most…beautiful woman I have ever seen. But it was more than that,

Edeline. We may have been together only a very short time, but every minute moved like a day. Everything was so…" He looked down.

"Magical?" she guessed.

He laughed. "Maybe." He thought about it as he watched her blue eyes sparkle with interest. "Yes, maybe."

Moistening her lips with the tip of her tongue, she ventured further. "How much more than attraction?"

"We were never alone, if that answers your question."

Her cheeks turned a bright shade of pink, but she didn't look away. "Who were the others?"

He told her about the knights, what they'd learned and what they'd encountered. He told her about the trip to her grandparents' villa, the Dogs and her father. He told her about their final moments on the cliffs below Brines Castle.

When he was done, she looked away. "I thought it would bring me relief, but instead I feel an even greater loss. I wish I could have known them — truly known them. I wish…"

The sorrow in her voice nearly ripped him in two.

Cupping her face in his hands, he brought her eyes back to his. He wanted her to see his sincerity. "I'm sorry, Edeline."

Covering his hands with hers, she looked at him as though confused. "Why would you be sorry? You brought me home."

"I promised myself I'd remember it all to share with you later. I thought that would be enough. It was an arrogant assumption. I realize that now."

"What more could you do? What more could you possibly give?"

Dropping his hold, he shrugged his shoulders. "Perhaps I should have left you with the choice. It was, after all, your land, your father, your time." It had haunted him since he'd returned. He had to tell her the truth. "Edeline, I didn't tell you. I didn't tell you what would happen — that you'd lose it all — every memory, every moment. I should have told you what to expect."

"Why didn't you?" There was no accusation in her words, only curiosity.

"I don't know. It seemed somehow cruel. But then, when you were pulled from my arms…" He could still remember it, and it still burned like a sword straight through his heart. He looked away.

"The look on your face, the hurt, the betrayal…I can't take it back. I know you're here with me now, but I can't help but feel that I failed you. I can't help but feel that I lost a part of you that day."

She leaned forward into his line of vision. Smiled. "Dane, I wouldn't have changed a thing. The idea may have frightened me, but I wouldn't have stayed. This is my world, Federic is my father, and I'm very glad to be in this time. It would have been my choice."

Her smile warmed his heart and freed a mind tormented by memories of that day in the portal. He couldn't have asked for a greater gift. He'd needed her forgiveness, more than he'd even realized.

"I have something for you," he said, reaching into his front pocket.

"Something for me?" Her hands clapped together as she followed his movements with a great deal of excitement, reminding him a little of a small child on Christmas morning.

"It belonged to your mother. Omont had it made especially for her." After grabbing the trinket, he pulled out his hand and uncurled his fist to display the brooch. "We found it at your grandparents' house that day. Your father—"

Catching her breath, she stared at him in amazement. "Did you say it was my mother's?"

"Yes, it was, but it's yours now."

"Given to her by my father?" Big blue eyes looked at him as though they were witnessing a miracle, and it suddenly dawned on him perhaps they were.

Smiling, he reached for her hand. Turning it over, he then placed the brooch in its palm. "Your father was delighted that it now belongs to you, as he was sure your mother would have been."

"My mother's," Edeline whispered, staring at the brooch as her eyes began to tear. "My mother's," she repeated before throwing her arms around him and kissing him soundly.

Just as he reached to hold her tight, she pulled back.

"Oh, Dane, I—I don't know what to say." She opened her hand to once more stare at the ornament, tears trickling down her cheeks. "My whole life I've longed to own anything of my mother's—anything at all. I can't believe it. I just…I can't believe it."

Holding the brooch up toward the light, she continued to stare at its rough gems and simple design. "It's the most beautiful thing I've ever seen."

"Jaquette le Picart," she said, testing her mother's name. "Omont Montague," she said, testing her father's. "A gift from both."

"Yes," he said, unable to take his eyes off the beauty of the moment.

A single tear ran down her cheek.

Wiping it away, he pulled her into his arms.

He felt her shake, heard her sniff.

He squeezed her tight.

"I'm not sad," she said, allowing her head to rest against his chest.

The words ringing all too familiar, he almost choked on the potency of the moment. "I know," he replied, his voice rough with emotion.

"I'm really quite happy." She looked up into his eyes, and there it was—the same look she had given him that day in the village of Vanac, the look that said clearly he had her trust and her affection.

"I know," he said, wiping away another tear.

This was his Edeline, the same woman he'd held that day, the same woman he'd feared he might have lost forever.

Pulling the brooch to her heart, she sighed. "Thank you, Dane, for everything."

"You're welcome, Edeline."

Taking a deep breath, she smiled up at him. "I kissed you."

His gaze moving to her lips, he swallowed. "I know."

The air around them charged with an all too familiar awareness. Placing his hands behind her neck, he pulled her in for another.

The doors to the chapel opened. Voices drifted into the silent room as Federic and Father Tom walked in.

Closing her eyes and pulling away, Edeline grimaced. By all appearances, she was as disappointed as he by the interruption.

When she opened her eyes again, she smiled. "I hope you keep that thought," she said, allowing her glance to drop once more to his lips. "I'd be terribly disappointed if you didn't."

Dane laughed. "There's little chance of that."

"Good," she said, quickly moving from his arms and running down the aisle, holding out the brooch for the men to see. "Look," she said, lifting the brooch for their inspection. "Dane brought it back for me. It was my mother's."

Both men studied the brooch and then smiled.

"It's wonderful, Eda," Father Tom said.

"The most beautiful jewel I've ever seen," Federic said, taking his daughter in his arms and squeezing her tight.

Dane moved from the pew and headed their way.

"Dad, I met them — Omont, Roncin, Hemart and Lucas. I met them all."

Federic's eyes widened with shock. He stared over her shoulder toward Dane. He'd known about Omont, but had not heard about the others. "You met them?"

"It's a long story, but yes, we met them. We actually couldn't have made it without their help. They were truly a gift from God. I have messages for you from all of them."

Suddenly it was Federic's eyes which watered with emotion. "They were remarkable men, every one of them."

"Yes," agreed Dane having reached them. "They are a true testament to your own valor."

"They are a testament to something much greater than that, my friend. I'm most eager to hear every detail, but I'm afraid now isn't the time." Patting Edeline's shoulders, Federic leaned forward to deposit a kiss upon her forehead. "They want us to gather our things. We're leaving for France."

Edeline lifted herself up in her seat, hoping for a better look down the aisle. Still there was no sign of Dane.

Letting out a worried breath, she sat back down.

He'd left their small group right as they'd started to board. Though he'd assured her he'd be right back, that had been several minutes ago. By the way everyone was shuffling around, closing departments and securing all loose items, she feared they were getting ready to take off. She was afraid the pilot might not realize they were waiting for another, and she needed him — Lieutenant Colonel Dane Walker. In fact, she was surprised to realize just how desperately she did need him there.

When exactly had he become so vital to her — not only as her guardian, but also as her friend, and in an odd way, her soul mate?

Leaning toward her father, she rested her head on his shoulder. "They wouldn't leave without him would they?"

Dealing with his own set of uncertainties, Federic flipped the page on the plane's *Safety Response Guide* and scowled. "Look at this photo, Edeline. It looks like they're pushing the poor chap out the side door."

Glancing down toward the manual, she eyed the photo demonstrating how to help another passenger exit the side doors. It did, indeed, appear the individual was being shoved out in midair. "Hmm, hopefully in the time of need, the operator stops to actually read the instructions."

"We're not the ones in the center aisle are we?" Federic leaned sideways in his seat, searching the central exit.

Having lost her headrest, Edeline sat back up, raising herself in her seat to once again check the entrance.

"Ah," Federic grunted, nodding up ahead to the exit. "We'll let them worry about the exit plan." Flipping the page, he scooted back in his seat.

Father Tom leaned across the aisle to grin at Federic. "You're the only person I've ever met who's actually read that thing from cover to cover."

Squeezing her father's hand, Edeline smiled. "Yes, but your diligence is to be commended. I feel much safer for your efforts."

Federic sighed. "Oh, I'd be a mess. You'd best hope for no true calamity. Swords and daggers I can handle, a plummeting tin bird is a little out of my comfort zone."

Edeline blinked. "You really know how to calm a girl's nerves, Dad."

"We'll be fine, Federic," Father Tom said, patting her father's shoulder.

"Dad, let me have the guide." Edeline held out her hand, but her father ignored it. "It's not doing you any good. It's just getting you upset."

Holding fast to the booklet, he continued to ignore her.

"How can a man who jumped off a cliff toward a turbulent sea, fear something as common day as flying?" she asked, withdrawing her hand.

"Faith in God is what took me over the cliff," Federic said, hitting his hands against the chair's armrests. "Here I'm putting my faith in man—a maker I'm a little less comfortable with. And this isn't a small jump anywhere, you know. We'll be doing a lot of flying… over a lot of ocean."

"Folks fly over water every day. We'll be fine," repeated the priest. "Look on the next page," he instructed, leaning even further across the aisle and turning the next page on the brochure. "It tells you all about how to handle a water landing. See," he said, pointing to the next illustration. "The cushions can be used as floatation devices."

"Oh yeah, look at that." Federic studied the photo, then turned around in his seat to test the seat's cushion.

Bravo, Father Tom.

He knew her father well. Hopefully Federic's curiosity would soon outweigh his fear. If it didn't, it was going to be a long ride for all of them.

Edeline sighed and began flipping through the few magazines scrunched inside the pouch on the back of the seat in front of her. Neither the traveler's guide, nor the book on economic forecasting promised to keep her amused, so she surrendered her search for entertainment and leaned back against her seat.

A dark head moved into the plane, sending her heart pounding a little harder as her stomach fluttered with a funny mixture of relief and excitement.

Stopping just inside the door, Dane spoke briefly with General Matthews, showing him something he held in his hand.

The general ran his hands through his hair as though frustrated and slowly shook his head. Then turning, he motioned for the soldier behind him to close the door and signal the pilot.

Dane looked back her way.

Their eyes met and held. The broad smile she could now feel plastered across her face was immediately mirrored on his.

"Federic," Father Tom said, "why don't you move over here by me where you can have the window seat?"

"I don't think so. But thanks all the same." Federic shook his head. "I'm staying right here and keeping Edeline company."

"I believe she'll have company, Federic." Father Tom nodded toward Dane.

Federic looked toward Dane and then back to her.

"Thanks, Dad," she said with a grin.

Her father grumbled. "Oh, all right," he said, standing and side-stepped across the aisle. "But scoot over. The last thing I need is to see how far we'll be falling."

"That's the spirit," Father Tom said with a chuckle, scooting over to the next seat as his friend begrudgingly moved into his.

Edeline watched as Dane threw his bag into the overhead compartment. He was a handsome man from any angle, but something in that moment simply took her breath away. He had loved her. Perhaps he hadn't said it outright, but she'd heard it in his words, seen it in his eyes. She had a very strong feeling she had loved him just the same. The knowledge was as thrilling as it was unbelievable. Would they find that love again? Did he love her even now?

He took the seat beside her and held out a photo in front of her.

The sweet face of the little girl from the mansion stared back at her.

"Oh, Dane, that's her. Who is she? How did you get this? Have they found her family?"

"Her name is Lucy. She went missing from the Sadie Milton Orphanage last Tuesday."

Edeline's eyes began to water. "I hate to think what could have happened to her. What monsters they are to do such a thing to a child." Unlike Edeline, who had been given the stone and then rushed to safety, Lucy's fate would have been left in the hands of men who lived without morals, acted without care.

"She's in good hands now," he reminded.

"The best." Until they discovered where the child belonged, she'd been placed with Pual and Amanda.

Dane handed her the photo and wrapped his arms around her shoulders. "This is going to work. We'll find the cradle, and we'll put an end to your nightmare once and for all."

"What if we don't find it, or what if we do and it doesn't work? Is there any other way to rid me of this power?"

"Not one I know of." His brown eyes dropped to the photo in her hands. "At least not one I'll ever allow."

"Dane," she said hesitantly, the idea of sharing what she'd experienced somewhat frightening. "I...I put the necklace on, only for a moment, but..."

Taking the photo from her hands, he then covered her hands with his. "It's all right, Edeline. You can tell me. I knew something unusual must have happened."

"You knew? How?"

"Well, for starters, you had the necklace, and I'm pretty sure they didn't simply hand it over. Whatever happened, it made you believe; otherwise you wouldn't have bothered to try to protect it. You also wouldn't have called it a power rather than a curse. Plus, you're no longer mocking it. Which means something's happened to make you see its value."

Nodding, she leaned in closer. "It's hard to describe what happened. The stone fell against my chest and instantly started to glow. But there was more than just the light. It had a wonderful kind of warmth about it, unlike anything I've ever felt before. And there was this wind, but I think it came from the room, or maybe it started from the picture."

He raised a curious brow.

She laughed. "Longer story, less pertinent."

"All right, so there was a wind…" he encouraged.

"Yes, it started like a breeze but then grew stronger. It seemed to pick me up, first carrying me into this tunnel and then onto a field. On the field there were these men — I didn't know them at all, yet I felt as though I'd known them my whole life. Somehow I could feel their strength, feel their devotion. In that moment, I wanted nothing more than to join them. They were headed someplace…well, important. I think maybe to battle." She looked away. "It sounds crazy, but it felt so real."

"It doesn't sound crazy to me," Dane said. "I've met the men, or at least men of such character."

She followed his gaze to her father, who was sitting back straight against his seat, his eyes scanning the plane, no doubt in search of other wonders as magnificent as floating cushions.

Dane smiled. "I'd love to have seen him in his younger days. The way the knights spoke of him…well, he must have really been something."

Edeline smiled toward her father. "He still is."

She looked back to Dane. "Do you believe in visions?"

"I do these days, but even more I believe in you. It was a vision, though I'm not sure yet what we're to make of it."

"With Martin gone, will they continue to look for me?"

Dane took a deep breath, nodding his head regretfully. "Martin was in no way the head of the Dogs. There will be many bigger and far fiercer where we're going. I won't lie to you and pretend it's not so. You need to be prepared."

"They'll try again to abduct me?"

He looked away, but not soon enough to hide the worry.

"Dane?"

"They may try and take you again…or not." He looked back her way. "Either way, they'll come after you." The fear she saw on his face made it all too clear. If they couldn't take her alive and use her at their will, it was in their best interest to see her dead.

She'd already known it was true, but realizing it had already escalated to that point was more than a little unnerving. "I see," she said, leaning back in her seat.

"I won't let them hurt you, Edeline," Dane said, once again pulling her into his arms. "I will never let them hurt you."

She had a feeling he wasn't only assuring her, but also reassuring himself. In his arms, pressed against his warmth, she believed they could overcome anything.

And they certainly weren't alone. Her gaze roamed across the aisle to her father and Father Tom. They had complete faith they would all be well looked after—faith in God, in each other and in the group of men who would be meeting them in Paris.

Edeline grimaced as she looked to the seat in front of her father.

Graham sat there more silent than a shadow. He was her only uncertainty.

Grabbing Dane's hand, she nudged her head Graham's direction. "Dane, are you certain about this?"

"Yes." He covered her hand with his own. "He may actually be our greatest ally. He knows what they're like and how they think. Believe me, we can trust him. After you, he just became their most wanted."

"He's so angry. Dane, I can feel it. It's frighteningly strong."

"Yes, and that kind of anger on an ordinary man would be far too unpredictable. But Graham's no ordinary man, I assure you. He can bottle that anger and use it like a bullet in more ways than you could possibly imagine."

"You're sure?"

"I've seen it. What fuels his anger has one face—and that's your enemy. Their destruction is his mission as well as his need."

"All right, everyone," yelled General Matthews from the front of the plane. "I'm afraid I'm as good-looking of a stewardess as you're going to get on this ride. Fasten your seatbelts. We're getting ready to roll."

Their seatbelts already fastened, Dane and Edeline simply sat back against their seats, leaned against each other and waited.

The plane moved slowly forward. Two fast moving military jets whizzed past them down the runway.

"Our escorts," Dane explained. "They'll be two behind us as well."

"Can this thing even land on water," Federic asked as the engines roared a little louder and the plane began picking up speed.

A few seconds later the plane tilted up, and they left the ground behind them.

"Oh, this is much worse than the portal," her father said, his knuckles white as his hands gripped the armrest.

Chapter Twenty-One

They arrived in France midafternoon the next day. Under a clear blue sky, the city of Paris spread out on both sides of the plane—ancient and new merged into one amazing metropolis. Edeline looked past Dane and across the aisle, eager to see her father's response.

His head was resting on his shoulder. His eyes were closed shut. The only thing moving was his chest, rising and falling in deep, steady motions. He'd worried himself to exhaustion several hours back but had fought against sleep for fear of missing the moment of their demise.

Edeline thought about waking him, but knew slumber would be the best place for her father as they made their approach.

Catching her glance, Father Tom gave her a thumbs-up.

She smiled and sat back, her eyes drifting to look back out at the amazing city beneath. She wondered how different it would have been back in the fourteenth century.

"It's magnificent, isn't it?" Dane leaned her way for a better view.

"Yes, very. I can't tell you how long I've dreamed of this moment. I've always wanted to come back, to stand once more in the land where I was born. I've been fascinated with France for years. I wish I knew what it was like back then, or better yet, back when my parents were young."

"If things go well, and it's deemed safe, I'd like you to stay here with me for a while, you and your father. There are things I'd like to show you, places only short hours away that meant something to you when we were here last, places that probably still mean something to your father today."

"They still stand?" Hope mixed with surprise. Her fingers played with the brooch on her blouse. He'd already salvaged for her so much, she was afraid to hope for more.

He watched her fingers twirl around the jewelry before looking back into her eyes. "Perhaps not in their best form," he said with a smile, "but there are likely remnants—certainly the land, villages that have been remarkably well preserved. France is a literal feast of ruins."

"You sound as though you've been here a lot?" Realizing it a silly question, she elaborated. "I meant in current times, not…business trips." She laughed outright, amused by the oddity of the statement.

His gaze fell to her lips. Instead of laughing with her, a solemn and somewhat sorrowful expression fell like a curtain across his face. He looked backed out the window.

"Dane, what is it?"

"There are times it's harder than others," he said, continuing to study the city.

"Harder?"

"To step back." Dark brown eyes, sincere and troubled, caught hers inside the window. "I loved you, Edeline. I love you still. You are, though you don't feel it, the same woman I held so often in my arms." He sat back in his seat and sighed.

Covering his hand with hers, she studied his somber profile. "I'm not without…feelings for you. From the first time I saw you inside the lab, I…" This time she sat back in her seat and sighed. "I feel as though I've been waiting for you a whole lifetime."

Thinking on it further, she was surprised by the depths of her feelings. "Actually it's more than that. I know it sounds corny, but I come alive when I'm with you." She looked back his way. "But I've a practical side which holds me back. This time, I need to allow *time* to catch up with me. I'm not asking you to wait for me. I'm asking you to wait with me."

Those same dark eyes seemed to penetrate clear to her soul. He turned his hand to capture hers. "I've already waited a few hundred years. What's a few more months?"

They both smiled.

No wonder she'd fallen in love with the man, he was everything she'd ever hoped for—strong, trustworthy and not afraid to give his heart completely to the woman he loved.

The plane began its descent. Dane squeezed her hand. "Edeline, you should be prepared for what we'll face."

"What we'll face?"

"General Matthews, the soldiers—they'll not be allowed to leave the plane. The protection you receive from this point forward will be different. I'm not even sure what to expect." He looked past her out the window. "We're touching down in the middle of a warzone, one where the battles and the enemy are less obvious than most. At the moment, you're right in the middle of a tug-a-war. Both sides are desperate. Both have a great deal to lose. It's unlikely everyone will play fair. The Dogs will do anything to get to you. The knights will do anything to see that they don't. Things will get ugly."

"I've already been through so much, Dane. How much worse could this possibly be?"

"It will be different," he said. "Men from both sides will likely die. You have to prepare yourself for anything. Whatever happens, you must keep going. You must do whatever it takes to stay alive. If something is to happen to me—"

"No!" Her heart skipped a beat before it started to pound heavy with the pain.

"Edeline, you need to face the possibility. *I* need to know you can handle it."

"I can't," she said, closing her eyes and pulling his hand against her middle. The groaning of the plane's wheels being lowered sounded beneath them. She looked back his way. "I'll be all right through all of this, as long as you promise you'll be there with me."

He stared at her silently a long moment, his face a visual reflection of the turmoil within. "I can't promise you that—not this time." He cupped the side of her face with his free hand. "I love you, Edeline, too much to ever again hold from you the truth."

He bent to kiss her.

The plane bounced as the wheels connected with asphalt. The loud groan of pressure fighting against the breaks rumbled through the cabin.

"What is it? What's happening?" Federic sat up straight in his seat.

Dane dropped his hold and pulled away, echoing her disappointment with one heavy sigh.

"It's all right, Federic," the priest said. "We've merely landed."

Edeline looked across the aisle to her father. "Welcome home, Daddy."

He smiled, though worry was all she could see in his eyes. "Welcome home, Edeline."

It was eerily quiet as they walked off the plane and hesitantly down the long aerobridge toward the terminal. With a carpeted walkway, not even their footsteps echoed through the tunnel's walls.

Edeline searched Dane's face for any show of concern and indeed found it leery.

"Where is everyone?" he asked no one in particular.

Father Tom shook his head, his eyes still searching the tunnel's end. "I'm not certain. I would have thought we'd have seen them by now. Don't worry. I'm certain they're here."

Leading their small party by several steps was her father. He stopped, bringing them all to a standstill. "Something's not right."

"Dane?" called General Matthews from the plane's entrance, his voice echoing the uncertainty gripping them all.

"They're here," Father Tom said with a sigh of relief. Without another word, he hurried down the jetway.

"I don't know," Federic said, obviously reluctant to step out of the tunnel and away from the safety of General Matthews and his men. His troubled eyes met hers. "Perhaps you should wait here, Edeline."

"No," Dane said, pulling her close. "At no point do I want her alone."

"I'll check things out," Graham said, stepping around the three of them to head fearlessly toward the terminal.

"That man's got a death wish," Federic mumbled as they all three nevertheless followed.

The buzz of a busy terminal rolled up the walkway to meet them, its sounds growing louder as they neared the end, defining themselves in ways which soon made them recognizable.

A tall, middle-aged man, dressed in casual attire had stepped forward to embrace Father Tom. "It's been far too long," he was saying as they approached.

Behind him, carefully scrutinizing the corridor along with Graham, stood two men wearing stoic expressions and headsets adorned with mouthpieces. Behind them all and moving in both directions, was a sea of travelers heading for various destinations, pulling with them a vast assortment of wheeled carry-ons.

A wide array of languages passed by as new swarms of travelers emerged in steady waves from every joining hall, shop and gateway. Dressed in business attire, blue jeans and occasionally even top-Paris fashions, they scurried by, uninterested in the huddled group congregating at the tunnel's end.

Edeline wasn't sure what she'd been expecting, but the normality of it all wasn't it.

"Everyone," Father Tom said, pulling her attention back to their small group. "Real briefly, I'd like you all to meet Cole Babin. He's the son of one of my dearest friends. He…and the others are going to be seeing us through the airport. We'll make time for formal introductions later."

"Ah…the others?" she asked out loud before mentally counting two. If these were the only others, she'd prefer they take a withdrawal from the plane behind them.

"There are more," Dane said, searching the terminal ahead as though some bionic eye was spotting what she couldn't.

If there were more, she'd have liked to have seen their faces. Having lived all the daring she cared to back at the mansion, she no longer dreaded security, she welcomed it…lots and lots of it. Cole and his two sidekicks, though seemingly hardy, were hardly her idea of coverage.

"Everyone ready?" Father Tom asked.

She looked to Dane, then her father, and even toward Graham. *Isn't someone going to say something…maybe like "No!"* But the men surrounding her seemed to be paying no attention to her at all. Each had shifted gears into what she could easily see was their offensive.

They moved forward, Father Tom and Cole taking the lead, while Dane and her father both guarded her sides. Graham, looking every inch the fierce-soldier, fell back to take the rear, his eyes, like Dane's and her father's, continuously scanning every inch of the terminal—every corner, every door, every stand and every crevice. Taking separate sides of the entourage, Cole's two men did the same, only they spoke nonstop into their mouthpieces.

"Father," a young man greeted Father Tom as he walked closely by their group. Not one of her chaperones seemed particularly interested in him. It was surprising, considering the man was built like a linebacker. He could have easily at least made a dent in their armor had he made an attempt.

Perhaps she was simply making too much out of everything. Nerves—they were the culprit, they or the lack thereof. The last few days had nearly been her undoing. All nerves remaining had been plenty frazzled.

What she needed was to get a grip. In truth, peril simply didn't fit with this everyday terminal scene. Danger didn't appear to be lurking, it was only paranoia, her own included, which was running wild.

Nothing seemed out of place. In fact, it was just like in the movies—bright lights above various fast food courts and gift shops decorated the walkway like a walk down Las Vegas Boulevard. Seating areas, check-in booths, large glass windows, and walls lined with vending machines and Wi-Fi ports were all crowded with a large assortment of customers. None of them seemed even remotely interested in her or any other member of their group.

Edeline tried to relax. She'd always enjoyed watching others and wondering who they were, where they were going and exactly what made up their lives. The terminal offered a virtual smorgasbord of people to watch and test her imaginings.

They were all fascinating enough.

Take the well-dressed man sitting beside the newspaper kiosk. By all appearances he had the world at his feet. What was he reading—the stock market, news of mergers and acquisitions? Not entirely absorbed in the paper he was reading, his glance kept drifting over its top, searching the crowds. Perhaps by finding his success, he'd lost something else. Was he searching for it here? Did he search for it everywhere?

Standing on a chair beside her mother, a little girl bounced up and down, smiling at those who passed, stealing their hearts while sending them off with a sweet smile.

Edeline grinned and went to glance away, but her eyes were stopped by the cold, dark glare of the man sitting on the seat straight across from the child. His eyes reminded her far too vividly of another very cold, very hollow set of eyes, eyes which had been entirely immune to the cries of a child, eyes which could have watched without sorrow the child's death.

She stumbled over her own two feet, nearly falling to the ground before Dane's strong hands reached out to correct her.

"Look," she said, her gaze and her finger shooting back to the seat where the man had been.

Empty. He had gone.

The child across from him continued to bounce, giggling and cooing without a care in the world.

"She's adorable, Edeline, but you need to stay focused. Watch your footing, not the children."

"But—" She sighed.

His attention had already been diverted to the task at hand.

Another quick search of the area found the man truly gone. How had he moved so quickly? Where had he gone? It could have been nothing but her overactive imagination. There was every possibility he was merely studying the electronic boards which hung above her head.

Yes, that was probably it, and his flight had most likely arrived. The man was no more watching her than the two men working the vending machines over to her left. They too seemed somewhat distracted, not by her but by the crowds around them. They were fascinated with people, because people were fascinating. Hadn't she just been thinking that herself?

The hairs at the back of her neck stood on ends. She could feel them—actually feel them—the prickly little strands. But that wasn't all she was feeling. She could also feel the eyes. They were everywhere, but nowhere to be seen.

Everything's fine…just fine.

Nausea rose high in her middle.

Nearing the end of the first corridor, they moved into the center of the exiting crowd.

A tall man with long, silver hair pulled back in a ponytail, pushed along a loaded waste-barrel headed the opposite direction. Something about him seemed familiar as well as oddly out of place. A coincidence, certainly, as the man paid them no mind at all.

Federic nodded toward the glass corridor overhead where people waited and watched for the new arrivals. "You watching?" he asked Dane.

"Don't worry," Cole said. "We've got it well covered."

Edeline eyed the glass walkway. Though she didn't see any sign of coverage, nothing appeared out of place. A quick glance to Dane showed him watching it nonetheless.

Up ahead, standing only a couple feet outside the security gates, another priest anxiously watched their arrival. With him, a half-dozen men dressed identically to Cole's two guards, stood carefully watching all those nearby.

"Who is he?" Dane asked.

"Father Richard," answered Father Tom before stepping past security and straight into the man's waiting arms.

Father Richard. She'd heard the name. He was to be her replacement.

"Oh, how I've missed you," the priest said, stepping back to studying Father Tom. "We've grown old, my friend."

Father Tom chuckled. "Twenty-two years is a very long time."

"That it is. Elliot's been simply beside himself. Have you seen him yet?"

"In passing."

"Who's Elliot," Edeline whispered to her father.

"You've met him. He's Father Tom's baby brother." He looked over her shoulder as though expecting to see him appear. "He's visited the parish a couple times through these years. We passed him a while back."

It came to her immediately.

"I knew he looked familiar," Edeline said, remembering the silver-haired man. It had been probably ten years since Elliot had last visited LA. Turning to search the terminal with her father, she asked the obvious question. "Why was he pushing a dumpster?"

"It's his job."

"He's a janitor?"

Federic laughed, bringing her into his arms and kissing her forehead. "He's a knight, Edeline, as was the man sitting beside the kiosk reading the newspaper and the two gentlemen working the vending machines. So was the young man who passed and greeted Father

Tom. And that man over there," he said, pointing to a man sitting on one of the benches outside the security checkpoint, watching the crowds as he tied his shoes.

"There were also several who passed us as travelers," Dane added, still diligently watching their surroundings. "I counted no less than twelve."

"Twelve! You mean to tell me you both know these men?"

"No," Federic said, now rushing her past security, "but we recognize them."

"Recognize them? But how, if you've—"

The men once guarding the priest now fell back to surround her. Her eyes swung to them in surprise. "What are they doing?"

"Also their jobs," Dane said, hastening her along as the now larger group made for the exit.

"Wait! What about our bags?"

"Taken care of," Elliot said, suddenly standing beside her father. The gray-pinstriped overalls he'd been wearing were gone and in their place he wore jeans, a T-shirt and headpiece resembling all the others.

He was a knight. Thinking back to the limited memories she had of the man, she wasn't all that surprised. There had always been an air about him, a sense of righteousness, a feeling that he was destined for something more amazing than normality.

Looking around the group, she realized they all carried that presence—one of nobility and fortitude. They were an intimidating group, the men who now surrounded her—so many stoic looking men moving together in a swarm of determination. They spoke very little, but held guard with a diligence which relayed neither fear nor uncertainty. They would be formidable against any threat which was out there.

No wonder Dane and her father had recognized them. They easily stood out with no effort at all.

The group stopped right in front of the exit.

"We'll wait here for the cars," Elliot said, reaching past Edeline to pat his brother's shoulder. "Thomas, my brother, I am glad you are here."

While the two men exchanged a brief greeting, Edeline turned to Dane. "Why the disguises? Why didn't they simply come forward from the start?"

Dane turned her to look behind them. "That's why," he said, pointing to where three men, all handcuffed, were being escorted down the passage by an odd assortment of men dressed as airport personnel.

One face among the prisoners stood out in particular. It was the man who'd been sitting across from the child.

"Are they…?"

"Dogs? That would be my guess."

Her stomach turned an impressive round of flips. How had they known she'd be here? What had they done to get caught? Why, exactly, were they here?

Catching her obvious distress, Dane leaned forward. "I'll find out more," he promised.

"They're here," said Cole, turning back from the window near the exit and waving them forward.

Still laughing at something his brother had said, Elliot looked up just as Cole headed for the doors. "Cole, have Andre check that tour bus."

Cole turned back to the window, lifting his phone just as the double-decker, red and green tour bus darted out from behind their long line of Suburbans.

"Everyone, down," Elliot screamed, right as Dane pushed Edeline to the ground and then fell to cover her like a shield.

Federic hit the floor right beside her, reaching out and taking her hand right as the first round of bullets descended, shattering glass and sending countless shreds of destruction into the air.

Screams echoed between walls as bystanders scattered and security guards shouted for the knights to drop their weapons. Orders which soon changed to encouragement as the next round of bullets flew into the room.

"They're stopping right outside the doors," one of the knights near the entrance warned.

All around the room, she could hear guns preparing.

"Cover your heads," Graham yelled, walking right past Edeline and Dane and directly toward the gunfire. Kneeling down beside one of the fallen guards, he grabbed his gun and took aim.

"Federic," Dane said, "wait until we start firing, then take Edeline and make a run for that kiosk." He pointed.

"Done," Federic said, still holding tight to her hand.

Elliot handed Dane a gun and together they moved to kneel beside the others.

"Fire," Elliot ordered, and shots rang from the room.

Bolting to their feet, Edeline and Federic darted to the kiosk to slide behind its cover.

Behind them shots were flying like pellets from a hailstorm. Screams and cries could be heard through the chaos, echoing her fears as she peeked back around the stall to look for Father Tom.

A sorrowful cry, born in the very depths of her soul, tore from her throat. The unthinkable lay directly in her view. Bodies, lying scattered across the room, still moved with the jolts of shrapnel which danced with the broken glass atop the foyer's floor.

Men, covered in blood, still knelt on their knees returning fire and dodging bullets.

Refusing to search the dead, Edeline search the faces of the living, looking for those she knew — Elliot, Graham, Cole and…finally, there he was…Dane.

But where were Father Tom and Father Richard?

"Edeline, get back," Federic said, pulling her back behind the metal stall.

"Everybody back," someone screamed from the lobby.

Federic wrapped his arms around her and held on tight.

A huge explosion roared from outside, spitting a fierce wind along with new pieces of debris in through the broken windows. The metal stall giving them cover groaned and lifted partially from its bolts, but thankfully never gave.

"Dane!"

Federic held her still when she would have ran without thought. Visions of the scene lying behind the stall flashed through her head. Holding tight to her father, she buried her face in his chest and prayed for a miracle.

As the debris from the explosion settled around them, silence filled the once tumultuous air. Slowly the sound of movement emerged from the other side of the kiosk. She looked to her father, both uncertain and afraid.

Shaking his head, he motioned for her to be still.

Footsteps, heading their way, crunched across broken glass.

Grabbing hold of a cloth which had fallen from the stall, Federic wrapped it around the palm of his hand and then took hold a sharp piece of glass.

They waited.

"Federic? Edeline?"

"Father Tom!" Relief flooded through her so powerfully she shook.

The priest rounded the corner as they made it to their feet. "Are you both all right?"

"We are," Federic said, wrapping his arms around his friend. "You're a sight for worried eyes. Does this mean it's over?"

"It's over. The explosion you heard was the tour bus. One of Elliot's men from the caravan was able to escape and plant an explosive."

"Did any live?"

"Of theirs, very few."

"And ours?"

The priest looked toward Edeline, hesitating a painful moment. "We took a brutal hit. You should prepare yourselves for what you'll see."

Sirens blared from every direction as their silver SUV merged with the traffic heading west. The men around her took up the same vigilance as they had walking her through the airport terminals — focused, determined. But Edeline simply sat quiet — troubled and once again numb to the threat which lingered all around. Nothing seemed real anymore. It felt more like a dream — a confusing, terrifying nightmare.

"Why didn't they question us?" her father asked, sitting in the front passenger seat beside Elliot as they flew toward the country and away from the gruesome scene.

"We have friends in high places," Elliot said, in way of explanation. Checking his rearview mirror, he then merged to follow the tan SUV currently serving as lead. "They actually knew there could be trouble, but for the sake of appearance, had to stand clear."

"Stand clear?" Edeline repeated, shocked out of her silence. "How could they stand by and simply do nothing? Innocent people were killed. If your *friends* knew it would happen, then why didn't they stop it?"

Compassionate blue eyes looked back at her through the rearview mirror. "No innocents died today, Edeline, only those who knew the risks and found them worthy."

Dane squeezed her hand. "Edeline, they're not to blame…and neither are you," he added, once again reading her far better than she'd imagined.

"He's right," Elliot said. "Despite all appearance, this really has very little to do with you."

"This is my fault," Graham said, shocking them all. Sitting at her left, diligently keeping guard; the man had, for the most part, remained notably silent.

Suddenly angry, Dane looked past Edeline to Graham. "I saw you today. You fought like a man searching for a bullet. If this is a suicide mission, stay the hell away from Edeline."

"I would never let anything happen to Edeline. I'm simply trying to make a wrong I've done her right." He took a deep breath, turning back toward the window. "I'm a bastard and a heathen, damned by the very men I handed the stone."

"This isn't a new war, Graham," Father Tom said from the seat behind them. "It's been raging for centuries. You are merely one of a thousand pawns, neither necessary nor responsible for their ambitions or their deeds."

"I handed them the stone. I laid it right into their hands."

"Quit giving yourself so much credit," Dane said. "If you hadn't done it, they'd have found another."

"True enough," said Elliot. "They can always find a weakness."

"Well, they certainly found mine."

"You were human," Dane said. "Torture's been around so long for one very good reason. It works. And I'd wager the Dogs know how to use it better than any. I wouldn't have wanted to trade you places."

"You wouldn't have cowered."

"No one knows what they'd do for sure in such a situation. One thing I do know, however, is that when we've needed you, when it's really mattered, you've put it all on the line to do what was right. That's not a coward."

Both Elliot and Federic chorused Dane's view.

Graham nodded halfheartedly. "I'm not sure how much help I'll be this round. They're stronger here, fiercer and there's a lot more of them. I won't know them all. I couldn't possibly."

"You'll do your best," Elliot said. "That's all we ask."

"I'm no longer afraid of dying."

"No," Dane said. "I know you're not, and that's what concerns me most. This is likely to become more a game of intellect than might. There will be no room for retribution or atonement."

"It was a bold attack they launched today," Federic said, still diligently watching the roads. "If they'd take such a risk in a public place, what will they do to stop us at the caves?"

"Anything," Graham said. "They'll do anything."

Glancing toward Elliot, Federic asked, "Can we handle them?"

"We're a huge force numbering in the thousands. We have wealth, power and courage in abundance, but it was luck that got us through today. Despite our best laid plans and even with surveillance, they still got through."

"Of course, we never considered they'd make such a brazen frontal attack," Father Richard said, sitting in the back seat beside Father Tom.

Elliot nodded. "In that, we were careless. We forgot how much they wanted this. It's a mistake we won't make twice."

"You're forgetting our greatest asset, my brother," Father Tom said.

Through the rearview mirror, Elliot looked back toward the priest with lifted brow.

"We have God," said Father Richard. "It wasn't luck, Elliot, which saw us through. It was the Lord's grace."

Elliot smiled. "How foolish I feel."

Chapter Twenty-Two

The two-hour drive from Paris to the northern shores of France was in no way relaxing, but at least the scenery offered a visual escape from the daunting reality that placed them there. An enchanting decoupage of woodlands and pasture, cities and villages, created a captivating distraction. It was an incredible world where history was held within the palm of a modern civilization.

Once again, Edeline wondered what it would have been like all those years ago. She mourned it, and she mourned for those whom she would have loved who were now buried beneath its soil.

Taking her hand in his, Dane seemed to sense her sadness.

There was a comfort in his touch which always brought her peace. She smiled. "It's truly beautiful here. Does any of it look the same?"

Following her gaze back out the window, he shrugged his shoulders. "Pieces, here and there, resemble things I've seen. But this was never a path I traveled. Most of the time, we stayed well hidden within the forests, studying the inhabitants and their lives from afar."

"Until I came along," she reminded.

"Yes, until you came along," he acknowledged with a grin. "You took me directly into their midst. I may have brought you home to my world, but you first introduced me to yours. The memories are my favorite, second only to one." The look in his eyes told her clearly she was that one.

Despite the unease of a life in chaos, for that moment she felt nothing but happiness.

"Tell me we'll be all right, Dane. Tell me we'll have the chance to build more memories together. Ones we can both remember and treasure. Tell me, and I'll believe you."

He held her hopeful stare for several long seconds. "You know I can't promise you, but I do believe it's true." Lifting his hand, he caressed her cheek. "Our fate doesn't lie in the hands of the men who pursue us. Our fate lies in the hands of those who stand in their way. The shield has the last say in any battle, and there is no stronger shield than the one which has us covered."

"He's right," Graham said. "The knights have the advantage of spirit. Those who serve the Dark Army are only haunted by memories of such. Though some still hold souls as dark as the world they strive for, most have simply succumbed to the madness which holds their reins. Their souls have been imprisoned by the darkness, given no hope and no choice but to obey."

Graham nodded toward the front seats. "That's not true of the Knights Templar. They are what they are because of what they believe. They give everything and ask for nothing. They simply give and give without regret. Their souls are not bartered, but their hearts are pledged. They believe that what they fight for is bigger than themselves."

"And they will succeed," Dane added, "because for them, there really is no other option."

"This is it," Elliot said, pulling the SUV to a stop in front of a heavily guarded gate.

Federic sat up in his seat, looking from his left to his right. "Is this…?" He turned a bewildered look to Elliot. "It is, isn't it? It's the road to the Castle Brines."

Elliot simply nodded before rolling down his window and exchanging a few words with the guards.

"Amazing," Federic muttered. "I can't believe she still stands."

"I do believe she's had her fair share of cosmetic surgery through the years," Father Richard said, "but yes, she does indeed still stand."

The gates opened, and their small caravan rolled through.

"This is where it all began," Federic said to Edeline. "It was from here we rode to the cliffs and into the lives we have today."

Tall, stately looking poplars lined the drive to the castle. Though yet unseen, peaks of the fortress's grandeur could be spotted in the near distance, rising high above the tips of the regal trees. Edeline leaned forward, laying her hand on Federic's shoulder.

His hand covered hers. A second later their path took a turn and opened up into a wide drive sitting in front of a scene from a fairy tale.

Edeline gasped. "It's beautiful."

Huge, round towers boxed in a castle made of stone, rising high into the air, a beautiful testament to man's early abilities. Small peep-holes appearing sporadically at different levels served as windows. Even color was used to an advantage—shades of red topping simple gray stone, creating an appealing contrast.

Federic patted her hand and then reached for the door's handle.

"Wait," Elliot warned, opening his own door first and stepping out onto the drive. Once again he exchanged words with security and then ducked back inside. "It's safe. Feel free to step out."

Soon they were all standing upon the immaculately manicured grounds, spinning circles, trying to capture the full extent of its magnificence.

Federic nodded his head in approval. "I'd say she's had her fair share of work, but the heart of her still stands."

"We've tried to preserve her the best we could through these many years," Elliot said. "She was pretty well destroyed through the pillaging which followed the fall of the Knights Templar. Many believed the treasures once held by the knights were buried somewhere within her walls."

"Destroying one treasure for another," Edeline said. "Only to find they were wrong all along."

"They *were* wrong," Elliot agreed with a mischievous smile. "The treasure never did lie within her belly."

"Of course not," Federic said, grunting his irritation at such a foolish notion.

"The knights would never have been so careless," Elliot said, "though the scavengers weren't really that far off."

Federic's head whipped toward the man at his side. "Meaning?"

"The treasure was here long before the castle. In fact, the castle was built to guard it—not in its walls, but beneath its floors."

"I lived here for years. There was nothing beneath her but dirt."

Elliot nodded. "And under the dirt were tunnels, an intricate web of tunnels. We think at one time they may have been accessible through the castle. That's not true today. You must enter through the caves beneath the cliffs."

"The treasure is still there?" Edeline asked.

"She's still there, untouched for hundreds of years, buried deep within a cave that will not open without a key," he said, smiling toward Edeline. "We have been waiting anxiously to see what lies within. Much sacrifice has been made to protect it, even more to obtain it. With so many years gone by and so much uncertainty around it, it's time we see exactly what *it* is we protect.

"It's also time we change the guardian and protect the stone. If they know its location—and I believe it's safe now to assume they do—then these are the only two keys our enemies must obtain. We need to take measures to ensure that they don't.

"When we're done here, a new guardian will be chosen, one whose identity will be as guarded as the stone, a stone which will then be moved and guarded by men who know and understand its true value."

"Why did you wait? Why didn't you bring me here before?"

"It would have done us no good without the stone. And the powers that held the stone feared only its threat to time. They would not release it, not while the portal was still active."

"They still haven't released it nor do they intend to," Dane said. "The fake is still locked safe and secure inside a vault. Only General Matthews and Professor Blaine know we have the real stone. Oddly enough, it's probably a good thing it was taken."

Shifting his weight to look Dane's direction, Graham's brows pulled as though doubtful. "Are you saying there was some good that came from what I did?"

Dane hesitated before nodding. "Yes. It was a bumpy trip getting here, but the stone is back where it belongs."

A warm breeze slapped sharply against the shimmering waters below, whipping up an ocean spray which released its scent before diving back into the vast blue pool. Scattered gulls squawked from their multiple perches along the rocks below as their white-bellied companions flew by wailing in response.

Standing at the cliff's edge, Dane closed his eyes and inhaled the fresh saltwater air.

It was the peace before the storm, and a storm was certainly coming. In the distance, dark clouds rolled slowly their way. Much like that day centuries ago, when he and Edeline had rode with the knights toward these very cliffs.

Though it seemed a lifetime ago, it had really only been weeks. Those last few hours still haunted him. Not only because his choices had been so hard, but also because it was the last time he'd really felt she was his. Despite her earlier words of reassurance, he knew their bond had not yet reached that which they had shared back in time. He missed her, or more precisely, he missed what they had been.

"A penny for your thoughts," said a soft voice at his side.

With a smile that came so easily in her presence, he turned. "A penny? Is that the best you can do?"

Laughing and shrugging her shoulders, she confessed, "Sadly, at the moment, I doubt I could even do that."

Reaching out his hands, he took hers captive. "Then we will have to barter. Shall we say a kiss?"

She reached up on her toes and kissed his cheek.

His lips were still poised as she pulled away. He scowled. "That will only buy you a small portion of my thoughts."

"Then I will have to make a larger purchase when my guardians are not present."

They both turned their heads back toward the path leading to the mansion. Federic and Father Tom quickly looked away.

"This feels oddly familiar," Dane said, remembering the night they had shared outside the cottage.

"Did you really think they'd let me come this far without protection?"

"I should have realized." Though the cliffs, like the yards, were well guarded and secure, the men behind them were no different than he. With Edeline, they would take no chances.

Linking her arm with his, she leaned in against him. "I've been here before."

He bent his head to rest against the soft blond curls at his side. "Are you sure this is the place you remember? You were awfully young when you last stayed at the castle?"

"I don't mean as a child. And I wasn't exactly here," she said, pointing to the cliffs further north. "I was there."

Dane followed her finger to the cliffs from which they'd jumped, and by "they" he meant him and the future Edeline. The present day Edeline hadn't been there.

"Edeline, how can that possibly be?"

She looked up and blinked. "It was a dream I had when I was being held at the mansion. But in my dream there was a forest right behind it."

He doubted strongly it was merely a dream. Choosing to ignore, at least for now, the unease which settled in his stomach, he pointed toward the northern ridge. "There was once a forest which ran right behind it. It's where we hid that night."

Edeline shivered. "In my dream, it was frightening."

Dane couldn't help but grin. "In my experience, it was the same."

"Perhaps it's best that it's gone," she said, looking back to the sea.

He followed her gaze back out toward the ocean. Its endless waters stretched far into the horizon, broken only by its sparkling waves and a few distant vessels. "Tell me about the dream."

"There wasn't much more to it. I was in the forest, I could hear voices behind me, but what called to me came from the cliffs. It was a woman's voice. She called me clear to the edge. I believe she wanted me to follow her into the sea."

"Into the sea!"

Edeline laughed at his look of concern. Squeezing his arm tight, she quickly reassured him. "I don't believe her intent was to harm me, though I'm not entirely sure what she was after."

"It was a vision."

"Yes, I believe it was."

"You've never had them before the mansion?"

"No, never."

He took a deep breath. "I was told your uncle was a man of vision. He had the gift long before he took custody of the stone. By the way they spoke of him—he must have been an incredible man." Leaning down, he kissed the top of her head. "Not so unlike his niece."

"I fear you give me too much credit. I'm merely a girl with a stone that works as some kind of magical key. I was not specially selected because of any remarkable traits. I was selected because I fit the bill and was there."

"It's not the stone which makes you special, Edeline. It's your soul. With or without the stone, you are a beautiful woman inside and out. You have a giving heart, true compassion and a strength which might surprise even you." He took her face in his hands and smiled. "Make me a promise."

She covered his hands with hers. "What kind of promise?"

"Promise me you won't follow any visions off a cliff."

Edeline wandered the long hall admiring the many paintings adorning its walls. Replicating work from the fourteenth-century renaissance period; most were depictions of faith, hope and promise.

"They're beautiful, aren't they?" Father Richard asked, walking down the hall her way. "I've always been particularly partial to the period."

"I'm partial to it myself, and these really are quite captivating. It's as if there's more to the picture than what is visually present in the scene." Edeline shook her head and laughed. "That sounds pretty silly, doesn't it?"

Stopping beside her, he studied the portrait. "Not at all. They speak of love. Love's an emotion that takes us beyond canvas and oil."

"Yes, I believe that's it." Edeline turned from the portrait to face the priest. "I get the feeling this isn't the first time you've seen them. Have you been here before?"

"Oh, yes, several times through the years—usually for business, but occasionally for pleasure. I find the castle enchanting and the area charming."

"It is. If it weren't for the circumstances, I'd feel like a princess in a fairy tale." She looked once more up and down the hall. "I'm curious—how did the Knights Templar manage to keep the castle for so many years?"

The priest grinned. "You forget, Edeline, the Knights Templar does not exist and hasn't, to the world's knowledge, for many centuries."

"Yes, but we both know that's not true."

"No, it's not true. It never was. In truth, it was both arrogant and naïve to assume such an order could be so easily dismissed and dissolved. The Knights Templar, even then, was a huge order, numbering in the thousands and filled with men built of strength and devotion. Of course they didn't crumble and fall. They simply reorganized and refocused their efforts on their original plight — service to the Lord."

"How did they regain the castle?"

"Most believed the order had, indeed, fallen. The castle, like many of the order's properties, was pillaged and nearly destroyed by those looking for the treasure. Knowing the treasure would never be found, we stayed away for many years, allowing the castle to fall near to ruins. It wasn't until the fifteenth century we dared return."

"And took claim?"

"Sir Michael Barton purchased the castle under the guise of an investment. No one ever knew of his relationship to the Knights Templar. Similar transactions have transpired through the years, moving the title from one household to another and keeping the castle from falling under suspicion.

"We are more than what you see here, Edeline. Our numbers are many, our members quite powerful. There isn't a lot we can't manage."

"How do you know the Dogs know the treasure is here?"

"They at least realize it's near, or there would have been no reason for them to take you back to fourteenth century France, nor would they have made such a desperate and brazen attempt to get to you at the airport. They know it's here, and they know why we're taking you to it."

"How do you think they found out?"

"The Knights Templar is thick in France. I imagine it was not so very difficult for them to figure it out. Over the last twenty-two years, we've been particularly strong here in this region."

"Twenty-two years?"

"Yes, we tightened our guard when we learned of your existence."

"Why?"

"Even a locked door needs security when the key is dangling near."

"Will they try and attack?"

Taking her hand, the priest wrapped it through his arm. "I'm surprised we haven't seen them already," he said, walking her back down the corridor.

Edeline swallowed. "You say it so calmly. Doesn't it scare you?"

"We won't lose, Edeline." He patted her hand. "It simply cannot be."

"How can you be so sure?"

"How can I not?" He stopped and swept his hand back toward the portraits so beautifully portraying the truth of God's love. The man had amazing faith.

"I wish I knew for sure it would work so easily for me. I fear this may be my life forever, with or without the power."

He stopped and turned to her, his eyes warm and full of compassion. "I understand why you'd feel that way. You've been through a lot, one terrifying ordeal after another. But I believe you will have your life back. Not only will the Dogs realize there's no longer any point in taking or harming you, but they're also about to have their priorities shifted.

"When this is over and the treasure secure, the Dogs will be on the run and not only from us, but also their own. We've taken too many alive who are bound to talk. Those of high-ranking will move quickly to silence those beneath who know their names and ties to the Dark Army. It will take years for an organization like theirs to rebuild the strength and power they have today."

She closed her eyes and imagined the life she'd once had, and then imagined it with Dane. She smiled and opened her eyes. "I hope you're right. I hope…" She looked back to the pictures. "I hope you're right about all of it."

Rushed steps sounded from the stairwell near the great hall.

Exchanging a brief glance, Edeline and Father Richard picked up their pace to hurry down the passageway. Neither wanted to miss hearing whatever news was in route.

Two messengers emerged from the steps and into the corridor only a couple long strides ahead of them. By the looks on their faces, the news wasn't good.

Looking past them and into the room, Edeline noted the men were still all huddled around the large table near the west corner, looking over old maps of the caves.

The two new arrivals stopped just inside the doors. "The caves have been infiltrated and the entrance sealed," the older of the two men announced.

Every head turned, looking their way.

Elliot split from the huddle to walk their way. "How?"

"From inside."

"From inside?" Father Richard repeated, looking past the men at the door to the men inside the room. "How can that be? We've had the entrance well secured."

"It wasn't our entrance they used," said the younger of the two messengers. "They found another entrance."

"There is no other entrance," Cole said. "We've searched high and low. There is but the one."

Raking his fingers roughly through his hair, Elliot sighed. "Yes, but we always knew we could build one. We just weren't willing to take the chance and risk losing or harming any part of the chamber."

"A concern they wouldn't share," Dane said, stepping up beside Elliot.

"I believe it's safe to assume that's what they've done." Elliot let his hand drop to his side. "What we need to find out is how and from where? They wouldn't use anything too powerful for fear of being caught, and anything less than explosives would take months, maybe years."

"They've certainly proven their patience," Dane said, stepping around the men at the door and heading toward Edeline. Taking her hand in his, he squeezed it reassuringly. "I'm guessing they're waiting for us to find the entrance and join them."

"They wouldn't bury themselves in the caves unless they were sure they could get out," Elliot said. Turning his back to them, he walked back into the room and across to the window. Placing his hands against the walls at its sides, he leaned forward, peering out into the yards. "They're waiting for us, all right, and whatever they've got planned, they believe it's infallible."

A couple hours later, Dane stood in front of the same window staring at the distant cliffs and wondering what kind of hell hid beneath their unbreakable cover. The knights would be expected, and the Lord only knew exactly what that meant.

All they knew for sure was that a frontal assault was absolutely out of the question. There would be marksmen and traps covering the man-made entrance. The route offered only one certainty—slaughter.

The advantage had shifted and their opponents had the lead. They held the only access. They had plenty of time to plan. Worst of all, they had nothing to lose.

If the knights couldn't find a way to break through unseen, then they'd have to wait. What choice would they have? Explosives weren't an option. No one wanted to injure the chamber or do damage to the caves. Someone had suggested gas, but the choice was too obvious. The Dogs would have thought of it as well and adequately prepared. Waiting seemed their only option, and unfortunately, that would bring its own bucket of risks.

He looked back toward the long leather couch where Edeline lay facing the hearth. She was trying her best to fight off the sleep she so desperately needed. Her chest rose and fell slowly as her lids bounced up and down. It wouldn't be long, and the choice would be stolen.

A sharp wind blew against the castle's stone walls, howling its dissatisfaction at having its path disrupted. It caught Dane's attention and pulled his thoughts back to the night in the woods when five men had risked their lives to save the woman he loved. He wondered, not for the first time, what had become of his friends. Searching the well-guarded yards outside, he half-expected the brave warriors to appear.

"My eyes are starting to blur," Federic said from across the room.

Dane turned back to the table where the men still stood studying the maps hoping for a stroke of genius to give them a way in.

Graham tapped his finger against one of the maps and looked up. "Are we certain these are good?"

"They're precise," Elliot assured. "We've had our experts look at them several times. If there's an easy way in, they never found one. The caves are all deep, their walls as solid as they come. Any quick way in would likely jeopardize the structure, and in this case, announce our arrival."

Graham's hands swept the maps lying across the table. "If we can just get inside, there are several paths we can choose from—paths they wouldn't have adequately covered."

Dane looked to Elliot. "You said at one time there was access through the castle."

"There were rumors," Elliot said, "most likely speculation. If there ever was such an entrance, we've never found it, and believe me—we've searched every corner, every crevice." He shrugged his shoulders. "Nothing."

"We can't waste time looking for hidden passages that may have never been," Graham said, already focusing back on the maps. "What we need to do is find a weak spot we can break through and send in a reconnaissance team to find out what they're up to."

Elliot glanced back up toward Dane. "I agree. There's been much renovation through the years. If an entrance was there, it's more likely than not that we would have found it."

Federic grunted. "So much has changed. So much has been covered. The stone floors which run throughout the first story were once nothing but beaten dirt." He looked up toward the plastered walls. "And those were merely stone and mortar. If there was an entrance from the castle, it's most likely been buried."

"I can't disagree," Dane said. "Still, I don't think it hurts to consider it."

Still leaning across the table studying the cave's paths which lay far beneath the castle, Father Tom righted himself to standing. Moving his hands to rub his lower back, he stretched. "I could stand an excuse to move around a bit. We could go take a look. Have you any idea where to start?"

Dane gave it some thought and looked toward Federic. "Who in the castle would've been trusted with such information? Where was their chamber?"

Federic exchanged a fleeting glance with Father Tom.

"The priests," both men chorused.

"Their chamber sat right below the chapel," Federic said.

"Which would be another likely place to consider," Father Richard suggested.

Edeline sat up on the couch, pushing back the quilt Federic had placed over her when she'd first lain down. "I'll help," she said, her lids still drooping.

Moving across to the sofa, Dane bent to his knees. "Edeline, you're exhausted. You should try and sleep."

"I'm fine, really." Those same heavy lids fell across tired blue eyes. Covering her mouth, she yawned.

Fluffing the pillow beside her, he motioned for her to lie back down. "No arguing. You need your sleep."

She yawned again and lay back down. "I really am tired."

Leaning forward, he kissed her brow. "Sweet dreams, my love."

"My love," she repeated, a faint smile touching her lips. A second later she was lost to sleep.

"My love."

The endearment wrapped itself around her, filling her with joy as it soothed her nerves and carried her into peaceful sleep.

"My love."

It echoed through her mind and into her dreams. She was so blessed, so loved, so lucky to be cherished by these many wonderful men.

A hand touched her face.

"My love," the words played back in feminine tones.

Edeline smiled, remembering the soft, gentle voice from her time at the mansion.

"Come with me," it called to her, and without hesitation, she went.

Down the spiraling steps and out the castle's doors, she followed. The path moving faster than her feet, she seemed to simply glide across the grass and down the rugged cliffs.

The ocean's peaceful melody played all around her — restful, lapping waves rolling into sand. A warm breeze lifted her curls and tossed them behind her. Throwing out her arms, she met the wind on a run, the sand cushioning her steps before suddenly disappearing. Wind whipped through her toes, and she looked down to find herself flying.

Free of all chains, her load was carried by faith.

There was no fear, only peace surrounded her. No voices taunted. No chants rocked the earth. In her heart, she knew she was protected — loved by those who surrounded her, both the living and the dead. The earth was her home, but so were the heavens.

Flying high above fields, over farms, past small villas, she took in their splendor and inhaled their sweet scents. The hills turned into a meadow, the meadow into a field. Horses' hooves beat the ground as men stormed across the land. There was beauty in the moment and upon the faces of the men. They rode not for glory, yet glory echoed in their wake.

The thundering hooves turned to the quaking of leaves as the field turned back into rolling hills and the rolling hills into rolling seas. Now the smell as well as the sound of the ocean surrounded her.

Suddenly she realized she was not truly alone. The woman from the cliffs had been at her side. As the mirror image of her own blue eyes looked directly back at her, a love that she had before only imagined filled Edeline's heart and warmed her soul. This was her mother.

Taking the woman's hand in hers, she flew toward the rugged cliffs, soaring like an eagle over their mighty peaks before dipping down toward the sparkling sands below. The sands turned to rocks and the hillsides to stone. In the very next instant, they were inside a cave. A wild wind whipped around them as shadows of men and beasts flew beside them on the stone walls. Cries, captured in the wind, were echoed throughout the passage.

Her mother led her through a broken crevice and into a small passage within the stone walls. Lower and lower they descended down a spiraling stone corridor, deep into the belly of the cavern. They entered a room Edeline felt more than saw. Together they flew circles around it. What sounded like hundreds of voices began circling with them, each with a story begging to be told.

In the next instant they flew out of the room and back into the passage. Toward the end of the corridor, the woman led Edeline up and into the shadows of the ceiling. The passage began to rumble, the stone above them started to fall. Instead of stopping, the woman flew directly through the falling rock and into a large chamber where the three men most vital to Edeline's mortal world stood staring at the walls.

Edeline woke with a start.

Pushing away the large quilt wrapped tightly around her, she stood and scanned the room trying to get her bearings. Several confused faces stared at her from across the room.

Father Richard moved her direction. "Edeline, is everything all right?"

"I—I believe so." With her heart still soaring, she found she wasn't sure. "My father—where is he?"

"I do believe Federic is right," Father Tom said, standing in the middle of what was now the library but had once been the priests' chambers. "If there was an entrance here, it's long been buried."

Following the priest's gaze around the room, Dane found he could only agree. "We'd have to rip the walls and floor completely apart to know for sure."

"It's under the hearth."

They all three turned toward the entrance where Edeline now stood with Elliot and Graham directly behind her.

"The hearth?" Father Tom repeated before looking around the room. "What hearth?"

"There was a hearth," Edeline said, pointing to the far left corner. "It was over there."

"How did you know that?" Federic asked, staring at the now empty corner.

"I saw it in a dream."

Scratching his head, Federic continued to look suspiciously toward the corner. "A hearth did indeed sit there at one time. It wasn't much of anything really, basically just a hole in a stone wall. I don't even recall a fire ever burning. I wonder why you'd remember something so simple."

"It's not a memory, Dad. It came to me in a dream."

"A dream surely pulled from a memory," Federic said. "One of those…" He looked toward Father Tom. "What is it they call them—suppressed memories." Not waiting for a response, he nodded his head as though approving of the answer. "Yes, that must be it. Being back at the castle has probably dusted loose some memories."

"I'm not remembering something from my past. It was a sign, and the hearth was right there," she said, pointing once again to the corner. "I flew straight through it from the caves below no more than five minutes ago."

Federic blinked. Rubbing his hand slowly back and forth across his chin, he raised a sardonic brow. "Did you bump your head before or after the flight?"

Edeline looked toward Dane for help.

"I believe what Edeline means is that she had a vision," Dane said, before looking to Elliot. "We haven't anything to lose by testing its validity."

Elliot stared across the room toward the empty corner, then nodded his head in agreement. "Stranger things have happened. And you're right—we have nothing to lose for trying."

"We'll need tools to do the job," Graham said.

"Luckily, we've got an entire barn full of tools." Elliot motioned for the men to follow.

One by one everyone disappeared, leaving Dane and Edeline alone.

Stepping across the room, he drew her into his arms. "Did you see anything else in your dream?"

Resting her head against his chest, she sighed. "It was much like before. There were the warriors in the field and a flight through dark caverns." She looked up. "And the woman from the cliffs—Dane, I think she's my mother."

"What makes you think so?"

"She looks very much like me."

He smiled and cupped her face. "Beautiful?"

"She was beautiful," Edeline said, too humble to verbalize the compliment in his words. "I wish she could have stayed. I wish…" She bowed her head.

"She's still here, Edeline." He looked around the room. "I think they're all probably here—watching us, protecting us. There are times I'd swear—if I could only turn quick enough—I'd find them right behind me."

"I feel them too, or I think I do. I suppose I could simply be imagining it. I want it so badly." She leaned her head once more against his chest. "I know I'm right about the entrance though. I know I am. It's there. We're going to find it, and we're going to find the cradle."

"Yes," Dane said, but in truth he had doubts. The Dogs would have had plenty of time in the caverns and their interest in the caves had nothing to do with preservation. It was impossible to know what they had planned and impossible to know how it all would end.

Bright blue eyes looked hopefully into his. "Tell me again about the knights and my father. Do you think they survived? Do you imagine we'll ever know for sure?"

"I can't imagine them failing. They were incredible men, Edeline, not so unlike the men here today. But sadly, I doubt we'll ever know for sure if they survived."

He bent low, pressing his lips against hers, kissing her softly.

It was heaven holding her in his arms once again, feeling her body so close to his and enjoying her warmth. She was everything to him. A life without her would be no life at all. He would do anything to keep her safe—walk through hell or storm through fire. Whatever the Dogs had planned, he'd face it, fight it, overcome it or die trying.

Edeline peeked around the corner. Brick, drywall, plaster and stone lay in the middle of the dustbowl that used to be a room. Standing on the opposite side of the rubble, was her father and Father Tom. "Any luck?" she asked.

A dust-coated face looked up from the hole. "Just another layer of stone," Dane said. He lifted one of the flat stones at his side and wiped off a layer of grime. It turned out the gray looking stone was actually red. "We're almost through, I'd say. This is without question medieval."

Federic took the stone and turned it from side to side. "I believe this fella' might actually be older than me."

Dane grinned and wiped his dust-coated arm across his brow. "Want to take a look inside?" he asked Edeline.

"Sure," she said, stepping around the corner and into the room.

"Be careful," Federic warned, now standing dead-center in the middle of the wreckage.

Edeline tiptoed across the debris to look down past Dane into the hole. Layer after layer of flat stone went down at least ten feet. Every four feet the men had left footholds, narrowing the hole as they descended.

Graham stood at the bottom, handing another brick to the young knight positioned between him and Dane. "We've reached dirt."

"Is it solid?" Elliot asked, coming up behind Edeline.

Standing on the last established foothold, Graham braced himself between the stone walls and kicked. "It's solid."

Elliot frowned and ran his hand through his hair. "Let's clear a five foot square. If we don't find—"

"I've got something," Graham said, his voice rising with excitement. He handed up two more stones. "Right at the edge, I can reach clear through."

A round of excited chatter rang through the room.

Elliot hurried across the debris laden floor to the covered desk where a long metal wand lay. "Before we get too excited or do something stupid, let's put a scope down there and get some pictures." He handed Dane the wand before hurrying back to the desk and his laptop.

"It's in," Dane said.

Elliot tapped a few keys on the laptop. "Got it," he said, turning the screen so everyone could see.

At first it was hard to make out the scene, but slowly Edeline's eyes adjusted to the odd colors and dim lighting. "Are those stairs?"

Elliot looked her way and grinned. "So to speak."

"I'm sure that was their purpose," Father Tom said.

Wrapping his arm around her, Federic patted her shoulder. "You did it, Edeline. You found the back door. I never doubted you for a minute."

She shook her head and moaned. "Really, Dad?"

"It looks clear," Dane said, now standing behind them studying the screen.

"What little we can see," Elliot agreed. He handed the laptop to Father Tom, then turned to Edeline. "I need you to think back to your dream. Is there anything you haven't told us?"

"No, I've told you everything. We weren't in there very long, and we were moving very fast."

"But you're sure the opening was hidden?"

"At least in the dream. It was hidden within the shadows of the ceiling."

"And the room, the one you believe holds the treasure, it was also hidden?"

"Yes, down a long corridor hidden behind a thin crevice."

Dane's gaze fell to Elliot. "What are you thinking?"

"I'm wondering if we can pull this off without waking the hounds."

Chapter Twenty-Three

Less than an hour later, they'd broken through the earth below and straight into what was indeed a tight stairwell. Edeline stood beside Dane overlooking the hole. She was both eager and apprehensive about entering the unknown.

If Graham was nervous at all, it didn't show. Determined to be the first man down, he stood outside the small opening, strapping the rope securely around his middle. The flashlight, hanging from a cord wrapped around his neck, swayed back and forth, shedding light sporadically down into the darkness. He braced himself against the narrow stone walls before looking back up to Dane. "Ready."

"Be careful," Dane said. "Just because we don't see them, it doesn't mean they're not there."

"I'll be careful," Graham assured.

The men working the rope gave him some slack.

One small step at a time, Graham lowered himself down. Just before he completely disappeared into the darkness, he stopped and looked up. "If you don't feel the second tug, stay the hell out."

Dane nodded. "If the worst happens, do your best to stay alive."

"If the worst happens, I'm taking as many of them down with me as I can." A second later he'd disappeared into the black chasm.

Edeline slipped her hand into Dane's. "He'll be all right?"

A heavy scowl appeared between his brows as he watched warily the hole. "The plan is a good one," he said, not really answering the question.

The plan was simple—get in, secure the chamber, pass the stone and get out. They were wagering their lives on the hopes of a dream—her dream to be exact. In her dream the chamber was at the end of a hidden passage, easily sealed off from the rest of the cave. They'd studied the maps and determined it plausible. Even if the Dogs had rigged the caves to explode, the chamber could be salvaged…if it hadn't been found.

The rope pulled, indicating Graham had reached the bottom of the steps and was ready to descend into the cave.

"Hold tight," Elliot instructed. A few seconds later the rope tugged again.

They all took deep breaths and exchanged encouraging nods.

One by one, their small party descended down into the cave. By the time Edeline was allowed to join them, they were already busy securing the area and blocking off the crevice leading to the passage.

Shadows danced up and around stone as the small army of flashlights stuck to heads, dangling from limbs and moving sporadically in hands met, merged and departed along the cave's jaunting walls. Although nothing as surreal as the figures which ran and cried along the walls in her dream, the vision was still unnerving.

Moving closer to Dane, she took his hand in hers. "You won't leave me?"

The smile which touched his lips was warmed by the affection which shined in his eyes. "Never."

Elliot stepped away from the back crevice and joined them. "The entry to the cavern is secure. No one's getting in."

"Will it withstand an explosion?" Federic asked, helping Father Richard as he made the drop from the stairwell down into the cavern.

Elliot looked back toward the sealed entrance and grimaced. "Not a direct one. We need to get this done and get out of here before whatever luck it is that's been carrying us decides to run out."

"Moving," Graham said, once more taking the lead.

Slowly they made their way through the winding passage. It was cold, damp and dark despite the artificial lighting bouncing off the walls.

Edeline moved closely behind Dane, following his lead as he stepped over and around the scattered rock formations rising as though out of nowhere from the cave's floor. Moisture dripped from the multiple cracks in the rock ceiling above, inevitably landing on their heads and falling down their backs. At points along the passage, it could be seen running like a leaking faucet down the stone's rugged sides. Her clothes hung wet and uncomfortable against her skin as the journey began to take its toll on her tired limbs. It hadn't seemed so far in her dream.

The path twisted yet again, and once again Elliot signaled to his men to take the next turn. A handful at a time they disappeared around the corner, their swords held ready in their hands. Swords, Dane had explained, required greater skill and closer proximity than guns, but they held one distinct advantage — their strike could be controlled. In surroundings such as this, bullets carried the very real threat of ricochet.

The last group of men came back and nodded for them to follow. Once again they began to move. Like the wary tiptoeing past the gates of hell, they made their way through the dimly lit passage and into the deep chambers of the unknown.

They were nearing the end of the passage when a cold chill, born not of the elements but of something far more sinister, rolled into their path. It came out of nowhere as though exhaled from the invisible souls of the undead.

It rang the first warning.

Second to chime were the howls of the damned, tearing through the tunnels and halting the knights in their tracks.

As lights flashed instantly down the cavern walls, the stone they'd thought was their cover, crumbled and changed to the form of faces, bodies and swords. From the granite walls, a dark army emerged.

The sound of swords being drawn echoed in circles around her. Soon the cries of one were followed by the shouts of another, then another and yet another.

The surprise belonged to the enemy — an advantage the Dogs, by their numbers, did not appear to need.

As the knights drew together to form a circle, Dane wrapped his arm around her to move her into its center, protecting her with a massive wall of might. Her father, Dane and at least a dozen others stood as shields around her, waiting for the charge—a charge sure to come with a wrath brewed through centuries.

And so they came—wave after wave of merciless heathens hellbent on hell itself. Though they wore the flesh of men, they carried the souls of demons—beasts determined to see the spoils of victory and eager to see the blood of the righteous spread before the very cavern they were duty-bound to protect.

Swords flying and cries rumbling—the frightening face of battle emerged from every angle. As metal clashed with metal and bodies rose and fell, she could do nothing but watch. Her safety was her prison, and those whom she loved, stood as her bars.

The clanging of swords resounded like bells off the walls of stone. Soon the bright flashes of silver faded to dull under dark coatings of red. Blood fell like rain, wet but warm against her skin.

She wasn't sure what she'd expected, but nothing could have prepared her for what it was. Good and evil, death and survival—they were writing their story right before her eyes. Echoing life, their tales were grim and their destiny uncertain, but their point was unquestionably clear.

These two worlds had been combined on Earth so that both could see clearly they could never unite. Earth was the learning ground between Heaven and Hell, where both were allowed to roam free until a victor was claimed. And here, in the darkness of an underworld unknown to those above, one side would take the lead.

Though it was hard to tell for certain, it seemed the knights fared well, for the faces of their foe came steady and swift, but none flashed but once before her eyes. The knights stood well in the light of their legend. Remarkable skill and unyielding courage lied as the foundation for each and every one.

She had to remind herself to breathe as whatever protection her guardians had once had was quickly drawn away and they, too, were forced to step directly into the fight. She watched with horror as her father was attacked from two directions. But with amazing speed and agility, he moved his sword to disarm the first, quickly pulling the man into the other's sword.

A large blade plummeted down toward Dane. Turning and dropping to one knee, he avoided the piercing and plunged his own sword deep into his assailant's chest.

To his side, a beaten face with a crooked jaw and frightening snarl emerged. The man's gaze locked with hers. Ducking beneath what was left of the small circle of warriors, he reached inside to grab her. A bloodied sword flew down from the circle, severing the hand only inches from her arm.

Closing her eyes, Edeline shrank back further toward the ground, feeling sick, terrified and worst of all — useless.

Unable to bear not knowing, she quickly reopened her eyes.

The man had disappeared but the hand remained, an unsoiled silver knife clenched in its fist which now lay at her feet. Her gaze circled her surroundings and the war that raged. Deep inside her soul, courage took breath. Pulling the knife from the severed hand, she rose to her feet.

No more would she cower.

The daughter of warriors and a woman of faith, in a life much blessed, she had been given but one task. In order to see it through, she needed to stay alive.

From the corner of his eye, Dane spotted the man slithering toward the ground and past their protective cover. With a hardy yank, he managed to pull his sword from the entrails of another, raising it high and swinging down low to effectively sever the man's hand from its intent.

The monster's proximity to his beloved shook him badly and distracted him long enough to allow another to get too close. The sharp piercing end of a blade came directly at his throat. With no time to either move or strike, he simply acknowledged the inevitable and waited for the sting.

An anguished cry sounded to his side as Edeline flew past him and directly into his attacker. The sword may as well have done its damage, for his heart stopped nonetheless as he watched his true-love take on his fate.

But when the two forms parted, it wasn't Edeline who fell. And when she stepped back, she didn't step behind their protective circle, she moved to join it.

Determined to protect her, he stepped back into the fight…but the fight had vanished. The next wave of faces he saw were those of his comrades. Covered in blood and sweat, they too searched the room for any foe that might remain.

"Is that it?" Federic asked, still posed to do battle.

"Check the walls," Elliot ordered. "Make sure no more are hiding."

The men raised their lights, some searching the walls while others ran down the passage. Only seconds later, they had all returned.

"It's clear," Graham said, arriving back with the others.

Father Richard scanned the floors, shaking his head at the ugliness of it all. "Who are these lost souls?"

"Thankfully not ours," Elliot said, looking back to his men and assessing their injuries. "We've been blessed this round."

"Let's hope the blessings continue," Dane said, pulling Edeline into his arms. "I'm ready to get this thing over with."

Federic laid his hand on Dane's shoulder. "We all are, son."

Graham nodded over his shoulder toward the passageway where he'd just been. "There's not a lot left to it. There's a small empty cavern at the end, and that's it."

"Let's hope it's what we're searching for," Elliot said, looking back down toward the dead lying at his feet. "I'm certain there are more of their kind scattered throughout the cave. If they heard the skirmish or received any kind of warning, then surely they're on their way."

Graham wiped his blade against his already soiled jeans. "We'll be ready."

"Luck rarely holds when paired with futility," Elliot advised. "If they're coming, they're coming in numbers not even we can hold."

"So what do we do?"

"If the cavern fails to produce, we need to leave and leave quickly."

"Then we'd best get started," Father Richard said.

Federic looked once more around the floor. "I could do with a change of scenery," he said, starting them all moving by stepping past Graham and down the dark corridor.

It wasn't what she'd expected—the empty walls no more spectacular than any other. In her dream, she couldn't see much, but she was certain the walls had glistened. These walls were dull. Not even the moisture dripping through their cracks added sparkle to their dim.

The men scattered around the room, checking crevices and pushing against stone.

"I don't see anything," one of the knights said, having already circled the cavern.

"That's because you need better lighting." Elliot reached inside his pocket and pulled out the stone. He stepped across the room to Edeline and placed it around her neck.

It fell against her chest and instantly began to glow, spreading its warmth and its light like a burst of sunlight boldly stepping out from behind a dark cloud. From nowhere that made any kind of sense, a soft breeze began to blow, picking up the stone's radiance and tossing it against the somber walls, changing their drab demeanor into a striking and glimmering mass.

The breeze picked up its force, swirling dust throughout the cavern. The walls began to shake, and from their rumbles, voices emerged—cries of glory, hope and promise mixed with the tales of countless woes.

With the beating of the wind, the walls transformed, shedding their guise to reveal their true form. Upon their face, emerged a cross as tall as the cavern and as wide as its end.

"Look, there in its center," Graham said, pointing to the cross.

And there it was—a simple holder no less ordinary than the stone without its guardian and made of the same common marble.

"Are you ready, Edeline?" Father Richard asked, holding out his hand for hers.

Looking first toward Dane and then to her father, and receiving affirmative nods from both, she placed her hand in the priest's and moved with him toward the back wall.

It was exactly what she had wanted, so why it now seemed so hard, was impossible to fathom. But without question, a part of her was reluctant to let the stone go.

"It's a great responsibility you were given," Father Richard said as they stood before the cradle. "Such tasks are often the hardest to surrender."

"I want my life back." Her hand trembled in his as she looked down. "But it was a gift."

"They would understand, Edeline. It was not the stone they gifted you. It was the world it protected. Now it is time to exchange the one for the other."

The truth of his words was the path to her freedom. Lifting the stone from around her neck, she placed it into the cradle. Over her hand, was placed the hand of a pure and honest soul.

The wind stopped and an even brighter light swept from the stone, down the cradle and out onto the walls. Nothing it touched was left as it had been. The cradle turned to gold as did the cross which held it. Odd drawings and writings appeared on the walls. The voices which lingered faded to whispers which read from the script now lining the cavern.

Inside the cradle, the priest's hand squeezed hers. When she looked his way, he was reading the walls, tears filling his eyes.

"What does it say?"

"It says it is not darkness which rids the light, but rather light which rids the darkness."

"Is it talking about the war?"

"It's talking about eternity," he said, still scanning the script. "These walls tell not of an end, only a passage. I have a feeling the end is still being written. Fate is, as it always has been, held in the hands of man."

"There's a passage," Elliot said, squeezing through a narrow crevice now revealed behind the cross. Federic, Father Tom and several of the knights followed.

Dane stepped to Edeline's side and held out his hand. "I believe you have a right to know what it is you've been protecting."

She looked to Father Richard.

"You can go," he assured.

Turning her hand inside the cradle, she opened her palm, handing the priest the stone. As it left her hand, her body cooled.

Eyes closed, the priest sighed. "Ah, I wondered if I'd feel different."

"Thank you," she said, the feelings inside her hard to describe. She felt as though she could cry, but she wasn't exactly sure if it was sadness or relief.

The priest smiled. "You're welcome, Edeline." He nodded behind her. "You should hurry."

She moved with Dane through the crevice and into a wider cavern glistening with silver and gold. Mounds and mounds of treasure lined the walls. Numerous chests decorated with gems sat throughout the room filled with what she wasn't certain. Gold and silver coins, candlesticks, silver swords, jewels, golden images, cups and plates were piled everywhere—the assortment seemed endless.

"There's…so much," she said, making a circle.

Father Tom ran his hand down the spine of a gold-trimmed ledger—one of several sitting amongst the riches. He looked back to Elliot and smiled. "Do you see the resemblance?"

"They look like the one our father found."

"We should hurry," Dane reminded.

Elliot sighed. "He's right, as much as I know we'd all love to explore and see what treasures lie beneath, we can't. We can't afford the time."

As the last man stepped back out into the first cavern, Dane stopped and looked back. "What about the priest's vision—what about the weapons which were to be found on the cavern's floor?"

Father Richard smiled. "Our greatest weapon stands upon these floors, but it's not the treasure we protect. It's what protects the treasure." He looked into the face of each soul standing. "Courage is our greatest weapon. It and our faith will be what wins the war."

"To courage," said Graham, raising his sword. "To faith," replied Federic setting his sword to Graham's.

A chorus of cheers echoed around the cavern.

Wrapping his hand tight around the stone, Father Richard removed it from the cradle. Instantly the cavern transformed to stone. No more did the cradle sparkle. No more did the walls glow.

The secrets of the Knights Templar once again lay hidden behind the guard of a simple stone.

Edeline watched as Federic paced the floor in front of her, flipping his watch every so often and grunting his impatience.

"Why don't you sit down, Dad? Visit with me. It will make the time go faster."

He flipped his watch once more to check the time and then looked back out the window. His shoulders slumped. "Perhaps I should try something different."

The sound of approaching vehicles hummed into the quiet of the outside.

"They're back," said Federic, running right past her and straight for the stairs.

Edeline followed behind him.

Stepping out of the castle, they were met with a succession of slamming doors. No less than twelve vehicles lined the drive. Dane and Father Tom were the first to reach them. Their smiles laid the first clue.

"You were successful?" Federic asked.

Father Tom beamed. "It couldn't have gone better."

"We found their entrance," Elliot said, coming up behind his brother. "It was actually quite clever—a boathouse just a few miles down from the cave's opening. They went in from under the water. That's why we never heard them."

"They had to have been working on it for years," Father Tom added.

Elliot nodded. "They've certainly shown their patience. It's a strength we will from here on after give due credit."

"Did they get away?" Edeline asked.

"Not a one. They must not have been given warning. They all seemed plenty surprised. Once the opening was cleared, the men we already had in place were able to make their move, storming the passages from every direction but the one they were expecting. They didn't even try to fight, they merely made a run for it—right back out through the boathouse and into our custody. We took in huge numbers. Many are already talking."

Father Tom took Edeline's hand into his. "It will cripple their order for years to come."

"Is she safe?" Federic asked.

Dane stepped forward to wrap his arms around her. "She's safe."

Epilogue

Edeline peeked through the closed flaps of the tent and smiled. She couldn't imagine a more beautiful scene or a day more perfect. Tall wisps of grass bowed for miles over the rolling hills, all stretching their slight forms toward the gathering near the ruins of Vanac. It was as though they had gathered and declared the event worthy of their attention, or perhaps they were merely drawn by the music. Tender and rich, the satin-smooth notes of a well-played harp blessed the peaceful valley currently housing the makeshift altar and small army of invited guests.

This was her life, past and present, captured in one unforgettable moment. It held the sum of all her treasures, all her hopes, all her dreams.

Somewhere, on one of the surrounding hills, her mother was buried. Edeline felt her presence even though she could no longer see her face. Closing her eyes, she took a moment to imagine her mother there, standing on the hills, her hand secure in the hand of a handsome warrior with long blond curls.

They were there, she was certain, them and three knights Edeline had never really known yet could never forget.

She opened her eyes, and her two worlds met.

Heading down the aisle, her hand tightly held in Amanda's, was Lucy. Not a petal had left the basket, but it didn't really matter, the guests were completely charmed, as were her parents.

It had been love at first sight for Amanda and Paul. The moment Edeline handed Lucy into their arms, the little girl's future had been sealed. She'd found her home atop a used bookstore in the center of Morrow's Haven and deep in the hearts of two kind and loving souls.

"Ack. This tie is choking me," Federic complained from behind.

Edeline dropped the tent's flaps, turned and batted away his hands from his satin foe. "It's almost over, Dad," she said, loosening and then readjusting the offending material. "Then I promise I won't ask you to endure this torture again, at least not this trip."

"Thanks. Can I have that in writing?"

She laughed.

Her father's eyes grew serious. "You look beautiful, Edeline. If I haven't told you enough, I love you. No father could be prouder of any daughter than I am of you. You have brought me more joy than I can ever say."

Patting the now well-behaved tie, she fought back the tears. "And I am so very proud to be your daughter. I love you too, Dad."

The music stopped, then quickly started again, this time filling the hills with the joyous melody of the Bridal March.

"That's our cue," Federic said, taking Edeline's arm and wrapping it through his. He kissed her cheek and then pushed back the tent's opening. "Sure you're ready for this?" he asked, looking a bit pale himself.

"I'm sure," she said, spotting the handsome soldier who had fought for her freedom, only to turn around and steal her heart. "I've never been more ready for anything in my life."

Arm in arm, they stepped out of the tent and toward the aisle.

Chairs squeaked and clanked and an audible *swoosh* sounded as guests rose from their seats to turn and look her way.

She swallowed and stepped forward, her heart soaring as she caught Dane's eyes upon her. Just like that first day in the lab, his feelings were written clearly across his face and in the depths of his eyes — she was his. Nothing and no one would ever keep them apart.

As the sun shed its warmth and promise across the hills of France, they pledged their lives and their hearts to each other. When the "I dos" were passed and their worlds combined, they turned to face their honored guests.

From the crowd, forty swords were drawn and brought together, their chimes echoing through the hills of present and past. And through the arch of their bright silver glory, Edeline and Dane made their way into the future.

Acknowledgments

To my much appreciated editor, Sean Riley, for being a great coach and director.

To the team at Omnific for giving a newbie a chance.

About the Author

Amity Grays is an accountant by day, romance writer by night. She lives in Southern Idaho with her husband, two daughters, two sweet dogs and one snobbish cat.

True to the nature of an accountant, Amity is a list builder, budget monitor, and proud owner of a 2005 Camry, which she's holding onto for another 140K miles because the salesman assured her she'd get 300K, and she feels the need to test his accuracy.

On the flip side of her obsessive nature is a desire to let go — to spin a globe, point a finger and explore the world, to walk through haunted castles and to jump into time warps. She enjoys exploring emotion and capturing its intensity inside the written word.